ALL OF OUR SINS

DARK LEGACIES
BOOK 2

YUVAL KORDOV

For Ester, my matriarch.

PART 1
EXODUS

HELIO

THE SPACES BETWEEN

The meager sun hovered low on the horizon, painting the monochrome wastelands a bloody shade of red. Below the empty heavens, a cemetery of banded sandstone hoodoos reached up like totems to a dead god, shrouded in wind-borne clouds of their own silty skin. The dust squall whistled and shrieked as it snaked between them, flaying away their desiccated flesh and depositing it, particle by anonymous particle, into the barren salt flats beyond. Helio Ramirez winced as the torrid current beat about his face, pitching his long locks of black-and-blonde hair into fits. Like a malignant spirit, the wind made every effort to distract him from the intruder in the canyon below.

He peered through his binoculars as she stumbled her way through the second gorge of the Devil's Claw. Helio was intimate with all four of the region's conjoined canyons—its "fingers"— but this one he knew all too well. It was a graveyard. A misty scrubland dense with dagger-sharp brambles tipped with neurotoxins, poisonous shrubs, and hidden bogs that could swallow an inattentive hunter in an instant. None of that seemed to matter to the oblivious black-haired wanderer, who flitted in and out of its thick, sulfuric fog like a wayward wraith, repeatedly backtracking from the finger's maze of impassable dead ends.

It was the only hunting ground within practical range of Newhaven. Most of the animals here were edible, even the hideously deformed ones. That's what he was here for. But not all of them were placid. Hellhounds stalked the area—demented wolves and coyotes and whatever other kind of dog the Hellmouth had corrupted into even deadlier predators. Traveling alone, as she was, or without experience, which she clearly lacked, was suicide. The hunter became the hunted.

She was something else, but exactly *what* he wasn't sure. Her zigzagging route suggested she hadn't been here before, and she had no gear other than the drab beige cloak on her back.

There was also something about the way she moved.

Despite her haphazard progression, the woman glided past the larger, more obvious hazards with a weird fluidity—blink and you'd miss it. His stomach clenched each time it happened, warning him that maybe he shouldn't be up here spying on her. Childhood terrors tickled at the base of his neck.

"Who the hell are you..." he mumbled to himself, his words carried down the gorge by the superheated eddies of the desert wind.

The woman stopped in her tracks.

Helio froze, his white-knuckled grip like a vise on the binoculars. There was no way she could have heard him from this far away. Instinct pressed him uselessly into the dry, impermeable clay on which he was sprawled. He should have taken proper cover behind one of the outcroppings atop the canyon instead of relying on distance like a rookie. Long seconds passed, breathless. Unprepared lungs smoldered painfully in his chest.

"Don't look up," he whispered.

"Helio, come back."

The timing was impeccable.

Helio rolled away from the ledge, baleful eyes landing on the radio receiver of his parked Runner, where the static-soaked voice had emerged. He low-crawled a few meters, wincing at the dragging screech of his patchwork armor on the ground, then sprang to his feet for a mad dash to the vehicle. Fumbling at the receiver dial, he yanked the volume down and hunkered into the metal floor of the caged cockpit, corded handset held tight to his mouth.

"This is Helio," he hissed. "What the fuck?"

A low rumble burbled from the speaker as the message relayed back to base along ancient hardware, interspersed with bursts of semi-structured noise. The bare skin of his arms puckered into goosebumps. He waited anxiously for a response, each abraded, whisper-like blip tying a new knot in his stomach.

Helio hated using radios in the wastelands and suffered no shortage of mockery for it. He couldn't abide the spaces between —that expansive void where demons were lurking, listening, eager to follow electromagnetic waves back to their source. No one had ever verified such a thing was possible, but he was sure of it. Sierra understood his fears full well and normally wouldn't have called him unless it was an emergency. He glanced back at the ledge, confirming the intruder hadn't climbed all the way up the escarpment in those few brutally loud seconds. The only thing moving was a rusty red haze of dust on the wind.

The reply finally came back, clipped into robotic staccato. "Sorry, Cousin. Getting... late... worried..."

The Runner's dashboard chronometer validated her concerns. It was an hour to sundown and a quarter more to get back home at safe speed. He had clearly lost track of time following the mystery woman, when he should have been hunting game. The meat cooler tucked between the vehicle's fuel tanks was woefully empty. He chewed on his lower lip and raked a hand nervously over the thick stubble of his cheeks and chin, debating whether to tell his cousin what he was up to.

The wobble in his gut wasn't just from the radio (which some giant hellspawn was definitely using to triangulate his position this very moment). It was the woman. There were no communities this far west, only a long stretch of cracked earth and rotted highway. Then Cathedral.

Helio replayed the memory of her movements, the mirage of black streaks that trailed her when she dodged past an obstacle. He had never seen a revenant sister before, but every ranger was taught what to look for just in case: corpse-gray skin, unnaturally vivid eyes, and their black habits; blessed with the power to blink across great distances in an instant or rip out your spine with their bare hands.

Assuming that was the case here, which seemed impossible, why was this one so underdressed, and what was she doing so far from home?

He depressed the Send button. "I'll be back soon." Blurted out, before he could change his mind.

Helio switched the radio off and leaned his forehead against the cool metal of the vehicle's roll cage, restraining the urge to drum his fingers on its welded bars. "Stupidly curious" was the term the elders used for him. They weren't completely wrong—the need to know gnawed at him like a ravenous, insatiable hunger—but if not for his curiosity, they never would have found Bastion or half of the other "lucky" discoveries that helped stave off Clan Ramirez's extinction. He could afford a few more minutes and still get back before dark if he punched it.

Lifting himself carefully from the cockpit, he paused to consider the array of meticulously maintained weapons stowed in the passenger nook—all useless if she was what he thought she was. Hopping out empty-handed, he crouched low behind a boulder this time and lifted his binoculars to his face, scanning the area where he had last seen the woman.

She wasn't there.

The sharp talons clawing at his gut dug deeper as he panned over a thick swath of gnarled bramble and billowing fog. This finger was infamous for its drowning pools, noxious ponds of bubbling brown liquid surrounded by a wide radius of inconspicuous quicksand. Without a partner and a tow line or a grappling hook, escaping their sucking grip was impossible. He'd rather be eviscerated by a demon than suffer that slow, choking death.

An animalistic cry echoed from the end of the gorge—farther than anyone could realistically traverse in the short time he was occupied. He swiveled his head around, adjusting the zoom rings on his binoculars to a higher magnification. The canyon walls lurched back and forth in the viewport as he found his bearings and the woman, standing atop an angled promontory, her back to a drowning pool, surrounded by half a dozen hellhounds.

"Shit," he whispered, his vision beginning to blur as the binoculars shook in his hands. Like demons, there was no commonality between them: some were furred, some scaled; others wore mottled flesh over their disfigured frames. Fortunately, unlike demons, they were just animals—mostly. But they were deadly in packs.

Helio's left leg bounced, urging him to action, but he was too far away. If the woman wasn't one of these fabled priestesses, she'd be dead any second. If she was... well, then he wanted to see what she could do, to see if the legends were true. The pack's alpha was creeping toward her, its broad triangular head hanging low between pinched shoulders. It was twice as large as any wolf had a right to be and coated in leathery green skin pulled taut across its oversized skeleton. He tried to swallow but his parched throat only clicked.

An explosion of pink mist erupted from the back of the pack. Helio swung his binoculars around but overshot, losing the melee for precious seconds before finding the combatants again. The alpha was still atop the promontory, sniffing at the rock confusedly, but the woman was now behind them. Helio watched in awe as she darted forward, striking impossibly fast and hard with her bare hands. Another of the creatures exploded, painting the barbed brush a sickly brownish red.

As she continued to blink from one spot to the next, leaping and attacking to disastrous effect, he realized she was not only unarmed but completely naked beneath her cloak. Arousal mixed with horror as he considered the carnage that could follow her if she made it all the way to Newhaven. He locked his eyes open, unwilling to lose a single moment of the impossible scene before him. As a ranger, he was lucky to have never had the misfortune of encountering an actual demon, but he knew they were real—one only had to look south. The elders' descriptions of the Revenant Sisterhood, however, always felt exaggerated. Bogeymen to support the narrative of their people's exile.

The alpha pounced, launching from the outcropping with its own unnatural speed and slamming with vicious impact into the woman's back. Helio's heart lurched as she went down hard. For the first time, he heard her cry out, a hateful curse that sent shockwaves rippling along the understory and up the canyon's walls. The inhuman roar cascaded over his skin, lifting the hairs of his arms on currents of static electricity. A manic thrashing ensued as the woman wrestled with a beast twice her size, frantically fending off razor-sharp claws and venomous incisors. He leaned forward for a better angle, heart pounding in his chest now, but could barely make them out through the brush. There were whirls of severed fabric, claws, and tail, then silence.

"C'mon," he muttered, fingers drumming impatiently atop his binoculars. "Stand up."

He didn't know why he cared so much, only that he did. Leaving another human, however "blessed," to die in a place like this wasn't right. He did some quick calculations based on their positions, figuring it would take at least ten minutes to drive around the canyon and down to its mouth, then maybe another twenty minutes to hike out to her. Which meant he might be camping here overnight.

Camping in the Devil's Claw.

Sierra was going to kill him, assuming the hellhounds didn't do it first.

HELIO

QUAGMIRE

Mia sang as Helio raced down the broken lanes of sedimentary rock, the sonorous roar of her engine melding with the drumbeat of chattering suspension. His whole body shook, hands vise-gripped to the steering wheel. Helio wasn't just known for being stupidly curious, he was also derided as unnecessarily reckless. There was a time and a place for caution, he supposed; this wasn't it. He glanced down at the tachometer, straining against its limits as he navigated the thicket of sandstone pillars in low gear. They were getting shorter, meaning the canyon mouth was close. It was properly dark now, the starless void peeling open above him. The Runner's headlights beamed out just far enough to keep him from killing himself—

A wall of rock burst from the road ahead.

Helio took the corner at speed, skidding to a screeching halt as the dry wash gave way to scrubland. Dust filled his nostrils, clawing past the edges of his bandana. Sand caked his driving goggles, reducing his vision to a narrow tunnel. *Mia* chugged impatiently, but the jolt of the near collision shook him more than her rough idling.

He had reached the end of the road. The caustic depths of

the second finger lay ahead. Helio hesitated, struck by how much worse it looked at dusk, how much like a trap for an overzealous ranger.

"I should leave," he muttered, smacking his goggles clear of debris.

His survivalist mindset was recoiling. He could still turn around, drive as fast as possible. If he was lucky, he'd make it back in one piece, then warn the elders about the woman, like he should have hours ago.

Helio shut off the engine quickly, before he could change his mind. The fog had started to creep forward—a trick of his head-lights maybe. He climbed out of the cockpit and grabbed some gear from the back: a cumbersome rescue bag, hatchet, and rifle. There was no time to camouflage the vehicle, not that it mattered much at this point. His hand hesitated over the light switch, waiting for one more particulate-soaked breath. Then a second. Then a third before slapping them off and rushing forward into the quagmire.

———

Newhaven—home—felt impossibly far away as he navigated the brush, pushing ever deeper into the putrid bowels of the earth. Normally, Helio would have been happy for the distance. Each time he drove back into the decrepit mine his people called home, he felt like he was climbing into an open grave. Any mission he could take to get away, he took: exploratories, procurement of artifacts for trade with the Americans, and risky hunts like this. Usually, they were preferable to home. Preferable to slow death alongside his clanfolk.

Usually.

Maybe not this time.

This place was even worse. Everything was worse at night,

but this place especially. It spoke to his chief's desperation that such a hellhole had been declared an essential resource pool instead of being cordoned off behind barbed wire and warning placards. The name alone should have been a giveaway.

Helio barely remembered Hub—he was only five when his people left for Newhaven—but a few etched memories of contentedness stuck with him. Security that could only be found tucked well away from the cursed earth. Without fail, the spaces between civilization—so-called natural areas that had survived or could be nurtured back to life—should have been left to the Adversary, no matter how plentiful they seemed from afar.

The dire wood shimmered around him. He plowed forward, guided by his rifle light, a hand compass, and a swell of adrenaline, but his momentum slowed the closer he got to the woman's position. The canyon looked bad enough from the outside. Trapped within its suffocating brush, it became abundantly clear no human should ever be here alone, at night. It was silent save for the muted rustling of the wind and the crunch of his own booted footsteps. No insects or birds. Visibility extended only a few meters out. Without his compass, Helio would have been completely lost, backtracking as his target had, with less time to spare. Even still, he waved his light along the ground every few steps to make sure he wasn't stumbling into quicksand. A wide nylon belt hugged his chest, attached with carabiners to a long loop of paracord and a grappling hook jammed into the top of his backpack. If he started to sink, he'd have a chance, but it wasn't something he was eager to test out.

The clearing came up fast. One moment he was chopping and ducking his way through an archway of tangled foliage whose taloned branches too closely resembled flayed human limbs, and the next he was facing the snarling maw of the alpha. Its sallow, soulless eyes glowed yellow in the glare of his flashlight. It looked like some sort of nightmarish snake, its giant head protruding from a length of detached spinal column. Very dead. The rest of its body was nowhere to be seen but likely scattered around the clearing along with the brutalized remains of its pack.

Lying face up on the rocky promontory, like a sacrifice to the void, was the woman.

Helio swallowed hard and straightened, unfurling himself with a grunt from the compacted posture of his trek. With clammy hands, he swung his rifle over the scene to make sure nothing was still alive. Curiosity and instinct had driven him here, but now that he was steps away, he hesitated. The air tasted sour. An inappropriate rumble of hunger grumbled in his empty belly, reminding him he should be flush with kills by now, instead of traipsing through this hellhole. Finding his second wind, Helio navigated forward, carefully testing every step along the way.

The woman's pallid face glowed pink in the dying light of the sun. Her complexion was otherwise gray and colorless as death, but her chest cycled up and down with the heavy breath of sleep. Vicious slash wounds marred the length and breadth of her flesh, most of which was on display now that her cloak had been rendered to rags. Despite the recency of the attack and the alpha's still-pooling blood, her wounds looked clotted, hardening over with scabs.

The elders were right.

Helio's eyes widened as he glided his rifle light over her scarred torso and legs, pausing for a moment at the coal-black mound between her legs, then continuing down to her bare blistered feet. Had she really walked all this way from Cathedral? Despite everything, he found himself aroused by the sight of her statuesque figure.

He directed the rifle light back to her face, heart shaped with strong cheekbones and a delicate jaw. She bore no wrinkles or blemishes, no signposts of years past. Her short bob of raven hair glowed with an inner radiance, as though reflecting absent moonlight. She was beautiful, ageless. He lingered on her eyelashes, wondering again at the elders' words: *"Eyes of purple and gold that can sway the hearts of men."* It seemed like another impossible tale, and yet here he was.

Dusk had turned to night. Helio didn't need to look up—didn't want to look up—to know the sun was gone, to feel the shrinking of his soul as his adrenaline ran dry. He pulled a double headlamp from a cargo pocket and strapped it to his forehead, thumbing it on as he lowered his rifle to the ground.

Sway the hearts of men? Or rip them out?

"I should make sure..."

Helio slowly reached for her shoulder, then pulled back with a yelp as a shock ran through his fingers. Her body hummed with electrical energy, like a miswired machine. He could see it now that he had more light: a shimmering vibration all around her. Reaching out a second time, he let his hand linger, bracing against a ticklish discomfort more alien than painful. He squeezed her arm, kneading it back and forth, but she was out cold.

Shrugging his rescue pack off his shoulders, Helio opened the main flap and pulled out an emergency fold-out stretcher. It was going to be a bumpy ride, hopefully ending with both of them still intact.

Moving the revenant sister took frustratingly long. She was far heavier than she looked, and her aura set his nerves on edge. Finally, he got her situated head up—to avoid knocking her brains out on the way back.

Slinging his gear as tight to his body as possible, Helio took off with the woman bouncing behind him. Cramps were already snatching at his biceps, but he pressed forward, driven by a renewed fear of the dark. Twin beams of light guided the way.

Every few steps, he glanced down at the compass bound to his left wrist. Still on course. It had taken him about fifteen minutes to find the clearing from the entrance, so it would take at least half again as long to get back.

"Then what?" he huffed to himself.

He hadn't planned that far out. There was an alchemical kit in the rescue bag that contained stimulants among other things, so he could stay alert at least while securing their location, then see what the morning brought. Assuming he made it to morning. The adventurous bravado that normally powered him through away missions was coming up short. He had never faced a threat like this, or an unknown so... *unknown!* Even Bastion, his biggest find yet—maybe anyone's biggest—had been lower risk, its oblivious soldiers unlikely to track him back to his home and murder him in his sleep.

A snap echoed ahead, flash-freezing the waterfall of sweat soaking his back and neck. Helio stood completely still, waiting for a repeat, then realized whatever was out there could still see him no matter how little he moved. He dropped the stretcher and swung his rifle up, activating its light to join the others. The fog was relentless, like toxic smoke boiling off a chemical fire. All he could see was yellow haze and dense brush.

A hoot rang out from his left, casting prickles of terror over his skin. He lurched around, almost tripping over a clump of gnarled roots as the weight of his pack swung him too far.

"Fuck!"

He fumbled at the buckle, pushing hard with his left hand until it snapped open. With a heave, he dropped the priceless bag to the ground.

Branches snapped to his right. He swung back the other way with another involuntary cry. The eyeshine of an army of beasts stared back at him. Helio's breath rattled loudly in the sandpaper lining of his throat. Stupidly curious—that pretty much summed it up. Sparing a glance down at the hastily abandoned mystery woman, he confirmed she was still very unconscious. This was on him, all on him.

Helio thumbed his fire selector to three-round burst and pulled the stock tight into his shoulder. His mind turned over the dilemma of attacking now or waiting. He was a ranger, an explorer scout, not a fighter, and would rather not have to attack at all, would rather these little fuckers (big fuckers, actually) lumber back to their hidey-holes and leave him alone.

He waited. As soon as he fired, he'd be announcing his location to every hellhound in the region. A primordial itching in his legs was telling him to run, to leave the woman behind and save himself, but he couldn't outrun a wolf.

A scaled snout protruded from the wall of fog, followed by two rows of ungodly huge teeth.

"Fuck it."

Helio yelled and opened fire.

Ten.

Deafening roars smashed his ears as he laid into the woods to his left and right.

Nine, eight, seven.

Each pull of the trigger brought him closer to that horrible moment when his gun would run dry. Speed reload techniques spun in his mind, learned during combat training but never used. Would he fumble? Would they rush him at that moment?

Six, five, four.

What did being mauled to death feel like?

Three, two.

A spray of gnarled bark flew back at him and up into the air, but most of his bullets simply evaporated into the fog.

One.

Click.

Empty.

Helio blinked—confused for a split second while his brain caught up—then hit the release button. His left hand found a new mag quickly enough, but he couldn't get it in. The opening was too small, too slippery. Instead of watching the enemy, or his own rifle, he stared uselessly at the ground. If he couldn't see them, maybe they wouldn't see him.

Snap.

The magazine was in. He slammed back the bolt and raised his weapon.

There was nothing there. The woods were empty.

————

Helio's lungs burned as hot as the coal furnaces back home. He didn't dare stop, rushing, stumbling, and at times fully falling toward the canyon mouth. The stretcher bounced the whole way behind him, thankfully only jolting the woman's already bloodied feet rather than her head. But his emergency pack had been abandoned, meaning no stimulants. Visions of giant disembodied teeth pressed him forward. By the time he surged out of the scrub, sprawling exhaustedly against the cool metal of *Mia's* frame, he was gasping for breath.

The unfortunate part of surviving was that he had to figure out what to do next. The Runner was equipped with decent enough headlights and a supplementary bar on the roof, but all that forward-facing illumination wouldn't help navigate corners in pitch black. No one was supposed to drive out in the open past sundown, ever. One missed turn and they'd roll over, or worse. Fatigue was also an issue. While he was currently wide-the-fuck-awake thanks to the self-preserving power of adrenaline, his supply was running low.

Then there were the demons. As scary as hellhounds were, they were still just animals. There was *really* no running away from demons. Or from the revenant sister in his back seat, mistakenly thinking him her captor and promptly ripping out his spine.

"What the hell am I doing?" he groaned.

Sierra always teased him for thinking out loud. He couldn't help it, especially under stress. He wished she were here now, watching his back.

There was only one option: stay put, try to stay awake, and hope that either his unwitting companion remained unconscious or that when she woke up, she would give him more than two seconds to explain his intentions. Helio pushed himself off the side of the Runner, grimacing at the deep ache in his arms, and got to work.

Preparedness was a core value for all Scavrats, exiles and Unionists alike. Unfortunately, redundancy was secondary to scarcity. In addition to losing all his medical supplies, he was out of rations and had only as much water as was left in his canteen. What he did have was a diverse assortment of traps and alarms intended for hunting, plus enough fuel for a presumed return trip. And his radio.

Helio stared at the deactivated device, wondering what Sierra was doing right now. For once, he took comfort in his cousin's very different, ultra-cautious disposition. As worried as she most definitely was, it was highly unlikely she'd commandeer a vehicle for a middle-of-the-night rescue, but there was no doubt she would have alerted their sector administrator. That meant Grandfather—Chief Neron Ramirez—was probably already cursing his name. He considered turning the radio back on, just long enough to reach out and let her know he was okay, but there would be too much explaining to do. Also, demons.

He set about laying as wide a safety net as he could, placing trip wires connected to warning bells, simple snares, a handful of claw traps, and two makeshift boobytraps using grenades passed down to him by his father. He always took the explosives with him on missions, for luck—something he needed a lot of right now. Reasonably satisfied with the defensive perimeter—though slightly worried he was as likely to blow himself up as his feral visitors—he shifted his attention to the Runner. A woven net interlaced with strips of tan fabric served as both camouflage and a modicum of shelter, obscuring the empty heavens if nothing else. He hurriedly draped it over the vehicle, trying not to think of the void above.

Guarding the whole canyon mouth was impossible, but unless one of the beasts was determined to go the long way round to murder him, there was a solid chance that something would trigger. The only thing left to do was hunker down and wait.

In the dark.

A fire was out of the question, despite the urging of his primitive instincts. The revenant sister lay stock-still beneath a burlap blanket. Her wounds were healing fast; hopefully not too fast, not before dawn. As long as he could stay awake, there would be time to explain.

Helio climbed into the cockpit, rifle slung tightly to his chest, and set to the task of waiting.

HELIO

LET'S EAT!

It was a party, and their whole clanhome was invited. Helio jostled around on his father's shoulders, bouncing and weaving high in the air as their group danced in a circle. A web of string lights glowed hazy orange above him, knotted into star fields along the hewn rock ceiling. Every so often, a constellation emerged, shining brighter than the rest. They alternated between the shapes of animals: crows, vultures, bulls.

Wolves.

Each time the wolf appeared, the music got louder. Too loud. It hurt his ears, but he forced a smile. Everyone looked so happy. They were all smiling, even those without eyes.

Helio tried to blink the horror away, but his own eyes were fixed.

Sierra was down below, smiling widely as Helio's mother swayed back and forth, pirouetting her into dizzy spins. Her long blonde hair gleamed brighter than the sun, brighter than the false stars. His whole family was there, and his family's family, and their cousins. From his lofty vantage, he could see them all. Helio didn't know what they were celebrating, but it was good, and *good* didn't happen often. It wouldn't happen again.

A bell began to ring, its tinny cadence cutting through the noise. A constellation buzzed into life—the wolf.

"Let's eat!" it called, eyes blinking hungrily.

No one stopped. The dancing only grew more frantic. Helio looked around for something to eat but could only see people, an ocean of them, hands and heads jutting and lurching. Not all of them attached to bodies.

Rows of teeth within teeth, grinning in the dark.

The bell grew persistent, chipping off bits of his face with each metallic clang. Helio slammed his hands over his ears, unmooring himself from his father. When he tried to clamp on with his knees, they only glided through darkened air, the spectral shadow of a man long dead.

The bell grew even louder; the room spun faster. Sierra was gone, reduced to golden threads of light. The string lights blazed, substituting constellations with a hundred glistening eyes. Hungry for meat.

Helio had nothing to hold on to. He fell. Into the sea. Into oblivion.

Suffocating.

"No!" he cried out, confusedly emerging from the darkness of the dream to the darkness of night. The sound of his panicked breathing was like a bellows beneath the net.

The hollow tone of an alarm bell tinkled in the distance. Helio froze, overcome by a wave of pins and needles that cascaded from his numb feet all the way to his crooked neck. Every hair on his body was lifted in terror. He couldn't see anything. He didn't want to see anything, especially teeth in the dark. But if he didn't leave his cocoon, he'd die—horribly.

The alarm stopped.

Helio reached up with sluggish arms to where he thought

his head was, fumbling around for his headlamps. The Runner's cockpit bloomed to life without consideration for his sleep-crusted eyes. He squinted against the brightness and gagged with the narrowing of his constricted throat. Breath came in thin, strangled wheezes as he tried to pull his shit together. No part of his body was cooperating. Eventually, he managed to squeeze himself up and out of the driver seat, poking through the square access flap above.

It was pitch black outside and, as far as he could tell, no nearer to sunrise than when he had accidentally fallen asleep. Dream fragments slithered in his memory, stabbing at his guts. A damp wind blew upon his face, carrying the putrid aroma of the quagmire: sulfur, muck, deceitful fruits. He wrangled his rifle out of the tent and onto his shoulder, thumbing its flashlight on to join the others. A trinity of light beamed forward then died, dissipating uselessly into the endless night. The driver seat groaned on rusty springs as he sidestepped along its surface, turning in a slow arc to the first row of alarms.

A mob of glistening yellow orbs stared back at him. They just hovered there, less than twenty meters away, waiting. To eat. The combined snorting and huffing of the pack sounded like a convoy of idling engines. He tried to count—to assign some quantitative measure to the horror—but there were too many of them.

The revenant sister!

Helio whipped his head around, directing his headlamps to the spot where he had left the stretcher. It was empty save for a burlap blanket rustling in the building wind. The woman was gone.

He was alone. In the dark. Surrounded.

For nothing.

"I'm on my way back." It was all he had to say. Sector admin would have broken his balls over his empty cooler, but he'd be

alive, eating gruel with his cousin, bitching about Grandfather. Watching his people go extinct.

Despondence took the place of fear. It sucked at his soul, like the viscous sludge of a drowning pool. He was going to die. And within a few years, his clan was going to die. There would be nothing left of anyone. The great Ramirez legacy, eroded into oblivion by one bad decision after another. He regretted not pushing his grandfather harder to make amends with the Union, regretted shirking his birthright, regretted the untapped potential of Bastion in the east.

Helio's last thought as he turned toward the hellhounds—stupidly curious though it may have been—was regret at not learning the woman's name.

He thumbed the rifle to automatic. Only two magazines remained, but he had coupled them together so that his one and only reload would be as fast as possible. He wouldn't botch it this time. A large, serrated knife hung from his hip. His hunting crossbow, powerful but useless in close quarters, sat in the footwell of the Runner.

Maybe he was a fighter after all.

"Come on then, you fuckers," he called out. There was no more stopping time. "Come a little closer..."

He stared at them through his irons, both eyes open and waiting.

A loud metallic snap rang out to his left, followed by a hideous howl of pain.

One down.

The creature's baying was joined by the rest of the pack. As one, they sent their guttural cries into the void, seeking the moon that had abandoned them centuries ago and finding nothing. For a moment he felt bad for them, empathetic to their sense of homelessness. Then he opened fire.

A whirlwind of bodies surged from the darkness, flitting in

and out of his lights, screaming as bullets hit home and as they stumbled into the rest of his traps. Strangled screams died at his throat, unable to bypass a jaw clamped shut for courage.

A hairless runt flew sideways across the camp, caught up in one of the catapult snares he had set. Another canine, much larger and swathed in what looked like sword-length quills, burst directly into his field of view before flipping tail over head as one of its legs was snatched by a second claw trap. It thrashed wildly on the ground, shooting quills in every direction. Two of its packmates were impaled. The remainder of its razor-sharp projectiles sliced open the netting just below his stomach. Their howls coagulated into a wall of noise, rendered indistinct by the concussion of gunfire in his ringing ears.

The second-last magazine ran dry. Helio felt it more than heard it but was faster this time: release, swap, slam it home. Flush with ammo, he fired at anything he could see through increasingly watering eyes. The claw trap line was expended. There was only one thing left—two, actually.

Anticipation did little to protect him from the proximity of the thermal grenade's detonation. The explosion knocked him backward, slamming his head hard against the roll cage as he dropped through the tent flap. For a moment he hung there suspended on the netting, dangling from his tangled rifle sling. Dizzy, blurry eyed. He tried to swear, but his tongue wouldn't cooperate. Finally, he tore free, falling the rest of the way into the cockpit. His upper body landed in the footwell while his legs flopped awkwardly outside the vehicle.

Everything went dark. An excruciating wave of pain surged from the base of his neck, erupting into a chain reaction of neon starbursts. Helio struggled to stay afloat, gasping for breath as oblivion clawed at him. If he gave up now, he would never wake up—or he might one last time, just long enough to feel himself get eaten alive. A plodding drumbeat thumped in his eardrums, deafening him to whatever was happening outside.

The second grenade detonated just as he crunched up to get his bearings. He screamed, instinctively shielding his head with his arms, but this explosion was mercifully farther away than the first. He hadn't fucked that one up, at least. Its incendiary residue radiated through the smoldering netting, bright enough that he was able to see again. One of his headlamps was on the driver seat, still alight but facedown. The other, along with his rifle, was nowhere to be seen. He contorted his body around and, with a joint-wrenching stretch, managed to grasp the strap, pulling the lamp back onto his forehead.

Something grabbed his boot.

"What?" he gasped.

He swung his headlamp around to where his legs were protruding from the edge of the crumpled netting. The thing yanked him forward.

"No!"

He clutched onto the Runner's frame with both hands, trying and failing to winch himself back in. Another yank and he was pulled almost all the way out of the cockpit.

"No, no, no!" he cried, uselessly, grabbing for anything to hold on to. His right hand found the handle of his crossbow.

A third yank and he was dragged completely from the illusory protection of the camouflage tent. He pulled the crossbow tight to his chest, so it wouldn't get snagged. The back of his head scraped painfully along the ground, slicing open on fragments of shrapnel. Then he was out in the black, pinned beneath the illuminated gaze and dripping fangs of an impossibly huge hellhound. For a second, he thought it was the alpha, not dead after all, come back to haunt him. It had the same mottled skin and massive jaws, but he quickly realized this creature was even larger—the real alpha.

Helio pulled the trigger without thinking and watched, mortified, as the crossbow bolt cleaved straight through the monster's soft palate and out the side of its skull, spraying his face with hot blood. But it didn't die. Primal terror overtook him as the hellhound reared, gurgling past its pried-open mouth before slamming its anvil-like claws back down onto his body. He tried to push the crossbow up like a shield, but it evaporated. A hundred daggers stabbed down into the side of his head.

The world went sideways. Somehow his headlamp was still on, but the picture it showed didn't look right. It was skewed, two-dimensional, like squinting through a cracked rifle scope. His cheek was wet and sticky. Someone was screaming in the distance, their voice hoarse with agony. A knife had made its way into his hand and was stabbing over and over into the beast, each thrust ejecting a heave of rotten breath onto his face. Teeth and blood were all he could see now. There was nowhere to go, no way to breathe pinned under its bulk. His heart was pounding, desperate for oxygen, but there was none. His thoughts, reduced to animal instinct, cycled between desperation to live and for the suffering to end. All light in the world was reduced to a distant speck, a golden thread.

Helio fell into the void.

"Mama..." he croaked.

She wasn't there. Nothing was there.

Only pressure. Compacting him back to dust.

And the thread. Circling, considering. Biding its time. He couldn't see it, but he could feel it—electrical, alien. Swirling around him—around the campsite—before annihilating everything in its path. Pained howls sliced into the dark. The thread grew brighter, blinding as it severed the heavens and earth.

Helio gasped, superheated air filling his lungs. His breath sounded wretched, like a hellhound. Like the beast that had nearly crushed the life from him. It was gone now, replaced by something else. An apparition had materialized above him, a fuzzy silver figure in the void.

Drawing on his last slivers of energy, Helio refocused what vision he had left and saw that it was a woman, naked, engulfed in a blistering aura of blue energy. She stared down at him with luminescent purple eyes, her coal-black hair lifted like a halo on a field of static. Golden fireflies danced in the darkness, sparkling in the thin thread of light that connected them.

Then she was gone, and so was he.

HELIO

SIERRA

A sea of bodies gyrated around him. Everyone was trying to get out of the communal mess hall, bottlenecked at the doors. No one panicked. No one screamed. No one said anything at all. There was only the sound of body parts pressing against each other, a throbbing susurration that drowned out the distant alarm bell.

Helio clung to his mother's chest, latching onto the steady rhythm of her heartbeat. She clung back. Every stroke of her fingers was like a cool cloth, siphoning the fever of fear from his burning forehead. They bobbed on the surface together, swaying in the tide. Slowly, steadily, they bubbled toward the exit, spilling out into the adjacent tunnelway.

"What's happening, Mama?" he asked.

They were running now, no longer froth on the sea. Back toward their clanhome.

"Hush, *mi tesoro*," she crooned, tucking his head under her chin as she ran.

Shadows ran past them, figments of warriors already dead. Greybulls. Their silhouetted heads swelled with abbreviated screams, fragments of lips and eyes stuck into sucking black whirlpools.

A familiar voice echoed from up ahead. It was shouting.

"Daddy!" he cried.

"Not now, Helio," his mother chided.

Grandfather was there too, angry like always, waving his arms wildly and yelling—growling wolf sounds. The old man turned as they passed. He had no eyes, only cavernous black saucers cored into his skull, oozing oily tears.

Helio squeezed his eyes shut, burying himself deeper into his mother's chest. When he opened them again, they were in their tenement. His mother tried to set him down on the family bed, but he gripped tighter.

"Whatever you do, Helio, don't come out."

"No, stay with me!"

She kissed his forehead, threw a blanket over him, and stepped away, her silhouette dissolving into the dark of the room. He sat there alone, shivering under the coarse linen, desperate to see what was happening. But the door was too far away, infinitely far. He lay down instead, pressing into the mattress in place of her. A vibration carried through the springs. Carried him away.

Vehicles.

Rumbling engines accompanied by shouting, voices.

Familiar voices.

Sierra?

He tried to call for his cousin, but his mouth wouldn't move.

Helio's eyes grew heavy. He fought each blink, but it was useless.

"You'll be okay, Cousin."

Sensation. Swinging back and forth, suspended in the air on his own stretcher. The distant vibration of booted feet pounding on the ground. Stale air filling his nostrils. Something was pulling at his face—*clawing at his eyes!*—but he couldn't see it, couldn't hear it. A heavy weight pressed down on him, pinning him—*the hellhound's jaws quivered over his head like a claw trap, its acidic saliva dripping onto his eyeballs, scorching them, melting them*—then hands on his forehead and shoulders.

Something gurgled in his ears, the rising crescendo of a scream, the same voice he had heard earlier. Then other voices, muffled shouts warbling in and out of coherence.

"Keep him still!"

Mama...

He was too deep to see, too deep to be, entombed too far down in the drowning pool to fight back, but the pain came for him anyway. It unfurled from the void like the petals of a flower, orange and black, shuddering with explosive radiance, all consuming. Until it was too much.

HELIO

NEWHAVEN

No one paid Helio any attention. The grown-ups were all too busy running to or from the vehicle hangar. Still, he kept to the shadows, cloaked in his blanket. There was a crowd ahead, but he snuck past them, crawling through a meandering tunnel of legs until he emerged into the open.

The massive hangar yawned open before him, illuminated under an array of floodlamps as bright as he imagined the sun must be. He squinted against the glare, rubbing little fists against his eyes, but his vision stayed blurry no matter how hard he pressed. Another group was up ahead—fighters standing in a circle with their guns pointed inward. They had no shadows.

Navigating back through the grove of booted feet, his hands and knees sinking into the muck, Helio found his way to a gnarled tree jammed up against the sandstone wall. Knifelike barbs protruded across the length of its scabby bark, but he had to see what was happening. Swallowing his fear, he clambered up, narrowly scraping past each deadly branch, ignoring the echoing howls of wolves in the distance.

Halfway there, he twisted back toward the hangar. It was dark now, save for a shimmering silver ring encompassing the fighters and a black-cloaked figure between them. He blinked against his failing vision, straining to see this new person. Her cowl tilted back, revealing luminous purple eyes. Staring back at him across the expanse.

A crackling groan sent him flailing for purchase. The tree lurched sideways, then began to drop. Helio shot a glance downward, but where the hangar floor once butted up against the tree there was now a drowning pool. Ochre bubbles ballooned from the depths.

He looked desperately back at the woman, and she smiled, but her smile wasn't human; it kept growing, splitting her face all the way to her ears. Searing arcs of energy crested from her head to the Hangarway ceiling as her distended mouth convulsed open, into the monstrous grin of a hellhound. Her massive incisors dripped with poison and charged violence.

"No!"

Helio lurched halfway out of bed, screaming, then promptly fell back onto his cot as the room started to spin. The corrugated steel walls of his tiny residential module rippled in the glimmer of an oil lamp on his bedside table. His head weighed twice as much as normal, and his mouth was bone dry.

The door burst open, making way for his cousin.

Sierra.

His nightmare faded at the sight of her. He was home.

She hesitated there for a moment before kneeling at his bed, scanning him nervously.

Helio tried to smile but couldn't make his face work. He was also having trouble seeing. His cousin's perpetually concerned face blurred in and out of focus, eventually settling somewhere in the middle. Her brows were furrowed even more than usual, and she twirled the end of her brassy-blonde ponytail the way she always did when she was worried.

"Is he awake?"

A new face appeared at the door: Elias. His best friend clamped the doorframe with a white-knuckled hand, stuck between coming and going.

"Eli," Helio croaked, then immediately began coughing, each expulsion of air a dagger driven into the side of his face. Sierra pulled a canteen from her belt and lifted it to his lips, cradling his bandaged head so he could drink. The insides of his mouth prickled in protest as he gulped down the acrid water.

"How are you feeling?" she asked.

He pushed away the canteen and forced himself up, grimacing as the room threatened to go askew again. Every tiny movement pulled his head down like an anchor. A loose corner of bandage tickled at his ear. He reached up to his face, tentatively patting the thick bands of cloth wrapped over his forehead and left eye.

"My eye…"

Sierra shook her head, lips pursed, tears budding in her eyes. He realized then he had never seen his cousin cry, not even when his parents—who were basically her parents as well—died shortly after their exodus from Hub. He wished his mother were here now. The whole clan had been hit by a wasting bacterial infection after moving into the mine. His mother died in the first year, his father the year after, though he was convinced that was due more to heartbreak than the disease—they had been inseparable.

"You're lucky to be alive," she reprimanded, but her voice wavered with restrained emotion. "What were you doing out there? Why didn't you come home when I called you?"

His fingers twitched as they probed a damp circle of gauze over his left eye—where it used to be. Scavrats never got through life unmarred and rarely died of old age. Survival was a daily struggle, and spending as much time as they did around antique machinery meant that injury, often gruesome, was the norm. Alchemy could only go so far. Still, this wasn't supposed to happen to him, not yet.

Sierra gently grasped his arm and pulled it down.

"You'll be okay," she said softly.

Helio tried to focus on the fact that he was alive, and he *could* still see, swallowing a wave of panic rising from his stomach to his throat. Even if everything looked strangely flat.

Sierra ushered Elias inside. His friend's paler than normal cheeks flushed pink, but he yielded, peering nervously behind him as he closed the door.

"What do you remember?" Sierra asked.

Teeth and blood, lit by gunfire.

Nearly dying.

Her.

Helio shuddered, but there was no avoiding it—deciding what to reveal and what not to. Maybe it didn't matter, since the revenant sister was long gone. Regardless, he had never been very good at lying to his cousin. She was only a few years his elder but had basically raised him after his parents died, and had an uncanny ability to extract the truth just by staring and waiting until he gave in. Had she been born farther west, she would have fit right into the sisterhood.

And so, he confessed, detailing the full events of his abbreviated hunt, rescuing the strange woman, and her apparent rescue of him, though he faltered when recounting his final terrifying encounter with the hellhound. Broken regulations were irrelevant at this point. What he had done was so far out of bounds as to merit punishments that didn't even exist. He took comfort in the fact that the truth would be safe with them. Sierra and Elias were the only two people in the world that he trusted—loved—but Grandfather would want answers. They stayed silent throughout the retelling, only becoming agitated near the end. A concerned look passed between them.

"Is *Mia* okay?" he asked, thinking back to his last memories of the Runner, steaming under the smoldering net. He had spent years upgrading her, sneaking parts wherever and whenever he could. She was the fastest vehicle in the clan as far as he was concerned. One day he'd prove it with a proper race—one day in his dreams, where fuel wasn't rationed tighter than water.

"No, Helio," Sierra replied, her concern visibly deepening. "It burned out."

"Burned... out." His lower lip trembled as accumulated shock took its toll. Everything could be fixed. A checklist of repair and maintenance items popped up in his head but quickly crumbled as reality set in. Years of work—his independence—up in smoke. "Wait," he said, double-checking his injuries, "if it burned... why didn't I?"

Sierra looked askance at Elias, who nodded back at her.

"We didn't find you with your Runner," she said. "We found you on the road, being carried back home by the revenant sister."

———

Getting dressed was much harder than Helio remembered. Even climbing out of bed took an extreme force of will, plus four helping if reluctant hands. Requisition must have messed up the last clothing order, swapping out his coveralls for a size down. Time and again he overshot a sleeve or tripped over a leg, cursing progressively louder. His left arm refused to cooperate, swinging wildly within his new blind spot.

"Fuck's sakes!"

The painkillers didn't help. They dialed his pain down to a semi-livable level, but at the cost of equally dulled motor skills and waves of vertigo.

He missed the left sleeve for the hundredth time, nearly pitching over in the process.

"Here, let me," Sierra said.

Helio clenched his jaw as his cousin finished dressing him, a flush in his cheeks.

"They won't let you see her," Elias protested. "Not yet."

The fact that the council had imprisoned their guest in the dungeon was not surprising; that she let them do so was. According to Sierra, the woman had refused to speak to anyone but him, even when denied food and water. He couldn't help but smile as he imagined his grandfather's rage—no one ever said no to the chief.

Helio had to see her. He wasn't sure why exactly, only that he felt responsible for her—and a longing that he couldn't admit to anyone, even those closest to him.

"We have orders to bring you to the council as soon as you can walk," Sierra said.

Helio winced, grabbing at his locker door as the module tilted just so.

"It was either us or Grandfather's enforcers." She looked no happier than him.

Great Chief Neron Ramirez. He frowned as he thought of his paternal grandfather, colloquially "Grandfather" to the clan. Of course he'd be summoned. The geriatric bastard had ruled over them with an iron fist for decades, both in Hub and Newhaven; there was no keeping him waiting.

He'd had the good fortune of not having to interact with the chief for months, to not have to relive the trauma each visit inflicted. It was Neron who had convinced the Greybulls to shirk the tithe, feeding them grandiose promises of independence. It was Neron who made the call to abandon the Union after the massacre that followed. It was Neron who was responsible for the death of his parents.

A haggard vision stared back at him from the mirrored surface of his locker. Disheveled, gaunt, the little color he had drained from his skin. His head looked like an enormous, angry mushroom. Sierra was right, of course; she was always right. His birthright was no protection from Grandfather, who would move the clan a second time before according any kind of special treatment to his only remaining heir.

"Fine," he conceded. "Let's go."

———

It didn't take long before Helio's hunger overtook his nausea; he had been laid up for three days after surgery and was starving. The queue at the kitchens was short today, maybe because the portions being doled out were so small. He stared at his half-full tin, waiting for the surly sector cook to deposit another scoop of fungal sludge. There wasn't a spot of color in it.

"That's it?" he asked.

The squat man waved his hand dismissively. "Keep moving."

There hadn't been meat in weeks, no thanks to him. Even still, he got two-thirds last time; he was sure of it. Sector 12 was starving. Every body that squeezed past him was scrawny, their hollow coveralls blowing about in the dank, forced air. The habitat modules weren't faring any better, pockmarked red with rust under the glow of drooping string lights. Decay was everywhere.

Helio peered downtunnel between slurps, counting how many bulbs were actually lit—less than last time, like his food ration. Sierra and Elias shuffled around while he ate, mostly running defense against overly curious clanfolk.

The three of them had moved to Sector 12 last year after Sector 11 collapsed, killing everyone who wasn't on shift. They had been lucky. Twelve was the same as the rest: an ancient tunnelway converted into a residential district, one of the many spokes that constituted their new hub. Even on the Scavrat scale of accommodations, it was tight. No sector was better than any other, but theirs was looking especially bad thanks to his compacted vision. Somehow seeing less also made the air feel thinner than usual. Like the lights, half of the HVAC was dead.

Helio coughed, choking on an errant waft of chemical fume.

"You okay?" Elias asked.

He could still see.

He could still see. As shitty as the view was.

Helio caught his breath after a couple attempts, then chugged the rest of his meal. Beyond the kitchen was a smaller tunnelway that would take them to the council, to Grandfather.

"Yeah," he said, clipping the emptied tin onto his harness. "Let's go."

All the residential sectors were the same, except for those reserved for the elders, of course—the aged sycophants who comprised Grandfather's court. They had the unique privilege of private quarters, located in the original crew areas on the mine's second level. Helio would never see luxury like that. If his grandfather ever did actually die, the chieftainship would likely fall to one of them instead of to him.

"Ghouls," he muttered, eliciting a concerned glance from Sierra.

The walk there was long and difficult. His feet felt detached from his body, lack of depth perception causing him to stumble constantly. More than once, he had to accept an elbow of support from Elias, who looked genuinely concerned—for his health or because of their impending audience, he didn't know. Elias had been his best friend since childhood but was as uncomfortable as his cousin with Helio's risk-taking. Still, they were a family and were together now, which meant a lot—meant everything in the absence of his parents.

Council chambers loomed up ahead. A pair of enforcers greeted them with flat expressions. They looked well fed, no sign of bagginess in their armor-plated fatigues.

"Wait here," grumbled the first, turning around to mumble something into an intercom panel.

Behind them were two massive steel doors: the entranceway to the Ancestral Council. This was the portal between the citizenry and its leadership, the only place where one could converse directly with the other. It felt more like the Hellmouth.

Sierra had radioed ahead to notify the guards of their arrival, but they were determined to make a fuss over the short notice. This, too, was Neron's doing. Helio's father spoke fondly of "better days" before he died. Theirs was a proud and stubborn people, resistant to taking orders from others, so maybe their exodus was inevitable, but they were always deeply united. Somehow, Grandfather had managed to divide their dwindling society when they needed that unity more than ever. Helio hated him for it, always would.

They waited in the foyer for half an hour, pacing and shuffling, before being admitted. In the interim, they were joined by Rico and Isabel, two more rangers who had accompanied Sierra and Elias on the rescue mission. The newcomers gave cursory greetings but mostly kept as far away from Helio as possible. He realized then how much leeway his friends were giving him considering the circumstances—considering *her*. The guards parted with ceremonious pomp as the portal opened behind them.

Helio had the misfortune of visiting his grandfather frequently enough to grow accustomed to the ostentatious trappings of his domicile. Neron had almost thirty years to transform it from an unremarkable concrete meeting room into a temple that was both lavish and intimidating. For all his acclaimed resistance to the Revenant Sisterhood, the chief had ended up no less a theocrat, except that his religion was self-worship.

It was even more baroque than last time. Burnished copper beamed from every surface, weaved into iron latticework along the walls and spiraling like electromagnetic coils around superficial plaster columns. A stepped stage topped with four high-backed padded chairs occupied the back of the room and was reserved for Grandfather and his fellow elders, intentionally elevated over opposing rows of bare-metal pews intended for petitioners. Hanging from the roof like chandeliers were hundreds of lengths of iron chain, intermixed with electric lamps turned bright enough to highlight the stage while keeping the audience in the dark. Finishing off the whole arrangement were enormous quilts fabricated from soft fur pelts, which hung like drapes at the corners. Helio scowled, his decades-old, reallocated coveralls suddenly more itchy than usual.

His crew seated themselves on the lefthand pew while the other two took the right. Two more rifle-wielding enforcers stood to either side of the raised platform. As the guests sat, a young page bedecked in furs marched onto the stage from behind the curtains, swaying under the weight of a large coil spring he wore like a sash. Helio did a double take. There were barely any children in Newhaven, certainly none he had seen in council chambers before. The boy was pale like all clanfolk, white-haired, and painfully thin, his narrowness exacerbated by Helio's monocular vision. Waiting until the room was completely silent, he raised a metal baton above his head, then dragged it along the spring, casting a deep atonal drone through the chamber.

"All rise!" called the enforcer on the left, and they did so—Helio a little more slowly than the others, bracing for the unwelcome sight of his last living ancestor. There would be no sitting back down during the interrogation, and he wondered uneasily how long his painkillers would last.

As the child exited the stage, a familiar mechanical whine emanated from the darkness beyond, paired with a loud rhythmic thump that sent a jingle of agitation through the hanging chains.

Whir, thump, whir, thump.

Ḥelio swallowed nervously as a monstrous silhouette coalesced out of the shadows. The chain links gyrated more vigorously as it approached, banging against each other like eager supplicants.

Whir, thump, whir, thump.

The platform groaned as a hulking titanium exosuit stepped into the light, two and a half meters tall, twice as wide as any man, and draped over with a giant gray fur cloak. It lumbered with the staccato jerkiness of a marionette. Grandfather's withered, ghostlike face—the only part of him visible within the machine, maybe the only human part of him left—peered out from the cavernous folds of its cowl, his sunken eyes beaming like searchlights. Neron was in his eighties or nineties—no one knew exactly—and long past conveying himself naturally. But he wouldn't relinquish control of the clan until he was dead; maybe not even then if the suit could still carry his rotting carcass around.

Helio swallowed again. Normally, he was undaunted by the chief's dramatic appearances. But this time something was different; he looked upon the cadaverous face within the fur-lined hood and saw his own face trapped within the killing jaws of the alpha. Beads of sweat were pooling around his bandaged eye, and his stomach gurgled uneasily. He clenched his fists and blinked the damp away, struggling not to appear intimidated by the old man—not now.

A cadre of similarly cloaked men unfurled around the chief,

each almost as old as Grandfather but not so decrepit that they needed a machine to transport them. Ironically, the lot of them looked how he imagined Cathedral's inner circle must—a gaggle of imperious witches handing down proclamations. As one, they sat in their thrones.

The young boy emerged once more, thrummed his instrument a second time, and departed. As the resonance of the metallic drone faded from the chamber, Grandfather leaned forward, the aged servos of his priceless exosuit whining their accommodation.

"Ranger Helio," he began. Neron never addressed his grandson as a relative. To do so would be acknowledgment of a birthright he had no intention of honoring. His voice was amplified for effect. "You have a lot of explaining to do."

———

Helio's nausea was worsening by the minute. Between his halved eyesight, the resumption of phantom dagger strikes into his skull, and his grandfather's booming voice, he was the least sure of himself than he'd ever been. Sierra stood somewhere to his left in his blind spot, and Elias was behind him and to the right. In this moment, he was alone—*but I can still see*, he reminded himself, necessarily to stave off creeping panic.

"Do you know what your stupid curiosity has brought into our midst?" Grandfather continued, his distorted, speaker-amplified snarl echoing around the chamber. Whereas the chief's eyes smoldered with anger, the faces of the other elders were drawn in various degrees of trepidation.

He looked desperately back at the woman, and she smiled, but her smile wasn't human; it kept growing, splitting her face open all the way to her ears.

The recalled dream assailed his nerves, prickling the hair on the back of his bruised scalp, but it also gave him an opening.

"The Chiefslayer," he replied, not overly loud; and as he said it, the murderous truth of the woman he had gone out of his way to rescue sank in. Not a revenant sister, but a revenant mother. He had snuck out of his home the day of the massacre and watched the horrible spectacle unfold from atop a stack of cargo crates. The Greybulls were reckless, provocative, driven by misplaced confidence—confidence instilled by Clan Ramirez. Chief Aubrey Greybull and an entire war party paid for that mistake with their lives. So much blood, so many body parts. The gruesome physical spectacle of it had been suppressed from his psyche until now.

"The Chiefslayer!" Grandfather repeated, unwilling to let Helio steal his thunder but scowling, nonetheless.

As though on cue, the other elders began to mumble concernedly and wring their hands. All theater aside, they must have been terrified. If they had been able to simply kill the revenant mother—Neron's legacy come back to haunt them—he was sure they would have done so by now. Instead, she lurked in their midst, untouchable and unknowable.

Helio waited for the hubbub to die down; this was his grandfather's show, after all. The best he could hope for was...

What? His eye glazed over as he considered what he'd gotten himself into, driven entirely by impulse. He had no idea what to hope for at this point, other than a chance to see the woman again, regardless of her bloody history, or maybe because of it.

"So!" the chief continued, leaning back and extending his enormous mechanical arms halfway across the platform. "The question is why." His eyes burned with frustrated uncertainty—and a little fear.

Helio knew his grandfather's mind and thus knew the real question was whether he had brought the woman back to

Newhaven to finish the job, to kill the right chief this time, the one who originally conspired to betray Cathedral.

"Explorer Scout Rico," called one of the elders. "Did Helio appear *bewitched* when you found him on the road?"

Helio's eye widened in alarm as everyone turned toward Rico. The man's mouth opened dumbly, eyes darting back and forth between him and the elder.

"El... Elder," he stumbled, "Helio was unconscious when we found... them. He was being carried."

"Carried..." continued an elder on Grandfather's opposite side. "So, you couldn't know if she had cast a spell on him or not."

The other ranger was clearly struggling between stating facts and pleasing his superiors.

"No," he concluded, "I couldn't—"

"Helio is himself!" Sierra called out, startling him as she stepped into his peripheral vision. "I've been with him since he got back, and there's no sign of corruption—"

"Are you an expert on the matter?" chided another of the elders.

Helio's jaw clenched with irritation at the man's strangle-worthy tone. It was an impossible question since no one was an expert. There was little distinction between fact and myth when it came to the priestesses of Cathedral.

Sierra chewed on her lip, retreating to cautious silence.

"So," Grandfather continued, "the lot of you found one of our people in the wastes"—Helio couldn't help but wince at the impersonal reference—"cradled in the arms of a *maldita* revenant *madre*, and thought it was wise to bring them both back to our home."

"He was dying!" protested Elias. Helio was surprised by his friend's impertinence, grimacing as he imagined the gentle man trembling under the council's ire. "She wouldn't put him down," he continued more quietly.

"We had no choice," Sierra confirmed.

The same elder that had addressed Rico flapped his arm at the ranger again, ignoring Sierra. "Is this true?"

Rico swallowed and flashed a glance at his companion, who stared straight ahead, unwilling to involve herself if she didn't have to. "Yes. Before I realized... what she was, I raised my weapon. Then I felt her eyes on me—"

"She rescued me," Helio interrupted, clamoring to redirect the council's indignation and hopefully banish any thread of conversation about him being fucking *possessed*. Grandfather squinted with annoyance but refrained from shutting him down, unable to deny his own curiosity.

"I got careless in the Devil's Claw. I was tracking a family of hares and got ambushed by hellhounds." A half-lie, but at least they were listening. "I escaped to my Runner, but the sun was down by then, so I had to make camp. They attacked in the night, almost killed me, then she appeared. I saw her kill them with her bare hands."

There was a collective muttering from the elders as myth became fact. Grandfather stood completely still, calculating his response.

"Why?" came his singular question.

"*Why?*" repeated Helio.

"All of it!" his grandfather retorted, clearly fuming at the woman's refusal to talk to him and his inability to coerce her. "Why would a revenant mother be out here in the first place? And why would *this* one in particular bother to save a Scavrat?"

Helio shook his head. He had omitted the part of the story where he'd rescued her first. Given the council's paranoia, it would have served as proof of him being charmed in some way

—assuming he wasn't. His reunion with the woman would have taken place from an adjacent cell.

"I don't know," he said, which wasn't overly far from the truth. "But I can find out."

Grandfather's face contorted into a sneer, but his small eyes darted around in thought. With a loud clunk and whine, his exosuit lowered itself so that his head was even with the rest of the elders. They hunched forward in their thrones and began to prattle in the ancestral tongue, thinking themselves impervious to eavesdropping. They had no idea that Helio's father had secretly taught it to him and Sierra when they were little, precisely so that Grandfather and his ilk could never keep secrets from them.

The old men argued for several minutes, exchanging theories on the woman being an assassin, but failing to reconcile why she had been so passive; or a spy, which was much more likely, but even that didn't make a lot of sense since the Matriarch wasn't known to bother with sneaking around. One of the elders suggested setting up an ambush: lead the revenant mother out into a residential sector, then attack, "fully prepared" this time. They debated the idea for a nerve-racking minute but deemed it too risky—for now. The lack of conclusion—and control—was ruinous to Grandfather, whose impatience only grew as they deliberated. At the end of the day, he had no choice but to relay his questions through Helio, and he loathed it with every shred of his malevolent soul.

The conclave disbanded with much less fanfare than it had begun, Chief Neron essentially storming off the stage after declaring that Helio would speak to the woman and relay back his findings. What happened after depended on what he learned. His body was vibrating as he left the audience chambers, from nervous excitement, fear, and stimulant aftereffects.

He was finally going to meet the Chiefslayer.

HELIO

NOWHERE ELSE TO GO

A grid of dimly lit iron cages extended ahead, stacked two-high against the cavern walls. Like the habitats, they were rusted red, though the rot penetrated much deeper here. All save one were empty. The revenant mother sat on her knees in the last cell on the left, palms up, eyes shut. Helio's coveralls clung to his back, damp with nervous sweat and moisture from the adjacent fungal farms. Two very nervous-looking enforcers hovered by the exit.

He hesitated, struck by the way the light contorted in her presence, refracting into dizzying colors. Something to do with his head injury, maybe. As much as he blinked, the effect remained. She was wearing standard-issue tan coveralls, which seemed entirely inappropriate. Sierra had said she was naked when the rescue party found her, carrying his unconscious body along the road. Just as she had been at the campsite, standing over him, bare skin as luminescent as the moon of old. Blood rushed to his groin as he recalled the sight of her.

Her eyes sprang open, freezing him in mid-reverie. Even from this distance, with only one eye, he was trapped by their otherworldly radiance. The air between them glowed purple and gold. There was no malice in it, just... power, teasing the hair from his skin.

Surreptitiously adjusting his coveralls, he turned and looked askance at the first enforcer. "Helio, here to see the prisoner."

The man had a permanent frown etched into his face. Rangers and enforcers didn't mix; it was just the way things were, maybe because Helio's kind spent so much time above-ground. Open spaces were unknowable, not to be trusted, as evidenced by the outsider in their midst.

"I know who you are."

The enforcer shared a look with his partner, then a fleeting glance toward the end of the dungeon, before nodding permission.

Helio stumbled forward, less gracefully than he would have liked, tripping once on the uneven stone floor as his depth perception failed him. Both enforcers followed him, but from a distance. The woman's eyes were on his the whole time, reeling him winch-like into their infinite depths. All other senses faded: sound, scent, the feel of his clumsy feet on the ground. Then she was there, gazing up at him past the auburn crust of her cage.

Helio crouched, wincing past exhausted nerves until they were face-to-face. Hers looked the same as it did that night: beautiful but weirdly transposed, devoid of color like the rest of her body. Her presence in this place felt like a dream, compounded by the stew of medicinals coursing through his blood. Ethereal yellow fog boiled in the corners of his vision, upset by the heavy breath of panting hellhounds.

An inadequate selection of words tumbled through his mind as she waited.

"Your wounds have healed," he blurted at last, stating the obvious.

"Yes, thank the Messiah," she responded immediately, her sonorous accented voice resonating in his ears—and his soul.

The enforcers, already stopped at a distance, fell back a few more steps. It was the first thing she had said since her arrival. They were probably expecting an invocation of some kind, followed by demons bursting from the ground. "Yours have not," she continued, her all-seeing eyes drilling past his bandage, into the empty socket below. The sutures there tingled.

"No," he replied quietly, his left hand brushing his face. "We're not so blessed as you..."

She nodded in stoic agreement, but a series of rapid blinks—a nervous tic, perhaps—suggested a hint of regret.

Helio cleared his throat, continuing to struggle for the right words. "Are they treating you well?" he asked.

"No," she replied brusquely, looking over his shoulder, her pupils dilating to minuscule black vortexes within an angry purple ocean. The shuffle of scurrying boots echoed through the dungeon as the enforcers retreated all the way back to the entrance. "Great Chief Neron likely thinks I came here to murder him."

"Did you?" he asked reflexively, more curious than concerned.

She faced him again, her still-withdrawn pupils dragging him physically forward—*past teeth the size of daggers, into her monstrous mouth, flushed dark pink and wet with desire.*

Helio gasped, clutching the cell door for balance. A flash of concern—so brief it may have been imagined—crossed the revenant mother's face, and her pupils widened back to normal, releasing their grasp on his soul. He sank to his knees, grimacing as he mirrored the uncomfortable posture she seemed like she could hold for an eternity.

"No," she replied tersely. "I thought him long dead by now."

He huffed for breath, wishing he had visited an alchemist for more analgesics before coming here.

"But it *was* you... wasn't it? Back at Hub."

She remained silent, but he was sure she understood his question: Was she the Chiefslayer? Her jaw clenched several times, then something appeared to pass before her faraway stare, some other recalled regret.

"We rarely determine our own fates," she finally said, wistfully.

It was an unsatisfying response from the clan's—the Union's even—most infamous villain. She was the face of Cathedral, living proof of his people's indentured servitude. His lustful fascination with the woman was overtaken by irritation—he wanted clarity for his reawakened but indistinct trauma. Was she a mass murderer or was she provoked? Or both?

A shooting pain stabbed through his skull, reminding him he didn't have much time left and had best get to the point.

"So, why did you come here?" he asked. "What do you want?"

"Why did I come here..." she repeated, trailing off, her eyes dipping away from his for the first time. "I suppose to return the favor."

"The favor?" he asked, then immediately regretted the question.

"Saving my life," she said. The words came slowly and with perceptible distaste.

Helio flinched, hoping the enforcers were far enough out of earshot not to catch his omission spoken aloud. He caught her eyes this time and subtly shook his head. A raised eyebrow suggested that she understood, unsurprisingly; was there any secret she couldn't discern simply by staring into his soul?

"I had nowhere else to go," she clarified, another series of rapid blinks betraying her displeasure at the revelation.

"To go..." he mumbled, confused. Why was she *going* anywhere? He recalled her bare, lacerated feet and the drab beige cloak she traveled in, wandering through the dire wood—

aimlessly. Flashes of childhood memory sprang into his mind, final goodbyes from friends he'd never be allowed to see again. Yelling at his father to stay. Crying into his mother's chest.

"You're an exile," he whispered, eye widening in disbelief. The irony of their shared fates seemed absurd.

The woman nodded slowly. For an instant she looked old, terribly old, her true age betrayed by unimaginable fatigue.

"The Chiefslayer couldn't exactly show up at Hub," she said, her perfectly symmetrical lips curling up in the barest hint of a smile. "Nor was I about to take up with the remnant." Helio shuddered. He had encountered their kind on a couple of exploratories: subhuman, barely removed from wild animals. "I knew there was a community east of Cathedral. Well east..." She trailed off, recalling a journey no normal human could have survived on foot, half-naked. "But I didn't know it was you."

Helio's heart fluttered as her eyes captured his again.

"I've never heard of such a thing," he said, dumbfounded.

"No."

"What did you do?"

The woman's lips moved silently, her hands clenching and unclenching in her lap as she considered whether to answer the question. Her pupils shuddered and the ends of her coal-black hair floated aloft like charred grass in the wind.

His teeth felt suddenly itchy.

"I betrayed my covenant," she said at last, her static-charged halo flattening with the admission.

Helio could already anticipate his chief's rage. Grandfather wasn't likely to be satisfied with the woman's lack of actual motive—*the woman*. No one had bothered to ask her name when she was busy butchering their people. All they had was a moniker, a murderer's name.

"What should I call you?"

She paused again, reluctant despite having revealed so much to him already.

"Rebekah."

A human name. Not what he expected.

"Rebekah. I'm Helio."

She nodded.

A wave of chilling nausea swelled in his gut, followed up with another shooting pain in his skull. Mixed emotions battled with physical pain, leaving him exhausted. Unable to sit any longer, he pushed himself up to standing, swaying queasily as his focus kept drifting. Rebekah didn't move but her eyes followed him.

"I need to report back to the council, then rest," he said.

She nodded again, mute as he stumbled toward the exit.

One of the enforcers grunted as he passed. Helio didn't stop.

"Wait," the guard said, stepping close enough that they shared breath.

Helio frowned at the man. "What?"

"What did she say?" the enforcer asked, not rudely. If anything, he seemed awestruck.

"Say?"

"The Chiefslayer," the man hissed, darting his eyes around but too scared to look back.

Helio looked back at the revenant mother—at Rebekah. Beautiful and terrible. Powerful but without purpose. The answer—her own answer—seemed impossible.

"She had nowhere else to go."

HELIO

AN EMERGENT MOON

Helio trudged through the dire wood, seeking. The sky was gone, replaced with a ravenous vortex of black on black that spanned the heavens. Each time his gaze wandered upward, he felt its hunger—infinite, rotating for all eternity. It emitted no light, no natural light. Even so, he could discern the silhouettes of the ghostly aspen surrounding him. Their sagging boughs glowed bioluminescent yellow, enmeshed into a winding tunnel that conducted him forward, deeper into the forest. He had been walking for as long as he could remember, his bare feet reduced to bloody lumps of meat.

A silver light bloomed up ahead, but he wasn't startled. It was here for him, as it had been each time before—each newborn passage through the woods. He belonged with the light —with *her*—but the way was closed. A second thicket blockaded the path, humanoid trees composited from the bodies of her victims. Lording over the stand was a mutilated old chief-tree, still wearing a golden circlet atop its head. Its multifold branch-bones spread out like great skeletal wings. A deformed child-thing huddled below, its thrice-twisted spinal column scabbed over with ashen bark. Branches of sinew lashed out from the lot of them, dozens of once-arms and once-legs barring the way.

As the wind came up, the thicket's shriveled face-leaves shaped it into a whispered warning. "Go back."

He wouldn't, couldn't.

Helio cut at them with his knife, severing their arms.

And arms.

And arms...

Cutting away the remnants of their faces so they couldn't leer at him. Thick brown blood bubbled from the people-trees' savaged bodies, smothering the ground and sucking at his feet as he plowed through their remains.

Ahead was the angled wedge of a rocky promontory, offering sanctuary upon a bed of quartz. It fluoresced silvery white under the light of an emergent moon. The muck dragged at him, but he persevered, dragging one bloodied stump after the other until able to heave himself onto its smooth surface.

Helio lay back and closed his eye, but the glare persisted. When he opened it again, there was no heavenly satellite above him, only her—only Rebekah. Her slender body was aglow, radiant silver bisected by veins as black as the void above, eyes crystalized into purple geodes. She was on top of him, and he was inside her, pulled deeper with every blink. He yearned to touch her light but was pinned. Coal-tipped breasts pierced his chest, and jagged claws burrowed deep into his shoulders. Panic surged in his groin. Rebekah smiled, so wide that her alabaster face began to crack, recomposing into the monstrous sculpt of a hellhound's jaws.

Breathless, unable to scream, he stared into her alien eyes and was consumed, until all that remained was the void—

"No!"

Helio sprang up to seated, just as he had last time. Mother Rebekah was standing at the end of his bed, watching him.

Blinking confusedly, he edged backward, stuck between nightmare and reality. But she didn't disappear in a puff of smoke, nor did she transform into a hellhound and saunter out the door. She was actually there, in his habitat.

"What the fuck," he croaked, unable to make sense of what he was seeing.

The door flung open, rebounding noisily from the structure's flimsy steel walls, and Sierra stormed in. A crowd stirred in the tunnelway behind her, held at bay by a pair of enforcers, then disappeared again as she slammed the door shut.

"Get away from—" Sierra's outburst was cut short as Rebekah turned her attention on his cousin, freezing her in place.

"I'm okay!" he managed to blurt out, still struggling to understand what the hell was going on. He was drenched in sweat, and a cloying stickiness congealed in his underwear. The damp bedsheets were twisted into a thick roll over his groin.

Sierra swallowed hard, her hand hovering over a pistol at her hip. The revenant mother shook her head, slowly, the jet-black tips of her hair starting to rise.

"Just. Stop," he said past a mouth dry and thick with sleep, trying to defuse whatever was happening here.

Sierra lowered her hand but to her credit didn't relinquish her glare upon the priestess.

"When did they release you?" he asked Rebekah, perplexed.

Sierra snorted. "They didn't," she said. "She released herself."

"What?"

"She walked right out, then came here. Followed your scent maybe," she sneered.

"My scent...?"

He shuddered, nerves frayed by both memory and dreams.

Maybe this mystery woman was a hellhound after all, able to change form as she pleased.

Rebekah turned to face him. "I had nowhere else to go," she intoned. "Isn't that right?"

Prickles of anxiety stabbed along his clammy arms and legs. "But Grandfather—"

"Is powerless," she finished.

He buzzed with reflexive glee at her rebuke of Neron, but it didn't last. Elation promptly became trepidation as he realized they were *all* powerless in her presence, as evidenced by her unfettered ascent into the residential sectors. It must have been chaos out there. The fact that no one was killed—

"Was anyone hurt?" he asked his cousin apprehensively.

"No," she replied. "Not yet."

—was a miracle.

The Ancestral Council had declared itself "in session until further notice" after his meeting, meaning his dictated report was relayed via his sector's administrative office. Helio had primarily urged against any kind of rash response to the revenant mother's presence. Liberties were taken, including the assertion that as an exile of Cathedral, Rebekah was an enemy of their enemy and therefore an asset, if not a friend—she could never be that. By allowing her to stay, he explained, they could acquire useful information on both Cathedral and Hub (neither of which Grandfather had any interest in). He considered adding a note about provocation playing a role in her past crimes but decided it would have made no difference. It was only a matter of time before Grandfather acted to remove her from their home, one way or the other. There was a kingdom of meager subsistence under his rule to get back to, and she had no place in it.

"So," he said, "what now?"

Her unemotional façade fractured for a moment as she considered. "I'm unused to being idle."

Helio squinted at her. "I don't think Grandfather would approve of you setting up a church down here."

Rebekah's nostrils flared. "The New Covenant is not for the likes of you," she said, in exactly the imperious tone he would have expected from her ilk.

"The likes of me," he repeated, not without some hurt.

She seemed to pick up on his dejection, blinking several times in rapid succession and softening her tone. "Did your people bring any of the Union's Archive with you?" she asked. "Perhaps I could help... analyze it."

To say his life had been uneventful to this point would have been incorrect. Surviving the cursed earth was enough of a challenge, never mind close encounters with demons, hellhounds, and Old World deathtraps. But at no point would Helio have imagined playing chaperone to a revenant mother—or having feelings for one.

"Grandfather will never let you near it," Sierra interjected.

He nodded. "She's right. He'll definitely think you're a spy then."

Quiet fell on the room, Rebekah's gaze becoming distant. He knew what it was like to lose his home, but only as a child and with family intact—for a time, anyway. She had lost everything. It must have been catastrophic.

A discordant hum emanated through the walls from outside, more than the usual buzz of perpetual labor. As disturbed as Sector 12 was, the council must have been losing their shit.

"Then guide my hand," Rebekah said at last.

A flash of recalled dream and subsequent heat coursed through him. Helio turned to look askance at his cousin, but she just shrugged, as lost as he was.

HELIO
PETRIFIED GIANTS

The Ancestral Council remained off-limits even after Rebekah's "escape," which was concerning. The only message from them was a terse three-line directive waiting for him at the sector administrator's office:

> **Ancestral Council still debating.** (When to strike, no doubt.)
> **You will be monitored.** (Already obvious, from the enforcers that trailed them everywhere they went.)
> **Duties restricted to Newhaven.**

This last directive came as little surprise. As a ranger, Helio's duties included hunting, scouting, and looting. He was glad for a reprieve from haunted forests, and most of their clan's "scouting" involved breaking into facilities that the Americans back at Hub secretly relayed to them—not information that Grandfather wanted to share with a revenant mother, exiled or otherwise.

It was a longstanding arrangement: hit sites before they're registered with Hub's Council of Chiefs (and therefore Cathedral), loot the highest-value items they can find, and exchange them at designated drop points for raw resources—food and fuel, mostly. Without the clandestine support of their estranged allies, which was a secret within Hub and within the general populace of their own clanhome, Clan Ramirez could never have survived; this was Neron's great lie to his people. But it was also expected that they wouldn't keep any advanced military hardware for themselves—one exosuit aside—which made the deal look very much like another tithe. As much as Helio yearned for his clan to rejoin the Union, it felt too much like servitude. In this regard, he was aligned with his chief, though he feared what the alternative might look like. More than once, he had overheard elders tabling the idea of raiding Union convoys to Cathedral.

No mention of their special guest was made during the sector's daily broadcasts, but word spread quickly enough after her first appearance. Even dressed in full coveralls and goggles to conceal her eyes, crowds parted for them. Those who practiced the old faiths made signs on their chests to ward themselves against evil. Mother Rebekah was unaffected—at first.

Being confined to the clanhome meant maintenance duty plus the usual sundry tasks each citizen was responsible for: reclamation, fabrication, sanitation, and endless upkeep of their ancient machinery. The work of living was never ending. Most of his training attempts failed, his charge simply refusing to cooperate. At one point he suggested she make use of her supernatural strength to expedite delivery of a cartload of steel beams to another sector. It was the first time since the campsite that he had felt true fear in her presence.

"The Messiah's blessings are no parlor trick," she had retorted, her lip curled back like the alpha's.

After he backed off, she muttered something about her power being a finite resource, to be tapped into only when no other means availed itself. It felt like an excuse, but for what he didn't know.

Eventually, he discovered Rebekah had an uncanny and seemingly uncharacteristic aptitude with vehicles. When asked about it, she explained that the Matriarch's servants were occasionally sent out of the city on long-distance missions. That required proficiency with both driving and repair, given the consequences of becoming stranded in the wastes. Her longest tour had been to Hub, the fact of which ended their first real conversation in short order.

In any case, she clearly didn't enjoy menial labor. It was a distraction, and her despondence grew by the day. Each evening, the revenant mother dispatched herself back to the dungeon, but on the third day she retired early, and on the fourth she didn't show up at all. Helio had grown as accustomed as one could waking to her standing silently at the end of his bed—Sierra had long since given up on keeping her out—so when he woke to an empty habitat, his immediate assumption was that Grandfather had made his move.

After hurriedly dressing, he raced to the dungeon, plowing through the crowds as he chased his fears. When he arrived, dizzy and out of breath, he was relieved to find Rebekah sitting in her cell as she had that first day, except instead of her hands resting calmly on her lap, they were clasped tightly together in prayer, her gray skin compressed to pure white at the knuckles. Her eyes were closed, eyelids jittering with rapid movements. He waited, trying but failing to read the silent invocation on her lips. All at once her hands released and her eyes opened, prayer completed, but she continued to stare forward instead of at him.

"You didn't come to the sector today," he said, stupidly.

"No."

He hadn't learned much more about her in the few days they had spent together, except that she ate twice as much as a normal person when given the opportunity and tired much more slowly. As eager as she seemed to be to prove to herself that she was still a functioning member of society—even one that wasn't her own—she was deeply introverted, tortured. There was nothing about her homeland or her exile. Most of their "conversation" thus far had been instruction, leaving his stupid curiosities unsated.

"Are you feeling okay?" he asked.

Rebekah swallowed, raising her head to take in her surroundings as though for the first time, enigmatic purple eyes scanning the ceiling.

"The walls close in," she said. "I miss the sky."

It made sense. As powerful as this woman was, she wouldn't be accustomed to the Scavrat life. Still, he wondered how much of her suffering was due to living belowground as opposed to living in a place where she was hated rather than adored—if such was even the case back in Cathedral.

Helio, too, was getting itchy for a change of scenery, not just because he craved the open road but because the absence of follow-up messages from the council was concerning. He had no idea what they were up to and his sector administrator, with whom he'd had a decent relationship up until recently, offered no insights. He had never felt less safe in his own clanhome.

"None of it will matter soon, anyway," she mumbled, as though reading his mind, her hands flexing in her lap.

She moved like the wind, her black body in multiple places at once, connected by streaks of darkness ripped from the void. And everywhere she went, death followed.

He shivered as the childhood memory assaulted him. It couldn't be allowed to happen again. He glanced back at the enforcers, who kept their posts despite their impotence.

Something had to give.

"Meet me at the vehicle bay in an hour."

———

Sierra wouldn't have approved. His cousin had barely said two words to him since he took Rebekah under his wing, but as rangers they couldn't escape each other. Luckily, she was on a hunt today.

Helio breathed deeply of the almost-fresh air that crept in past the steel-gated exit ramp, flavored with the comforting musk of oil and hot metal. Just like in Hub, the vehicle bay served as the primary way in and out of Newhaven and was the clanhome's outermost structure. Beyond it, a defensive corral plotted with intentional dead ends and laden with mines wound through the gutted aboveground excavation site, terminating in another gate that opened to the wastes. That was his destination.

"Grandfather's gonna lose his shit," Elias grumbled, wiping his greasy gloves on a shop rag.

"He's already lost his shit," Helio countered, double-checking the fuel lines on the Runner. "If something doesn't change soon, it'll be a bloodbath."

"What about your confinement orders?"

He chewed on his lip, searching for resolve and finding it in Rebekah's words.

"Neron is powerless."

Maybe against her, but not him. Still...

"Fuck my orders."

His friend's complexion paled more than usual, eyes darting around the hangar as Helio moved to check the tires. No enforcers were present yet on account of the revenant mother's absence, but they wouldn't be far behind when she got there.

"Besides, he should be happy that I'm getting her outside," he continued, frowning at the mediocre state of his friend's vehicle. He missed *Mia*.

"Happy enough to lock the gate shut behind you," Elias mumbled.

Helio snorted. "I just need a little distraction."

"Distraction... and if they do lock you out, who's going to get *me* out of the dungeon?"

"You'll be fine," he said, standing. "And if not, all the enforcers are scared of Sierra."

Elias couldn't suppress a grin, but it didn't last. The lithe man tilted his head, scanning Helio with his piercing blue eyes. "What do you want, Helio?"

"Want?"

"From *her*."

Helio flushed at the question, knowing he could never answer it honestly, even to his best friend. Yes, he wanted to know the truth behind the massacre. Yes, he wanted to know more about the woman's sisterhood and how exactly she was able to do what she did. But mostly it wasn't about what he wanted *from* her—it was that he wanted *her*.

"Answers."

It wasn't a lie, at least.

Elias shook his head. "You sound like your grandfather."

Helio grimaced as he lovingly grasped his friend's shoulders.

Rebekah glided into the hangar behind them.

"It's time," Helio said.

Elias turned, his expression pensive as they both stared at the woman. "I hope you know what you're doing, brother."

"So do I."

———

Leaving was easy. The council had done its best to lock down local operations, but it hadn't bothered to block egress in any way. He didn't see the enforcers' faces when he and Rebekah raced out of the hangar, making their escape while Elias and the maintenance crew "battled" a small oil fire, but he imagined they looked relieved.

Helio's people worked around the clock in the subterranean caverns of their clanhome, and his shift coincided with early evening aboveground. It was already growing dark, the earth the same cast of burnt orange as on his last outing. He focused his newly narrowed vision on the road ahead, fighting back a surge of mental and physical distress. The sensation was bizarre; he couldn't remember what things used to look like before, but now it felt as though his body was an overly large exosuit that he— the *he* inside the suit—was looking out of through a very small window. The driving goggles didn't help matters. Was this how Grandfather felt?

Dust devils writhed along the cracked earth to either side of the roadway, glittering red in the sparse light of the sun. Hot blasts of wind and sand beat against his face. The *outside* wasn't safe. He knew this as every Scavrat did, but to him it was beautiful at this hour, peaceably empty save for the endless migration of tumbleweeds. Rebekah was silent behind him, but he could feel her legs pressed tight against his seatback in the cramped cockpit.

Up ahead, the ancient asphalt broke apart, forking into one dirt road leading northwest to the Devil's Claw and another south to his destination. He turned south, driving fast and hard over the sunbaked desert flats. Within minutes they were descending into a winding canyon pathway. The Runner's suspension shuddered as they dove into the prehistoric depths of the earth, the rocky plateau gradually weathering down into dense fields of enormous sandstone hoodoos.

Petrified giants stared down at them as they passed, guardians of the only place in the world he felt something approaching religious reverence. He had originally scouted the area to look for an Old World town mentioned in the Archive but instead found a temple, a sacred and private place he came back to whenever he could. The great striped pillars seemed intentionally placed for contemplation under the sun. One in particular he had dedicated to his mother, his most precious ancestor. It was under that tower—resplendent in variegated stripes of gray, brown, and red—that they stopped.

Helio exited first, wobbling as his lagging focus reoriented. Rebekah pulled off her goggles as she clambered out after him, scanning the tight-ringed clearing with her otherworldly eyes. Did she see something different from him? A secret world lurking above, or below, this one? The gray skin of her cheeks glistened silver under the dusty rays of fading sunlight. She closed her eyes for a moment, rigid features giving way to rapture. He couldn't help but stare. Her tan coveralls rippled in the breeze, like shifting dunes under the wind. They were zipped tight at the neck, the same way she would have worn her habit, but he had already seen what lay beneath, had imprinted her nakedness into his memory. He wanted to see it again, pressed against the pillar—wanted to feel it.

"This is your holy place," she said, turning to look at him.

He snapped out of his lustful daydream. "Why do you say that?" he asked, flushing.

She gestured at Aria, the tallest of the hoodoos he had privately named after his mother, then turned to point at each of the others in turn.

"Eight of them stand in this clearing."

He frowned, confused. "So?"

She completed her circle and stared at him again, adding the furrow of her brow to his own. He squirmed under her scrutiny, suddenly feeling very much the savage heathen she undoubtedly considered him to be.

"Why did you bring me here?" she asked, not clarifying.

He licked his lips, suddenly self-conscious. Her apparent bliss had disappeared as quickly as it arrived. What was this dry, desolate place to her compared to Cathedral?

"Follow me."

Aria was tall, maybe three times his own height, but had enough handholds on its silty surface to climb. He had no doubt the revenant mother would be capable of scaling it, assuming she didn't just magically levitate to the top. After a somewhat precarious minute of vertigo, punctuated by several of the more brittle handholds crumbling away into dust, he sat atop its smooth, pebble-like cap. Rebekah appeared beside him as though conjured from thin air, mercifully in full view to his right. The closer they got to the sun, the more beautiful she was.

Sprawling out before them were hundreds more stone giants. Each was a shard of reflected light from the fading sun, waxing and waning under the fast-moving shadows of the clouds above. There was no life here, not even a blade of wild grass, but in this moment it felt like a normal world, uncorrupted by the Hellmouth.

Helio glanced at his companion, her craned knees brushing against his as they crowded together on the small pillar top, and was relieved to see some of his own reverence mirrored in her wide alien eyes. She turned her gaze to him, and his heart leapt even though her pupils remained fixed. He gripped the stone more tightly, worried that his suddenly clammy hands might send him into the abyss.

"I'm surprised," she said, eyes still holding his. "I thought your people were scared of open spaces."

Your people. His elation crashed again. Would he ever be anything but a Scavrat in her eyes?

He turned to look back upon the rock field.

"My *people*," he said with emphasis, "had to adapt. Newhaven is nothing like Hub." Rebekah blinked rapidly at the mention of his ancestral home. "It never will be."

How many years did Clan Ramirez have left before it petrified and died? Its citizens no more meaningful to the world than these anonymous statues, bereft of their legacy. The frail page boy at the council chambers materialized in his memory, his too-small body traipsed around like a puppet for his grandfather's benefit. Sector 12 had no children, which was probably for the best. To birth a child into their world would be a crime.

"You want to go back," she said. "To the Union."

"Yes... but it's forbidden. And even if we managed to convince them, Gran—Neron is too proud."

Of all his familial conflicts, this was undoubtedly the greatest. Helio had gained some ground over the years with the Americans—Greybull and Vega—and even made inroads with Clan Harper, but theirs was purely a mercantile arrangement. Still, there had to be a way.

Greybull...

"I need to know," he said bluntly.

Rebekah nodded, eyes seeking west, back to her own former home.

"We were informed. About the tithe being broken—"

"Informed?" he interjected, dubious.

"Not all of your clans are so independently minded. Most of you understand our..." She paused, stumbling uncomfortably over her own words. "That the arrangement benefits everyone."

He bit down on his tongue, resisting the urge to protest. Newhaven's failure was proof enough of his people's inability to go it alone.

"So, your matriarch sent you to punish us."

Rebekah flinched at the mention of her former mistress.

"Yes. But only their chief."

Their chief, meaning Aubrey Greybull, unwitting and unwise pupil to Neron Ramirez.

"Only!"

"If we didn't set an example, everything would have fallen apart. Hub would have ended up like Newhaven."

He flushed at the revenant mother's appropriation of his own sentiments to defend her past actions. The worst part was that it made sense. Or was his desire getting in the way of his judgment?

"What about the others?"

Where before, his dream had shown their deaths, he now heard them: warriors and civilians alike—a dozen? two dozen? more?—screaming in horrible, abbreviated agony as Mother Rebekah brought a brutal end to all who stood against her. She moved among them like a wolf among rats.

But there was something that came before that, something he hadn't noticed the first time—gunshots. And before that the fuzzy memory of his grandfather arguing with Chief Greybull as his mother rushed him home. Neron was yelling at the other chief to stand for his principles, while Helio's father pleaded with them both for calm.

He answered his own question. "They attacked first."

Rebekah was staring straight forward, blinking continuously. They sat in silence for a minute, interrupted only by the dissonant whistling of the wind among the hoodoos and the heavy, steady breaths of the woman beside him. He wanted to embrace her as much as he wanted to push her off the top.

"I had no choice," she said quietly, as much to herself as to him.

The towers closest to the horizon had submerged into darkness. There were so many more things he wanted to ask her, things he *needed* to know, but time was running out. An unasked question from the dungeon flashed in his memory, suddenly urgent.

"What did you mean before when you said none of this will matter?"

Rebekah straightened her slumped shoulders and reset her expression back to its usual formality. Her lips parted, but she hesitated while deciding how much to share. An exile, yes, but maybe not long enough removed to reveal all her secrets.

"Something is coming."

"Something...?"

"You know about battle walkers, from the Old World?"

Helio stiffened and nodded in mute response.

"We—the Matriarch... has eight of them."

His vision skewed, as though the stone pillar he was very precariously perched upon had tilted sideways.

"Her God-engines. And she means to use them to cleanse the world of her enemies, demon and human alike."

Eight! Was this why the Americans were so agitated lately? Not that it mattered. They were fucked, no matter how far underground his people burrowed. Nothing they had discovered could stand up to a single battle walker, let alone a fleet.

Almost nothing.

He turned to his unlikely companion.

"I have to show you something."

HELIO

BASTION

"What *is* this?" Rebekah asked.

They were huddled around a pristine metal table in the Archive: Rebekah, Helio, and Sofia, the cripplingly nervous archeolog on shift. She was a friendly, but that didn't mean she was happy sharing their most precious secrets with a revenant mother.

A small army of rifle-wielding enforcers had been waiting for them when they got back, barring the entrance back into the vehicle hangar. Their commanding officer, a power-hungry sycophant named Hugo, headed the formation. Helio had often fantasized about punching the man in the face. "Chief Neron has declared that... the witch"—this part mumbled with nervous hesitation—"is not welcome back inside Newhaven." The standoff didn't last long.

"This," Helio said, tapping the photo for emphasis, "is Bastion."

He hadn't even felt Rebekah get out of the Runner. She was sitting there with him one minute, and the next she was in the middle of the squad, half of them disarmed and the other half sprawled in a pile on the ground. It was the first time he had seen her move like that since she took on the hellhounds and it was no less awe inspiring, her inhuman speed and power overwhelming his confused senses.

"Bastion?" she asked, fanning out a batch of black-and-white photographs on the table. The archeolog was gesticulating—timidly—for her to be careful with the evidence. "A city from the Old World?"

One of the enforcers had moved to trigger an alarm but was stopped short by a blowtorch-wielding Elias. The other mechanists present didn't know what to do, so had watched silently as Helio and Rebekah ran past them into the tunnelway and onto the Archive, repository of all clan knowledge. Their time was limited, but it always had been. Whether Rebekah had been allowed to stay one day more or ten, it was inevitable that Grandfather would make a move, either out of personal vendetta or some misguided notion of trading her to the Americans. He only had to make sure that once they finished here, he didn't end up taking her place in the dungeon.

"Not from the Old World," he replied. "From last year."

The grainy photographs showed a distant city, bordered by a broken mountain range on one side and curtain walls on the others.

"That's... impossible."

"I discovered it on an extended scouting mission out east. Newhaven was going through hard times—harder than usual—so I left, hoping to find something we missed. I almost didn't make it back."

"Great Mother spoke of other communities, after the War, but mostly the remnant. Nothing like this..."

Helio watched Rebekah as she cycled repeatedly through the evidence with trembling hands—from dwindling adrenaline or fear he couldn't tell.

"There's more," he said, motioning to Sofia for the second box.

The archeolog extended one hand to retrieve the first stash before dispensing another, as was Archive policy, then quickly withdrew it and handed over a second metal box. He opened it, revealing a small stack of heavily reused and yellowed logbooks and another batch of photographs, which he set down beside the first. They showed the same scene but from much closer.

"We set up a monitoring outpost. Telescopic lenses and a communications rig to intercept their radio signals. That's when we saw this."

He pushed away the top few photographs, his own hand shaking this time, until he got to a close-up. Pictured on it, noisy and poorly focused, was the unmistakable silhouette of a large flatbed truck with a completely intact battle walker strapped onto its trailer.

———

There had been four battle walkers in all, captured at different times but all identical in appearance, bearing Old World insignias.

"Have they fielded them?"

"No, not yet."

It was the first time he had seen Rebekah truly shocked. Not only was her precious Last City not the last city at all, but its God-engines were not the only battle walkers to survive the World War. If it had been anyone but him showing her this, she probably would have thought them a lying heretic (and ripped their spine out).

"Most of the radio comms we picked up have been from their military. Not encrypted because they have no idea anyone else is out here. But when these photos were taken, the channels were empty. No one was saying anything."

"A secret?"

"I think so. And whoever took them either hasn't figured out where the On switch is or…"

"Or?"

"Or they're too scared to turn them on."

Sofia was listening intently, wide eyes switching back and forth between them. Helio knew she was documenting everything the revenant mother said for later transcription. He paused to observe the meticulous chamber that contained the sum total of his clan's knowledge. It was a different world from the rest of Newhaven—the habitation sectors anyway. The past was the future and it had to be preserved accordingly. Long rows of well-lit metal shelving climbed all the way to the smooth concrete ceiling, each exactingly catalogued by date, subject, and region. The chamber was clean, sealed, and climate controlled. Deposits were available to everyone, rangers mostly, but withdrawals required administrative approval. Helio's limited sway as grandson to the chief had bought him some favor, but having a revenant mother in tow also helped.

No one had come for them yet, but it was only a matter of time. There was no audible alarm—that would cause too much panic—but there was almost certainly a force on the way.

"Does Neron know?" Rebekah asked.

"He knows everything."

"And?"

"And nothing. Too far away. Too dangerous. He'd rather raid our own people than take any risks."

Rebekah looked up at him, calculating. "He's not wrong."

Helio sighed and rubbed his stubbled cheeks, hand moving unconsciously to stroke his bandage. The skin underneath was starting to grow itchy. He wanted nothing more than to rip it off but wasn't prepared yet to face the facts of his loss. "No, he's not…"

"Did you figure out where they found them?"

"No. Somewhere farther east maybe."

"Or southeast…"

"The Deadlands?" Helio's spine tingled uncomfortably. He had traveled far and wide on behalf of the Americans and in his own pursuit for something that could turn the tide of entropy, but never there. He'd rather face the Hellmouth head on.

"This could change everything," Rebekah said, barely above a whisper.

A loud series of bangs hit the outer door. They turned as one, eyes on the slab of steel that sealed them in.

"Come out now!" came a distorted voice, unrecognizable behind its electronic amplification. "Come out now and no one will get hurt."

Helio's heart started to pound, his eardrums thumping along in a panicked rhythm. Visions of dead clanfolk passed before his eyes. He looked at Rebekah, looked at her hands, her instruments of death, and grasped them without thinking. They were supple, warm despite their waxen tone. She looked at him, saw his fears, and grasped back, her fingers interlocking with his.

"Please, Reb—"

"Don't worry," she interjected. "I won't." Rebekah turned to the archeolog. "Open the door."

Sofia gave the precious evidence one last harried glance, then darted away, scuttling from the viewing room to the access console at the front of the Archive. Helio and Rebekah uncoupled and followed after her in lockstep, continuing to the door.

The archeolog entered a long disengagement sequence, culminating in an overly jolly confirmation jingle. A series of loud *thunks* erupted along the bottom of the door, followed by a hiss of air as its pneumatic locks released. She glanced back at them for confirmation, hand hovering over a large button illuminated red.

Helio took a deep breath and nodded.

Sofia pressed down. The door lurched, then rolled back noisily along its tracks. Standing outside was every enforcer in Newhaven, armed and crouched behind mobile barricades. In their center was Grandfather.

Helio's eye widened. The chief almost never left Level 2. He ruled entirely by proxy, sequestered within the sustainment apparatus of his exosuit. The ancient machine-man towered over his enforcers, his fur cowl grazing the tunnelway's ceiling. Grandfather's disembodied head stared down at him from within. From this close, Helio couldn't help but be reminded of their uncomfortable family resemblance. He saw his own face there, trapped under the jaws of the hellhound.

The chief had reconfigured his body for the occasion, swapping out robotic arms and hands for two belt-fed rotary autocannons—the kind of advanced weaponry they typically only "acquired" on behalf of the Americans. Once again, Clan Ramirez was betraying a tithe. The cannons were aimed directly at him and Rebekah, gleaming with murderous intent under the orange glow of the ceiling lamps.

Hugo stood next to Grandfather, scowling within the protective shadow of his liege. Helio clamped down on his own hatred. As much as he wanted serious harm levied against this piece-of-shit minion, he was terrified that one wrong move would set Rebekah off. He could already feel the familiar buzz of static electricity building around them, his long streaked hair lifting like an angry serpent from the back of his head.

The enforcer carried an umbilical handset in one hand,

connecting him to the exosuit's communication systems, and an exotic-looking automatic shotgun in the other. It was then that Helio realized all the enforcers—the frontline at least—were wearing a type of high-tech combat armor he had never seen before: olive-green bodysuits with interlocking ceramic plates over the chest and limbs, plus reinforced joint sleeves. Some wore fully enclosed helmets that didn't even have a visor. They looked pristine.

"Step aside, Helio," Hugo snarled. "We'll deal with you later."

His vision skewed again, but not because of his lost eye. The air pressure in the tunnel had increased, accompanied by a tooth-chattering vibration. It felt as though a tunneling machine was burrowing toward them from farther belowground. One of the overhead lamps surged bright yellow before exploding, then another and another until the only thing illuminating the tunnel was the backlight from the Archive—and the bright blue arcs of electricity dancing over Rebekah's body. Reality quaked in the revenant mother's presence. Rivulets of impenetrable black cracked open in the space around her, bleeding out disjointed beams of prismatic color that seemed to also be... screaming.

Helio's heart stopped.

The enforcers' guns were up. The ones whose faces he could see looked terrified. If any of them fired, especially Grandfather, the Archive could be destroyed—their whole legacy. Was his chief really so eager to erase the past?

"Rebekah," he whispered, barely, vocal cords straining to activate. "Rebekah!"

The vibration stopped as suddenly as it had begun.

"You can lower your weapons," she said calmly, as though a small army's worth of firepower wasn't leveled at her.

"Oh, can we," Hugo retorted, the sweaty sheen of his face at odds with the confident tone of his amplified voice.

"I'm leaving."

Hugo looked confused. An older voice blistered from the speakers—Grandfather's. "And where exactly are you leaving to?" he asked, incredulous.

Rebekah glanced at Helio, and for the first time he saw a glimmer of hope in her alien eyes. She stepped forward, unintimidated by the towering death machine before her.

"To Bastion."

PART 2
HERESY

MOTHER REBEKAH
CHAOS AND ORDER

It was a trap.

She should have expected it. Too many days had passed without contact from the archon, too many nights spent in tortured contemplation in her guest quarters, aimless, unsure what to do next, growing weaker as her accelerant faded. Contact had been made with the Union, and the bunker key given, but she knew little else. Finally, she had been summoned under the cover of night for a follow-up meeting with the entire Ascendancy to discuss the next phase of their plan.

A red-robed orderly guided her through a maze of empty corridors and winding staircases. Both of them were cowled like crimson ghouls, silently traversing the Grand Citadel's unfamiliar halls under the solitary glow of the man's oil lamp. The way was long, labyrinthine, and entirely disorienting no matter how hard she tried to imprint the many steps and turns into her memory. It was like the Devil's Claw all over again but shrouded in blinding incense instead of fog.

Chaos and uncertainty. This was the totality of her life now, and she was the harbinger of it. Should the Union actually succeed in evening the odds against Cathedral, nothing would ever be the same again. Should they fail, the Matriarch's punishment would be severe. In either case, the future of her adoptive clan—of Helio—was at risk. In moments like this, her plan seemed ludicrous. She was just a servant, after all.

A pair of armed paladins emerged ahead, right as she was about to ask if they had repeated their circuit. The stoic figures stood to either side of a set of heavy steel doors emblazed with heptagrams. She eyed them warily. Up until now, the archon had been quite accommodating. She supposed their inner circle was routinely guarded, bereft of Messiah's blessing. How weak they must feel, these men of God.

Nodding silently, the guardsmen pushed the doors open and stepped aside as she entered. The place was empty. Instead of the archon or his inner circle, there stood only a single man at the far end of the vast chamber. She halted as she saw him, smarting as the doors slammed shut behind her. He was dressed in a red chasuble embroidered with silver, stretched taut by a suit of formfitting black armor worn beneath it. His face was young, but his eyes burned with an intensity beyond his years. A severe wedge of prematurely whitened hair sat atop his head like a crown, aglow in the light of a sconced torch that blazed upon the stone wall behind him.

"Ahh, welcome," he began, his voice echoing from the vaulted ceiling above. "Oh, great and terrible Mother Rebekah."

"What is this? Who are you?" Mother Rebekah shifted uncomfortably in her borrowed red robes, inching backward.

"Who am I?" he asked, mockingly. "I... am Bastion's salvation."

"Where is Holy Father?" she demanded, channeling a lifetime of falsified confidence into her voice—so practiced that it almost felt real.

"Indisposed."

Indisposed?

She had crossed the world to get here, and this was their thanks. A font of primordial power stirred deep in her chest, threatening to geyser out into her veins. It scalded her guts, clamoring for release. She clenched her hands into tight fists, fighting back her murderous desire with nails in flesh.

"I am to meet with the Ascendancy," she said through lips pursed with restrained rage.

The man raised his arms out to his side, palms up. "And so you have."

More men stepped out of the shadows, surrounding her, all dressed in black armor, all wielding long blades. She should have seen them! Mother Rebekah blinked, as though to clear the creeping weakness from her starbound eyes.

Chaos called to her, begging to be shaped into lethal focus, demanding she strike down this heretic. Killing—it was her lot in life.

"Did you really think you could just walk in here and tell us what to do?" he sneered.

She breathed heavily, as every sister was taught to reclaim their calm, but each inhalation was a gale that stoked the furnace smoldering within her. The sconced torch flared brighter.

"She is coming!" Mother Rebekah shouted, her outbreath a thunderclap.

The man blinked, head jerking nervously as his composure cracked. "She..."

"The Eternal One."

"The *Eternal* One," he repeated, his voice dripping with sarcasm. "The *Messiah*. Fancy trappings for a witch."

Her hands twitched, rejoicing in the muscle memory of past violence. "Ignore me at your peril."

His face twisted into a sneer. "You arrogant bitch."

Mother Rebekah unclenched her hands.

"Kill her!"

The torch exploded.

Rebekah lurched as the world fell away, plunging her into the tidal void. Oblivion pulled her down, the physical world dragged her back up. Cellular membranes screamed as she thrashed between the two, willing herself toward equilibrium, to the calm between chaos and order. The confluence where divine power took hold. Ecstasy.

A dozen blades struck out.

Rebekah's robe drifted to the floor, shed like an outgrown skin. Then came the screams.

The assassins dropped one by one. Even when their blades struck, they were too slow. Though she was weak, they were weaker. Mother Rebekah flowed between them, carried on the tide of her accelerant—striking, slashing. Hot death splashed upon her face, cauterized by the electric aura of her vengeance. They were no more to her than dogs, howling in death. Hellhounds in the dark.

Helio's empty eye socket gaped from the ruined side of his face. She watched in despair as it filled with blood.

A man's head was in her grasp. She didn't know him but had hatred enough to spare. His mouth twisted in terror as she detached his spine. Bronze skin faded to white as he died, the specter of a Greybull fighter. Bodies surrounded her, now and then, agitator and innocent alike.

Bodies. Her victims, their terrified endings illuminated in the light of the open chamber doors.

Mother Rebekah faltered. Was it any wonder her daughter so readily embraced her fate? They were killers, all.

Open doors?

Claws stabbed into her back, followed by the roar of gunfire.

"Demon!"

She twisted away from the carnage. The paladins had taken up positions at either side of the doors, rifle muzzles aflame with retribution. Their red cloaks billowed in the space between seconds. Waiting for the moment where the hall revealed itself, she extended her arms, blinked and was there. The armored men were on the ground, pulled off their feet as she passed.

Time returned, slamming her hard into the wall. Blood sprayed across the stone, coughed up from her punctured lungs. Rebekah sagged, shivering with shock. Her undergarments were soaked red. Turning her head, she saw the priest still standing at the end of the chamber, eyes wide, lips pressed together with hatred. She wanted to go back. To murder him. To feel his spine break in her hands. He was a heretic. Worthless. They were all worthless without the Messiah.

Without the Messiah. Without my sisters.

Am I worthless?

Self-doubt smashed into her, as hard as the wall.

"Run, Mother!"

Mother Rebekah dragged herself away, every breath agony. Something was lodged in one of her lungs—a bullet. This was the pain her daughter felt every day of her life, pressed against the cage of her own corrupted body. Alone in silent suffering.

Pain surrounded her, filled her.

The Grand Citadel unwound itself as she tried to retrace past steps, falling back repeatedly as one dead end after another blocked her way. Once more she was lost in the dire wood, alone in the fog, the alpha's claws tearing into her back. A muffled klaxon sounded from outside. The Church had awoken in all its righteous fury. There would be no more subtlety, no more assassins. She followed the sound, fixing her heightened senses on the hallways where it rang more clearly.

At last, she emerged onto the street. It was well past sundown, the sky a black void. But instead of an empty district, its inhabitants retreated to the safety of their dorms, it was abuzz with life. Squads of armed paladins marched in practiced formation throughout the campus, their way lit by spotlights projected from the Grand Citadel's towers. Robed priests accompanied them, eyes intense and seeking, their bolstering chants undone by the wailing siren.

She realized then her good fortune at having been kept secret. The alarm would be the same one used for a general incursion. It would bring action to the citadel district, but its stalwart defenders would be looking for a demon bursting from the earth, not a scantily clad woman, though she would hardly avoid scrutiny for long. A row of concrete pillars lined the outer foyer of the citadel, opening onto a broad and very exposed platform before stepping down into the main courtyard. Beyond that expanse lay the promise of concealment among the crowded buildings of the Church campus. Between here and there were scores of warrior priests.

She hadn't been outside since her last radio communication with Helio, hadn't seen him in person since he left to liaise with the Union. It was still another two days until their weekly relay. The thought of him made her heart ache, the part that had been cut open when her sisters abandoned her. She had to get back into the Metro, to her secret stash in the suburban line that had carried her into the city.

It was time to leave.

They had hidden a second Runner amidst the ruins, but she was in no shape to drive. She would have to hide out until she healed—assuming she did heal. She couldn't see the wounds, but she knew they were severe. The wheezing complaint of her own breath and the raging fire burning along her spine told her that. How much longer did she have? How many more times could she count on the Messiah's blessing before her time was up? Would she phase once too quickly, unthinkingly heave an obstacle one time too many, then suddenly crumble into ash? Thoughtless, soulless absent sanctification, lost amongst the dust squalls of Helio's temple.

Doubt ravaged her. Regret ate her from the inside out. This plan, if it could even qualify as such, was doomed from the get-go. She was no Great Mother. Powerful as she was, the notion of bending an entire nation to her will, on her own, was absurd. As much as the ascendant's words filled her with spite, they were accurate. All the existential threats in the world didn't make her any less a foreigner to these people, unworthy of their trust and fear. She had underestimated them, thinking them barely more civilized than the remnant.

The plan...

A wave of fear froze her in place, pressed against a towering column. Did the Ascendancy know about Newhaven, positioned as it was between Bastion and Cathedral? Did they know about Helio? He claimed they were ignorant of the monitoring stations, but what if they weren't?

What if he's already dead?

Despair and hatred churned in her blood. She had to move —fast—while also conserving her energy. The searchlights hadn't turned toward the entrance yet. Her foe was likely hoping to blockade her escape from the district without giving too much away to his own people. It wouldn't do to admit the Ascendancy was harboring a foreign heretic.

Mother Rebekah ran, jaw clenched against her own suffering, biting hard on her lip whenever a cry threatened to escape her lips. By the time she made it to the outermost pillar, the courtyard was even thicker with enemies. There must have been a hundred by now, and not just priests. Men of the Legion had joined their ranks, meaning the subway exit she was planning to take had been compromised. It was the only way she knew in and out of the citadel district. The gates would be locked, and the walls surrounding the holy city were too tall for even her to scale. Creeping panic swirled in her chest.

Every streetlamp had been lit, their luminescence added to the seeking eye of the Church. Flashlights beamed and twisted like angry knives, leaving tracers in her vision as they cut through the pitch. The only option was to try to make it past the courtyard into the campus, hide out until she could circle back and sneak into the Metro. One phase, one very long sprint through Hell to find salvation.

Collect yourself.

Focus.

She felt like a kettle boiling over, teeth chattering in her head as she strained to summon the pittance of accelerant in her veins. Her farseeing eyes found an unlit alley between two build-ings near the courtyard's edge, ingesting their every detail. Every line and pit of their scrubbed cinder block walls. The uneven slope of the paved earth as it slipped between them, falling into the black. Wisps of vapor seeping from a rusted steel ventilation spout, evaporated into nonexistence by the city's arid heat.

The world broke around her, the edges of *here* and *there* sparking against one another as her body followed the golden path of her gaze. Tunneling through space and time, clutching to her faith as a guide while the void sought to pull her in.

She almost made it.

Yells rose around her, indistinct. She was lying on her side, facing back toward the Grand Citadel. A long trail of gray skin marked the point where her phase had prematurely ended, sprawling at unnatural speed along the ground, shredding her bare arms and legs.

So close.

"Rise, Sister."

Rebekah blinked awake, waiting for another surge of pain, but it didn't come. Warm sunlight bathed her from the stained-glass dome overhead, Messiah's touch soothing her brow. Fireflies sparkled in the air. At each edge of her octagonal altar, a sister smiled, welcoming her home.

Rebekah flopped her head over to the other side, toward the alley. There was a face, disembodied in the darkness.

Great Mother stepped into view, her radiant gold-and-silver flecked eyes beaming with joy.

"Welcome, Sister Rebekah. We are so very glad to have you."

The spotlight found her, encased her, revealing her alienness for all to see. Several gasps blurted out into the night, followed by the clink and shuffle of raised weapons, but she only had eyes for the face in the alley. Faces. There were several now, plus more figures creeping along the rooftops.

"Rise, Sister."

Something flashed in the dark, then the courtyard behind her erupted in fire. Her hearing returned just in time to catch the thunderous detonation. A wave of heat and sour chemicals rolled over her. Gunfire erupted from both ends of the court-yard, then a second explosion, this one chorused with screams. The siren wailed.

Mother Rebekah pushed herself up, groaning as patches of flayed skin stretched taut between her legs and the ground. The face in the alley was gone. She stared straight ahead, stumbling forward to where it had been. Darkness enveloped her, then arms hoisting her forward.

Buildings rushed past, blurred between the slits of her failing vision. Windings streets, more shouting, shooting, a third explosion, then stairs, a ladder which she half managed to traverse before falling into a pool of muck. A pitch-black tunnel extended before her. There was only the smell, steaming effluent corroding her nostrils.

Gentle hands cupped her face, lifting her chin. The disembodied face—a woman's, pale and beautiful—beamed at her before dissolving along with everything else.

"We've got you, Sister."

Her eyes were purple flecked with gold.

MOTHER REBEKAH

KIN

Mother Rebekah awoke on her side, blinking at the dim light of the unfamiliar room. The plush pillow and soft bedding of the cot felt like her own bed. For a moment she exalted in the feel of it, escaping into a fantasy where she would rise and greet her fellow sisters. Another day of blessed purpose within the Spire. But the gray cinder block walls were wrong, resembling her cell in the Grand Citadel. A single lightbulb flickered overhead, its pull chain turning lazily on invisible currents. Instead of the constant drumming of rain there was a mechanical thrum, indistinct as though she lay in the belly of a machine. Newhaven? Worry fluttered in her chest as her cycling mind failed to identify her surroundings.

Grimacing in anticipation of pain, she pushed away from the bed but didn't get very far. The colorless duvet flopped aside, revealing arms and legs precisely wrapped in lengths of gauze. Her otherwise naked body was completely swaddled in bleached fabric, a thicker band at her torso. Untangling herself enough to move, she probed at her back and felt a small pillow there, placed so she wouldn't roll onto her wounded back as she slept. After one more awkward rock back and forth she managed to sit up, blinking again at her surroundings.

The room was small and hot, more utility closet than bedroom. A single embroidered rug topped an otherwise rough floor of broken concrete and gravel. Additional tapestries hung from each of the room's walls, presumably to soften its raw ugliness. In many ways, it reminded her of her daughter's room under the Spire, carefully decorated to make Rebekah-6 feel like she was something more than a lab animal. (It never worked—her daughter was too clever.) The textiles were woven from disordered bands of drab color and decorated with geometric designs: star and sun motifs, and scenes of women with hands raised to a central glowing figure.

Messiah?

Opposite the bed was a metal counter stacked with a small pile of clothing as well as a full crystal decanter and glass, adjacent to a row of lockers and a chamber pot. A shut steel door marked the exit, though it bore no handle or lock that she could see. A prisoner, again? A well-kept one, if so.

Mother Rebekah recalled her panic as she fell into the putrid sludge of the sewers. As she lost consciousness, she had worried her accelerant would be insufficient to stave off infection. The piss and feces of all those who hated her seeped into her wounds, seeking to destroy her from the inside out. But she had clearly been bathed as well as bandaged. An unfamiliar chemical smell emanated through her dressings. Vague memories of a cistern, hands scrubbing away the filth. Purple eyes. Had she imagined them, so desperate for her sisters that she projected them onto her liberators? The uncanny familiarity made her anxious, made the heat of the room more suffocating.

She stepped carefully out of the bed, testing herself and sighing with relief as her legs held. Her pain had diminished to a reasonable level, the call to ash suppressed for now. Brushed fabric caressed her feet as she approached the counter, eyeing the decanter. Though her skin had been cleansed, Rebekah's mouth tasted of stale blood and sleep. Pristine water shimmered within the crystalline jug. A moment of hesitation stilled her hand as she pondered whether someone would go to this much trouble just to poison her. Unlikely. She drank heavily, foregoing the glass, then promptly drained herself in the chamber pot, annoyedly yanking the bound pillow from her back. The ammonia stench of her urine added to the room's underlying malodor.

Duties done, Mother Rebekah examined the pile of black clothing left out for her. Peeking from the top fold was a nondescript metal jewelry box. Her brow furrowed with curiosity as she pried open the lid, revealing a simple gold band nestled upon a velvet cushion. Goosebumps prickled at her flesh. Helio had given her the ring before she left, an awkward exchange that felt much more precious in retrospect. It had been his mother's. She accepted the gift but never wore it; her body still belonged to Messiah. Instead, she had tucked it away with the rest of her supplies and a shortwave radio she smuggled into the city, hidden within a collapsed wall of the suburban Metro line.

There was no sign of her other possessions in the lockers. This circlet of precious metal was the only connection she had left to anything familiar, even if that thing was another temporary home where she was uniformly hated. She hesitated. Wearing jewelry was forbidden within the sisterhood, self-adoration that distracted from worship. She would be trading one loss for another in the wearing of it, but the gain seemed stronger in this moment. It slipped perfectly over her ring finger. Rebekah shut her eyes for a moment, awaiting retribution, but none came. She could take it off later.

The clothing left out for her was an expertly crafted two-piece outfit. The first piece was a formfitting sleeveless jumpsuit with a zippered back and high collar, the second a long hooded cape with voluminous sleeves. In combination, it looked halfway between a proper habit and the attire of the local priesthood. She admired the stitch and symmetry, on par with Cathedral's best artisans. Next to the clothing were her boots, cleaned and polished. They were another gift from Helio, which he had personally crafted from sturdy animal hide and dyed black to her tastes. He had delivered them along with a snide comment about not skulking around in bare feet this time around.

Rebekah squinted, trying to recall his actual words. Were they snide, or had she been too preoccupied with her own misery to appreciate his intent? She brushed her lips, recalling a final kiss in the shadow of the sundered Northern Ridge. She was trembling—from fatigue, assuredly. Slowly, she unwound the gauze from her body, blinking away the ripples of anxious heat that followed her hands—his hands.

Her arms and legs were largely unmarred, veined only with faint white lines where the assassins' blades had landed and from her unceremonious fall in the courtyard. No doubt, her back would be a different story. Tentatively, she reached around, running fingertips along puckered flesh. The paladins had fired their weapons with ruthless purpose, desperate to take her down even as they killed their own—assuming the warrior priests and assassins were on the same side; the Church's segregation by order was as alien to her as the rest of Bastion. Her breath came in shallow gasps as she probed, reluctant to extend lungs so recently violated. Grasping the countertop for preemptive support, she counted down from eight, then tried a proper inhale. Fire flared through her rib cage, eliciting a restrained cry.

How much longer did she have?

With measured movements, she donned the outfit, zipping the back one slow notch at a time. The cape was a blessing, an extra layer of defense against weakness. It was a perfect fit, satisfying even as its foreign cut unsettled her. She wished only for a mirror, to remind herself that she was in fact present, living, being, and not lost in darkness.

All that was left was to leave, or try to anyway. Composing herself as best she could, Mother Rebekah turned to inspect the exit. The steel door looked immensely heavy; her blood ached at the prospect of moving it. Just as she reached out, a bolt released on the other side. She stepped back as it swung silently outward on well-oiled hinges, revealing the woman from the alley.

They stared at each other. She had not been hallucinating— not entirely. The woman's skin was pale bronze, metallic but not quite gray. Her eyes were closer to violet than purple. And though the heavens sparkled therein, they were flecked silver rather than gold. Silver! Like a shadow of the Eternal One. She wore an identical habit to Rebekah's and had brown hair pulled back into a tight bun, emphasizing her wide eyes and face. Like all revenant sisters—*is she one?*—her age was indeterminate, but the maturity of her features suggested she was in her thirties, or had been, prior to acceleration. The familiar and unfamiliar parts of her warred in Mother Rebekah's mind.

"I'm happy to see you up and feeling better."

The woman's accented voice flowed like water. Without warning, she stepped forward and grasped Rebekah in a deep embrace. It was overly familiar. Uncomfortable.

Her hairs lifted at the memory of the wind-swept moraine outside Bastion, nestled in Helio's arms—

It wasn't appropriate.

—of the last time her hand had held her daughter's before they were forever separated.

The woman's touch felt like home.

—of this alien woman's hands on her body, gingerly lifting away bloodied rags and lowering her into a bath of not-quite water, which sealed her wounds and awoke the slumbering accelerant in her veins.

Undone by a simple embrace. Her memories and fears felt out of order, fragmented.

"Who—are you?" Mother Rebekah stuttered, prying herself away. "Where am I?"

The woman smiled. "I'm Sister Selene. You're with your kin."

Like her unsolicited embrace, the woman's tone felt too casual, especially when addressing a revenant mother. A former revenant mother. Whatever she was now.

"My kin... but that's impossible."

The woman turned and gestured to the broad hallway beyond. It resembled the Metro. They were clearly belowground.

"Walk with me. The others are waiting. They're anxious to meet you."

Mother Rebekah recalled other pale faces in the dark, wielding guns and explosives.

"The others..."

"Our sisterhood."

———

Vague memories of their descent into the city's underbelly played back as Selene led the way down the low-ceilinged thoroughfare. They had raced through basements connected by secret tunnels, ancient subbasements predating the city's rebirth, in and out of the sewer system—she shuddered at the foul memory of echoed vermin calls, retching violently at the sights and smells of the place—and across rusted, abandoned rail lines. To get here, wherever *here* was.

The same underlying tang of mildew from her cell permeated this place, as though it had been flooded for a century and only recently dried out. Where rectangular tiles still clung to the walls, they shone green and black with mold. Also like her cell, the spaces between had been lined with tapestries, hanging rugs, and sheets of assorted textiles that sought to obscure sagging concrete held back by rusted rebar. It was a miracle the walls hadn't completely caved in. Every so often, the broken mosaic tile floor branched off into archways cordoned off with more drapery.

"The Underground is our home. Before the world fell, it was a marketplace connected to the Metro—one of the dead lines, like the one you took to get into the city." Selene turned to glance at her, a smile at the edges of the woman's lips. Mother Rebekah bristled but held her tongue. "We've been watching you since you got here. You keep strange company."

"Watching me..." Mother Rebekah darted her eyes around, wondering if others were watching her now from behind drawn curtains. Where was the way out? There were no rays of natural light, no tributaries of fresh air to lead the way if she had to flee.

"Don't worry," Selene continued, "we're on the same side."

Sides. Did such a thing exist anymore? Whose side was she on?

Though this sisterhood's home was decrepit and presumably forgotten, it still seemed to be connected to the city grid. Long lines of cable extended the length of the pitted concrete ceiling, punctuated with electric bulbs placed just close enough together to light their way. And the water had tasted clean.

Selene noticed her taking in the scenery. "We're not without allies. The Triarchy's rule isn't as perfect as they think it is."

Allies. A cursed word.

"Where are we going?"

"Dinner."

It had been the middle of the night when she was rescued.

"How long—"

"Two days. Your wounds were severe, slow to heal."

Their casual conversation seemed suddenly absurd. Too much was unknown, the spaces between *newness* too short. The Revenant Sisterhood had no chapters outside of Cathedral. How could it, given that its home was the so-called last city, the solitary bedrock of true Messianism. The Union didn't count; they were one step removed from the remnant. (Were they? Was that old Rebekah talking or new?) Perhaps the Matriarch had dispatched a secret circle to make a foothold here. Or another exile made her way across the wastes. If so, who?

A new possibility bubbled up from her racing thoughts, drowning out the others: if this outpost was so removed from Cathedral's purview that they were not aware of her exile, maybe it was an opportunity—to stave off ash. Fear prickled up her mangled spine as she carefully picked her words.

"I am overdue for my re-accelerant."

"Yes," Selene replied. "Great Mother will provide."

Mother Rebekah stopped in her tracks.

Great Mother?

Her heart began beating as fast as her mind was spinning. The passageway narrowed around her, constricting her breath. The clamorous rhythm of her own blood in her ears sounded like a tidal wave, the flood that had once drowned this place returned to wash her away—

Selene's hand was on her face, cupping her cheek. Her palm was cool, soothing.

"Don't worry, Sister. Great Mother sees all. She told us of your arrival and of your betrayal. She watches over you as she watches over all of us. You'll see, in time. Come."

Selene stepped back, waiting under the pale yellow glow of an overhead lamp. The silver flecks in her eyes shone almost gold again. She looked celestial.

In time... What choice did she have?

Soon after, they emerged at the subway station. A row of concrete bulkheads had spilled onto the line at both ends, cutting it off from the Metro proper. Mother Rebekah closed her eyes, extending her senses beyond the platform. The faintest draft of fresh air greeted her, cooler than the surrounding furnace. A way out.

An ancient escalator led upward, its mechanical steps reddened into a sandstone staircase. Thick electrical cables replaced its flayed handrails. Everything about this place, save the omnipresent tapestries, reminded her of Newhaven, and Hub before it. Shabby. Uncivilized scavengers eking out meager existences in the crypts of the Old World. She had tasted actual civilization again in Bastion, but it wasn't for her, would never be.

A second escalator led down into darkness. Mother Rebekah peered into it but saw nothing, only a void. The hum was louder here. And another sound atop it: murmurs, the whispering of lapping water.

"Rebekah."

She swayed at its top, one foot stepping forward.

"Rebekah," Selene said. "This way."

Mother Rebekah blinked, glancing back over the rail line before joining the woman.

"This was precious to you?" Selene asked, gesturing at her hand.

Mother Rebekah frowned at the question, then realized she had been twisting Helio's ring around her finger. A flush of embarrassment warmed her face. "Yes," she blurted. "Thank you. Where is the rest of my gear?"

Selene's expression darkened. "It was destroyed when Gauthier's people collapsed the line."

Destroyed!

Collapsed the line...

She was truly trapped. The creeping pressure of claustrophobia returned, squeezing her from all sides. Her portable radio was her only contact with the outside world and with Helio, short of leaving the city. Which was apparently now sealed off. She had thought herself so clever, so superior, but apparently everyone in Bastion knew exactly what she was up to. For the briefest moment, she contemplated letting it all go, letting the wind take her as she dissolved to nothing—

"A sister found the ring in the rubble," Selene said.

The heat in Mother Rebekah's cheeks became scalding. "Gauthier?"

"Our adversary."

Adversary. Mother Rebekah flinched at the woman's casual use of the word. Thinking back to her attempted assassination, she retrieved the face of the man who had arranged it.

"Pale, with white hair past his age?"

"No," Selene replied, malice in her voice. "That's Ascendant Benoit. Two sides of the same coin. Come, let's not make our sisters wait." The woman gestured to the escalator, and Mother Rebekah followed.

Benoit. She had a name now to place her hatred upon.

More tapestries blanketed the adjacent wall, except these had different patterns. Instead of the sun and stars, they depicted female silhouettes, hands alternately linked and raised toward the ancient moon in all its phases. Like the other works, they were painstakingly crafted, but from a myriad of different materials—leftovers maybe.

A low chatter joined the background hum as they approached the landing, the creaking metal of the ancient escalator steps announcing their arrival. Female voices. Mother Rebekah's stomach cramped. The last time she had been surrounded by women, they were seeing her out of the Spire, out of Cathedral, each turning their back in sequence as she was ejected from all that she knew.

They landed in a cave-like plaza that had been converted into a dining hall. Whatever else once existed on this floor was walled off by a circular escarpment of collapsed rock. The ceiling was higher here than below, concealed behind innumerable crystal chandeliers of varying size and shape. They jutted into the man-made cavern like quartz stalactites. Only a few were lit, but their luminescence enveloped the entire room, bent into prismatic ripples that gave the sense of being underwater.

Aglow beneath the chandeliers were a myriad of violet eyes, all staring at her. Mother Rebekah hesitated, grasping the cable railing for strength. There must have been thirty of them, now silent and seated at round tables swathed in elaborate tablecloths and more crystalware. She saw faces young and old—much older than was normal for an accelerated sister—all pale and metallic like Selene.

"Introduce yourself, Sister."

Sister.

Absent habit and daughter. Whatever she portrayed to the Ascendancy, the mantle of motherhood had been taken from her when she was ejected from Cathedral. This was all she could ever be now.

"I am... Sister Rebekah."

They chanted as one, "Welcome, Sister Rebekah." Their faces beamed, each smiling.

The room skewed in all directions, bending with the light. Bile bubbled in her throat. How was this possible? Where was she? Who were these women?

Selene's hand on her arm brought her back, gently guiding her toward a half-occupied table and gesturing for her to sit. Staggering forward, she stared at her seat, a folding metal chair topped with patchwork vinyl. The cushion had frayed and been sewn shut again dozens of times, multicolored threads criss-crossing its ancient surface like sutures. Like her, it could never be new again. Strong hands pulled her down to seated.

Her place setting was mostly crystal plus silver cutlery and the strange addition of a sewing needle wrapped in a delicate bow of gauze. Centered on her plate was a pile of cubed white vegetables and some unidentifiable meat, smothered in a gelatinous brown sauce. Her stomach quivered with rejected hunger. Even as a "guest" of the Church, the meals they had prepared for her were more palatable. Two crystal glasses sat astride her plate: a tumbler and a small goblet, both filled with water.

Selene lifted a spoon and tapped once on her goblet, unnecessarily since everyone present was already rapt.

"Tonight," she said to those assembled, "we celebrate Remembrance: the story of how we became. As told to all our new sisters. Normally, we sit here together already knowing them from their past lives. But Rebekah comes to us from beyond the city, just as our Great Mother did."

As one, the women crossed their chests in the tradition of local priests warding themselves against evil. But they added an additional gesture, raising right hand to forehead then down to their lips, closing the movement with a kiss.

"We remember," incanted Selene.

"We remember," they repeated.

"We remember. Toiling day and night in the factories. Spinning thread while our fathers died. Spinning thread while our husbands died. Spinning thread while our sons died. Mothers and daughters of an endless war."

"Sisters," came the response.

"Toiling without rest."

Everyone raised their goblet and took a sip. Selene motioned to her to do the same.

Mother Rebekah drank thoughtlessly and bit back a grimace

—the water was heavily salted, like tears. Glancing furtively around the room, she noticed several couples clasping hands, their resemblance undeniable. Mothers and daughters bound together by the accelerant as sisters, beyond age and death. She quickly lowered her glass, lest her trembling hand be noticed. Mother Rebekah had prayed to God, Messiah, and Great Mother for such a thing, to no avail. To only greater misery. The unfairness of it stabbed at her, that these heretics could have what she could not.

Heretics? The thought came unbidden. Were they? Was she?

More than ever, she missed her daughter. Whatever fate Rebekah-6 had been bound to, their own bond could apparently not be severed, no matter how futile her yearning.

Where are you, Rebekah?

"And then the plague," Selene continued. Instead of responding, everyone looked down and closed their eyes for a breath. "It stalked our district like a beast, taking our youngest, our only futures. We watched, helpless."

"Helpless," came the response, followed by a second sip of salt water. Mother Rebekah was more cautious this time, just mouthing the rim.

"We were weak, alone, quarantined. Abandoned by the Church. Starved by the Legion. Ignored by Parliament. And then the plague came for *us.*"

Selene made a sweeping gesture to include the room, then shuffled out of her cape. Tracing all the way down the length of her arms were whorls of mottled skin, permanent scars from some kind of flesh-eating disease. Mother Rebekah's eyes opened wide, and she retreated into her chairback. The disease must have been dormant by now, tamed by the accelerant. But still... She squirmed, unconsciously holding her breath, following the jagged lines with anxious eyes. They were like a labyrinth, like the dire wood, pressing in on her, suffocating her—

"I was the first," Selene declared.

"The first," came the response.

Mother Rebekah blinked away her creeping terror but kept her breaths shallow as before.

"Lying in my cot in the factory. Delirious, racked with fever, my brain boiling in my head. Praying to God. Praying for salvation. And as I felt myself slip into death, I heard a voice."

"Her voice."

"Her voice. It whispered to me, soothing my pain, giving strength to my rotting limbs. Strength enough to wander, below the city, without light but still able to see. Until I found our home."

"Our home."

Selene was emotional, tears building in her eyes.

"Great Mother was here, waiting for me. Like us, she had been abandoned, hunted. She told me there was another way, without disease, without suffering. A power that resided in all women of faith. True faith. In her. Not the false god of the Church."

Once again, the women made their holy sign, arms crossed, ending in a kiss.

Mother Rebekah was paralyzed. She listened intently but couldn't reconcile the words she was hearing.

"The Lifeblood," Selene declared.

Lifeblood?

Accelerant?

This was wrong. However weakened her covenant, this was blasphemy. Accelerant was the Revenant Sisterhood's link with divinity, with the primordial, but without Messiah's blessing it was unclean, powerless. Worse than powerless—lethal. No wonder their supposed Great Mother had been exiled. But what of their eyes…?

Selene untied the bow around her needle, and the women followed suit. Pricking the tip of her finger, she squeezed a droplet of blood into her goblet. "Not you, Sister," she whispered to Mother Rebekah, who watched with growing discomfort. The salt water bloomed into a red haze, sparkling with kaleidoscopic light under the chandeliers. Each table passed their goblets around, collecting blood from every sister until their contents were black and viscous as drowning pools.

"But there was a price," Selene continued. "For a long life, a purposeful life, we bear the mark."

The women lifted hands to cup their own faces, metallic palms contrasting against brilliant eyes, and repeated, "We bear the mark."

"I died that night and was reborn, the first apostle. And just as one of us came to you"—she placed her hand on Mother Rebekah's shoulder, smiling warmly—"my life's task was to seek out others to join our holy sisterhood. To show them what power we could have. Power to shape our own destinies.

"Word of our new faith spread. Under the cover of night, we took back what was rightfully ours: food, medicine, arms—to distribute to women in need. Many lay sisters supported us from above, along with others who had been crushed by the Church. Those of us who were ready partook of the Lifeblood." Selene raised her goblet and the others followed. "Not all survived the changing, but they remain with us in spirit."

They all drank, a roomful of noisome slurping until the bloody water was drained.

Selene continued, a pale red ring now haloing her lips. "But our new faith became too powerful, and we were betrayed. By Gauthier, the Heretic. Quarantine was not enough. He came with his dark paladins, armed with fire. Our district burned. Our sisters burned. We burned."

"We burned."

"Great Mother wept, as did we all. Once more the true faith was buried. And so, we slept, waiting for a sign." Everyone turned to stare at Mother Rebekah, hope shining in their eyes. "And so, it has arrived."

———

Mother Rebekah excused herself early. The room had returned to idle chatter once the ceremony was complete, but every time she looked up, there were eyes on her. No one approached their table, presumably warned away in advance. It was all too much to process. Partaking of the bland meal would probably have restored some vitality, physically at least, but she couldn't bring herself to the task. Selene walked her back to her room, both silent along the way.

When they reached the door, Mother Rebekah noticed a pair of rectangular steel hoops pinioned into the surrounding wall and a heavy beam waiting alongside it.

"We have a lot in common, but we're also new friends." Once more, Selene had read her thoughts. "The Church would lie to you and call you their guest. I won't. Precautions have to be taken, for everyone's sake."

"I have questions," Mother Rebekah mumbled, her voice trailing off along with her energy.

"I'm sure you do. Rest some more, and in the morning I'll see if I can answer them for you." Selene pulled the door open and gestured for her to enter. "Goodnight, Sister."

Mother Rebekah shuffled into the room, flinching as the door closed behind her and the steel beam slid into place with a shriek of metal on metal. It might hold her in her current state;

she didn't want to try, in any case. One cell after another, this was her fate. Perhaps Cathedral was the last city after all, the last civilization at least. The farther away she traveled, the farther she descended into degradation. She stood at the exit for a minute, taking in her menial surroundings. Her chamber pot had been emptied and scrubbed and there was a crystalware pot of food on the counter next to the refilled decanter.

Ignoring the offering, she sat on her cot and pulled off her boots. Her pale gray feet were smooth and unblemished, betraying no testimony of her long walk, but it was an illusion. The journey was imprinted into her memory, as was the entirety of her century-long tenure with the sisterhood—the real sisterhood. She felt her age.

Memories of her first acceleration flooded her, as they did when she'd lain on the cobblestone outside the Grand Citadel. The feeling of limitless strength in her blood and bones. The unshakable sense of purpose in her heart as the Eternal One welcomed her officially into the Revenant Sisterhood, to guide others into the light as she was guided. To protect them from the hell on the horizon. This was her calling, all gone.

She pulled the blanket up around her chin despite the cloying heat. Revenant sisters did not have dreams; the accelerant banished them along with their wombs. When her day was filled with meaning, the restful emptiness was a solace, but tonight it felt like falling—falling with unheard screams into infinite nonexistence.

MOTHER REBEKAH
LIFEBLOOD

Selene's quarters looked familiar. Not because they resembled those of a revenant mother—which the woman seemed to be, for all intents and purposes—but rather the soulless office of one of Mother Rebekah's many civic intermediaries. It was spare, functional, fronted by a steel desk and little else. The only indication of this being a holy space was an enormous and elegant burgundy curtain that cut across the center of her abode, presumably dividing her workspace from a private bedroom. Flame motifs danced along the edges where it scuffed the floor, and curved valances hung from the top, tasseled with crystals. A matching and particularly ostentatious crystal chandelier dangled from the open-framed ceiling above. The preponderance of glass that this sisterhood cherished must have come from the Old World, something they found in the ancient market. But the drapery looked too new. It occurred to her that it resembled some of the ornate fabrics in the halls of the Grand Citadel.

They stared at each other across the desk, seated in threadbare red velvet chairs framed in actual wood. Selene lounged back, hands interlaced while her thumbs made circles over each other. Mother Rebekah felt somewhat stronger after another night's rest, her physical aptitude reinforcing her mental resilience. All she had wanted was to leave, to escape this infernal city and get back to... where? That option was gone now in any case. In its place, another opportunity, one she had never imagined finding in Bastion: the accelerant, served up by this enigmatic group of exiled sisters. The call of her weakening blood warred with her need for answers.

"What do you want, Sister?"

Mother Rebekah raised an eyebrow at the question. Once more, Selene had been waiting for her outside the cell door after she finished her morning toilet, as though the woman had never left. They had largely walked in silence until veering off into what she presumed was Selene's chambers. The dank hallway was quiet once more, save for the susurration of indistinct prayers bleeding out from behind drawn curtains.

What *did* she want? It was like her first conversation with Helio all over again, after carrying him back to Newhaven and being thrown in its dungeon as a reward for her good will. She had set herself to a long-shot plan of upending Cathedral, some sort of halfhearted revenge against the Matriarch. If nothing else, maybe she could put an end to the Symbiote Program by depriving them of new God-engines, so that other children would not have to suffer as her daughter did. Assuming they suffered at all, once "relieved" of their physical bodies. Rebekah-6 had embraced her fate; maybe the others were the same. Her betrayal seemed so futile now. Given a second chance...

"You don't know," said Selene, her tone sympathetic.

Mother Rebekah hated the truth of it. "What does your Great Mother say about it?"

It was an evasion but also an honest query. Before finally falling into the oblivion of sleep, her mind had spun with wondering over the origins of this alien sisterhood's patron.

Why wasn't the mysterious exile among her flock? She thought back to the escalator leading downward into darkness, and to her own Great Mother's reclusion. Was it the nature of all matriarchs to be alone?

Selene stilled her thumbs and leaned forward, the sleeves of her cape folding back as they dragged along the desk. Butterflies fluttered in Mother Rebekah's stomach at the thought of the latent disease beneath that fabric. "She says you yearn to belong but must be guided into the light."

"I have already been guided into the light."

"By those who betrayed you?" Selene asked, without malice.

Mother Rebekah chewed on her lip, focus drifting over the tapestry as her eyelids blinked away her insecurity.

"You can have a home, a real home. Here with us. We are the same."

"We are not the same," Mother Rebekah snapped.

Selene leaned farther forward. "We both bear the mark. That makes us the same."

Mother Rebekah pushed back into her chair, eager to maintain their distance. "Whatever *lifeblood* you have acquired, it is unclean. It may have colored your flesh, but it rots in your veins. Only the Messiah can light the way."

Selene sighed, pushing back her chair and lounging once more. "Messiah. God..." She trailed off. "Aren't our mothers our gods? Didn't your child worship you as her god?"

"My..." Mother Rebekah blinked, trapped in a cascade of confusion as the light of the chandelier strobed.

"Great Mother sees all. Our god sees all."

"Blasphemy!"

Mother Rebekah blinked again and noted for a fraction of a second that Selene was no longer seated in front of her. In her place was a fragmented black silhouette, folding back into nothingness. There was a knife at her throat. Selene was hunched behind her.

"What about now, Sister?" Selene hissed in her ear. "Do you still doubt we're the same?"

All she had was doubt, growing by the second. Belligerence bubbled up in her tightening throat. "Weapons are for mortals."

Selene slid the spine of the blade along Mother Rebekah's high collar, then drew it away and stood. Stepping back around the desk, the woman sat herself back down, pulling her sleeves straight in irritation. "Rules. So many rules. Where have they gotten you, Sister?"

Mother Rebekah's mind spun with possibilities. Their resemblance was more than skin deep, after all, but how?

"Your old sisterhood isn't yours anymore. But you can have a new one. We're small but you can help build our numbers. You can stand beside me as a leader once more."

Leader.

Her desire for it stung. "And what? We'll rule the sewers together? I've had enough cave dwelling for one lifetime."

"You think too small, still stuck in your own head. We're not alone in our resistance to the Church."

"Your allies."

"Yes. Every Sunday, the archon preaches of equality. Our shared nationhood. But equality has never existed here. Districts that contribute the most to the war effort get all the food and medicine. Those that fall behind rot and die, like ours did. Any form of protest is met with crippling punishment. There are others like us out there, waiting for a call to rise up."

"Rise up?"

"And destroy the false church. A new matriarchy can rise, in Bastion."

This woman was insane. Where Mother Rebekah had wanted to bring balance, Selene just wanted to destroy.

"You think I'm mad," Selene continued. Once more, her thoughts were laid bare. "Even though they tried to murder you."

Pinpricks of heat pattered up and down Mother Rebekah's spine as she recalled each bullet. The smug face of Ascendant Benoit, uncaring of the risks she took to get here, to empower their people against her own. Selene was right. She should want them to suffer, she should want to burn down their civilization. Her blood boiled with possibility. But her heart was empty.

"Whatever you think," Selene said, "you're not a prisoner here. But you know what awaits you if you leave."

Ash.

Indecision wormed its way through her guts, leaving her cramped and insecure. Her last plan had failed, but she was alone then. Was there really a home for her here? Whatever disparities existed between their faiths, maybe they could be bridged, maybe this was a road back to Messiah's grace. Could *she* bring *them* back to the light, as the Eternal One had saved humanity after the wars?

"And if I stay…"

Selene's posture eased, her alien eyes sparkling under the chandelier. "Every sister-to-be is tasked with a holy duty before they can receive the Lifeblood."

Lifeblood.

Accelerant.

Her body shook of its own accord, hungering.

"Tasks are commensurate with the candidate's abilities. Which means yours is special."

"Special…"

"We need to send a message. One that can't be ignored." Selene paused, licking her lips. "Kill Gauthier."

"What? I just escaped from their clutches."

"Which is exactly why you can do this. We can get you close, but only you know the inside of the Grand Citadel."

"But it's a fortress!"

"Yes, and so are you. Your body hungers but it's still strong. I can feel it."

Mother Rebekah recoiled at the idea of going back there. It felt like death. "I'm no assassin."

Selene stood again—at human speed this time—coming around the desk to kneel before her and clasp her hands. Mother Rebekah flinched with the uninvited intimacy, instinctively pulling back, but Selene held her fast. The woman's eyes searched her soul. Her touch was warm. Rebekah-6 had always wanted this. Each time they were in proximity, her daughter's hands would find their way to hers, brushing against them like a persistent fly to be batted away. How could she have been so cruel?

"Aren't you?" Selene asked.

Mother Rebekah had murdered six sisters in her futile effort to rescue her daughter, recognizing her inadequacies too late. Six. All good women, all of whom had at one point helped raise her child in her absence. Before that, eleven Scavrats. And within the week, three of Benoit's men. Twenty human souls had been delivered by her hand.

Compared with her age, it seemed a reasonable number. She had failed as a mother but excelled as a killer.

"This is your task. If you decide to stay. If you decide to come home."

MOTHER REBEKAH
SERVANT OF GOD

It was hot and dry, even this late into evening. Where the acid rain in Cathedral poured down without end, Bastion was so parched that Mother Rebekah wondered how its populace hadn't expired from dehydration long ago. Back home—she caught herself; Cathedral could never be that again—her soul was shielded from the empty heavens by the thick walls of the Spire first, and the constantly boiling cloud cover second.

Despite spending long months exposed in the wasteland, then here, she had a hard time acclimating to perpetually clear skies. Everyone living, save the Eternal One, had been born under that infinite void, but the absence of light in the night sky was so profoundly unnatural that even newborns instinctively knew it wasn't *right*. It was too dark, too empty. Only those with nefarious intent, like her, and the brave souls standing in their way, emerged from their shelters after nightfall.

Oppressive darkness permeated the citadel district, dispelled in pockets by the anemic glow of intermittent streetlamps. Swirls of polychromatic light emanated from stained-glass windows on the towers beyond, demarking the otherwise invisible silhouette of the Grand Citadel. The ragged crown of the

Northern Ridge overlooked it all. The Church, ever self-assured, considered the broken mountain a divine shield placed by God to ensure the safety of his disciples, but to her eye it looked more like a burial shroud, liable to collapse entirely one day and return this overly proud city to ruin. Selene wished as much.

None of it should have existed. Why hadn't the Matriarch told her about Bastion? It was absurd that such a thing would be discovered by a Scavrat—from an exiled clan, no less. Had the Eternal One sensed her betrayal from the beginning? Certainly, as far as Cathedral's citizens were concerned, theirs was the last city, founded by the singular leader of humanity and consecrated by the Messiah. The Grand Citadel rivaled the Spire yet was completely alien, incompatible with the divine right of the Revenant Sisterhood.

Where are you, Messiah?

No monuments. No mention in the scripture of her former hosts. Unknown to the strange sisters that had rescued her from this place. Did she still carry the Messiah in her heart, despite her crimes against her order, or did devotion die in isolation? Mother Rebekah paused, distracted from her cautious traversal across the district by her own wandering thoughts. This was the torture of exile: crippling self-doubt and abject solitude, amplified by the call to ash.

A patrol marched past the alley she was currently sheltering in: two paladins with rifles slung low and a red-robed priest wielding a censer in one hand and an oil lantern in the other. The incense fumes roiled in the air as they passed, tendrils snaking out, sniffing at the shadows.

There was no going back.

Selene had provided her with a shortcut into the Grand Citadel, a maintenance entrance located much closer to the surrounding campus than the one she had tried and failed to escape from. It lay twenty meters ahead. Doable.

Mother Rebekah lurched out of the alley and immediately phased across the expanse, the black wake of her accelerated passage concealed by the darkness. Her glee upon landing vanished as a shockwave of pain burst up her spine, forcing her to bite down a scream. She half collapsed against the concrete wall. Pink and red flares exploded at the corners of her enhanced vision.

"Messiah watch over me," she moaned, breathless. Excruciating seconds ticked by, exposed out in the open, as she waited for the sensation to pass.

A few more exertions. Just a few more.

The lock on the steel door whimpered then popped as she forced it open, slowly to avoid attention. She was in, greeted by a high-ceilinged passageway almost as dark as outside. Specks of meager light flickered at opposite ends of the hall, emanating from oil lanterns turned low for the late hour. Her pupils dilated, sucking in whatever scant particles they could. Gradually, her surroundings materialized into a grainy pastiche.

The surrounding citadel district housed the bulk of the nation's clergy, but their leaders languished in their respective private wings within the Grand Citadel alongside high-ranking aides and assistants. The archon had given her a sparing after-hours tour of the facility after she gained his trust—laughable, in retrospect. Only a small portion of the Church's headquarters was shared. The remainder, including Gauthier's wing, was accessible via a central nexus—her destination.

She crept silently through mostly dark halls, following pathways of memory from both before and after the night of her betrayal and subsequent escape. What patrols she encountered were easy to avoid, the citadel's guardians blinded by their own light as they marched past her with blithe confidence. It didn't take long to reach the nexus.

Unlike the rest of the grounds, the enormous chamber was

well lit, though mercifully absent any foot traffic. Its concrete walls extended all the way to the roof of the Grand Citadel, the windowed dome high above as black as the void beyond. She had emerged between the bottom two points of an enormous seven-pointed star, the symbol of Bastion's faith, tiled into an intricate black-and-white mosaic floor. Each point terminated in a monolithic entranceway, headed with a stamped steel placard bearing numerals I through VII. They were numbered as one would have drawn the heptagram's lines, with the first order of Archon Alexis Levesque at the "topmost" point across the chamber, Benoit's second order—the Order Sacramental—to her right, and Gauthier's seventh order—the Order Occult—to her left. The link between the latter two seemed inextricable, just as Selene had said, though they presumably represented deeply opposed viewpoints within the Church. It was a wonder a cohesive faith existed at all given how enamored its inner circle was with segregating themselves.

She lingered at the main entrance, fantasizing for a moment about going after Benoit instead of Gauthier. Of showing him the price of betrayal. Her vibrating body carried her one step to the right. Small blue arcs of static electricity crested and popped in her peripheral vision, lifting her hair from her scalp. This might be her only chance to exact revenge, finally.

No.

It wasn't her task.

What about the archon himself? They were all within reach. Assuming she could get through whatever guards he had in place, which was probably a great deal given her escape, she could confront him, demand to know why he had scuttled their plan. But she already knew the reason: she was a foreigner and a heretic. Had he shown up in Cathedral warning of a threat from the other side of the world, he probably would have been treated worse—far worse.

A vision of the lord commander appeared before her, the terror in his cataracted eyes as she held him fast. He was her enemy as much as these priests, but there was honor in him. Given the absurd structure of Bastion's government, it was possible he had no idea. It was possible their plan could proceed without her. Possible but improbable. She hated not knowing almost as much as she hated her growing weakness.

Yes, they were all within reach, but there was no choice if she wanted to live. Servitude was inescapable; it was her place.

Mother Rebekah turned and entered the inner sanctum of the Order Occult.

The wing was silent. She passed through rectories, eating halls, study areas, and shrines—all empty. Not a prayer nor a snore from behind closed doors. No one studying late into the night, no paladins walking their shifts. Just empty halls bearing tapestries upon their cold concrete walls, indiscernible in the grainy darkness. Gauthier's domicile was as dark as it was quiet, the last light she passed having been at the entranceway. Until now.

A single cowled figure stood at the end of a long hallway, bathed in the radiance of an overhead electric lamp—the first sign of modernity she had seen since entering the Grand Citadel. She watched him from a safe distance for several minutes, blended into shadow, but the man remained motionless. He was ensconced in thick folds of maroon and held some sort of polearm in his right hand, tipped with a metallic black cylinder rather than a blade. Behind him towered a grand stone archway whose keystone bore the exquisitely sculpted face of a bald, austere man with empty eye sockets—Gauthier, presumably. A portcullis of latticed iron blocked the way.

Was twenty-one so much worse than twenty...? Twenty-two including the ascendant.

Mother Rebekah gathered up her own red robes, conveniently provided for her by Selene, pulling the hood low over her head. She wouldn't get past the gateway unmolested, but her disguise might get her close enough that she could dispatch the guard without overexertion.

She proceeded down the hall, shuffling unhurriedly toward him. The engraved face seemed to follow her as she approached, its eyeless gaze seeing through her deception. Violence churned in her heart, sputtering like an ancient machine, sending pings of heat along exhausted nerves to the tips of her fingers.

"Welcome, Mother Rebekah."

She froze. The baritone greeting—slightly abraded, as though spoken through a mask—came from the guard, but he hadn't moved or shown any outward sign of alarm.

"His Eminence has been expecting you."

Expecting me?

The faceless man stepped aside with a soft jingle of chain, and as he did so, the portcullis slid silently up and away.

Pitch black lay beyond. She didn't dare move. The last time she had been invited into a space such as this, by these people, she almost died. She waited, anxious for clarification, but none was forthcoming. The guardian may as well have been a statue.

Empty eyes stared down at her. She glanced back the way she had come, squashing an urge to retreat to the nexus. Wherever she went now, she would be trapped.

Clenching her hands, she crept slowly forward, reciting prayers against fear.

Messiah is with me.

I shall not fear.

The words felt hollow—fake.

The guard remained still as she approached, showing no

fear, or any emotion at all, in her presence. A deep bronze hand —unlined, with perfect cuticles at the fingernails—gripped his staff, but his face remained obscured behind his tipped-down cowl.

"Expecting me?" she said, giving hesitant voice to her thoughts.

No reply. The tip of his polearm shimmered under the light, buzzing like a swarm of insects.

She wanted to wait—to hold out for some acknowledgment of her superior position. But every second in his presence was an eternity. She couldn't suppress a shudder. Already, the tables had turned. Mother Rebekah may have been a killer, but she made a terrible assassin.

The open archway waited ahead.

Breathing deeply, she stepped forward, bracing herself for the inevitable slam of the iron gate closing behind her. It never came. Another overhead lamp sparked into life, illuminating a minuscule patch of what appeared to be a much larger chamber than expected from the confined entranceway—too large. Long rows of priceless leather-bound books faded into darkness on either side of her.

"Just a library," she whispered, blinking reassurances to herself.

An unlikely spot for an ambush. And yet the path forward was impenetrable.

She glanced back again, but the guard hadn't moved. Her twitching hands flexed, drained of their urge to do violence, wishing instead for comfort. The memory of Helio's hand inter-linked in hers filled her with grief and longing, the rough calluses at the base of his fingers scrubbing against her smooth palm, the beat of his pulse against hers. She wished he was here in this moment, if only to remind her that she could still breathe no matter how enclosed the space.

Once more, she had nowhere else to go. The lamp behind her fizzled out as she stepped forward and a new one snapped to life, stopping her in her tracks again. The fixtures seemed to sense her presence. Looking up, she gasped as an intricate, geometrically paneled fresco unfurled from the illuminated portion of the ceiling. The craftsmanship was elaborate and terrible, depicting a black sea around the edge, triangular partitions filled with drowning limbs and faces. Fire raged in the center, all consuming.

She followed the spectacle to the edge of her circle of light, blinking as a new lamp surged awake and the old one died. Demons swirled in her vision now, their chaotic forms inlaid with a dizzying level of detail. Unyieldingly asymmetrical, sculpted from human nightmares, they spiraled around a stylized sun. Human limbs sprouted from their vile multicolored carapaces, grasping for the light.

A wave of vertigo crested over her, forcing her eyes closed. When she reopened them, swaying against nothingness, there was darkness in every direction beyond her pale yellow circle. The gateway was gone. Though the ceilings were high and the library's edge was concealed in shadow, the space around her felt too small. Like a subterranean cavern, barely large enough to accommodate her wriggling body. The muscles between her ribs were spasming, each breath into her damaged lungs more strained than the last.

She lurched forward again—at least she assumed it was forward—hurrying now and averting her eyes from the spectacle above as consecutive lamps flared and died. She focused instead on the perimeter, noting that in addition to vast bookshelves and reading pedestals there were steel tables laden with laboratory apparatus and rows of specimen jars stacked higher than she could see. A dank waft of vinegar breezed into her nostrils, coiling around an old memory as she gulped for breath.

She marched into the testing chamber, attached to the sacrificial demon by a pittance of chain. It clawed against her soul, shrieking silent curses, shredding layer after layer of accelerant-reinforced defenses.

Her pace quickened. Tangles of inhuman viscera floated within ochre fluids. Creeping from the edges of perception, they writhed within their prisons, then stilled again as particles of light smothered them in her wake.

Her sisters pulled the chain taut, and the demon became silent once more, subservient to their joint will, bowing before Messiah's chosen.

Another lamp burst to life as the last one died. A scratching sound from the shadows to her left—talons scraping along glass. Then tapping from her right: slow, methodical.

She lost count of how many more lamps came and went. An explosion of painted blood gushed from the ceiling as the War against Hell came to life, shimmering in the afterglow of the last lamp. Thousands of desperate faces attached to red-robed men and black-clad women, screaming in anguish as they threw themselves against the Hellmouth and were extinguished.

The Numbered child stood opposite their ranks, struggling to stay upright. This one was too little, too weak, but her cursed body could not hold her any longer. The golden flecks in her eyes churned and weaved like panicked fireflies.

An open archway materialized before her. At its side, another cowled figure holding a black-tipped polearm. She swallowed, disoriented, thinking herself turned around, then realized the passage beyond was different than the hallway she had entered from: an unfamiliar room, fully lit. Restless shadows dragged at her heels. She wanted to bolt.

"Proceed," intoned the guard, with the same muffled voice as the last.

She was no longer the aggressor. Her willfulness had been

siphoned, leaving behind a weakling servant. Hurrying through the archway, she prayed this time for its portcullis to fall, to remove her from her newfound terror, but again it remained open. The last lamp in the library extinguished itself, pitching the infernal place once more into total darkness.

Her eyes watered as they adjusted to the new room, a lavish space lit by standing lamps around the perimeter, painting the domed ceiling a myriad of dizzying colors. Eager to remove herself from the gaping door, she skirted the edge, her harried footfalls swallowed by tapestry-enshrouded walls. Scenes of terror played out along the rich fabric, as lifelike and forbidding as the library's illuminated frescoes. Once again, she found herself surrounded by scores of demons, their alien carapaces shimmering like oil on water. The level of detail seemed impossible—and familiar. Twin couches separated by an ornate iron table occupied the center of the room, upholstered in red velvet.

Unease ballooned in her stomach.

Minus the decay, this room looked like a mirror of Selene's quarters. Only the ever-present crystal was absent. And rather than mildew, there was an underlying floral musk, overlaying something darker, bitter. The origin eluded her. If only her daughter were here, she could...

Mother Rebekah blinked away the thought and inhaled deeply, catching a third scent: butter, sugar. The aroma pulled her toward the table, where she saw a silver platter of tiny foil bundles, alluring twists of blue and purple. Her mouth watered at the sight of them. She hadn't eaten in days.

Maybe just one.

"Help yourself, please."

She jumped at the voice, thinking it was the guard, then stared as a narrow, extraordinarily dark-skinned man appeared at the other end of the room. Ageless emerald eyes sparkled at her from an unlined face adjoined to an equally smooth scalp.

Like all the archpriests of his Church, he wore long red robes edged with silver runes. A hazy crimson halo rippled outward where its hem met the burnished tile floor, as though afloat on a pool of blood.

Gauthier.

"Or not," he said, his voice liquid. He bowed slightly and made a sweeping, dramatic gesture. "This is your chance, after all."

My chance.

Mother Rebekah realized she was crouched, hands instinctively clawed into scythes. Some violence left in her after all. Like his guards, he showed no fear. She should do it. One more to save herself from the ash. What was he to her? The same thing she was to them: a heretic, an obstacle, a foreigner that shouldn't even exist. This was her task.

But she hesitated—long enough for him to stroll past her, casually, as though his life was not forfeit. He plucked a sweet from the platter, hefted up his robes, and sat himself down on one of the couches.

"Perhaps a last meal, then," he said, holding up the sparkling violet package with a hint of a smile. It unfurled in his hands, releasing a delectable wave of caramel before the candy disappeared into his mouth. He let out a gluttonous sigh. "I'm still alive," he said through chews, "which means maybe we can come up with an alternate arrangement."

"Still alive," Mother Rebekah said, voice catching in her parched throat, "for now."

He motioned to the opposite couch. "Please."

The plush fabric called to her. She was exhausted, more than on her entire barefoot journey across the Devil's Claw. Though probably only spanning minutes, her passage through the library had felt like an age. She was also curious; this was not the welcome or reaction she had expected. Truly, nothing beyond Cathedral was what she expected.

Carefully circling her designated nemesis, she sat, crossing her arms. The cushions were astonishingly comfortable, enveloping her whole body. She sank willingly into their embrace.

"So, Selene sent you." He raised a hand as she stiffened again. "Don't worry, you haven't been betrayed. Not this time, anyway."

Not this time.

Benoit was the executioner, but this man sat on the Ascendancy alongside him. "Two sides of the same coin," Selene had said.

She hated them all.

"Haven't I?" she seethed.

Gauthier stared intently, bright green eyes swiveling back and forth over her face and hands. His left thumb rubbed compulsively on a pilled patch of fabric at the end of his sleeve, summing up a private tally of notable features. *Scritch, scratch,* like the disembodied experiments in the library, pressing against their prisons. His scrutiny cut into her like a scalpel.

"Would you like to take a picture? It will last longer."

He blinked and smiled, switching to a more human face. The shift was disorienting. His thumb ceased its counting. "Apologies. You are... This is only the second time I've seen one of your kind."

She imagined he'd much rather see her on the surface of a dissection table.

"Second?" she asked.

"Our mutual acquaintance."

Acquaintance.

Selene had lied to her, like everyone else—or at least divulged only half-truths. The familiar sting of it prickled her chest. She licked her lips, inadvertently tasting the lingering fragrance of butter in the air. It was bait, all of it. She wouldn't take it.

"How is it that an ascendant of the Church is so familiar with his enemy?"

"Enemy..." The word seemed to pain him. Gauthier's eyes darted around again as his cryptic brain calculated a response. "What did she tell you?"

"You first."

His head clicked sideways, emergent lines around his eyes quivering with irritation. "Fair enough. Selene wasn't always one of you—"

"She is not one of *me*."

Wasn't she?

Gauthier's eyes flared for a moment, like one of the library's sensory lamps. His robotic composure reminded her of the battle walker she had visited with the archon, its alien eye struggling to comprehend a world beyond Bastion's meager walls.

"Very well. Selene Carter was superintendent of textiles for District Thirteen. She was also one of my best students."

"Students? Since when does your church allow women into its ranks?"

He raised a sculpted eyebrow. "And yours men?"

Mother Rebekah huffed.

"She was special. Unlike her predecessors, she enjoyed servicing my order. She understood our true purpose."

"Which is what, exactly?"

"To understand the Adversary. In all its shapes and forms, that we might defeat it." It sounded like a practiced response. Clearly this was a position he'd had to defend on a regular basis. "We discussed theology at length: apocryphal works, the primordial spirit. She infused the word of God into all of her creations." Gauthier lifted his arms reverently toward the room's tapestries.

Mother Rebekah reluctantly turned her head, gritting her teeth at the uncanny images swaying around her. "I hardly see God in these."

"Selene saw God in all things. Too much, perhaps. She became obsessed, begged me to sponsor her for the clergy." He paused, looking with reverence upon Selene's work, a glimmer of regret in his eyes. "I had no choice but to remove her from her position. Shortly after, plague struck."

Visions of Selene's scars imposed themselves on her, trails of pestilence spiraling over her arms like the beasts of Hell that danced upon her weavings. Anxious to reinfect.

"Our constant companion, come with humanity to the holy land. The district was quarantined, as per regulations." Gauthier's right hand clenched tightly around the crinkling foil wrapper. "One night, I received a priority call. It was her—Selene. She was dying, begging me for help."

"Help... Using something from your library?"

His emerald eyes turned back to her, latching onto her own. They were full of secrets. She resisted the urge to blink her discomfort away.

"I couldn't help her. There is no cure for the plague, even within the Celestial Codices." He sighed, seemingly disappointed by his own statement. "I didn't hear from her again, so I assumed she died with the rest. Until she showed up here—where you sit now."

Mother Rebekah's eyes widened. Every accelerant-deprived cell in her body screamed at her to stand, to swat away whatever blight Selene had carried. She breathed, trying to remember that they had just recently shared air and she was still whole.

Gauthier noted her surprise, nodding in agreement. "I felt the same. Her eyes and skin had changed, much *like* yours," he said carefully. "She said she had been saved, her and some others. That there was a cure. Not just for the plague... but for death."

The ascendant's gaze faded along with his voice, receding into calculation.

Selene had offered this man accelerant, not understanding it would have been his death—an agonizing, pain-filled death. Or maybe she did.

"Bastion is a holy place, but our holiness is constantly tested. False faiths are everywhere. I assumed she had been taken by the Adversary and summoned my guards. She moved like a— like you. Escaped the citadel. Benoit burned down her district that same night."

Gauthier had indeed hurt Selene, grievously, but not in the way the woman had claimed—or known. The ascendant leaned out of his couch, leaving precious little distance between them.

"Tell me, Mother Rebekah. Are you truly a servant of God?"

The archon had asked the same when they met, clearly dubious, and had gone on to betray her. This man's tone was different—sincere.

"I am."

"Then, as two servants of God, let us help each other."

"You understand I came here to kill you."

Gauthier nodded, still unaffected. "Selene sought to tear down our civilization, to make way for another. Is that also your goal?"

Mother Rebekah swallowed. She felt as thin as the man before her, her veins empty. Selene had offered to fill them again, not just with power but with belonging. She recalled the beatific faces of the women at the remembrance ceremony, all sisters-to-be. Would she actually join them once she'd had her fill? Everything was moving too fast, in unfamiliar directions.

"I can help you get out of the city," he said. To Helio, her only constant. "If you bring me the Lifeblood."

"What of false faiths?"

"In the right hands, all tools can do good."

Should I tell him? Or should he suffer? Correctness warred against malice.

"The acc—the Lifeblood is not for men. It would kill you."

Gauthier frowned, his smooth scalp drawing down over his brows. "You've probably guessed by now that your proposition has been rejected. The Ascendancy knows about your Scavrat lover," he said, suddenly sounding a lot like Benoit. Her heart skipped a beat. "We know about his home in the mine. Given the Order Sacramental's fondness for foreign allies, I wouldn't expect them to be left alone much longer—"

She was on him. Ovals of blue and violet foil hung in the air, suspended between time. The iron table, now bent beyond recognition, groaned in staccato notes. Her heart pounded from the exertion, sending cascades of pain writhing down her limbs.

Something monstrous stirred at the edges of the room.

Gauthier's throat was in her hands, and still his eyes showed no fear. "I am not your enemy," he said, voice barely muted though he was half-choked.

The sweets clattered to the floor.

Mother Rebekah squirmed, frustrated by the man's lack of reaction despite the wrenching pain in her own chest. He should be terrified, groveling. She released her grip, standing clumsily away from him.

His eyes followed her, but he didn't bother to adjust his disheveled robes. He continued to sit as he had, unaffected. In this moment, more powerful than a revenant mother. His emerald eyes caught hers just as fiercely. She felt enveloped by them, reduced by them. Judged by them.

"What say you, servant of God?"

MOTHER REBEKAH
STARING INTO THE SUN

"Will it hurt?"

Her heart broke at her daughter's question, posed to the Great Mother when the head of their order had come to announce Rebekah-6's symbiosis day. She looked so small, cocooned and shivering in her blanket after her final test. A hundred years prior, Rebekah—not yet sister or mother, but proselyte—had asked the same question when faced with her own transformation. A transformation that was denied her only surviving child in favor of something far worse.

"Will it hurt?" she asked.

"Yes."

Then, too, the Great Mother, the Eternal One, had answered directly. The way of the revenant sister was not easy. Messiah and God alike demanded sacrifices.

She lay upon the altar, naked beneath a ritual cloth of black edged in golden geometry. Her hair was still damp from the bath, chilled by the obsidian stone beneath her body. A kaleidoscope of colors drifted along her chest, beaming down from the stained glass above. She blinked at the radiance of sacred women—her sisterhood—battling the Adversary, pushing the demonic horde back against a great rift in the sky. Multifold pincers and tentacles lashed out, enveloping them, but they fought on, for humanity. This was her legacy and her destiny.

"You will feel your body die."

The words were terrifying, would have sent her staggering from the altar if spoken by anyone else. But Great Mother's voice was a song, a psalm, her immortality reassurance to every proselyte that had lain on this altar before her. She was resplendent in her black habit and cloak, eight gold flames extending from her high collar like a halo. They shimmered under the light of the dome, burning into Rebekah's hazel irises as though she were staring into the sun.

Eight more sisters surrounded her, each of them with hands placed upon her sheathed skin. Pressing her down. There was no escape in any case.

"The accelerant will fill you, just as it filled me and your sisters, and you will be reborn. To serve, joined to Messiah."

"Bless the Eternal One!" came the response of her sisters.

The Eternal One nodded once. Rebekah peered out the corner of her eye, where an intravenous line had been inserted into her left hand. A viscous tendril of black fluid wriggled its way down the tube, carried by a chorus of escalating prayer. Her sisters' chanting grew louder, deafening. Their hands pressed harder, pinning her, until she felt her bones might crack against the stone. The accelerant was almost at her vein.

"Remember your prayers."

It took her then, and everything changed.

Faith had been difficult for Rebekah the proselyte. Though she was an adept student, it was not until her own acceleration that she truly *believed*. God was the creator, the destroyer, present in all things but ever invisible. God alone was never enough for her.

It was Messiah that consecrated the blood of demons—also

God's creation—into the accelerant, so that mortal women could join with the divine. The accelerant was a conduit to the primordial, an escape from the crisis of mortality. It was Messiah, whose arrival had been foretold by the old faiths, that brought light to darkness through the Great Mother.

But ultimately, it was the Great Mother herself—whose immortality and power were undeniable, physical, material—that made faith possible. Finally possessing that power made faith easy for Sister Rebekah—a miracle made manifest. It was easy to forget God when each new day was guaranteed, when she had the power to shape the world as a servant—to her matriarch, to her divine sisterhood, and ultimately to the accelerant.

Always a servant.

"We bear the mark."

Selene's words—truths. The accelerant was all consuming. It filled her: body, mind, and soul. Only as she felt it slip completely from her veins did she begin to comprehend what that sacred servitude had also taken from her—from all of them. Not just dreams, but love.

Family.

"They are an affront against God."

God.

How could her daughter have been anything other than a blessing? Birthed in the twilight between divinity and mortality, the last time her accelerant had been depleted—purposely, as part of the Great Mother's design.

Why did her increasingly human heart yearn for a man she barely knew?

Why wasn't Gauthier scared when she had straddled him, prepared to rip his spine from his body? All she had was fear. His faith was strong, even absent Messiah, absent the conduit. He had asked if she was a servant of God. Reflexively, she'd said yes. But was she? Or was she the heretic the Church thought her to be?

Mother Rebekah twirled Gauthier's signet ring between her fingers, rubbing her thumb over the numeral printed on its thick silver head. An errant wind, also lost in the Metro, whistled mournfully along the rusted girders of the collapsed ceiling. On the other side of the hidden passageway lay a choice that once seemed obvious—accept the Lifeblood, stave off ash—only leaving the after part to sort out. She looked down at the gold ring on her left hand, bright and yellow as her daughter's shorn hair.

The Lifeblood would save her body, but at what cost to her soul?

————

The Underground was quiet, its nocturnal inhabitants out on whatever sundry errands occupied Selene's enigmatic cult. For all the woman's boastful talk about uprooting their society, it was not clear what that entailed on a daily basis. They had no intermediaries to manage, no city to run, no populace to shepherd, and yet for all her time here, she had never seen any of her new sisters-to-be sitting idle. She had barely seen them at all.

Mother Rebekah paused as she passed the escalators, her gaze lingering on the one that led down. It was pitch black past the first few rusted steps. There was no sight, nor sound, nor smell beyond the pervasive mildew of the place, just a void as empty as the night sky. Her hand gripped the railing, latched there like an anchor as her body swayed around it. Flashes of frescoed ceiling erupted in her memory, painting the nothingness with streaks of violent color.

"Who are you?" she whispered.

The sound of her own voice roused her, along with a series

of cleansing blinks. Turning on her heel, Mother Rebekah expedited herself through the thoroughfare to Selene's quarters. Her host would be expecting her.

The claustrophobic walkway did not seem nearly as oppressive this time, compared with the nightmare of Gauthier's library. Remarkably, it felt almost comfortable, familiar at least. She had been invited, could stay here as long as she liked without worrying about being murdered in her sleep. She snorted at the ridiculous reality of her new day-to-day baseline. How had it come to this?

She arrived quicker than she would have liked, not yet having fully suppressed her earlier doubt. It sat in her stomach like a malignancy, souring her breath.

"Come," Selene called from behind the curtain.

Mother Rebekah hesitated. The signet ring flexed in her grip, dug into her palm.

Nowhere else to go.

The room felt different this time, as though she had stepped back into the Grand Citadel. Only the dinginess distinguished it. Selene, too, seemed different, honorable. The head of this strange sisterhood had been steeped in faith—not Messianic, of course, but religion nonetheless. It curtailed some of her perceived wildness. She stood in front of her desk, shrouded in her formfitting black habit. Mother Rebekah plucked anxiously at the sleeves of her own attire, suddenly uncomfortable in the borrowed red robes.

"We heard the alarms," Selene said.

Mother Rebekah nodded and unfurled her hand. Gauthier's ring sparkled under the shifting light of the crystal chandelier. It felt unusually heavy, as though eager to sink back into her skin —away from Selene.

The woman's expression was hard to read. She stared at it, silver meeting silver. Her lips were pursed but trembling slightly.

When she had sent Mother Rebekah on this errand, it seemed a directive born out of raw hatred, vengeance against those who had hurt her and her sisters. But it was so much more. Given a different choice—a different church—this woman could have walked among the clergy. In the light.

"I see..." Selene's voice trailed off as she stepped forward, eyes locked on the ring.

She cupped her hands under Mother Rebekah's, as though unable to support its weight on her own. Her touch was gentle, loving—wrong. But maybe in a world full of wrong, it could be right. They were alike in so many ways: rejected, betrayed, flailing for their own faith.

"I wanted this for so long," Selene said. Tears welled in her violet eyes, blinked away as quickly as they appeared. Her hands closed, leaving the ring with Mother Rebekah. "This is yours now. A trophy to mark the day you joined our sisterhood."

"I have completed my task." Elation filled Mother Rebekah as she spoke the words. Elation and dread.

"You have," Selene replied quietly.

Silence simmered between them. Was there something more?

The constant background thrum of the place was in her bones. She had to clench her whole body to stop it from vibrating.

Don't make me beg for it.

"It's late," Selene continued. "For you at least. Rest now. Tomorrow will be a big day."

"Tomorrow..." Mother Rebekah repeated, barely a whisper.

Selene did not trust her. She would check.

Control. Control at all costs, lest chaos take her. She forced a slow nod, swallowing past the snap of compressed nerves.

The entranceway curtains felt heavy as lead as she navigated out of the room, shuffling toward her cell. Another night of dreamless nonexistence. How many more nights before that nonexistence became an eternity? She imagined herself crumbling into a pile of colorless ash, smothered under dual bands of silver and gold. Smothered under the celestial aspect of the Great Mother, who brought her into this world and would take her from it.

MOTHER REBEKAH
GREAT MOTHER

"Awaken."

Mother Rebekah gasped back to life, lurching up to seated. Her legs swung around, clambering for the stinging reassurance of the broken floor upon her feet.

Nothingness, absolute and infinite. It had almost taken her.

A ragged breath blew out of her mouth, followed by a cry. She doubled over, hugging herself, fingernails digging into her bare arms. Her body shook with sobs. Every pore ached. Every nerve flared in a cycle of heat and cold, numbing pins and needles followed by serrated blades vivisecting her from the inside out.

She was dying.

A shrunken partition of her brain, still able to problem-solve through the pain, searched for an appropriate prayer, to reinforce her against darkness. There were none. There were only her feet on the floor, her habit on the table, and whatever fate awaited her beyond the escalator. She was a proselyte once more.

She drank, pissed, dressed, and stood obediently at the door. Selene would be waiting for her. It was inevitable.

The beam slid from the doorframe on cue. Mother Rebekah cleared the last of her emotion from her throat. She was an empty vessel.

The steel door swung open, revealing Selene and all her sisters. They lined the edges of the tunnel, standing in rigid formation with arms crossed over chests but heads turned toward her. Brass, bronze, and pewter faces, all smiling. Her focus failed past the first few, but every set of silver-flecked eyes she could see was wet with tears.

"They're here for you, Sister," Selene said. "We all are. It's time."

The woman grasped her quivering hand, gently interlacing fingers. An electric trickle of energy filled her, prickling through parchment skin into her shallow veins. It would be enough.

They walked hand in hand down the hall. Time evaporated. Each span between ceiling lamps felt like an eternity, one unfeeling step placed after the other, smiling disembodied faces to either side, yet before she could blink, they had arrived at the escalators. The background thrum was nearly an earthquake, its epicenter directly below them.

"We go to the Great Mother the same way we were birthed."

Two women approached from the landing and began undressing them, gently prying the perfectly tailored fabric from their bodies. Mother Rebekah stared at Selene as their clothing was removed, the space between them swirling with gold and silver light. Reams of skin peeled away despite the tenderness of her sisters' attentions, but so long as she held that gaze, there was no pain, only numbness. Gray ash lined her discarded habit. Toenails separated from her feet as her boots were removed. But still, she felt nothing.

Selene's metallic skin swirled with the scars of ancient disease. They ran the lengths of her arms, legs, and torso like runes upon a tablet. And yet she was whole.

Deep in the speculative, suffocating part of her brain, Mother Rebekah imagined limping down the steps only to be greeted by Holy Esther, her Great Mother. The *only* Great Mother.

This is a lie.

Esther, the Eternal One, somehow at once here and in Cathedral. She would look upon Rebekah the proselyte with disgust, at the gall of claiming the accelerant as an outcast. It would be the last thing she saw on the face of her former matriarch—her god—before being torn apart.

Selene took her hand. Doubt dissolved, joining the ash of her crumbling body.

They were walking down the escalator. She couldn't see, but Selene could. She could barely feel, only enough to realize they were descending into a pool. The same not-quite water in which she had been healed after escaping the Grand Citadel, slippery and stringy, no cooler or warmer than the air that preceded it. By the time they reached the floor, it was at their shoulders.

Selene continued to guide her forward, deeper into the void. Mother Rebekah clutched the woman's hands, which had become hot in hers except for a patch around Helio's ring. As with the hallway, the journey seemed to last for days only to end suddenly.

"We're here," Selene declared, her voice echoing into the distant depths.

"Here..." Mother Rebekah repeated. Her head swiveled from side to side, despite there being no light with which to see.

"We will bathe in the living waters and pray for the Great Mother's blessing."

Selene's hands withdrew, and Mother Rebekah fell. The water took her, beating against her ears, flooding into her nostrils—

Then she was breathing again, gasping against darkness.

"Repeat after me, Sister," Selene said, and she did.

"Blessed are you, Great Mother,

who has sanctified us through your commandments,

and commands us to immerse."

The blessing was familiar, almost right. Ancient words dragged through different times and faiths, patched and reshaped to new ends.

The water came for her again. She did not resist, the space between breathing and not breathing lost along with her vision.

"Blessed are you, Great Mother,

who makes us holy by embracing us in living waters."

Her own voice sounded distant, lips moving of their own volition. She fell a third time. Something sparkled at the edges of consciousness, then she was out.

"Blessed are you, Great Mother,

who has given us life and sustained us,

and enabled us to reach this sacred day."

The sparkles grew, specks of light bubbling up from beneath her. Tiny starbursts flared in her vision as they reached the surface and popped. All around her, the water began to boil, the ever-present thrum of the place elevated to a persistent rumble.

Lines appeared, then shapes: the silhouette of Selene's face, dim bands of prismatic color upon the water's surface, a cavernous ceiling of jagged crystal spars. All illuminated from below, from deep within the water.

The illuminated circle grew brighter as the water churned. Selene's hand was in hers again.

"Be brave, Sister."

Something splashed directly ahead of her. She swayed forward but was held fast. The light became blinding, searing silver-white, too great a contrast from the pitch.

It burst from the deep.

"Great Mother," she breathed.

It was beautiful and terrifying. A towering pyramid of metallic white flesh, pockmarked with craterlike scars, like the moon returned to the heavens. Captured radiance beamed from every pore.

No—

Its entire body was bulbous folds, quaking against one another with infinite love—

Lust—

Each fold encircled with charcoal teats, dripping with thick black milk.

The Lifeblood.

Welcoming arms extended from its sides—

Too many.

More than her mind could process. Mother Rebekah doubled over, shuddering violently as her bowels emptied themselves into the water.

Not arms.

Not arms!

Tentacles. Decorated with the same runic swirls that covered Selene's body.

Selene.

No longer beside her. Her sister was embraced in its arms, curled like an infant. Suckling.

Tentacles. Tipped with mechanical pincers like those that had encircled her daughter's neck.

It was the most beautiful thing she had ever—

No! This wasn't—

Selene's body glowed as she fed, outlining the runes on her back. Her skin puckered, peeling away from her spine. Edges of scar tissue swam in a spiral, coalescing into a new shape—a face, dark and beautiful, more than beautiful. Its eyes and mouth were raw sinew.

"Come home," it sang—Esther sang—calling her into the

fold.

Into its folds.

Mother Rebekah swayed forward, unanchored. Her weak human blood begged for it. Its arms beckoned her forward.

Its arms.

Its claws.

Around her daughter's neck.

"Rebekah…" she whispered.

She saw past the false face, to the perfect face of her child. Frameless without her mane of honey-blonde hair. Her tiny body, laid upon the operating table—

"Come to me, child," it crooned. "Drink."

—a miracle made manifest, even as the accelerant sought to prevent it.

My child.

Not an affront against God. Proof of God.

Something grew inside her, filling the void in her veins. Truth. Glory. Filling her until she felt she would explode. She was sacred violence.

Mother Rebekah's fist punched through Selene's spine and out the other side. Her sister died instantly, eyes fixed upward in rapture. The beast screamed as her clawing hand dug into its malignant innards. Unholy wails burst her eardrums, flayed the last strips of skin from her body. Eruptions of shattered crystal sliced at her from above. But she pressed on. Past the woman's corpse, hunting, seeking with divine clarity. It was there: a thrum, pounding beneath her fingers, growing in intensity. The demon's heart quaked within her grasp, then was torn free.

Its wail ceased abruptly, along with its light. Bubbling folds of diseased flesh collapsed around her, sinking back into the water, now barely luminescent. Selene floated alongside the beast, her face locked in a final expression of surprise and sorrow, then she too sank.

Mother Rebekah stood alone in the encroaching darkness. In her hands was everything she had wanted: life, power. Faith.

"Esther pulled forth the heart of the Beast,

And Messiah declared:

Eat of the flesh,

that you should be joined to me."

Joined to Messiah. Not to God.

The heart shuddered in her hands, impossibly heavy. Impossibly powerful. It looked more geometric than organic, trembling with an alien life of its own. Infinity lay within. Life everlasting.

"Dear God—" Her voice broke. Fear replaced truth. Doubt replaced glory. "Dear God. Guide my hand..."

The cavern was silent save for the bubbling of the beast's slow capsize.

"Guide. My. Hand!"

Silence. Deafening.

The choice was hers alone.

Mother Rebekah screamed in frustration and remembered agony. Her hands shook, clawing, crushing, destroying the hellish thing in her hands with the last of her strength. She shut her eyes against it, refusing it.

"I am with you."

An electric shock jolted through her body. The pulped organ was writhing, pulsing in her hands—no, not in her hands, in her blood.

Her eyes opened in horror—

Exultation.

—as its black blood pressed against her open wounds, finding her veins.

She stared at it in rapture. In terror. She could still drop it. There was time.

No time!

Only ash.

Her arms shot upward instead, clutching the heart high above her head. It pulsed harder, squeezing its contents into her, past her hands, into her arms, to her heart. Violating her soul.

Mother Rebekah screamed, cleaved in two by anguish and ecstasy.

The Lifeblood smothered her, coating her hands in a glove-like sheen. Her ring—Helio's ring—sizzled beneath it, crumbling into dust.

The accelerant flowed into her. She resisted, tried to pull away from the intravenous line, but the press of her sisters was too strong. It surged inside her, took her. All she could do was scream as her humanity died, replaced with the primordial. Replaced with the Messiah.

Helio's face faded from her memory.

Her daughter died a second death, drowned in the abyssal waters below Bastion.

Mother Rebekah was born again.

———

Forty?

Fifty?

It no longer mattered. She had ceased counting those dead at her hands, directly or otherwise. The women of the Underground had not attacked. They merely watched her leave, pleading for the stranger who had shattered their lives to stay, to be their new guide. They would not die by violence but by solitude, until ash took them.

The Metro stretched out behind her, the screech of distant handcars echoing along its ancient walls. It was ironic that so much of civilization lay belowground, away from the sun, away from life. But the primordial lived deep in the earth, alluring with promises of safety, power, certainty, ever drawing mankind farther from the light. Resistance was fleeting.

Her gaze ran the length of the red-and-white level-crossing barriers. They were nothing to her, a play at power by the powerless. Still, this was not the time for more chaos. A message needed to be sent. Mother Rebekah depressed the switch on the call box. Moments later, a spotlight downrail sprang to life, enveloping her.

"Who goes there?" came a tinny, agitated voice through the speaker.

Mother Rebekah breathed deeply, flexing her rejuvenated body within her new habit. It felt good. It felt right.

"My name is Mother Rebekah. I've come to see the lord commander."

PART 3
REVOLUTION

JULIA
WAR CRY

Julia Harper's father had once described a God-engine to her. It stood like a gargoyle outside the gates of Cathedral, still and silent but very much alive. An intentional display of the Matriarch's superiority, to be relayed back home so the relationship between their two nations was crystal clear. She never fully appreciated how terrifying the sight must have been—until now. And this time there were two of them, striding out of nowhere like beasts of Hell.

Everyone was just staring up at them, Julia included, entranced as though by a demon's crooning. But unlike hellspawn, which were pure chaos, these machines were all hard-edged symmetry, identical models. They had enormous hawklike legs like the unfinished battle walker she and her father had discovered, joined by a buttressed torso to a viciously sloped upper body. A malevolent red eye beamed from their prows, and enormous cannons protruded from their shoulders. In their own way, they were beautiful. Every ornamented panel of their hulking, black-on-black bodies had been painstakingly sculpted to present the maximum degree of intimidation, and it worked.

Julia's whole body was shaking. One of them had spoken, demanding their surrender. No one expected that, not to say anyone knew what to expect at this point. Its voice was alien, ear-splitting even out in the open. Clipped bursts of distorted but intelligible noise—not human but not entirely mechanical either. Julia wasn't sure, but it sounded female—young. What were they? *Who* were they?

Baptiste's men weren't faring any better. The lot of them were frozen like stalagmites, gray armor blending into the gray nothingness of the landscape outside the bunker. Only Kai was stirring, his mouth making silent motions while he stroked a golden ornament fastened to the end of his beard—it looked important, like something she should have recognized. His eyes briefly caught hers across the field, and a mournful smile crossed his face, in that moment looking so much like his younger brother.

She wished Roen was with her now. They had known each other since adolescence, were inseparable companions, part-ners, lovers. Their marriage had been a formality because *of course* they would spend their lives together—a formality and a curse.

Kai stepped forward, walking slowly away from Lieutenant Baptiste, toward the battle walkers. His smile faded, contorting into a hateful scowl.

He wouldn't...

Kai yelled—the savage, beastly scream of a predator. No echo called back to him from the Deadlands. His fists were clenched tight as though he would take on the death machines bare-handed. He yelled again, and this time his call was joined by others. Half of them were still in the *Ironclads*—the Greybull infantry fighting vehicles—while the others milled about like hungry wolves. They all started hooting in a rhythmic war cry, beating their weapons against their chests and the sides of their vehicles. One of the Ironclads' cannons turned toward the enemy. Julia's arms bristled with terrified goosebumps.

The Bastionites started to back up, edging toward the hangar door. Her father stared alternatingly between Kai and the God-engines, mouth agape. His ambition had gotten her husband killed, and now, between him and her crazed brother-in-law, it was going to kill the rest of them. She should have hated him for it, but all she felt was emptiness, hollow as the surrounding gray. He peered around as his human shield began to retreat, looking intently from the Greybulls to the Harpers to her. They locked eyes, and as they did so, he mouthed the words, "I'm sorry."

Anticipatory terror beat in her chest.

Straightening out of his stooped posture, Sophus brought his hands to his mouth like a megaphone. "Scatter!"

It was a command every Scavrat knew: split up and make as many small targets as possible, like rats. Julia was paralyzed by indecision, stuck halfway between the convoy and the bunker. The vehicles were sitting ducks, the hangar entrance was a death trap, and the gray offered no cover. Everyone else was moving in all directions. One of the AARVs started rolling, turning in a wide arc to retreat the way it came. Someone was shouting her name, then the shooting started.

The God-engine that had "spoken" stepped backward with a monstrous thud, surprisingly fast as it lumbered to bring its long cannons within range. Twin machine guns, emplaced like fangs below its baleful eye, were spitting out violence, swiveling manically to find targets. The other machine wasn't moving, weirdly stationary despite Kai's provocation, as though it had been turned off.

Two of the Greybull vehicles leapt forward in an angry plume of diesel smoke, racing to make distance between them and the battle walkers before circling back in a double-flanking maneuver.

The Bastionites were in full retreat, racing to find cover within the bunker entrance. Their formation split as one of the APCs poked out from the door, both of its cannons forward and pointed at the attacking God-engine. They looked tiny compared to the battle walker's, like toys, but their pulsing chant rang out nonetheless, firing in alternating sequence at the machine. Julia turned her head, following the lines of fire to the enemy, and watched entranced as it brought both of its main cannons to bear, shaking off the barrage without missing a step, and fired back.

The vehicle blew apart, instantly deconstructed into a nebula of twisted metal, tires, and body parts. The explosion expanded slowly before her, frame by frame, as though restrained by the insistent stillness of the Deadlands. She watched wide-eyed as the fireball rolled outward from the bunker, smothering the men who had almost made it back, thinking themselves protected. Killing every last one of them.

Julia floundered under a deluge of unanswerable questions: Would they feel the flame melting their flesh before they died? Did they have time for last thoughts? Did they have families back home?

Her eyes burned beneath the spectacle, but she couldn't turn away. She was anchored in place.

"Move!"

Something slammed into her—Mace, carrying her in a running bear hug.

"Get her out of here!" someone shouted.

A swarm of them surrounded her: Mace, Baptiste, several of his soldiers, and Kai.

She watched, numb, over her bodyguard's shoulder as the God-engine swung around, stepping away from the bunker, drawing its aim onto the fleeing AARV.

No...

Both of its cannons lurched back with a murderous boom. She clamped her eyes shut, but it didn't save her from the soul-shattering sound of the second explosion. Her people, her family—gone in a flash.

Why?

Why was this happening?

A cascade of bullets crashed around them as the God-engine turned again and brought its heavy machine guns to bear. One of the men fell, then another. Her eyes sprang open as a different sound assailed her ears: the swarming Greybull Ironclads, bringing their own cannons into the fray. Still half the size of the Sisterhood's ungodly weapons but a good deal larger than the ineffective Bastionites. They were circling fast at close to point-blank range. The God-engine staggered, falling back as it struggled to find a target. It seemed reluctant to leave the side of its mate, which was still just standing there, guns up but motionless.

Malfunctioning?

"Lieutenant, you have to go!"

She was being pushed into the last Ironclad, while people yelled all around her. Baptiste was arguing with one of his sergeants.

"No, I have to stay!"

"We're dead! You have to get word back!"

"The delegation—"

"They're in the other IFV!"

Lafayette's face was in hers, his breath hot and rancid with stress. "Take care of them," he hissed, his words drowning in the din of battle. "Go now! Now!" He smacked the side of the vehicle, then dashed back toward the bunker.

Mace was kneeling on the gray earth in front of her, head drooped. He wasn't moving. Julia wondered if he was praying, then saw the holes in his ruined back and the guts cradled in his dead hands.

"Mace!" she cried, stepping forward.

Someone inside grabbed her, reeling her back in.

"Give me the package!" Kai yelled. A Greybull fighter tossed him a heavy-looking backpack, which he caught in one arm and swung over his shoulder. In his other hand was a walkie-talkie.

"Kai?"

He looked up at her. She caught his eyes, azure as the glowing caves beneath Hub, and was transported back in time.

Delving together—her and Roen, with Kai as chaperone—into unexplored depths to find ancient treasure. Laughing together as they nearly got themselves killed, time and again. Lying together while naming bioluminescent constellations, to distract themselves from their empty bellies. As long as they were together, they were safe.

"I'm sorry, little sister," he said, eyes wavering. Then he was gone.

The deployment ramp came up, locking her in.

"Kai! Kai!" she screamed, tears welling in her eyes as she pounded the metal.

Julia was thrown back as the vehicle jolted forward with a growl.

"No! Go back!"

They didn't.

Julia gazed at her surroundings, numb. The passenger compartment was much tighter than the crew cabin of an AARV, its occupants seated shoulder to shoulder amidst protruding steel bulkheads and webs of drooping cable. The haunted faces of those around her glowed red under the dim cabin light. Baptiste's head was in his hands.

She had to see what was happening.

Julia roused herself, clambering over the other passengers, then yelping as a sudden maneuver tossed her against the outcropping of a wheel well. Supporting hands reached out but she dodged past them, making her way to the front of the vehicle, where the periscope was.

"Let me in!"

The vehicle commander turned at her yell and helped pull her past several more jostling bodies. They were already crouched but ducked instinctively as the turret above them boomed, sending a pressure wave through the cabin. It felt like someone had clapped their hands over her ears, sending her reeling. She fought back the urge to throw up, clutching onto the periscope tube. The commander, a Greybull fighter like most of those crammed inside the over-capacity vehicle, looked equally nauseated—and terrified. He couldn't have been more than eighteen.

Julia pushed him aside and hustled into the standing harness, blinking the tears from her eyes as she leaned into the goggles. At first all she saw was a blurry gray field, peaceably free of carnage. With a swivel of the periscope, she saw what the driver was up to. The other Ironclads were engaging the God-engine, trading fire and mostly missing as they danced figure eights around each other at perilously close range. Even still, the battle walker had taken damage. The right side of its body was smeared silver, its internal structure exposed under a crater of peeled-away black armor. A growing plume of purplish smoke was billowing from its left shoulder, the cannon on that side stuck in position.

Their own vehicle was moving away from the fracas, but at low speed. Sprinting alongside them, hidden from view of the God-engine, was Kai.

A thunderous blast rang out, followed by the groaning of metal as their vehicle staggered under a shockwave, momentarily lifted off its left-side tires. Shouts filled the cabin as it dropped back down. One of the Ironclads had been hit hard, knocked onto its side, and cracked almost in two. It wasn't on fire yet, but she also couldn't see any hatches popping, any sign of life. Julia reluctantly rotated her view between the scene of destruction and Kai, who had banked off and was running for the second God-engine. It still hadn't attacked.

What are you doing?

The AIs had all gone insane, so legend went. Even if some had persevered, their mechanical bodies were hundreds of years old. However skilled Cathedral's own mechanists were, things went sideways in battle. Maybe the second one had overheated. Maybe its ammo feeds had jammed. Then she remembered the voice. Was it an *it* at all?

She watched the God-engine through the periscope. It wasn't walking but it wasn't completely stationary either. It seemed to be shuffling on the spot, as though indecisive. Stuck in a logic loop. Its upper torso twitched, as much as something that massive could. How many more twitches before it sorted itself out? One system reboot could kill them all.

The package...

Julia flinched away from the goggles as a burst of noise crackled from the young commander's headset. He grimaced, eyes darting back and forth as the broken message came through. She couldn't make it out. Turning back to her viewport, she saw Kai still running but talking into his handset. He was almost at his target.

The commander banged on the metal wall dividing them from the cocooned driver up ahead. "Get us out of here!"

Out of here?

She thumbed the periscope controls and saw that the other surviving Ironclad was bolting away at full speed, weaving back and forth so its rear end wasn't an easy target. The second AARV was nowhere to be seen. The injured God-engine twisted its torso back toward the bunker—toward Kai.

Julia had to continuously adjust her focus as they sped away from the scene. She wanted to shout at them to turn back, to yell and scream, but that would be suicide. There was no turning back. Her husband was gone, her father was gone, and now Kai... She watched in horror as the tiny speck of him scrambled up the beast's legs, toward its torso. Where its reactor was.

She knew what he was doing, even as they moved out of range. She couldn't see him anymore, but she could feel him looking back at her, saying goodbye as he pressed the detonator.

"An eagle," Kai said, pointing at a cluster of azure blobs on the ceiling, glowing brighter than the rest.

"What?" she and Roen said together, giggling.

"There." He was serious. Kai was always serious lately.

Julia squinted, anxious to see what he saw. At first, there was only chaos, but gradually a shape appeared in its midst. Vast wings unfurled from the bioluminescence, rippling across the breadth of the ceiling. Feathers shimmering, as though they would lift the whole of Hub away and her with it.

Julia closed her eyes.

The Deadlands turned white, brighter than the sun.

BAPTISTE

THE MIDDLE OF NOWHERE

They didn't get far before having to stop. The second Scavrat vehicle was damaged, losing fuel—from the battle or the explosion he didn't know. He didn't care. Baptiste had been the first one out, retreating to the rear of their small convoy. Julia warned him not to leave, to just let the mechanists do their repairs. She was going to swap crew for the rest of his delegation—Father Ollet and Vice Chancellor Stern—but he didn't want to see them. Not yet. The ghosts of his men would be waiting in their eyes.

Also, he didn't want Julia to see him throw up.

A minute of dry heaving later, he gave up, turning to face the way they had come. There was nothing behind them, of course. No enemies in sight. No smoke, fire, or mushroom cloud rising into the drab sky. No bunker, even. Baptiste searched the horizon and found only the Deadlands, in all its monotonous entirety.

No survivors followed after them.

"Lieutenant?"

"Sir, what do we do?"

"Should I radio the gunners?"

"Sir!"

Private Reese had died first. Then Thomas, torn in half.

Autocannon shells blazed over his head. Everyone was running, but death came for them. Fire, rolling across the gray like a thunderhead. Inevitable.

Stratton had fallen at his feet, steam hissing from a dozen holes in his armor.

"Get him out of here!"

Lafayette had saved him. Baptiste argued out loud, resisted when the sergeant shoved him into the vehicle. But in his heart, he was already long gone; he had abandoned his men the moment he froze on the battlefield.

They drove, hard, while Julia stared through the periscope. He couldn't see her eyes but the anguish in her body told him everything. He knew suffering, knew how it manifested in the bones and skin and sinews. In her seized posture he saw what she saw: utter destruction.

The shockwave followed.

It was barely a vibration at first, muted like everything else in this place. But even the Deadlands couldn't hold back such primordial violence. Within seconds, everything shook, everything screamed—everyone screamed. The vehicle swerved, tossing bodies around. Their power failed, pitching the cabin into blackness. Julia found his arms and thrashed in them, caught between opposing terrors of fire and suffocation. Hot tears and cold sweat filled his mouth. The world reared as though dying a third time.

Then it was over, muted at last. Bodies retreated to their seats. Words died on lips pursed with grief. They rolled quietly to a stop, in this place—no different than any other place to the border of the infernal plain. Gray above and below.

As he looked upon the emptiness, Baptiste wondered which apocalypse had been worse, man's or God's. The World War killed billions, though such a number seemed absurd. How could the earth hold so many? It couldn't, apparently. God just wiped away the ruins, relegating that which humanity had already destroyed to Hell. Bastion—and Cathedral, he supposed—were the exceptions. Most of the world was like this place: broken, lifeless, empty. Maybe this was the natural order, not civilization.

Nothingness clawed at his soul, and he let it. His soul was already dying, cut away one maimed and murdered soldier at a time. There was little left to lose. He just wanted to walk. He could live without a soul, but his legs would atrophy to stumps if neglected much longer.

Gabriel would have scolded him for such blasphemy.

Baptiste grimaced at the persistent itch of his talisman—the last fragment of his brother's armor, and existence—crammed beneath his own armor. His skin curdled wherever it touched, chest hair caught on its jagged edges. Instead of calming, it burned, distracted. He scratched uselessly at his battle-scarred cuirass, coming away with a handful of blood and grease; human remains, rendered by the flame. Half of Black Watch was dead—under his leadership. Baptiste tried to rub the stain away, but it only piled more thickly upon his fingers, charcoal gravestones under his fingernails.

He had to move. It was suffocating here, beside the others—someone else's army. He had to walk, just a little, to clear his head. A few steps, a few counts to pull him out of the abyss. The drive back would be so long, wherever *back* was.

Unless Julia was lying to him.

Baptiste thought back to their last conversation before her people showed up. It wouldn't be the first time. She and Mace were always whispering when he walked in on them.

Conspiring.

There was something in the bunker they weren't telling him

about. "Help them," the old man had said. Maybe they found what they were looking for and were done with Bastion. Maybe the Scavrats were rounding his people up so they could execute them along the way.

"They'll murder you."

Baptiste whirled around. The hairs on his neck stood at attention.

"What?" he blurted.

The voice had been close, right behind him, but everyone who had ventured outside was heads down doing repairs. Under the vehicle? He stepped away from it.

"Lieutenant?" Julia eyed him across the encampment.

She knew he knew. Her eyes were filled with lies.

"Run," it whispered. *"Get away while you can."*

He had to get away.

"Lieutenant! Baptiste, come back!"

Everyone was shouting at him, but he ignored them. They were just trying to trick him. Back into the vehicle, where they'd slit his throat.

"No, don't!" Julia called.

Liar.

His talisman was scalding, but he ignored it. Gabriel was wrong this time.

Baptiste turned and ran—

And emerged into nothing.

———

The horizon looked the same as before. Looked the same but wasn't. He turned around. The same as before, except it was everywhere. Gray all around. No vehicles, no crews.

Only him, shadowless.

He blinked—and caught a flash of armor slab. Another

blink, and a silhouette lurched from the void before fading back into dust.

Baptiste spun around again. He was in the middle of nowhere. Terror pressed in on him. His skin recoiled from his body. Blood boiled in his temples.

What have I done?

He had run away. He had run into the Deadlands.

"No..." he whispered.

"Baptiste!" The voice was distorted, scattered across time.

Infinity passed between breaths.

"Julia?" His voice terminated at his mouth, as though sucked into a vacuum.

Every second blink brought them back. Then every third, fourth...

Until he was completely alone.

A smell, or the memory of one. Bitter, choking—fleeting, pushed away by the nothing. Baptiste shambled toward it, desperate for anything.

Andrite was there, standing with him on the gray. Staring silently past him.

"Father?"

The chaplain's robes suddenly caught fire, engulfing his body in flame. His wiry hair flared into a crimson halo. His eyeballs dribbled from their sockets. He was screaming, his whole body black as the void, his voice the scream of the world as it died twice over.

Baptiste screamed with him, eyes burning with smoke and tears.

Red-robed hands protruded from the chaplain's charred body, grasping him around the waist.

Andrite was gone.

There was something on him—a steel cable, looped into a belt, extending outward to the limits of his vision. It shimmered as though vibrating, cutting the gray. It didn't belong here.

"Take it off!" the voice demanded. It was everywhere now, in the sky and the earth and the nonexistent wind.

He reached for it but jerked back as the talisman latched painfully to his chest.

"Pull!"

He was yanked almost from his feet, catching himself at the last. Prayer filled his ears. The bitter scent grew stronger, nauseating. Baptiste wretched, hot bile finally spilling over his chin. He tried to blink away the tears. Julia was there, then not. A startled shout, followed by a rumbling engine. Then gray. He blinked again.

Father Ollet stood before him, clutching the cable in one hand and a smoking censer in the other. They were all there—both crews—as they had been the whole time, *behind* the nothing. Baptiste's gaze followed the cable past the priest, where it terminated in the winch of Julia's vehicle. At some point they had turned the vehicle around.

"Praise God," Ollet said.

"Commander?" asked one of the Scavrats. He had a crossbow in his hands.

A fierce-faced woman pushed the weapon down. "Cool it, Boris."

"How do we know he's okay?" another one hissed.

They were all so pale, so narrow. If he turned his head just so, they disappeared again, even though he was back.

Back.

What did that mean in this place? Breathless, he pressed his hand against his armor, pushing the talisman in deeper. Trying to expunge the sight of Andrite's immolation.

"As long as he's on the other wagon with the rest of his people, I don't care," the woman said.

Julia stepped forward, eyes wide, but stopped at arm's reach. An oily rag shook in her hand. "Here."

Baptiste looked at the rag, confused.

"Your face," she said.

"My face," he repeated, still trying to reconcile what had happened.

He patted his cheek, adding a wad of yellow phlegm to his already stained hands. Shame was the first emotion to return. It burned his cheeks. Shame and confusion. He snatched the rag, wiping himself down as Julia stepped closer to unhook him from the winch. For a second, they locked eyes, her arms around him. Bodies touching as they had when the shockwave promised their deaths. He no longer thought her a liar, but her arms felt... alien. The rag was too heavy in his hand. Nothing felt right.

"Reel it back in," she called to her people, stepping back. "Tala, repairs done?"

The other woman grunted acknowledgment.

Julia was searching his eyes, seeking out the broken bits inside. "Are you okay?"

She didn't want to kill him. She just wanted out of this place, like everyone else. Panic had taken him, again. And maybe something else—whatever had spoken to him.

Baptiste strained to pull himself up, ignoring the wrongness of his own limbs. There were still holes in him, gray spots left behind. And questions he didn't dare try to answer. The cable slithered ponderously along the ground, back into its reel. Snapping, wriggling.

He nodded.

"Then let's get the hell out of here."

"Don't have to ask me twice," Tala said, moving off.

A pair of glowering cave dwellers followed the woman to the other IFV—the swapped crew, relieved of their circumstantial camaraderie.

"What did you see?"

It was Ollet. He was still standing there, attention alternating between Baptiste and the *nothing* he had walked into. His voice, a blessedly rare thing, sounded strained.

"See?" Baptiste asked.

Ollet gestured over Baptiste's shoulder, as though urging him to turn around. His gut dropped at the idea. Though gray surrounded them, behind him was nonexistence. He could never go that way again.

"Nothing," Baptiste muttered.

"But you were gone..."

Baptiste shivered in his cold sweat, trying and failing to swallow his fear. His throat was dry with recalled ash. He *had* been gone. Barely a few steps away and nearly lost forever. He realized then that Ollet wasn't asking because he was afraid; the priest was excited, practically salivating.

Anger trickled into the gray spots. Had he been saved out of duty, or curiosity?

Saved... by a scribe. What did Ollet possess that Baptiste did not—faith?

Disgust followed anger.

As though he hadn't prayed enough. As though he hadn't suffered enough.

"Come on!" Julia called from the deployment ramp. Their vehicle was idling angrily, raring to go.

Baptiste strode forward, pulling his armor taut.

"Let's go, priest."

He could feel the man's scrutiny on his back. The same way he had felt Father Valmor's, and even Andrite's before him. They had no right. They were just men. Only God could judge him. And in this broken place, God was absent.

JULIA

THE WAY BACK

The rest of the way back was brutal. Everyone was doing their best, but it was barely enough given the circumstances. For Julia, the trauma of battle was still too raw. She had witnessed death before but never murder. Explosions rippled through her waking memory, one vehicle blowing apart after the next, their occupants' last experience a maelstrom of fire and fear. Soldiers running to their own deaths, faces melting, their armor-encased bodies bursting like overcooked sausages. Then Kai, screaming as he was incinerated, body and soul, the man-that-was rendered nonexistent. Over and over the grisly images repeated.

On the other side—in fitful sleep—Mace waited for her. He kneeled upon the gray sands, black pits where his eyes used to be, dead hands clasped tightly in prayer. The red eye of the God-engine hovered over his corpse—the eye of the sun, his Messiah. Julia reached for him, but his flesh was sand, crumbling to dust under her bloody fingers.

There were only nightmares now, escaped at the end with a choked cry. The crew had grown accustomed to it, too engrossed by their own suffering to be bothered with hers. All except for Baptiste, his tortured eyes peering at her from the shadows of the dimly lit cabin. He had been in a bad enough state before his... disappearance. He was worse now, somehow hollowed out. When not staring glassy eyed at the past, he hunched over with his head in his hands, occasionally kicking at something by his feet. As far as she could tell, he never actually slept.

She kept trying to tell herself the whole incident had been a trick of the eye—fatigue, maybe. She tried not to think about it. No one spoke of it. Denial kept them sane.

The same phenomenon must have been responsible for the missing Harper vehicle. According to the chronometer, their repairs—and Baptiste's sojourn—hadn't taken that long, though it felt torturous at the time. A few speed welds to keep Tala from bleeding out any more fuel. They punched it right after, risking some of that same fuel in exchange for speed, in hopes of catching up to the slower AARV. But it was gone.

She hated this place. A single mistake in navigation and you were lost forever. Linger too long and your mind went. It was *wrong*. Cartographers couldn't make any sense of it either. Every attempt the Union had made to map their way around the Deadlands failed, much to the misery of those involved. They never should have come.

Ollet was murmuring a prayer. His Bible sat open upon his lap, but the litany continued even when his eyes closed, even when it seemed he slept. He reminded her of Bertram. Her wandering thoughts turned to her former crew. There had been no time to ask her father about them before all hell broke loose, if they made their own journey back intact. Char hadn't been the same after her brother disappeared. She wondered if Jax was still wandering around out here, somewhere.

Better that he was dead.

Ollet snorted, turned the page of his holy book, then resumed his arcane muttering, eyes still closed. She envied the priest's supernatural calm, which persisted even after he had slipped into—

No.

Julia shook her head, trying to exorcise the memory, but it persisted.

She had seen it with her own eyes, felt the breath choked from her as Baptiste was there one moment and gone the next. The winch had been Ollet's idea, brilliant and terrifying. Nonsensical. He, too, had been there then gone, then there again with the lieutenant in tow. It was *wrong. He* was wrong, gleeful when anyone else would have crumbled under the pressure, when Baptiste had. Tala had wanted to leave them all there. Julia could see it in her eyes afterward. That and something else—a creeping hysteria, like Jax the night before he disappeared.

Julia pulled herself away from Ollet, directing her attention to the others. There was little else to do save stare out the periscope.

Evelyn, the politician, was near catatonic, hunched into a tiny ball for most of the drive. Occasionally, she erupted into twitching hand gestures and murmured dialogue, deeply engaged in conversation with herself. Each time, the priest laid his hands on her forehead, whispering into her ear until she calmed. Her bloodshot eyes bulged with resentment.

The few Greybulls left aboard after the exchange were having a rough go of it. None of them had been to the Deadlands before, nor did they expect to make a round trip with no reprieve in between. Caleb, the vehicle's former commander, was nearly undone by the stress of leadership. He had been relieved when she took command of both their vehicle and the convoy. Tala grumbled about it, but her complaint was half-hearted. Stubborn as they were, the Greybulls respected her "expertise."

Julia did her best to set an example, but in private she was buckling. Everything happened at the wrong speed. The things she had seen—and not seen—corroded her brain. The sheer monotony of their journey, horrible under any circumstances, clawed at her nerves. The passenger compartment was tight, halved by auxiliary fuel tanks, but sometimes it felt too tight, airless. Sometimes the roof was too distant, a grab bar the only thing keeping her from floating unmoored into the void. Hallucinations started to manifest alongside memories. She saw things in her peripheral vision: wrinkles in the air, eye floaters that elongated into black tendrils.

Her hearing, too, was playing tricks on her. Ever since stopping, an intermittent knocking had started up from the vehicle's underbody, as though something—or someone—was trapped beneath it. No one else could hear it. Eventually it had been too much, and she ordered the convoy to stop again so she could get out and check. Tala almost mutinied right then and there. Ollet had offered to accompany her, but she refused.

There was nothing there—of course, there was nothing anywhere. The wheels were clear. Nothing had adhered to the chassis, nothing she could see.

Nothing.

"You look worried," Baptiste said.

Julia blinked the tendrils away. They were staring at each other. He leaned forward as though they had been in conversation this whole time. Their foreheads were almost touching.

Her own lips were moving but making no sound. She couldn't talk.

She was still outside, waiting for the ramp to lower.

No.

They closed it after she got out to look. No one wanted to see the nothing again. The hydraulics were jammed. She wanted to yell, to pound on the door, but she had no voice, no hands. She was nothing.

No.

That was not now. That was before.

She had asked them to stop, to check the sound. Baptiste agreed but refused to go with her.

Ollet went instead. She had told him to stay but he came anyway. He watched her as she ran circles around the vehicle, searching, pulling, probing for whatever was fucking banging on the floor!

Stop it! Stop it! Stop it!

Nothing.

When she finally gave up, she tried to find the deployment ramp, but the vehicle was too gray. Every side of it looked the same, blended into the earth and sky. She turned to Ollet for help.

The priest was bleeding incense.

It gushed from every pore of his skin, burning through his robes. The essence of him fell upward until only a shadow remained—black, eyeless.

No.

That was not now. That was before.

Baptiste had dragged her back inside, screaming. The ramp was down the whole time—he wouldn't let Caleb close it on her. She was inside now. They were all inside. Together.

They were okay as long as they stayed together. But Roen and Kai were dead.

Fingernails dug into her palms. Her nails. Her hands. Her body. Slowly, she winched herself back, as Ollet had.

The priest sat across from her, beside Baptiste.

She wasn't outside.

Syllables churned in Julia's brain, tumbling together until words emerged.

"We're close," she wheezed, begging for it to be true.

They had been talking, but she couldn't remember any of

their conversation. Any of the rest of the trip. There was only outside—the first time and second time—and now, hours away from home.

Tears bubbled in her eyes. Her belly ached, bloated with anxiety and undigested rations.

"We're close," she said again, just to make sure she could.

Ollet watched her through half-lidded eyes.

Close—hopefully close enough.

Home. It was at one time, anyway.

She had no idea what she'd find there, or if anyone would be left alive at all. Chaos, left behind by her father and brother-in-law. A crater, surrounded by God-engines. Radio was useless in the Deadlands. They just had to keep driving. They had to get out.

Before the Deadlands took them all.

"They've set up a blockade…" Caleb was peering through the periscope, turned toward home.

Julia thought she had imagined every possible horror on returning home: massacre, forced exodus, nuclear fire. What she didn't expect was to see their own people barring the door. She rose from her seat, grasping an overhead rail for support as the driver slowed their approach. Her old self was slowly bubbling to the surface as the Deadlands receded behind them. Her hallucinations faded with the gray, but she could still feel their residue at the corners of her eyes. "Let me see."

Caleb moved off so she could take his place.

Normally Clan Vega ran interception protocols, but they were nowhere to be seen. Instead, a small fleet of Mercers had scuttled out of the canyon to block the main entrance. Their star-and-circle emblems shone red under the late-day sun. Clan Mercer was the titular head of the so-called loyalist bloc within the council. They handled most of the shipping runs between Hub and Cathedral, relayed communications between the two, and as far as Julia could tell did whatever the Matriarch told them to do. They were the antithesis of Clan Greybull, and as close to enemies as another clan could be.

"Four heavy Runners, armed. And"—Julia pressed herself into the goggles, wondering if she was hallucinating again—"a tank?"

It looked brand-new, desert tan, its cannon pointed in their direction. She stared, speechless.

"Ancestors..." Caleb muttered. "Wait, incoming message."

Julia pushed aside the periscope with trembling hands. Baptiste was staring at her again. Like her, he had perked up since they left the gray behind, though his normally dark skin hadn't recovered any of its color and his eyes seemed no less haunted. A low muttering thrummed through the cabin as Ollet recited psalms of protection, emboldened by the stress of his cabinmates.

"Put it in the cabin," she said.

Caleb toggled a switch on his control board, shunting the staticky signal to an overhead speaker.

"—is Mercer unit Alpha One to unauthorized Greybull forces, you are ordered to hold position and await further instruction."

"Ordered," Julia repeated, scowling. She was only half Greybull, but that half was starting to win out. Anger brought her into focus. She grabbed another headset from the console, snapping it over her ears.

Caleb looked relieved to defer responsibility for their current clusterfuck. He was soaked in sweat and stank of nerves.

"Should we stop?" he asked.

"No. Tell Tala to get behind us and follow our lead."

Caleb nodded, moving off to relay her instructions to the other Ironclad.

Julia depressed the transmit button on her earpiece. "This is

Acting Commander Julia Harper to Mercer blockade. What orders?"

There was a pause before the message came back.

"Commander, your other vehicle has been permitted entry and is currently quarantined." Julia sighed with relief; the AARV was safe—presumably. "But all Greybull forces are to wait at the perimeter for further instructions."

This was unprecedented. Access to the Hangarway was sacrosanct. Protected, always, but never forbidden to any clan. Disputes were always resolved inside, removed from the terrors of the wastes.

"Who is this? Who gave these orders?"

"Commander Rylan Mercer, acting on behalf of the council. Please shut down your engines."

On behalf of the council...

Caleb was swearing and tapping the side of his headset.

"What's wrong?" she asked.

He didn't answer immediately, at one point yanking the speaker away from his ear as a series of shouts clipped through.

"Caleb!"

"Tala's out..."

"Out?"

"I don't know. Sounds like she snapped. Boris is taking over."

Julia pressed back against the periscope, spinning it to their rear. The second Ironclad was wobbling back and forth, at one point veering completely off course before pulling back in behind them.

"Caleb?" she asked, glancing one-eyed at him.

"We're good. They're good. I think..." he muttered, his hands white-knuckled on his console.

Julia ground her teeth together. Shit timing. She rotated her view back around to the blockade, squinting to see their myste-rious opponent. Rylan... The name wasn't familiar, but she didn't know much about his clan other than epithets. She stayed as far away from politics—and loyalists—as she could. Her father would have known what to do, what to say. He claimed to hate politics, but he would have been a clear candidate for chief if not for failing every single Finder's Right. Bunker 23 was his last chance.

She turned toward Caleb, wishing for eyes in the back of her head. They were so close now, which only made things worse. Energy formerly reserved just to stay sane was now needed to actually do something, which allowed unhealed mental wounds to reopen. And Tala had been one of the tough ones. "How long 'til nightfall?"

He stared back dumbly for a few long seconds, then checked the chronometer on his console. "Hour and a half," he stammered, his red-rimmed eyes vibrating with stress.

"We can't stay out here," Baptiste said.

Julia jumped at the sound of the lieutenant's ghoulish voice. His cold eyes beamed at her from the shadows.

"Maybe I can speak with them," Evelyn offered, crawling from her cocoon. She looked like she regretted the words as soon as they sprang from her mouth. Her hands twitched uselessly.

Julia shook her head. "They don't know you."

Her father would have known what to do.

She saw him again, across the battlefield, painted with regret. His apology was swallowed by the din, but the pain on his face was plain to see. The failure. It stuck into her heart like shrapnel.

The Hangarway blurred before her. She blinked, hard and repeatedly, forcing the memories away, and clicked her transmitter back on. "How long are we supposed to wait?"

A wail of distortion came through the radio, skittering off the cabin walls. It sounded like the God-engine's dying scream—a torrent of noise channeled across every frequency, as black turned to blinding white. Julia lurched, but it was over by the time her hands made it to her ears.

"Unknown at this time. Cut your engines, now."

"Unknown... What are we supposed to do, camp out here?"

There was no reply, only a grating buzz left over from the prior burst. Julia ripped off her headset and grabbed the periscope handles, swiveling it around to their flanks. If the demons didn't get them, the God-engines would.

No...

A sacrifice? Not even loyalists would stoop to that... or would they?

"Ask Tal—ask whoever's in charge over there if they see anything on their scopes, due north-northwest."

She waited while Caleb checked in. The passenger cabin was in one of its too-small phases. Every brush against its steel bulkheads felt crushing, like exponential weight piling upon her shoulders.

"Nothing, Commander."

Nothing. Yet.

"Fuck this," she muttered.

They were close now.

"Caleb, put a call into the chief on a secure frequency. We're going to need reinforcements."

"Commander?"

"Do it!"

"Okay. But which chief?" he asked.

Julia grimaced. Born a Harper, married into Greybull, then widowed. She felt homeless most of the time, dispossessed. Since Roen died, she had spent most of her time at one forward operating base or another. Ironically, she had accepted her father's mission because it was an opportunity to get even farther away.

"Both."

Caleb nodded.

"Joro," she said, calling to the gunner stationed across from them. He was an older man, gruff, almost her father's age. Other than announcing his duty swaps with the driver, he had said nothing the whole trip. He mostly slept or stared idly through his viewport. "Bring up the turret, but do *not* shoot at anything unless they shoot at us first. Understand?"

He nodded and gripped the targeting joystick—a little too eagerly.

"Understand?" she repeated.

"Yes," he muttered, settling into his viewport.

Julia bristled. Taking command had been unorthodox, and not everyone approved. To most Greybulls, she was still a Harper.

She replaced the headset and stared through the periscope. "Full speed ahead. We're going in."

They were close now. The cavern entrance yawned open behind the heat-blurred specter of the Mercer forces.

The buzzing of the empty channel crackled into a panicked-sounding Rylan. "What are you doing, Julia? Stand down or we'll fire."

She didn't bother to turn on her transmitter. "I fucking dare you," she whispered.

Closer.

She could see them clearly now, including Rylan presumably. He was manning a machine gun atop the lead Runner, peering back at her through his own binoculars.

Next to the tank.

How had they managed to hold on to it? The war machine looked completely untouched by time, other than being rebranded in Mercer regalia. Greybull skirted the rules to keep the good stuff, but these people purportedly only did Cathedral's bidding. Which meant they had been given permission. The notion unsettled her to the core.

The periscope goggles sucked at her face, damp with sweat from her forehead. It had grown insufferably hot in the cabin. Every breath felt stale, a little less oxygen than the last.

Closer.

The Runners still weren't moving. Her convoy was headed right for them. The tank's main gun swiveled, the sight of it almost knocking her from her moorings.

"Easy, Joro," she said with forced calm. "Easy."

They wouldn't—

A deafening boom rang out, reverberating through the whole vehicle as though it had been struck by a massive hammer. Everyone lurched, ducked, or otherwise pressed themselves into whatever corner of imagined safety they could. The tank had fired! But the shell had gone high. A warning shot—a damned expensive one.

Joro held his fire.

No one protested. No one shouted for her to stop. She wished they would, to divert her from this very Kai-like behavior. They trusted her—mostly—which made everything much, much worse.

Closer.

Rylan was yelling something into a walkie-talkie. She could see his face, riven by fear as his driver accelerated hard. The Runners scattered in every direction. The tank heaved from its position, borne on an angry cloud of dust.

"Yes," she hissed. "Everything we've got, Caleb!"

He banged on the driver's compartment.

The world darkened around them. They drove hard into the Hangarway entrance, the metal panels beneath her shaking with the unshackled power of the Ironclad's big engine. Julia dropped back from the periscope, pressing herself into the bulkhead as they navigated the winding labyrinth at its mouth. Pained creaks whined from the vehicle's twisting chassis. Her whole body was vibrating of its own accord.

"Oh no," Caleb muttered. "Joro, who's on home defense right now?"

They were both staring at the roof. Julia's stomach clenched as she followed their gaze.

Home defense was a standing rotation, evenly distributed between the Union's clans, as all things officially were. If whoever was in charge now thought Hub was threatened, they could open fire or even collapse sections of the Hangarway right on top of their heads. She hadn't even considered it.

"I don't know..." Joro said.

Baptiste was staring at her, one eye twitching. The last time they touched death together—when the God-engine exploded—they had found each other's arms. Her face had pressed against his neck. Conjoined, they could withstand the pressure. Her body ached for it now even as her mind rejected it.

A muted voice buzzed from Caleb's headset. He cupped a hand over his ear and nodded. "We're being followed in," he said.

Not likely they were going to get blasted to bits, then—not yet at least. Julia sighed with relief.

"Thank the ancestors," Joro whispered.

Julia held on tight as they neared the exit. Her Greybull crewmates were cheerful, but the Bastionites looked uncertain, sharing nervous glances. She felt as much a foreigner as them. This wasn't home to them, and it no longer was to her. Hub was a graveyard, filled with the ghosts of her past. She was alone here. She was alone everywhere.

———

Julia had moved up to the driver compartment, anxiously peering through the slit of its windows as they approached the Greybull bay. Her heart was racing. The missing Harper AARV was there, apparently repatriated. But all around it was destruction. Caleb had filled her in on the battle with the revenant mother, something that up until a few days ago seemed as impossible as battling God-engines. She had hoped he was exaggerating. He wasn't.

The floor outside the mangled perimeter fence was cratered and stained black from heavy weapons fire. Bullet holes riddled the sandstone wall separating it from the Harpers and cut both their flags to tatters. It looked like a war zone, about to be revisited.

Swarms of clanfolk were pouring in from the hangar tunnels. She spotted a cornucopia of animal totems on their fatigues, representing the entire extended family of the American movement; in addition to Greybull and Harper, there was Vega, Asher, Bridger, and Cheyenne. Most were armed, but only a handful of those looked like actual fighters. They parted to allow the convoy into the vehicle bay, then closed ranks, forming a wall between their vehicles and the incoming Mercer forces.

"Shit. Open the ramp!"

Anxiety throbbed in her temples as she clambered back through the vehicle. They had enough to worry about, even before this mess. The Union persisted mostly as a matter of luck, always on the verge of starvation, death by disease, or simply dying out for lack of living children. She was nearly proof enough of that. Were they going to kill each other now? Civil war was what got humanity here—her own clans preached it often enough.

Guilt ate at her. Maybe she should have just waited outside after all.

Baptiste had latched onto a grab bar and was pulling himself out of his seat.

"No," she said, scrambling over until her face was in his—too close, but too late to back up. Her voice caught in her throat. "Not yet. You're the last thing they need to see right now."

His face contorted, a cascade of frustrated emotions pulling against his pursed lips. She had delivered him from one war zone into another.

"This isn't your fight," she said, placing her hand over his. It burned as hot as an ember.

Slowly, he released his grip.

The deployment ramp juddered open with a whining screech. The priest was chanting a prayer, beseeching God's protection. For once, she welcomed it.

"Stay put."

She ducked out the door, hopped clumsily to the ground, and was immediately struck with dizziness. Her vision dimmed, then brightened to blinding as her blood shuffled around her body.

"Julia," a voice said through the pounding of her ears. "Julia."

Everything came back into focus, milling bodies everywhere. Her old chief, Magnus Harper, appeared beside her, looking especially harried. Behind him, the crew of the AARV was being helped off—one of them unwillingly.

"It's good to see you," he said, quickly grasping her elbows and touching his forehead to hers. "Where's your father?"

The words struck her like a blow. She pulled away, silent.

Magnus's brows came together as realization set in. He took a step back, nearly stumbling. A low keening bubbled up from behind him. The broken crew member had been stretchered and was thrashing against her restraints.

"I... I have to take care of our people." Magnus turned and left.

Another sound was approaching: distant engines. Julia darted around the steaming vehicles, out of the bay, and into the throng—the army she had summoned. She pushed, pulled, and swore her way through until finally emerging onto the front line.

Aubrey II, chief of Clan Greybull, was there, standing a head taller than everyone else. He wore a light-gray cloak over a bulky suit of dull white power armor, its faceted surface scarred by forgotten battles from another world. Julia did a double take. She had seen a lot of Old World tech, but this was unfamiliar—yet again—and definitely something that should have been tithed. Along with their IFVs and Clan Mercer's tank, it seemed everyone was happily putting their contraband on display, consequences be damned.

The chief cradled an enormous battle-axe in his servo-enhanced arms. He nodded at her as she sidled up next to him, his disfigured face stuck in a permanent scowl.

The scream of engines rang through the hangar as their pursuers emerged from the other side, the Runners first, followed by the tank. Shocked murmurs frothed across the crowd as the war machine lumbered forward. Up close, it looked far more intimidating than through the periscope. She swallowed hard, beset by her own idiocy at playing chicken with it. Aubrey's scowl deepened.

The Mercers skidded to a halt, forming a semicircle around her ad hoc army. A billow of diesel fumes and sand rolled over the assembled forces, eliciting a chorus of nervous coughs. Rylan was perched in the back of his Runner, holding fast to the handles of his heavy machine gun. He stared at them—at Aubrey, in particular—through his driving goggles.

Julia couldn't help but notice all the dark patches staining the ground between them, each burgundy blotch marking the grave of a fallen Greybull fighter. Caleb had described a great victory over the revenant mother, but it looked more like a massacre, no better than the last—maybe worse, given the consequences of "winning." Looking up at her father-in-law's face, she saw only hatred—and accusation—in his pale blue eyes. She wanted to touch his shoulder, to beg for calm, but if Kai was stubborn, his father was impenetrable. She also knew that the moment his attention turned to her, she would have to tell him his son was dead. If that happened now, another massacre would surely follow. At least no one was pointing their weapons at each other—yet.

"Rylan!" Aubrey shouted, his voice reverberating along the cavernous walls of the hangar. "Where's your mother?"

The idling Mercer machines barked in fits and grunts. Rylan pushed up his goggles and lifted a handset to his mouth. His response came through a speaker mounted to his Runner's roll cage. "I need you to hand over Kai," he said.

Julia's stomach flipped.

"You really think I'm going to give *you* my son?" Aubrey retorted, the right side of his bisected face opening into a toothy snarl. His axe came up, followed by the weapons of those standing in the front line. The tank's cannon budged, then halted as Rylan's hand shot up.

Doubt tore at Julia. This was her extended family—born into one, married into the other, cousins with the rest—but Clan Greybull's impulsiveness never suited her. It permeated the American movement, which she had always argued was counterproductive. She was too much like her father, too practical. Roen had been different too, able to walk both lines. Whatever the Mercers were up to, at least they weren't rushing to kill their own.

"If we don't give Cathedral something, we're all going to suffer the consequences," Rylan said.

Julia detected movement behind her: a handful of fighters slipping back toward the vehicle bay.

"Give them something," Aubrey said, his chin lifting in disdain. He tilted his axe toward the war machine in their midst. "How many revenant sisters did you have to eat out to keep that tank?"

Rylan's pale face flushed pink. "*You're* calling *me* a traitor?"

A ripple surged through their ranks, depositing two large men to either side of Aubrey. Each was wielding some kind of heavy anti-vehicle weapon, a meter long.

"Fucking hell," Julia whispered, horrified, stepping back. Everyone around her followed suit, not wanting to be incinerated by the backblast.

Two of the Mercer gunners swiveled their machine guns toward them, but Rylan raised his hand again. "Stop! Fuck—just stop!" he yelled.

"It looks like you're outgunned, fancy tank and all," Aubrey shouted. "So why don't you saunter off back to your bay and we'll go back to ours, and we'll let the council decide what's what."

This was crazy. Julia knew Aubrey had no intention of giving in, whatever the council said. She needed answers—on all of it. Before Hub imploded.

Rylan stared at the forces arrayed before him, still clutching his handset. His gaze paused as it crossed hers.

She had to talk to him.

He called out an order to his driver, and they lurched away. The others followed at speed, leaving her ragtag army in the dust. A handful of halfhearted jeers tittered through the crowd.

Aubrey grunted with satisfaction and lumbered around. "I need volunteers to stay and guard the bays. The rest of you, go home."

The crowd dissipated, self-organizing into those who would stay and those who headed back for their clanhomes, clear relief on their faces.

Aubrey spared a final bitter glance in the direction of the fleeing Mercers, then turned to Julia. The right side of his mouth fractured into a crooked smile. "So, where is my son? He can stop hiding now."

Julia mouthed words but nothing came out.

Aubrey's smile disappeared. He peered past her, through the emptying courtyard to the vehicle bay. She followed his gaze. The surviving Ironclads looked ragged, caked in dust and ash. Tala's was heavily pockmarked.

"We sent three," he mumbled.

The Deadlands turned white, brighter than the sun.

Julia tried to speak again, but grief choked her words.

"I'm sorry, little sister."

Tears blistered in her eyes. She couldn't hold them back anymore.

"No," Aubrey whispered, his axe dropping to the ground with a muted thud. The myriad scars of his face converged into a grimace of pain, aging him before her eyes. "No…"

She remembered the man's sorrow when Roen died—sorrow and seething rage, directed at her own father, who was ultimately responsible. It had almost torn their peoples' alliance apart, and though he never said it out loud, she knew Aubrey's resentment trickled down to her by association. But Kai was his firstborn. As painful as that loss was, this was worse.

The chief stood stock-still, warring against his own emotions. Had he not been supported by his armor, Julia imagined he'd be on his knees.

"How," he whispered past a trembling jaw. His neck muscles twitched in grief denied his body. His attention fixed on the vehicles, as though he could will his son to walk down one of their deployment ramps.

"We were ambushed. At the bunker," she said.

"Ambushed…" he repeated, eyes glazed over.

"God-engines. Two of them."

Aubrey blinked, his brow furrowing as he turned to look at her. "What?"

"They demanded our surrender. K—" She paused, swallowing hard. "Kai attacked."

The chief's eyes widened, his lips parting in awe. "Ancestors…"

"He killed one of them. He sacrificed himself so the rest of us could escape. Kai saved us all."

Kai damned us all.

The thought came unbidden. First the revenant mother, then the God-engine. Kai had single-handedly declared war against Cathedral on the Union's behalf, just as Aubrey the First had prior to the last massacre.

"Killed a God-engine," Aubrey repeated, the anguish on his face turning to wonder.

Julia stared at him, trapped between words of reconciliation and budding resentment. He couldn't hate the sisterhood that much. This wasn't a fair trade.

Aubrey's expression darkened. "Mercer…" He peered down at his axe.

This was what she was afraid of.

"We don't know that," she said.

"I should have killed Rylan where he stood."

"Please!"

Aubrey locked eyes with her, his voice breaking again. "They took my son. My legacy."

"The Matriarch took your son!" Julia caught herself. Whatever started here when the revenant mother attacked, there was no going back now. They lived in the wake of actions that could not be undone. It was also the only thing she could think of on the spot to avoid a bloodbath. Chief Greybull was like an unstable explosive, liable to go off any second. She had to reel him back from the edge, even if it was to push him toward another. "You still have a legacy. You still have a daughter."

Aubrey's eyes shimmered with restrained tears. Momentarily relieved of his hatred, he once more resembled her dead husband—half of him, anyway. The other half of his face was permanently locked in a scowl thanks to the Chiefslayer. His armored hands came up, grasping her shivering elbows; his forehead touched hers. Julia sighed with exhausted relief, allowing the churn of agitated bodies to melt away for a few precious seconds.

"You need to rest," he said, pulling back.

She did, she really did. Collapse wasn't far off. But there was so much else as well, the crushing weight of responsibilities she never wanted. She had a foreign delegation to introduce to the Council of Chiefs, which seemed to want nothing to do with them. She had to keep Clan Greybull from going to war with everyone. But mostly, she had to figure out what the hell was going on. Their mission, the revenant mother, the ambush—it all had to be connected. And once word got back to Cathedral, it would get much worse.

Julia had never seen Hub so skittish, its tunnelways so empty. It had been almost a week since the revenant mother's appearance and miraculous defeat at the hands of Kai Greybull, and everyone was waiting for the tempest that would follow.

The council had unanimously voted to halt all missions beyond Union territory, which was remarkable since the council never unanimously agreed on anything. Also remarkable was the council's sanctioning of the American bloc, "temporarily" restricting council participation, voting rights, and operational access. Her clans were cut off while everyone waited for the Matriarch's next move. The last and only time that had happened was with Clan Ramirez, prior to their self-imposed exile. As much as Julia took solace in working far from Hub, hiding away her feelings in one forward operating base after another, the idea of her people being forced from their homeland was terrifying. Aubrey II would die before he let that happen.

She had to talk to Rylan before everything burned down, but their lines of communication had been severed. Finding someone willing to play negotiator between them was difficult.

Word of their curtailed brawl had spread quickly, coursing like a disease from one clanhome to the next. Emergency protocols were already in play, putting even more strain than usual on the communal resource sharing that allowed Hub to function. Many clans had chosen to close their doors altogether, retreating to their own subterranean sectors to wait things out. Most of the rest wanted nothing to do with internal conflict. Finally, her appeal was answered by Clan Dakota, a neutral bloc member that had benefited more than once from illicit trading with the Harpers. The promise of future shares from their next trade with Clan Ramirez sealed the deal.

The designated meeting place was a small, nondescript cafeteria in Dakota territory. Their tunnelways had been cleared of traffic, ensuring only those invited could get in or out. A rectangular table occupied most of the room. She sat at the end farthest from the door, waiting. The Mercers were already twenty minutes late according to an ancient analog clock hanging on the wall. On either side of her were Chiefs Magnus Harper and Teo Vega.

Magnus was dressed in what looked like a brand-new set of coveralls, dark blue, presumably pre-apocalypse. Though he seemed proud of the attire, repeatedly brushing invisible lint from the sleeves, he shifted uncomfortably in his chair, grumbling under his breath about his boney ass cheeks.

Teo was dressed in his council finery: a leather cloak sewn in with brown and black feathers. In combination with his sunken cheeks and hawk nose, he looked very much like a carrion bird. Unlike his counterpart, he sat stock-still, hands clasped over the table.

Vega had suffered greatly for their association with the Americans. In many ways, this meeting was not just about clearing the air with the loyalists, but about mending those bonds.

"Where are they," Magnus muttered.

"Patience," Teo said, as irritated by the complaint as the waiting.

"I should have brought coffee," Magnus said.

Teo snorted. Julia's stomach gurgled unhappily. Her old chief had been an alchemist before climbing the ranks. Perhaps his penchant for mixing up questionable concoctions would have been better suited for their labs than politics.

"Chiefs." One of the Dakota guards crept from the doorway, a crossbow slung over his shoulder. Not only was everyone cagey, almost everyone was armed of late, even in their own residences. "They're here."

Julia stood, hands fidgeting uselessly at her sides. Her companions turned to watch but remained seated.

Rylan entered first, pausing at the entrance. A camo satchel hung over his arm. He scanned the room, looking past its occupants for signs of subterfuge. Given the events of the last twenty-four hours, she supposed she couldn't blame him.

"Do you think we snuck in an army?" Magnus chirped.

"Wouldn't be the first time," Rylan replied.

Magnus grunted, repositioning himself again.

Julia peered at Rylan. It was the first time she had seen their nemesis up close, and something about his features struck her as odd, something she couldn't place at first until she realized he looked... healthy. His skin was unblemished, sun-kissed, and a full head of dark blonde hair fell around his shoulders. His desert-tan fatigues were new, and even his black leather boots shone. Envy clawed at her throat.

He turned his attention to her, eyes as blue and uncorrupted as an Old World sky. "Where's Aubrey?"

Julia blinked, consciously relaxing hands that had curled into fists. She had asked Aubrey's permission to attend the meet in his place. He agreed without protest, retreating to his clanhome to grieve. "I will be representing Clan Greybull in this matter," she said.

Rylan raised an eyebrow but didn't seem upset by the news.

"And your chief?" she asked.

Aubrey had described Chief Morgan Mercer to her as a "vicious bitch," which was about what she expected him to say. *"Beware of that one. She'll trap you with words as easily as a revenant mother can with her eyes."*

A short, wiry woman pushed past Rylan. Unlike her second, she looked like any other Scavrat, save for a lethal gleam in her eyes. Where every other clan was weakening with successive generations, Mercer seemed to be the opposite. Generational prosperity, courtesy of Cathedral. The jealousy growing in Julia's heart clawed deeper, upsetting the charitable mindset she had worked so hard to foster since the blockade.

"You?" Morgan said, looking Julia up and down.

Julia wanted very much to be somewhere else. The room was too bright, the electric buzz of its lights too loud. Morgan was shorter than her, yet Julia felt tiny in her presence, the bagginess of her fatigues only serving to accentuate her smallness.

"Would you rather we summon Aubrey?" Magnus cut in, graciously snapping her from an anxiety loop. Teo, too, was eyeing the woman, his normally neutral expression exchanged for something more predatory.

Morgan switched her attention to Magnus, thin eyebrows knitting together in disdain. "Fine."

The two of them walked in, taking their seats at the opposite end of the table. Everyone watched as Rylan lowered his bag carefully to the floor. Weapons? Restraints? None of them were armed, as per the agreement. Magnus and Teo shared a concerned look.

Julia sat down, relieved for the security of her own thighs to hold on to.

"This is highly unusual," Morgan said, crossing her arms over her chest. "I'm only here because my second insisted."

Rylan was scrutinizing Julia, clearly on edge as he waited for her Greybull wildness to burst forth.

"You didn't leave us much choice," Julia said. "It's not like we could bring this to council."

Morgan ignored the jab. "And what exactly is *this*?"

Julia glanced around the room. They hadn't killed each other yet, which was a positive. "An exchange of information, for the sake of our Union."

Rylan leaned forward to speak, but Morgan cut him off. "The only exchange needed here is Kai Greybull."

Julia winced at the sound of her brother-in-law's name. It was still too raw when spoken aloud. The sleep she had managed in her father's cot was barely better than on the journey back, leaving her little recovered. Mace and Kai both haunted her dreams, screaming in their replayed moments of death for her to come back—to come back to the Deadlands, where they were waiting for her. Before lurching awake for the last time, she saw them seated with her father at the same table they had shared with the Bastionites, his body a shuddering black silhouette. Reduced. Inhuman.

"Come back."

"Julia?"

The table was too long. She was falling upward.

There was a hand on hers, extending all the way from a distant concrete horizon.

"Julia."

The room rushed back in. Everyone was staring at her.

Julia swallowed back the residual vertigo. "Sorry."

A few hours of sleep and a mugful of medicinals were keeping her conscious, but only barely.

They had managed to keep the battle at Bunker 23 secret so

far; it helped that Clan Greybull had effectively been quarantined. Other than crews sworn to secrecy and the American chiefs, no one knew about the God-engines—or about Kai. Julia hated it, but the blowback from his killing of the revenant mother was bad enough. The whole truth couldn't come out until there was a guarantee they wouldn't all be executed on the spot—justifiably or not.

"Kai Greybull is dead," she said.

"What?" asked Rylan, incredulous. "You brought us all the way here to start lying again?"

Morgan's head was tilted, eyes like microscopes upon her. "No," she said, much to her second's surprise. "She's not."

Rylan's face fell, eyes clouding over with imagined horrors. "Then he's taken us all with him."

"What is it with you Americans?" Morgan asked, practically spitting the words out. Her momentary compassion for Julia's loss disappeared as quickly as it had appeared.

Magnus scowled. "And if we had given him up, what would you have done with him? Turn him over to Cathedral? Since when do even loyalists stoop that low?"

Teo's jaw was clenched, but he continued to stare down at his hands.

"What choice do we have?" Rylan retorted. "Watching you flaunt the tithe over and over!"

Teo's gaze came up, meeting Magnus across the table.

"You think we don't know?" Morgan asked.

Julia looked from person to person. Her hands were soaked with sweat, leaving dark patches on her pants. The HVAC must have been on the fritz. It took her a moment to catch up to the Mercers' accusation. Was it possible they knew the truth about the bunker? About the human-piloted battle walker they found there?

"Everyone holds back a little gear," she said.

"A little?" Rylan repeated. His formerly calm demeanor was quickly deteriorating into outright panic. "We've seen your little. And your not so little. We're not idiots, we just chose to let it slide."

"How very gracious of you," Teo intoned.

Julia couldn't tell if the chief was being sarcastic or not. Clan Vega had always been a reluctant partner in their franchise, more so after their people were slaughtered on account of Kai's indulgence. Old bonds were breaking.

Magnus continued to fidget. He had confessed everything to Julia, including the involvement of Clan Ramirez in their ill-fated mission. It gushed out of him, as though in penance for the doom he had laid upon her father.

"We know about Ramirez," Morgan said.

Magnus stopped moving.

Rylan heaved his satchel onto the table, unceremoniously tearing the zipper open. Julia flinched, the sound of it cutting into her like a knife. They all watched as he pulled out a familiar-looking metal cylinder and placed it on the table before him.

Morgan was staring at Magnus now. "Wasn't one massacre enough for you?" she asked.

Rylan pushed the cylinder, sending it rolling quietly down the table. Dread filled her as it turned end over end, the scab of a red wax seal clearly visible where the lid had previously been opened. She caught it with shaking hands before it could fall onto her lap.

Impossible...

It looked exactly like the case the Bastionites had given them outside Bunker 23. The one her father had taken with him when he returned to Hub for reinforcements, along with the bulk of its contents. She had kept only a handful of schematics to get things operational in his absence. Magnus would never have let such an artifact out of his sight.

"Where did you get this?" she asked, barely above a whisper.

"Open it," Morgan said.

Teo stared intently, half standing out of his chair. Magnus was sweating more than she was.

Her left hand slid slowly up to the lid; it felt detached from the rest of her body, as though guided by someone else. Nothing was reflected in the gunmetal-gray of the case. Nor could she see her reflection on the table.

Nothingness surrounded her, gray to the ends of the earth.

The lid opened with an explosive pop. Julia winced, exhaling against the crisp fume of hard copy that surged into her nostrils. She carefully tipped the cylinder sideways, unfurling a sheaf of fresh white paper onto the table. Familiar diagrams flicked past her, animating the bunker's innards for all to see, battle walker bays included. It was an identical set to the documents Baptiste had delivered to them—the key, in its entirety.

"What..."

Julia squinted confusedly at the pile, thumbing back a handful of pages. They were *all* there, including the schematics she had taken.

Mercer hadn't stolen anything. This was a copy.

"Where did you get this?" she asked again.

The Mercers looked uncomfortable in the artifact's presence. Rylan's agitation had withered into simmering discontent. "You don't deny it, then."

"At least we know you're not a liar," Morgan added, a hint of relief in her tone.

Rylan reached into his bag and drew out another stack— photographs, which he dealt down the table one at a time. Julia stared at a snapshot of herself, alone within a field of gray. Her heart was pounding in her temples. Then another, capturing her father and the rest of their crew and vehicles. One of Baptiste and his men, Deckard handing over a case identical to the one on the table. Their APC, with the bunker entrance looming in the background. The truth spilled out before her photograph by photograph.

There were no photos of the second Bastionite vehicle.

Julia peered at her interrogators. "Who gave these to you?"

Morgan glanced at her second, who was looking almost as distraught as Julia felt.

"The same foreigners that gave you the first one," he said.

The blood beating in her skull was making it hard to think. Baptiste? Had the Harpers been completely fooled? Had she?

"It's one thing to steal guns, armored vehicles even," Morgan said. "But battle walkers! Making deals with foreigners we know nothing about? You people are insane."

Spoken out loud, by someone other than her own chiefs, it did sound insane. It always had, but they carried on like it was just another lucky find.

Julia pried herself from the photographs to Magnus, who was staring wide-eyed at the evidence.

"Bring them in."

———

Morgan was on her feet, hands hovering over an empty holster at her waist where a sidearm had been relinquished. Julia imagined it was the first time in ages that Clan Mercer's chief had been truly shocked. Rylan was frozen in place. Magnus sat himself back down and resumed his fidgeting.

"How did they get here?" Morgan asked.

Lieutenant Baptiste eyed the lot of them, equally uneasy bereft a weapon or familiar territory. The priest and politician crowded in behind him. Of the three of them, only Ollet looked eager to be there, silently ingesting every detail. Currently, he seemed enraptured by the feathered visage of Teo Vega. Teo scowled in response, hunching deeper into his cloak.

"They were granted safe haven within Harper territory," Julia said. She eyed the lieutenant, trying to spot signs of recognition —of betrayal. There were none.

"Safe haven?" Morgan asked, aghast.

"Are we on trial here?" Baptiste asked, his voice low. Even unarmed, he looked formidable in the heavy plate armor he had refused to remove.

Evelyn stepped forward, placing a hand on Baptiste's arm. Her ambitions had apparently been restored. "Please, Lieutenant."

He acquiesced—reluctantly.

"I am Vice Chancellor Evelyn Stern. This is Lieutenant Baptiste and Father Ollet. In the name of Bastion and the Holy Triarchy, we greet you."

Morgan and Rylan shared a look but said nothing.

"I have been sent by my government to discuss terms of our alliance," she continued.

"Alliance..." Rylan repeated.

Morgan stepped right up to the table's edge. "You must be fucking joking."

Evelyn's face fell.

Baptiste bristled, shedding his fatigue as anger took over. "My men died to save your people."

"What?" Morgan asked. "How?"

"Your Revenant Sisterhood, that's how!"

Rylan paled, finally assuming a proper Scavrat complexion. Morgan opened her mouth to respond, then clamped it shut again.

"God-engines," Julia said. "The Matriarch sent God-engines to the bunker."

Any pretense of confidence Rylan had worn coming into the meeting completely disintegrated. "Ancestors…"

"We barely escaped. Thanks to the lieutenant and his men."

The Mercers glanced at each other, fear in their eyes—plus something else: a subtle head shake from the chief.

Julia snatched a photograph from the table, the one clearly depicting the Bastionite APC.

"We are all betrayed," she said, handing it over. Baptiste eyed it confusedly, then the others on the table. "Who was in the second vehicle, Lieutenant?"

Fire flared in Baptiste's eyes. He turned to Ollet, snatching the startled man's robes up in his fist. "Priest. Tell me you know nothing of this."

The priest remained impossibly calm, even lifted halfway from the floor. His eyes swiveled slowly from the photos to the lieutenant. "I'm just a scribe," he said.

"Lieutenant!" Evelyn called.

"Just a scribe," Baptiste muttered, releasing his grip. He glared intently at the Mercers. "The people who gave these to you, what did they look like?"

"Like you," Rylan said, then pointed at the disheveled priest. "Like him. Red robes, gray armored cars."

"Bastards," Baptiste muttered.

Evelyn closed ranks. "What's going on, Lieutenant?"

"We *are* betrayed. By our own. Rayos…"

"Rayos?" Evelyn asked.

"Order Sacramental."

Evelyn stammered out half a "why," but nothing more came forth.

"When did this happen?" Julia asked, fixing all her energy on Rylan as momentum shifted in her favor.

"A week and a half ago. On a trade run."

"They just showed up?"

Rylan straightened in his chair. "We were caught off guard. At first, we thought it was a Ramirez raid—"

"Raid?" Magnus cut in.

Morgan scowled. "You're a shitty judge of character, Magnus."

Teo sighed in irritation, cracking his neck from side to side. He was one flap of his cloak from flying off.

Rylan continued. "They surrounded us. It wasn't until they dismounted that we realized they weren't clanfolk, exiled or otherwise."

"Then what? They just handed this over?" Julia asked, pointing at the artifact.

"Basically." He shrugged. "They warned of grave consequences if we didn't intervene. A new army rising in the east."

"Your fucking army," Morgan added.

"And what did they want in return?" Julia asked.

Rylan didn't answer right away, rubbing the thin stubble on his face and neck. "Nothing."

"Nothing..."

Rylan nodded.

"And you just trusted them?" Julia asked, recognizing the irony in her accusation. Hadn't her father done the same when Baptiste's men showed up at the bunker? Was the Union so desperate for handouts that they'd take them from anyone at this point, unquestioned?

"The evidence was undeniable. The timing matched up with your mission into the Deadlands. And those," he said, pointing at the photos.

"I need to get back," Baptiste said. He caught Julia's gaze, imploring. "I need to warn the Legion."

"Wait." Julia did the math in her head. A trade run, meaning Clan Mercer was en route to Cathedral. Plus a day or two for transit. Reality crashed into her, painfully obvious in retrospect. "You told her... You told the Matriarch where we were going."

All eyes turned to Rylan, save Morgan, who was chewing on her lip.

"You fucking told her?" Magnus shouted.

Teo wrinkled his beak in disgust. "You sold us out."

"She promised clemency," Rylan said, finally choking out the truth. "I bargained on our behalf—"

"*Our* behalf?" Teo asked.

"She agreed to limit her retribution," Rylan finished.

"Limit," Magnus said, disgusted. "Just those responsible, right? Like last time."

The Chiefslayer. She had been dispatched to Hub when Clans Ramirez and Greybull broke the tithe the last time, before Julia was born. Aubrey—Aubrey the First—was the intended target. It didn't go as planned—not then or now.

Julia felt dizzy. A cluster of black tendrils danced in her peripheral vision. She blinked hard, but they persisted.

"How dare you blame us," Morgan said, leaning toward Chief Harper, her small hands planted on the table. "Clan Greybull is a curse upon the Union. They. You"—she pointed at Julia, her voice rising to a yell—"brought on Cathedral's wrath last time, *and* the massacre that came of it. And you've done it again! Only this time you fucking killed one of her inner circle! Do you have any idea what that means?"

Everyone was silent.

"My men know what it means," Baptiste muttered.

Julia could see her own trauma reflected in the man's eyes.

Magnus was flexing his hands on the table. Any fussing over his appearance had long since been smothered by bubbling rage. "Does she know? Does the Matriarch know about the revenant mother? That we killed her."

No one said anything.

Magnus lifted slowly from his chair, the muscles of his neck bulging. "Does she know?" he whispered, his voice caustic.

Morgan swallowed loudly, her throat as parched as her pale, cracked lips. "Yes. We had to save the Union. If we didn—"

"You've *destroyed* the Union!" Magnus shouted, slamming his fists on the table.

Morgan jumped. Rylan shot upward, instinctively positioning himself in front of his mother.

"Do you think her God-engines will stop at the bunker?" Magnus asked. "They'll come for us next. For all of us—"

"Chieftains!" It was the Dakota guard. He plowed into the room, out of breath. A walkie-talkie was clutched tight in his hand. He paused as half a dozen angry faces turned his way.

"Out with it," Morgan snapped.

The tabletop began to lengthen, a featureless expanse of cold gray extending to the horizon. Julia grabbed the edge for balance. She barely heard the guard's words; he was too far away.

"We're under attack."

The meeting ended without resolution. Instead of taking the message together—whatever that message was—everyone bailed out, awkwardly avoiding one another as they rushed back to their own clanhomes. Teo Vega stormed off without a peep. Only Rylan hesitated, a pained look on his face as he tried to form last words, cut off by his chief's summons. Julia instinctively followed Magnus back to Harper territory. The Bastionites followed close behind, two borrowed Greybull fighters acting as rearguard.

The chief was seething, alternately grumbling to himself and descending into long bouts of silence. She had never seen him so tormented. Then again, she had also never spent as much time with him as now—that was her father's role.

Baptiste's people were silent, but she could feel the lieutenant's gaze burning into her back. All she had done was lie to him, or obfuscate the truth at the very best. His patience would run out eventually. The guilt of it hurt more than expected.

The way back was as quiet as the way there, ominously so. Normally, Hub's outer sprawl was abuzz with activity. There was always work to be done, trades to be made, the endless drone of manufacturing and excavation. But other than skeletal mainte-nance crews and the occasional courier, it was dead. The hand-cranked elevators that shuttled between the sprawl and clan sectors had been abandoned, leaving her party huffing up and down an endless array of narrow stairwells.

The air was getting thinner, hotter, with each delve. There were too many people in her party too close together in too crowded a space. She felt... smothered. The sensation was unfa-miliar, deeply unsettling. Though Julia had spent the last two years away from Hub, she grew up in subterranean confinement. *Closeness* was never something that she had considered until recently. But as they submerged deeper belowground, hustling single file through one dimly lit, low-ceilinged corridor after another, a familiar pressure built in her head—the same oppres-sive heaviness she had felt on the journey back through the Deadlands. She wanted to say something, if only to unload some of the weight, but was too mired in looping memories of her conversation with the Mercers.

Was this all our fault? She couldn't shake the possibility. Her grief over Kai's death was becoming tangled with resentment, leaving her as emotionally unsettled as her chief.

As they made their way to the central landing, a small gaggle of mechanists came into view, loitering around the freight elevator cranks. Julia made out a panicked curse as the neglectful crew spotted their chief marching in from the direc-tion of the stairwell.

"Why the fuck isn't anyone up top?" Magnus asked.

A grease-stained woman piped up in reply, kneading her hands anxiously, "We—we heard a rumor—"

Magnus raised both hands, shutting down her protest. He closed his eyes and breathed deeply before continuing. "Go. Now, *please.*"

Two of the four hopped forward and out the way they came.

"Ancestors, we'll kill ourselves from panic before the Matriarch has to raise a hand."

The Matriarch. It must have been. Did the surviving God-engine follow them back? More dispatched from Cathedral?

The muted bustle of her ancestral clanhome came as a relief. There were still people here, living their lives, persisting civilization in the abandoned shell of the past. Concrete tunnels and hewn passageways struck out in every direction. Short trains of bedraggled Harpers shuffled to and fro, tending to their communal chores. Somewhere downtunnel, a solitary baby was wailing.

Magnus turned to their Greybull escort. "Bring our guests back to their quarters."

"That's it?" Evelyn asked, pushing away one of her over-eager guards. Her cool was long lost. "Back to our prison?"

The chief wasn't having it. Whatever grace he bore coming into this endeavor had been whittled down to the nub. There was also the matter of an urgent, unknown attack on their territory. "Is there somewhere else you'd rather go?"

The politician pursed her lips, her dusky skin flushing pink.

Baptiste gently grasped her arm, stepping past her into Magnus's face. "Whatever happens next, don't forget our people died to save yours." He glanced at Julia, then led the way toward their quarters, dragging Evelyn alongside him. The priest followed without protest. One of the guards gave Magnus a look, which he returned with a raised eyebrow before dismissing them.

"Well then," he said, "let's find out what's going on."

———

"Attention all command personnel, this is an emergency alert. Please report to your tactical operation rooms for debriefing."

The message was coming from the overhead speakers, repeated every thirty seconds.

They were crowded into a radio room: Magnus, Julia, Aron and Gwen—two senior mechanists about her father's age—and Bertram, working the console. She had beamed when she first saw her crewmate, but that joy promptly fizzled as she got closer. The man's quirky demeanor was gone. His eyes were dead—*had they always been gray?* The space around him felt *wrong*—too quiet, somehow insulated from the rest of the room. He moved robotically over his controls, showing no sign of recognition as she hovered over him. Guilt piled upon guilt. Julia had failed to check in on her former crew when she got back. She didn't even know if Char was alive. And Jax...

"What is that?" Magnus asked.

Julia dragged herself away from the console, once again shoving the pain down so she could focus. "Maybe a prerecorded alert, triggered from one of the FOBs."

Magnus frowned. "I don't know. I've never heard it before."

Aron and Gwen were shaking their heads. They both stood well away from Bertram, as though afraid to get too close.

"Play the other transmission," Aron said.

Bertram typed something into his keyboard, summoning a squat waveform onto a small monochromatic display. He pressed another key, and a burst of distortion cascaded through the room. Julia grimaced, reaching for a grab bar—

Not a grab bar.

She shook her head, trying to regain her bearings. She wasn't in the Ironclad anymore.

Reaching for the wall—for support.

The noise became grainy, chunked into discordant syllables before eventually smoothing into legible words.

"This...Eastport...und...attack—"

The transmission collapsed into a hiss.

"Eastport," Julia repeated. It was one of their most distant forward operating bases, used for refueling and layovers on exploratories.

"That's it?" Magnus asked.

Gwen was nervously pulling at her lip. "That's it."

"Have you tried contacting them?"

"Yes. No reply."

Magnus scratched at his neck, irritably unzipping the top of his jumpsuit. "What about Ridgeline?"

Another forward operating base, equidistant to Hub and Eastport.

The mechanists shuffled uncomfortably. Aron eyed his counterpart. "No reply..."

Magnus tented his hands over his temples and shut his eyes. "Shit. The others?"

"Everyone else within range has reported back," Gwen said.

"Well, that's something at least."

Julia watched the screen. Another waveform, mostly flat, was being transcribed live from the radio. They were there, just silent. Every so often it blipped upward, sending an electric shock through her nerves. The gray concrete wall felt damp under her hand, as though back at Bunker 23. Nothingness pressed down on her from above.

"You should get some rest." Magnus was standing in front of her.

Julia squinted. "How did you get out here?"

"What?"

She blinked, as confused as he was by her question. She was in Hub, not the bunker.

Magnus gently grasped her arms. "Should I call an alchemist?"

Julia pushed herself upright. "No. No..."

"There's nothing more you can do here, and you look like shit. Go. Get some rest."

"What about the other bases? Should we evacuate our people?"

"Not yet. Go. I'll call you if anything changes."

Julia's gaze fell once more upon Bertram's back. He was staring straight forward, motionless. "Okay."

The journey back to her temporary quarters—her father's dorm—was a blur. A sea of bodies, pressing too close to her as she churned past. Gray coveralls pressing against her skin. Cold gray eyes staring at her from the froth. She was out of breath by the time she got there. The loud *clang* of the door came as a relief.

She looked idly around. Her exhaustion the prior night spared little time for examination. In any case, staying here made her deeply uncomfortable. She had no idea if her father was alive or dead. In some ways he had already died long ago, the same day as Roen. Whatever bond they had built up to that point—fragmented from the outset by the fact of her mother's death at the cost of her birth—had been completely broken. His request for her accompaniment to Bunker 23 had come as a surprise. At the time, she'd assumed it was a pragmatic choice—selfish, even—based solely on the experience she could offer as crew leader. But maybe there was something more to it, an attempt at reconciliation.

The concrete room was small, sparsely decorated for a senior mechanist. Only a handful of Old World trophies were scattered about, and those were mostly mundane: a toaster, two shelves' worth of bird statuettes, and what appeared to be a solid-gold-handled toilet plunger beaming from the water closet.

Her father's ancestral altar caught her eye from atop an

ancient wooden dresser. She stepped cautiously toward it. On one side was a plastic camera in perfect condition, on the other a metal box—photos she didn't dare look at. Centered between them, within a circle of paraffin candles, was an intricately wound copper wire sculpture of a tree bearing family heirlooms on its branches. Some she recognized: her mother's wedding band, a pair of impossibly small knitted socks she must have worn as a child. Others she didn't. Her father had never spoken of his own parents, and she had no memory of them.

Atop the tree, perched like a once-living crown, was a small bundle of dried-out herbs and flower petals, impossibly colorful even in death. He had presented it to her as a wedding gift after returning from an exploratory. Where he had found living flowers was anyone's guess.

"It's an Old World wedding tradition. Button it to Roen's chest."

Julia had refused, mostly out of youthful obstinance. She would make her own traditions. It had broken her father's heart, and now it broke hers.

The pain was too much. Sobs racked Julia's chest, shaking her until she fell back onto the bunk. She clawed at the quilt, pressing her face into its coarse patchwork so no one would hear. Tears flowed freely, washing away the cracks that persisted at the edges of her vision. The mattress squeaked in protest as she punched it repeatedly, cursing the world for its unfairness. Her husband, her crew, her father, and now maybe everyone else—taken from her. Grief poured out, and as it did, the room fell away with it. Endless gray darkened into a black, dreamless sleep.

———

"Come back, Julia."

Her eyes popped open, then immediately shut halfway

against the glare of the still-lit room. She was lying in the same position she had fallen asleep in. A red glow crept into her peripheral vision, flashing at her for attention—her walkie-talkie. She shot upright and pulled it from her waistband, depressing the talk button.

"I'm here."

"We lost another one." It was Magnus.

"Fuck. How long was I out?"

"Two hours. Are you feeling better?"

"Was it Ridgeline?" she asked, ignoring his question.

"We still haven't heard from Ridgeline. This came from Mercer. They haven't told us which base yet."

Mercer?

"Hardly the time for secrets," she muttered.

"I know. They've called a council meeting. Everyone's invited, including our new allies."

"Invited? I thought we were sanctioned."

Dead air. Julia stared impatiently at the walkie-talkie.

"Chief?"

"The sanctions have been lifted. On one condition."

———

The Greybull clanhome was very different from the Harpers'. Where her birth clan had left their ancient accommodations largely unchanged, compressing themselves to fit within its boundaries, Greybull had cored out almost every corner of their abode. Tunnelways were wider and ceilings taller. Mechanical conveyances had been installed wherever possible to shuttle their population between floors and across wide-open, seemingly bottomless excavations. Its people, too, were generally rowdier. But today, its people were grieving.

A mournful harmony echoed down the corridor from

Aubrey's chambers, carried on the breath of a drone flute. The hewn walls hummed, transmitting their leader's grief for all to hear. Her passage slowed as each pained note crested above the underlying drone, threatening more tears, but she mashed down her feelings—this was Aubrey's time. Each person she passed bore a small cut under their right eye, signifying the clan's shared loss. Some still had a scar from the last son lost. She shuffled more quickly past those.

The double doors to the chief's chambers—more cave than room—were wide open. It was dark, lit only by the flickering of a large gas fireplace at the back. Julia hesitated. The last time she had been here was the day of her wedding. Two short pews occupied the front. Beyond them, elevated upon a podium, Aubrey II sat in his grand throne of carved bone and steel. He looked smaller than usual, huddled in a white-and-gray fur housecoat. A large wooden instrument was cradled in his thin-skinned hands.

He paused without looking up. "Come."

Julia took a seat at the front pew, pressing her hands hard into her thighs as he resumed his dirge. Occupying most of the wall behind the throne was a faded flag of old America. This room—the crown of Clan Greybull going back generations—was where the Movement began, to restore the past in order to save the future. It was also where that grandiose plan might end. Arrayed around the flag were oil portraits of past Greybull chiefs, each of them captured in their youth by the prior chief, in anticipation of their transition of power. Transient flares from the fireplace imbued life onto their pale faces, drawing out the generational anger present in every single set of eyes.

Kai's face stared back at her.

He would have been next in succession. Julia dug her fingers harder into her legs, holding on for control as Aubrey finished his tribute, sinking back into his throne.

"Once more, I have no body to bury, to give back to our people," he said.

Julia remained silent.

"Do you believe in curses, Julia?"

"Chief?"

"Curses. Darkest, blackest magic. I survived the massacre, mostly"—he gestured at his face, disfigured in the attack—"but the witch's touch penetrated deeper than my skin. The Eternal One is a demon, possessing her sisters at will. Through her minion, she planted her corrupt seed in my line, to ensure its end."

He relocated the flute to an adjacent table, setting it down with care.

"I'm sorry." Useless, but the only thing she could think to say. Her gaze drifted back to the portrait of Kai.

Aubrey followed, the right side of his mouth curling up in a sad smile.

"He loved you. Maybe more than he loved his own brother. When he asked to join the rescue mission, I felt it, I knew he wouldn't come back. He was so happy for his victory. So proud." The smile disappeared. "But the witch's blood was poison on his hands. The demon's curse was complete."

Aubrey slouched in his chair, staring down at his own hands. The fire blazed silently behind him, painting a gaunt silhouette upon the floor.

Julia squirmed in her seat, struggling to balance the urgency of her visit with her father-in-law's grief. There was no room in her head for revenant mothers, Chiefslayer or otherwise.

"Father," she stuttered. The word had never felt right for Aubrey, not even when she was still married to his son. Her actual father occupied too much of that space already. "I don't have much time—"

"I know. The Mercer bitch called me herself. Can you believe that?" he said with a snort. "Such an honor."

"It's impossible, of course."

Julia hadn't believed her ears when Magnus told her the council's conditions for reentrance: Aubrey II deposed, Julia to take his place as chief of Clan Greybull.

"It's the only thing that *is* possible. My bloodline is ended—the curse made sure of that. But as you reminded me, I still have a child. A daughter, not of my blood. Safe from the demon's grasp."

Julia shook her head. All she had wanted was answers, to restore reason, so her people wouldn't slaughter each other. Everything was moving so fast, and she was still so tired. The nap had blunted her exhaustion, but she could feel darkness creeping back into her peripheral vision.

Aubrey glanced at the other paintings. "I'll need to get started on a new portrait."

"How can I possibly be a chief?" she asked. "I couldn't even take care of my crew."

Aubrey hoisted himself from his throne and lumbered down the steps to the pew, taking a seat beside her. "Wisdom comes from failure. You just have to recognize it and do better next time."

They stared at the fireplace together.

"So, I'm the perfect candidate because I'm a failure?"

He smiled, and for a moment it seemed to cross his whole face. "How do you think I got the job?"

Aubrey's closeness only made her miss her real father more. The realization hit like a mudslide, drowning her in even more feelings she had no time for.

Into the bottle they went.

"I'll send word," he continued. "We'll delay the ceremony for now."

"What will you do?" Julia asked.

"That depends on what you do." He stood, sighing, eyes fixed on the ancient flag. Its threadbare stars glowed in the void. "All I ask is that you don't forget our dream. It's all we have now. Don't let it die."

BAPTISTE

SOMETHING ANCIENT

"That went well," Baptiste muttered, slouching on the lower berth of his bunk bed.

Evelyn was pacing back and forth in their shared quarters, twitching like a cornered rat. Once her voice came back, she hadn't stopped complaining, not even after they were interred. Every word out of her mouth was accompanied by exaggerated gestures, as though she could mesmerize her audience in the absence of having anything worthwhile to say.

"What did you expect?" she said, waving her hands at the door.

Baptiste cared for politicians about as much as he cared for priests. There were exceptions—Andrite, mostly—but not her. His men had done well to save them; they followed their orders and were heroes for it. But if it were his choice, any of them would be sitting here with him now instead of these two. Any of them would be alive.

"I've never done this before," she continued, gesticulating. "I'm used to settling trade disputes between districts, not negotiating alliances with other nations. I didn't even know there *were* other nations until this mission."

Ollet surveyed the room from the second bed—Baptiste had refused to bunk with him. He had procured a journal from somewhere deep in his robes and was taking notes. Somehow the priest was constantly enraptured by his surroundings, even a featureless cell such as this. Their accommodations were hardly that: two bunk beds crammed into opposite sides of a closet-sized concrete room, a narrow metal table and chair along the wall, and two lockers at the foot of each bed. No toilet. It resembled a barracks pod in the Metro, only smaller.

"What is that smell, anyway?" Evelyn asked, sniffing loudly. "And why is it so damned hot in this place?"

The vice chancellor was sweating profusely, dark circles staining the armpits of her rigid gray uniform.

"You've never been in a Metro barracks, have you?" he asked.

Evelyn paused her circuit, just long enough to look down her nose at him. "My understanding is you haven't been in them recently, either."

Baptiste grimaced, cries of agony echoing in his mind. His own within the sanatorium; his men's after the attack on the drilling station and again as they were cut down outside the bunker; Andrite's—or his doppelganger—forever burning in the Deadlands. His life had become a succession of catastrophes. He had already been growing numb to them when the *nothing* took him; it just finished the job. Anguish fled from his enervated soul, sinking instead into his constantly aching bones.

"I didn't want to be here," Evelyn continued. "It was your lord commander that asked for me, like always when the Church isn't playing nice."

"Mind your disrespect," Baptiste said.

Evelyn's sneer faded as she reconsidered her irreverence, given present company. She moved to sit in the chair, arms crossed.

"You know I'm right. The Ascendancy has lit a fire and your old man is playing with it."

"Something ancient." The lord commander's obtuse confession after half of Baptiste's platoon was killed. That was the extent of it, and in all their time together at the bunker, it was apparent that Evelyn knew little more. He was glad for that, but just as frustrated.

The battle walkers—God-engines, the Scavrats called them—rose like obsidian monoliths in his memory. He had never seen anything like them before, beautiful and terrible. There was something about the way they moved... like a hybrid of machine and demon. The Scavrats had proved Bastion was not alone, but the God-engines were the first real evidence of Cathedral's existence. When the lord commander first briefed him on an enemy in the west, he secretly thought it a lie—bluster to cover up some other inconvenient truth. Now he wished that had been the case.

Something ancient.

Was it possible? His mission under Captain Ballard. The flatbeds—

"What about the photos?" she asked. It was the first time any of them had broached the subject since their awkward meeting with the Scavrat chiefs. Ollet's pen stilled.

The photos. Endless lies, spilling like acid from the lips of Bastion's leadership, burning everything back to chaos. Even when his great-uncle had finally apologized for a guardianship rife with cruelty, he hadn't divulged anything new. And now, this: the Order Sacramental, or Rayos at the very least, sent on a follow-up mission. For what. To undo the work of the Legion? To bring down the enemy's wrath? It made no sense. Baptiste had tried to warn his great-uncle of the risk, of starting a war. And now war was exactly what they had.

"The Church can't be trusted," he mumbled, his thoughts given license.

"You know I can hear you," Ollet said, scrutiny alternating between his counterparts.

"He speaks!" Evelyn declared.

The priest stared right through her. "Those who speak the most often have the least to say."

"Suitably cryptic," she muttered, shifting uncomfortably in her chair.

Evelyn retreated to her thoughts, mercifully quiet. Ollet resumed his scribbling. Baptiste simmered, replaying the moment the Crusader exploded; his men dying around him; Lafayette shoving him into the Scavrat vehicle. Their relationship started poorly thanks to his great-uncle's imposition, but he had grown to respect and depend on the sergeant. Baptiste pressed a hand against his cuirass, compressing his brother's talisman against his skin, and prayed. He prayed for Ferris Lafayette, for any of his men to have somehow survived. He prayed for a way out of this place to find them. And he even prayed for Bastion, as Gabriel would have had him do.

He needed to get back.

Baptiste heaved himself up from the bed, adjusted his armor, and banged on the steel door.

"What are you doing?" Evelyn asked.

A viewport slid open, sunken eyes staring back at him.

"Any word from Julia?" Baptiste asked.

"No."

"How long are we to wait in this cell?"

"Do you need something?"

"We *need* to leave."

The viewport slammed shut.

"Dammit," Baptiste cursed, clenching hands grown stiff from disuse. The urge to pace trembled in his legs, but he held fast, leaning back against the door. Pushing hard to restrain himself. The last walk he took hadn't served him well...

"We can't leave, anyway," Evelyn said. "Even if they offered to shuttle us home now, the alliance is more important."

"Don't tell me what's important," Baptiste snapped.

"They're your own orders."

"They *were* our orders."

"I understand you're—"

"Don't," Baptiste cut in. "Just don't."

She was right, of course. Everything was playing out as the lord commander had feared, meaning they needed these allies more than ever. Still, it chafed. His whole body itched, anxious to bolt home and warn the Legion that traitors were afoot. His platoon had already run out their expected mission time prior to the attack, so hopefully a rescue party had been dispatched to the bunker by now. Hopefully they would find more than ash.

All he could do was wait. Baptiste shut his eyes and counted, seeking solace in imagined footsteps through the distant Metro.

———

The shuffling of a bolt roused him from his meditation.

"Praise God," Evelyn muttered from one of the top bunks.

He moved away from the door as it swung open, revealing Julia.

"I'm sorry," she said, eyes on him. "You weren't supposed to be waiting that long."

Relief washed over Baptiste, as well as a reflexive twinge of joy at seeing the Scavrat woman again. She wore the slightness of her people well. Her alien features had unsettled him at first —her skin, eyes, hair were all too pale—but a great deal of time had passed since then. Also, their moment of panicked closeness when the shockwave hit. A second wave of heat coursed through his body.

"Indeed," Evelyn said. She was also staring at him.

Baptiste blushed and cleared his throat. The right words escaped him in the moment, just as they had at the bunker. "What's going on?" he asked.

"We're under attack—our forward operating bases. A council has been convened and I've been asked to bring your delegation."

Evelyn hopped down from the bed. "About time."

Ollet joined her.

"Wait," Baptiste said, raising a fist as though still commanding a section. "Why?"

Julia looked confused, maybe even wounded. "You started this relationship."

"Yes, we did," Evelyn said, "and we intend to see it through. Lead the way."

Julia spared one more glance for Baptiste, then spun on her heel. "Follow me."

Baptiste, Evelyn, and Ollet followed her as they navigated their way through the labyrinthine complex, Julia and a guard in the lead, another guard trailing.

Evelyn crept up beside Baptiste. "I see how you look at her," she hissed.

Baptiste felt his cheeks warm but continued to stare straight forward.

"The Church would not approve."

His nose wrinkled in disgust. "Damn the Church," he said, quickening his pace to put distance between himself and the vice chancellor.

Julia noticed his approach and waved for the front guard to swap places with him. They walked alongside each other in silence for several minutes. For his part, Baptiste was just happy to be moving. In a relatively normal place that at least vaguely resembled the Metro. There wasn't much foot traffic at this hour —whatever hour it was. Those they passed kept their gazes averted, pinning themselves to the walls.

"Look," she said, finally. "You were right before. We started that fight, very stupidly. Your people could have run, but they didn't. And my people are alive because of it—some of them. I owe you. *We* owe you." She glanced at him from the corner of her eye.

Baptiste mulled the words—maybe the most she had ever said to him. "You're welcome."

She snorted, a fleeting smile touching her lips before becoming serious again. "Be warned: the rest of the council won't trust you. Your politician might be disappointed."

"There's not a lot of trust going around these days."

"No," she agreed. "And I don't imagine that's going to change any time soon."

Julia led their party from the concrete passageway into a much narrower tunnel, Evelyn's curses echoing around them as she tripped on the transition. The space between them shrank. Julia grew silent again, until they emerged into another concourse, but she made no move to distance herself from him. There was a scent about her, past the sweat and grime that afflicted them all—earthy, arid, like a flowering plant that didn't exist anymore. His olfactory palette was too basic, limited to oil and gunpowder, but it reminded him of home. Something stirred in the cold of his heart.

"It's confusing," he said, stuck for a second as his words caught up with his emotions. "You call yourselves a union. But from the moment we got here, you've been at each other's throats."

Julia glanced at him, then back to the rest of his delegation. "It seems like we have that in common."

She wasn't wrong. Maybe Bastion and the Union weren't that different. Maybe they were too similar for their own good.

The freight elevator appeared as they rounded a corner, its operators hurrying to their stations.

"Ready?" she asked.

Cold settled back into his chest as its iron doors creaked open to let them in. It reminded him of the elevator down to Central Command, and the broken men that guarded it. Banished to their box after being traumatized by the outside. Except this time, he was the broken man.

Julia stared in awe. She had never seen the council chambers, had only ever heard it described before today. It looked nothing like the rest of Hub, or any standing Old World facility she had encountered. The cylindrical man-made cavern resembled a giant turbine engine, completely framed in metal and bracketed on all sides by the twenty-two flags of the Union. An intricate latticework of steel girders and crossbeams fanned out across the lofty ceiling, extending like blades from a protruding central hub. Looming below it was an amphitheater consisting of three concentric circles, segmented into four quadrants that housed the various chiefs and their seconds. Myriad disembodied faces shimmered in the scattered glow of overhead spotlights, watching her. Waiting.

Julia faltered by the entrance, gripping the massive doorframe for support. She hurriedly scanned the unfamiliar faces, looking for Magnus. He would be seated with the rest of the American clans in the first quadrant to her left, across the speaker circle from Clan Mercer. An ethereal hand waved at her from much too far away, beckoning her into the darkness. Baptiste's breath was hot on the back of her neck, insistent. Julia wiped her sweating hands on her legs and stepped out onto the terraced catwalk, directing the Bastionite delegation to the dimly lit gallery behind the uppermost row.

Deathly silence gave way to a background hum of concerned muttering at the foreigners' presence. She was grateful for the diversion as her tromping footfalls echoed around the chamber. Majestic cloaks, jeweled crowns, and power armor glimmered at her from each level. Every chief, even those of the smaller clans, was dressed in their best finery. She suddenly felt naked in her tan fatigues.

"Julia, over here," a voice whispered.

Magnus and Teo stood over their seats at the front row of their quadrant, each with a seated second acting as advisor and secretary. Gwen nodded at her from Magnus's far side, while a severe man that could have been Teo's twin sat at his. Julia crowded in, taking the empty spot to their right.

Each of their coats of arms was stamped into removable panels upon the concave desktop. All the American clans sported animal totems: a windswept crow for Harper, a vulture-shaped constellation for Vega, and of course a bull for Greybull. The bovine skull stared back at her from the table, ominously haloed with crossed battle-axes. Bulls no longer existed in nature, as it was, but she had read about them. When Julia was a child, she would inundate her father with questions about animals from the Old World, begging him to sneak out zoological encyclopediae from the Archive. They were stubborn beasts: aggressive, territorial, prone to destroying China shops, whatever those were—all appropriate.

The murmuring quieted. A man was methodically making his way from the quadrant at their left to the brightly illuminated speaker circle. He was modestly dressed in a dark tunic and leatherette breeches, all his splendor reserved for the meticulously sculpted metal of his powered prosthetic legs. They glimmered as he walked, twinkling copper and silver. As Julia followed him down, she saw Morgan and Rylan Mercer, staring at her from across the way. Both were dressed in red leather greatcoats, Morgan imperious and Rylan looking as troubled as when she left him.

"This council commences." The man's voice reverberated along the chamber's metal skin. "Clan Helthorn assumes the role of speaker, as eleventh clan for the eleventh session of the cycle. All in favor?"

Julia jumped as the chamber erupted into chaos, each clan chief thumping their desk in consensus.

"All against?"

Silence, other than a residual ringing in her ears.

"Very well. We meet under dire circumstances. Again."

The chief walked a small, loping circle as he addressed the chamber, slowing past her quadrant. The servo whine of his legs grated at her. The room's attention on her was crushing.

"Due to the urgency of these circumstances, I relinquish the circle to Clan Mercer."

A series of mutterings bubbled up around the chamber, mostly constrained to those nearby. As Morgan moved from her seat to the speaker circle, the susurrations coalesced into curses: "loyalist," "charlatan," "traitor." Across the circle, an opposing sea of illuminated faces was also churning: "idiots," "savages."

Julia ground her teeth together. The Union had come into existence out of necessity, not without bloodshed. For generations they had survived, together. All she saw here was disunion, independent of Cathedral's meddling influence. How long would it be before the promise of joint security was no longer enough to keep the clans from each other's throats?

Chief Helthorn weaved his way back to his seat.

Morgan clasped her hands behind her back, straightening to the limits of her diminutive stature. "Welcome back, distinguished chiefs. And a special welcome to our new Chief Greybull."

More murmuring. Julia shrank into her seat.

"As Chief Helthorn said, extraordinary circumstances are upon us again. Circumstances that require unity."

Magnus growled under his breath.

"As you all know by now, our forward operating bases have come under attack. We lost contact with Eastport and Ridgeline earlier today, and I can now confirm we have lost contact with Blacklake."

The assembled chiefs gasped almost as one. Blacklake was their main refinery—defended almost as well as Hub because of its criticality to operations. Every mechanist did a tour there at some point in their career. It was one of Julia's first stops after Roen died. She knew people there.

Harried voices called out from every quadrant, shouting questions over each other.

"Attacked by who?"

"A swarm?"

"The remnant?"

"Cathedral?"

The last question silenced the chamber.

Morgan turned to her second. "Play the recording."

A nondescript black playback unit sat in front of Rylan—Julia hadn't noticed it before. He depressed a button, eliciting a loud pop and hiss from its speaker. Everyone hunched over their desks, rapt. It was a radio transmission, barely legible. A low, continuous rumble permeated the background, interwoven with garbled voices. Julia cocked her head, trying to make out what they were saying. The signal gradually cleared as the original operator filtered it, revealing voices—shouting voices, begging for help, ordering others to their stations. It sounded like chaos. Gunfire, a blast of static, then a long, painful period of emptiness before a familiar-sounding synthetic voice tore into Julia's soul: "in... name of... Matriarch—"

The recording ended with a snap.

The ceiling was too close. Julia's hands clung to the desk, numb all the way to her forearms, but if she let go, she would float upward. Past the ceiling, past the ancient crust of the earth, into the void. The chamber was too big—infinite—and yet there wasn't enough air. There was only pressure, packed against her eardrums.

The God-engine's words rang in her ears, stolen from the guarded recesses of her memory: *"In the name of the Eternal One, Great Mother of the Revenant Sisterhood, Matriarch of Cathedral, we order you to surrender!"*

No one spoke. To do so would be to admit a horrible, impossible reality: the Union was under attack by its own benefactors.

Morgan continued. "The last time we convened—in smaller numbers—was to discuss the murder of the revenant mother within our territory." *Murder.* Is that what it was? Caleb had told her the priestess struck first. "As agreed, we relayed the news back to Cathedral, in hopes of averting total disaster."

"What..." Magnus whispered.

Teo was mumbling in a language she didn't recognize.

Julia fast-forwarded to the present, struggling to digest the words. It wasn't just Mercer that had capitulated. It was the whole council—minus the Americans.

"Our messengers have not returned."

Morgan walked the speaker circle as the prior chief had, indecision twisting at her lips. When she stopped, she stood directly in front of Magnus.

"Earlier today, my clan met with the instigators of this incident. Our American friends, recently returned from their illicit mission to the Deadlands. Returned after coming under attack by God-engines, which now attack our homeland."

The chamber remained silent, but all eyes were on their quadrant—on this faction that once more had brought woe to the rest of their people.

This was starting to feel more like a trial than an assembly of equals. When the ultimatum came for her to take Aubrey's throne, she assumed it was because Clan Mercer sought a less hot-headed partner. But maybe the whole thing was a ruse, designed to weaken their movement. Dwindling numbers already put Greybull under threat of assimilation into a larger clan.

"Now we must decide what to do," Morgan said. "Together."

A quiver ran down the woman's clenched jaw. She was scared. Aubrey might have relished the moment, but it terrified Julia. Whatever Clan Mercer or the other loyalists were, they represented the status quo. That was gone now.

Magnus cleared his throat. "Eastport and Ridgeline are our farthest bases from Cathedral. Blacklake is our fuel. The Matriarch is cutting us off at the knees."

"Nothing new there," someone called out from behind them.

"What about Aubrey's son?" Julia looked for the speaker, but he had shrunk back into the quadrant to her right. Anger prickled up her spine. They were all so eager to sell each other out, for what—scraps of mercy?

"Lost in transit," Morgan returned.

"How about Aubrey himself?" The same voice.

Julia spotted him this time: a weasel of a man arrayed in high-collared leathers like some Messianic sycophant. Hatred passed between them, unsettling those chiefs in its path.

Teo unfurled from his seat like a gargoyle come to life. "Scum."

Panic crashed through the assembly as terrified indecision turned to desperation.

"We have to give her something!" came another voice from their left.

"Maybe she'll stop at Blacklake."

"We can wait it out."

"What about our people?"

"We can't risk going out there."

"Coward!"

"Greybull has to go."

"Traitor!"

"She'll kill us all!"

Julia floated to her feet, hands outstretched for balance. She sought Kai's face in her memory and found it painted in oil—proud, uncompromising. He had sacrificed himself for them, given up his soul to oblivion. For them. Aubrey's final words surged through her blood, anchoring her body to the floor: *"Don't forget our dream. Don't let it die."*

"We fight," she said.

Half the room quieted, while the others continued their ranting.

"We fight!"

Her shout boomed from the ceiling, walls, and floor, silencing the rest. She could feel Magnus watching her. Her old chief stood, followed by every other chief and second in her quadrant. They were all watching her. Somehow, they were all waiting for her—for this moment.

Julia stepped out of her row, forcing her feet to carry her to the speaker circle. She should have asked permission, but that time was over. The dim glow of her clan seat receded, replaced by the glaring brightness of the circle.

Morgan's fear had fully enveloped her, collapsing the woman back into her smaller self. Her eyes were bulging, lips pursed. She stepped back at Julia's approach, half in and half out of the light.

Julia's heart was pounding. The vastness of the chamber was so much worse at its center. With great effort, she pulled her gaze away from the American quadrant, turning as the other speakers had, to present herself to the entire council. Ethereal faces bore down on her, riven with fear. Words smashed around in her skull, looking for purchase. She had one chance.

"God-engines can be killed. My brother, Kai Greybull, did not die in transit. He died in battle."

Fearful murmurs sprang up from every seat, threatening to devolve into chaos again.

"They are just machines!" she shouted, exerting herself against the rising tide.

She was lying.

The God-engine's voice called to her again. The air had rippled black in its wake as it turned about, lining up its cannons to murder her fleeing people. Julia had never seen a revenant sister in real life, but most clanfolk, and certainly every Greybull, knew the tales of the Chiefslayer. The world had torn open around her as she murdered their people, tracers as black as the void following wherever she went. God-engines may be machines, but only in part.

Was this the job of every chief? To lie for the greater good?

"We are people of science, yet we allow ourselves to be cowed into superstition."

She was good at it after all.

An elderly man cloaked in black stood from the front row of the loyalist side, next to Rylan. "Was it *superstition* that killed a dozen of your own clanfolk in the hangar?"

Teo grimaced. His people had fared poorly when the revenant mother attacked. They bailed on the rescue mission and almost on the whole movement.

"You're right, the Revenant Sisterhood is powerful. But they are not immortal. Kai killed their emissary as well. One man did all that."

"And he died for it," the man retorted.

The Deadlands turned white, brighter than the sun.

Julia swallowed back her anger. "Yes, he died. For us. For you."

The man scowled but resumed his seat.

Julia continued her slow circle, pulling at her wrinkled jumpsuit. The ceiling girders seemed to be rotating in the opposite direction of the chamber floor, skewing her stomach sideways. She focused on the flags lining its walls, on the people they represented, inside and outside of Hub. It could have been her dying at Blacklake or any of the other distant bases she hid away in.

"This is our home, our civilization. When the world died, our ancestors came together in this place. They set aside their differences, not just to survive but with the hope of a better future. The Union was never meant to be constrained to Hub."

"We survive because of Cathedral!" someone shouted.

She kept moving. "We survive in *spite* of Cathedral. Before the Matriarch, before the tithe, we had already expanded beyond Hub. Civilization was in sight."

The cloaked man was on his feet again. "Empty words. What civilization can there be where demons roam free?"

Julia stopped her circuit, turning to look up at the gallery row where Baptiste's delegation was lurking. "Ask them."

Everyone turned to face the Bastionites. Word had spread since her meeting with Clan Mercer. All of Hub was abuzz over the news of another nation in the east. For many, that news brought fear, especially now—what made these new foreigners any different from Cathedral?

"I'd like to call Evelyn Stern to the speaker cir—"

"We can hear you just fine from up there," Morgan cut in.

Evelyn paused one step out from the gallery, looking for confirmation. Julia eyed Morgan, still hovering at the circle's edge. The chief glared back at her, uncompromising. Perhaps she had broken enough traditions—for now. She turned back to Evelyn and shook her head with a sigh.

Evelyn stood tall, rolling her shoulders back.

"Thank you, Chief Greybull. Thank you, distinguished chiefs of the Union."

A handful of chuckles echoed from below.

"My name is Evelyn Stern, Vice Chancellor of Bastion. Together with my colleagues from the Legion and Church, we represent the government of our people. I understand time is short, so let me be brief. I have been authorized to negotiate an alliance with your Union, based on simple terms: freedom of movement and salvage in our territory in exchange for technological assistance."

"Another tithe!" someone shouted.

"No," Evelyn said. Her calm despite the combined distrust of the room was impressive. Even her hands were still. "Not a tithe. Cooperation. A partnership of equals."

"Sounds like a business deal, not a mutual defense pact."

Baptiste stepped forward, displacing Evelyn from the top step. His scarred armor beamed from the shadow of the gallery. "When these so-called God-engines attacked, they did so on our land. They killed both our peoples, my men and yours. I assure you that makes it our fight as well."

Another round of muttering ensued from the assembly, but it felt different this time, marginally shifting from fear to consideration.

"And how far is your Bastion from here?" Morgan asked.

Baptiste shook his head, too far removed to know.

"Three days," Julia said with an involuntary wince.

"Three days," Morgan repeated, "through the Deadlands. May as well be in the Hellmouth."

"Maybe two—"

"And maybe their whole army gets lost en route, assuming they even have one!"

"Larger than yours, I would guess," Baptiste returned. Evelyn shuffled uncomfortably beside him.

A loud slam turned Julia around.

The black-cloaked man had both hands pressed to his desktop. His pale, wrinkled face was flushed pink with rage. "All this talk of armies is pointless," he said. "The Matriarch has no army to invade Hub, and we certainly don't need *theirs* either."

"You stupid old fuck!" Magnus shouted back. "The Matriarch doesn't need soldiers if she has God-engines. Once they're done wiping out our FOBs, they'll siege the canyon, collapse Hub from the outside."

"We can lock down. Withstand it!" the man countered.

"They'll just keep coming!" Magnus shouted.

"Unless they run out of ammunition."

Both men turned. It took a second for Julia to realize it was Rylan who spoke, concealed behind his angry neighbor.

"What?" she asked.

Rylan darted his eyes around the room before landing on his chief. Morgan recoiled into the darkness beyond the circle. His left hand rubbed at his lips, as though to keep them shut.

"As you said," he began, "God-engines are machines—war machines. They need ammunition like any other war machine. It wouldn't be practical to return to Cathedral each time they ran out." Rylan shifted in his seat. "They rely on a handful of automated hangars hidden in the wastes, used for rearming and repair."

"How do you know this?" Julia asked.

The cloaked man sat, leaving Rylan fully exposed within his cone of light.

"They're Old World tech. We helped rebuild them."

The chamber was silent. Magnus's lips were moving, readying an onslaught, but Teo silenced him with a hand on his shoulder. "What are you suggesting?"

Rylan's fingers twitched, moving to his neck, where they pulled nervously at his throat. "We destroy the hangars. Or sabotage them at least."

"*Destroy* them," Teo repeated.

Rylan nodded slowly.

"She won't see it coming," Magnus said, with equal parts hatred and glee.

Julia glanced at Morgan, but the woman's expression was unreadable in the dark. "You would actually help us with this?" she asked.

"It's always 'you' and 'us' with *you* Americans," Rylan retorted, speaking for his chief. "None among us is blind to the truth. Some of *us* just choose to think about it for a minute before we start a fight we can't win!"

Was he just saving face? Or was he right?

The other chiefs in her bloc were stirring, calling out questions.

"What if we run into them on the way?"

"We don't know how many are out there."

A young chief from the adjacent quadrant stood. "With Blacklake gone, our fuel supply is finite. We can't just run around out there forever."

The black-cloaked man looked dumbstruck. "You all can't be considering this."

"It's suicide!" The leather-bound weasel.

"Chief Harper!" Julia shouted, not quite sure how to proceed but knowing well enough that meekness now would scuttle any possibility of action. That this was Rylan's plan still amazed her.

Magnus stood tall at her summons.

Her summons.

Julia was suddenly struck dumb by the reality of her situation. She was a mechanist, not a tactician. Her father was supposed to become chief, not her. She hadn't earned it. She hadn't *learned* it. The old man was right—how could any of them be considering anything she was saying?

"Yes, Chief Greybull," Magnus said, prompting her out of her anxiety loop with a meaningful look.

Julia pressed her sweating hands against her thighs, trying to anchor herself. She nodded acknowledgment at Magnus and cleared the nervous gravel from her throat. "Assuming a delayed response from Bastion," she continued, "do we have enough fighting vehicles to attack directly?"

Magnus squinted, pinpointing Morgan in the dark. "Does her grace, Chief Mercer, know how many God-engines are out there?"

A shriveled silhouette stirred just out of sight. "Eight," came the reluctant answer.

Eight. The number echoed through the chamber, carried on the tremulous whispers of all present. Now seven, thanks to Kai —of the Old World's most powerful war machines. Even Julia knew they didn't stand a chance against those odds.

Teo shook his head.

"No," Magnus said. "But I know who might."

"And which new mystery ally would that be?" asked the old man.

"Clan Ramirez."

"What? Are you insane?"

"You know full well they're the strongest of us."

"Except no one's seen them in a generation!" the man yelled.

Julia was surprised by his ignorance. Morgan Mercer had declared at their last meeting that she knew about *all* of Clan Harper's indiscretions, including their associations with Clan Ramirez. Apparently, they kept their secrets as close to their chests as the Americans.

"We have," Magnus said. "We've been trading with them ever since they left. They're the ones that told us about the stasis bunker."

"Ancestors!" the old man cursed. "Do any of our laws matter to you?"

"The security of the Union matters to me," Magnus said. "Without those trades, we wouldn't have been able to hold half the FOBs we have now. Those bases serve all of us, fuel and feed all of us."

"Again," Rylan cut in, "that sounds more like a business deal. They already ran away once. Why would they help us now?"

"Their grass has not proved to be greener. They want back in," Magnus said.

"It can't be allowed," clamored the old man.

Morgan stepped back into the circle, like a red sun slowly rising from the void. The assembly hushed. "These are desperate times. Perhaps an exception can be made."

Julia stared at the enigmatic woman, whose moods seemed to shift with the wind. At least this time the wind was at their backs.

Help me, ancestors. Help me, Kai.

"I call a vote," she said. "To reunite the clans. To fight. And to take back what's ours."

———

"Congratulations," Baptiste said. "You've won us a war."

The numbers were close, but ultimately Chief Mercer's position swung the chamber. Julia was still shaking.

"Very funny," she said.

All the other chiefs had left, some still cursing on their way out. Next steps were to be decided in smaller groups, organized around those who could contribute to the action plan. All other clans were tasked with preparation for siege. Julia was to meet with Magnus once the Bastionite delegation was put away again, for safekeeping. For now, they huddled by the gallery.

"When do we leave?" Baptiste asked.

Evelyn blanched. The woman had survived two trips through the Deadlands but clearly didn't relish a third one so soon. Julia didn't blame her. Like the lieutenant, she felt *reduced* by her journey. Another one, especially so soon, would be suicide—or worse.

"They have to stay," Julia said.

Evelyn sighed with relief. The priest looked positively eager. Julia shuddered at the gleam in his eye, recalling visions she had hoped would fade with the nothingness.

"What do you mean?" Baptiste asked.

"There's no way we can make a trip all the way to Bastion, even with reserve tanks."

"I have to warn them."

"I know—"

"I thought you wanted us to help you win this war."

Julia shut her eyes for a second, breathing through her irritation. She owed him—she had said so herself and she meant it— but there were too many other things, too much pressure. "We have to see Ramirez first. You can come if you want. If they join us, we layover and refuel, then you can head to Bastion from there."

"And if they don't?"

"Then we're all dead."

The lieutenant's jaw stiffened. His body wanted to argue, but she could see fear in his bloodshot eyes. His face had become gaunt since their first encounter, his complexion more pale. Each day he looked more like a Scavrat. More like Roen.

"Maybe you can get your answers this way," Evelyn offered.

"Which ones?" Baptiste asked brusquely.

"Did the lord commander ever tell you how this arrangement was made in the first place?"

Baptiste frowned, turning to the vice chancellor. "What do you mean?"

"We never knew these people existed. My office certainly didn't. Yet we somehow sent them an invitation to our territory, via this exile clan. With key conveniently in hand for an asset we also just learned about."

Julia could see the hunger in his eyes. He desperately needed reconciliation for the loss of his men. "Magnus didn't know either," she said. "His Ramirez contacts said there would be help waiting for us at the bunker, but that was it. I didn't even know that much until we got back."

They all stood in silence for a minute. Finally, Baptiste lifted his hands to his temples, grinding them with callused fingertips. "Okay, then. Let's go get some answers."

PART 4
REVELATION

REBEKAH-6

A SIMPLE TEST

"Concentrate, R-6. Don't think about the wires."

Easy to say for the person not squashed in a metal cocoon, tangled like a human ball of yarn.

Don't look down.

Suspended above an abyss.

This lab wasn't anything like the others. It was more like a cave, broken off from an ancient subterranean tunnel system. Geometric runes were inlaid in gold along the rock wall, all the way to the point where it dropped off into a pit as wide as the Spire itself.

Don't look down.

She couldn't help it. The pit was bottomless as far as she could tell, a void from which nothing could ever return.

A special lab for a special test, Mother Leah had said. This being her eighth birthday, Rebekah-6 had been blessed with the opportunity to control an ancient exosuit, her largest machine yet. Just the top half, sadly—her heart had sunk when she was wheeled in and saw it, too, had no legs. Even still, it was massive and swayed ponderously at the precipice, where it—and therefore she—had been bolted into a much too slender metal railing.

Don't look down.

Those three words had become a mantra, repeated every time she pitched around on the machine's gimbals.

She was woven into a human chrysalis, barely able to move within the winding lengths of cable that comprised the exosuit's guts. The bigger the machine, the more contact she needed—this was the way of the Numbered. Electrodes were stuck into her scalp, arms, and chest, like fleas burrowing into her skin to suck at the juicy bits inside. Despite her predicament, Rebekah-6 wanted nothing more than to scratch at the bald spots that had been shaved into her hair. The itch was torture.

Don't look down.

Maybe it was a good thing she was strapped in so tight, even if it made breathing harder than normal. A watery gurgle emanated from her stomach. There had been no breakfast today or anything to eat the day before. A fast was required before every test, to clear her mind and "allow her to reflect on her spiritual purpose, removed from a body that would eventually serve no purpose." It was her least favorite part, even more than the scolding from the revenant mothers when she couldn't move the machines exactly the way they wanted. The stumps of her legs wiggled, anxious to walk her out of the cocoon and back to the fake comfort of her cell.

"You may begin," Mother Leah said.

Rebekah-6 was distracting herself, procrastinating. The discomfort, the itch, the hunger—they were all easier to suffer through than the thing before her. The real test. Mother Leah had said it would be simple: move an object from one spot to another. It didn't sound that bad until she saw what she had to move and from where.

She blinked several times over to clear the moisture in her

eyes. Her multi-jointed titanium arms extended out into the chasm. They were too long, too heavy, pivoting her too far forward any time she reached out. Telescoping out on either side of them, perched above the pit, were two circular steel-mesh platforms. The righthand platform was empty. On the left-hand platform was an unfamiliar creature, hunkered down as low as its diminutive body allowed, small head retracted into its shoulders.

Rebekah-6 squinted at it from her cocoon, lips quivering. It was... precious. Striped alternating grays with delicate white paws, orange eyes, and slitted pupils. She had never seen anything like it before.

She did want to reach out, but to stroke it, to feel its soft fur on her cheek. To cuddle it as she wanted to be cuddled. Like her, it appeared to be trying its hardest not to look down. To look down was to fall, to drown within the airless void of the pit.

A simple test: pick the creature up from one platform and deposit it onto the other, at which point it would retract into safety.

"Proceed, R-6."

Rebekah-6 flinched at the prompt, lost in the eyes of the "object" before her. Mother Leah stood out of sight behind her hulking frame, documenting her progress for the Great Mother. A spark of rebellion flared in her empty stomach.

"I don't want to," she muttered, as though quietly refusing would dull the revenant mother's indignance. It didn't.

"Proceed, R-6," Mother Leah repeated, more sternly this time.

The creature stared at her with its strange, unblinking orange eyes. She stared back, hoping to hold it in place with her gaze alone.

"Why are you making me do this?" she asked.

Mother Leah was beside her. She didn't dare avert her eyes,

but she could feel the woman's powerful aura scraping against her own. Scrutiny prickled at her skin.

"R-6," she said, not unkindly. "You might hold all our fates in your hands one day. This is necessary."

All our fates.

It was too much. She wished her mother had been here for this test. Did Mother Leah have her own child, in another cell below the Spire? Had Mother Rebekah watched Leah-2 (or 3 or 4) do the same test? Terrible visions spun through her young mind: a steaming mountain of bone, animal and human, piled high upon the molten core of the earth. Necessary sacrifices.

Stay with me. A prayer and a plea to the unwitting participant perched across from her.

A watery-eyed blink broke her stare. Her heart jumped, terrified that the brief detachment would send the creature spiraling downward. But it was still there, shaking. Hurriedly, she extended her consciousness into the exosuit, whimpering as the whole of her was compressed. The bald spots on her scalp bubbled with sweat as she strained to push herself inside of the machine, like a terrified rat squeezing through a too-small hole. Her body folded in upon itself, each bisection agony. Until finally she was running along copper roadways, swimming through rivers of light. Hot blood dripped onto her human lips, but she ignored it, stretching past the throbbing torrent of pressure.

Her robotic arms shivered and shuddered, clambering from their centuries-long slumber.

My hands.

Rotating on shrieking servomotors until palm up. Titanium slab fingers given grace, rippling in sequence as though playing an invisible instrument. Each movement accompanied by another drip.

Slowly, slowly, she lowered herself to the creature. Blue arcs danced between her fingertips, bristling against the fabric of reality.

Stay with me. Please.

The creature's back came up in an arch, its small mouth issuing a nervous hiss. Her hands hovered directly above it. If she was fast enough, she could scoop it to safety.

Its back was at the platform's edge.

If she was fast enough. If she was good enough.

But she was only eight.

Rebekah-6 wished for her mother.

Whispers called to her from the other side, the human body she had left behind. Prayers carried on bloodied lips.

She lurched forward.

————

Nothing had gone the way it was supposed to.

[R-6 > L-4: Respond!]

The heretics had not surrendered. They were running in every direction, back to their vehicles, to the bunker, to their deaths. A few misguided ones even ran into the gray. Targeting reticles swam and multiplied in her vision, like immune cells seeking out foreign bodies. They sought to outmaneuver her, thinking she could only see from her front, but she was not a half-blind girl anymore. Though eyeless, she was all-seeing. All-hearing.

But not all-knowing.

L-4 was not moving.

Rebekah-6 extended her telemetry to her sister. It was *different* than what her machine host had been designed to do, but the two of them connected nonetheless. Her consciousness flowed across L-4's titanium body, peeking in wherever her sister's neural network terminated: weapons online, reactor temperature normal, all systems operational. No anomalies detected. Wait—there was something there, amidst the signal. Fear. Doubt. Corruption within her organic data packets, like clotted blood, weighing down her limbs, pushing her back into the biological prison of her sepulcher.

If Rebekah-6 could shudder, she would have, recalling her own experiences of total sensory deprivation. First in the bath and again as her stripped body awoke within the lightless bowels of the battle walker. Was L-4 trapped? Was her companion's symbiosis failing? Could her own circuitry fail, leaving her stranded in the dark?

Something crashed into her from the front—

Tentacles whirled around her, exploding from the dry clay below, smashing into her back, barbed and vicious. Seeking, metal wrapped in putrescent flesh. Slithering past the ruse of her perfect exterior to violate the delicate mind within.

Light autocannon shells, no more than 25mm, pricking at her skin like electrodes.

She fired back instinctively and watched through her sensors, horrified, as the attacking craft exploded, consuming everything around it in flame. Volatile ammunition, surplus fuel —all notes in her hymn of destruction. They were once humans, now cinders.

Dead at her hands.

Metal hands, trembling as they neared the creature.

[R-6 > L-4: Are you there?]

The other vehicles were swarming now, crowding her, drawing her to violence. Another one exploded by her hand, and her visual sensors surged, zigzagging lines tearing across the gray, stabbing at her heart. They had been retreating, would have brought more back with them. It could not be allowed. They had to die.

"Set an example, so that others may be saved."

The Great Mother's command.

I'm killing people...

People not of faith. People whose unguarded souls would dissipate into oblivion, featureless grains of dust settling forever with billions of others in this purgatory.

Was L-4 right? Incapacitate, do not destroy. Force into submission. Turn the heretics from darkness to light. So that they may retrieve what lay within their bunker: a sister's body waiting to be born, another holy warrior to run alongside them, to help redeem the world.

Had they received different commands, revealed only at the last? Did the Great Mother doubt her sister?

[Leah-4 > Rebekah-6: I am here]

Two of the enemy vehicles were on her, pushing her away from her sister. A third was on its way.

They all have to die.

[Leah-4 > Rebekah-6: No sister. They are us]

Did L-4's telemetry extend into her thoughts? She felt foreign tendrils at the edges of her sepulcher, already past the firewall of her skin and intermediate mechanical viscera, swaying her circuitry.

Steel pitons gouged into her legs. The demon was climbing her, mounting her, seeking vengeance for its pulverized brethren. Before being pulverized itself, sundered by the holy flame of L-4's short-range missiles. The Numbered bathed together in cleansing fire.

[R-6 > L-4: What are you doing?]

Impact.

Impact.

Two of the enemy's shells struck one after the other. Gray landscape turned to red static as her flesh peeled apart over her chest, exposing the deformed rib cage beneath—

Struggling for breath within the subterranean temple, worshiping at the foot of the many-tongued demon.

Her left shoulder snapped back, punctured by a memory not her own.

Autocannon feed offline, articulation offline; chambered ammunition only.

For a moment she was the truncated human in the box.

The creature on the platform.

Shrunken, isolated, nowhere to go but down into the abyss.

"Don't think about the wires."

"Remember your prayers."

[R-6 > L4: ...]

Voiceless. Systems failure. She strained at her circuitry, to reestablish lines of communication with herself, with her sister. Strobing in and out of her sepulcher. Electrodes dug into her scalp—too deep, all the way in—and into the artificially sustained carcass of her dissected body.

Rebekah-6 arched her back—the creature arched its back; and hissed, their hisses accelerating into a singular scream.

Connection reestablished.

Her synapses opened, shot through the end of her remaining cannon in a roaring shriek. A third vehicle died, cracked open along its side. Human parts spilled forth from its ruined hull.

[R-6 > L-4: You must fight!]

[Leah-4 > Rebekah-6: No]

[R-6 > L-4: Great Mother commands it]

[Leah-4 > Rebekah-6: God commands otherwise]

"This is the fate of the Numbered. They are an affront... against God."

The Great Mother's words rang ominously within her memory.

Another vehicle had entered within range, encroaching on her disabled flank. And something else was moving on the other side of it.

Zoom and enhance: a man, mounting her sister as the demon had mounted her, carrying death.

[Leah > Rebekah-6: I am called]

Rebekah-6 was too alien, her metal hands not a promise of freedom but a monstrous prison. There was no comfort in her touch. The creature retreated and fell, yowling as it blinked out of existence, consumed by the pit.

[Leah > Rebekah: Run]

As she did, Rebekah-6 shuddered with loss, her exhausted heart heaving beneath layers of futile armor plates. The explosion turned her world brilliant white, but it brought no light to her darkness. Her skin flayed under the explosion, sensors dropping offline one by one, until she, too, was falling into the abyss, alone, surrounded by the corpses of all those she could not save.

He should have heard back by now.

Long-range communication was impossible in the Dead-lands, but Lucas Castillon had specifically asked his great-nephew to rotate out one of their Crusader sections after a week. That time had come and gone, which meant something was wrong. Still, he had refrained from sending out a second scout mission just yet. With the destruction of Drill Site 7, projected fuel supplies for the season were dangerously low. Also, the place was a curse. Every single man he sent there was one more soul he was potentially condemning to a fate worse than death.

The chancellor was getting antsy. He had shipped out her right hand alongside his soldiers, and Parliament was distinctly unused to that kind of risk. Together, they had opted to see this next mission through before escalating the overarching issue of Aleph and its "brothers" to a session of the Triarchy. There was no point in any of it if the bunker proved fruitless and their presumed allies disappeared back into the western wastes.

In the meantime, their resident battle walker was still confined below the mountain. There had been no communica-tion of significance between the Legion and the Church since the incident that killed a score of his men, certainly nothing between him and Alexis. He had even skipped last Sunday's Divine Liturgy, for the first time in his life. Rumors were spreading, despite efforts on both sides to contain them.

It couldn't go on like this much longer, but there was no clear way out now that he had personally unshackled the machine. Every night was riven by sweat-soaked nightmares of the thing bursting free and killing them all. In truth, he was surprised it hadn't—credit due to the archon. At least with the participation of all members of government—something he should have sought far earlier—there might be a way of proceeding, but slowly. Carefully, ensuring Bastion's longstanding balance of power was not altered—not against the Legion's favor, at least. Secretly, he was hoping the Union might have some means of turning Aleph off altogether.

Waiting. Damnable waiting. Even if everything was going according to plan, and Baptiste's rendezvous was bearing fruit this very moment, the stress of operating in the Deadlands was going to kill him. It was too opaque, like everything else these days.

Lucas thumbed his left armpit, grimacing at the tendrils of alternating pain and numbness that radiated into his arm. The armor he had worn with pride his entire adult life felt like a cage. Each morning, after scrubbing the pungent residue of the prior night's dreams from his body, he pondered going without. But there would be no clearer defeat, for him or the Legion. His armor was his station.

A nasal trio of beeps chirped from the speaker of his personal call box—the chancellor again, no doubt. The white-on-black panels of its flap display whirred and clacked as the line connected before settling on the number 19. Lucas sighed, pulled his rotary file from a drawer, and depressed the receiver button.

"Go ahead."

"Sir," came a female voice, young, "this is Operator Nineteen."

"One moment." Lucas held the file at arm's length, thumbing through the plastic cards until landing on the matching tab. George had come up with the new security measure given recent circumstances. It was irksome, but well intentioned. "Go ahead."

"Password of the day is 241-418," she said.

The numbers matched.

"Yes, go on," he replied impatiently, waving his hand at the call box.

"Sir?"

George had been specific about the protocol. "Password accepted," he added, feeling foolish.

"Sir, I have a call for you from Guardsman-Captain Ritchie at Central Command access. Flagged urgent."

Lucas furrowed his brow. There was nothing on the schedule.

"Urgent? Did he say what about?"

"No, sir. But..."

Lucas stared at the speaker, waiting for the operator to continue. They weren't typically so plodding. Dread began to creep from his armpit to the whole of his chest. "Out with it," he prodded.

"Sir. He sounded... scared."

Scared.

Guardsmen were never scared. Never supposed to be. Nor was he, yet his breath had started to catch painfully in his ribs. His armor was too tight. Lucas fumbled at his waist, exhaling with relief as he found the pitted wooden grip of his revolver. Centuries-old grooves slotted perfectly against the calluses of his hand, reassuring him he was where he was meant to be: at the helm, in control.

Now *he* was plodding.

Lucas cleared his throat and leaned forward. "Patch him through."

It was the nature of Central Command's layout that one couldn't make their way from the elevator into the meeting rooms without first navigating the Situation Room. This part of Bastion's key military infrastructure had been borrowed from what came before. There was no going around it, nor had it ever been a problem up until now.

Up until now.

"She says her name is Mother Rebekah," Ritchie had said. The operator was right. Lucas had never heard fear in one of his guardsmen until that moment. The man was barely keeping it together. "Sir, her eyes..."

He knew full well about her eyes. And her touch, a vise grip on his hand—the moment he first felt his vitality seep away, like blood to a leech. Blood that he never felt return to his veins, even now. Especially now. As bad as things had got with Alexis, something far worse must be afoot if the witch was coming to him directly.

Directly...

Lucas paused mid-step. He and George had linked up and were making their way to the elevator.

"Sir?"

Lucas tried to make sense of it. How was she here? They had only ever met at the Grand Citadel. Part of the deal brokered by his counterpart in the Church was that she would remain their "guest" for as long as she remained in Bastion. Had she escaped? Was this Alexis's doing? In either case, turning her away was not an option. She'd be as likely to murder his men and make her own way down. But revealing her to all of Central Command was also not an option. It was one thing for rumors of ancient technology and tension between the Legion and Church to be floating around. Those things existed within the reasonable bounds of everyday reality. The general public was not ready for Cathedral, and they certainly weren't ready for a revenant mother.

Lucas had looped the remainder of his senior staff into all things Aleph. They knew of its retrieval, activation, and the disaster that came of its inaugural mission. What they did not know was the instigating factor behind a possible general deployment: Cathedral, and more specifically Mother Rebekah. At the time, it had seemed one truth too far. Only George, his longest-standing guardsman and confidant, had been privy to all the facts. Lucas had needed a confessor—not of the priestly variety but someone he could actually trust—and it was the big man who took the brunt of it, without levying any judgment in return.

It made sense then to assign George with the task of triggering a surprise evacuation drill. There was shock and the expected protest of those operators on active calls with city defense, but they all eventually complied, with admirable efficiency.

The auditorium looked massive, the gleaming white of its walls blinding in the absence of its staff. The intricate magnetic statuettes representing friend and foe hovered in stasis upon the enormous city map, locked in combat. Too many chalk lines marked the fallen. Emptying this place felt like surrender. For some of those abandoned on the streets, cut off from communications and reinforcements, it would feel like death.

Lucas pulled himself away, hurrying toward the elevator with George in tow. Their guest would be arriving any second.

The guardsmen on duty at the access point were ordered to

accompany the revenant mother, after which a replacement section would be dispatched Metro-side. The damage there had been done. All Lucas could do now was try to nurture the men's trust by inviting them deeper into the awkward truth. He also felt marginally better knowing that he'd have more than a single bodyguard at his side.

The foyer unfurled before them. It was dim, deprived of half its ceiling lights. The ancient elevator screeched along its guide rails, gears and pulleys groaning as though overloaded, then landed with a thump.

Just in time. For what, he couldn't be sure.

A cloud of gold-tinged dust rolled from its base, scouring his eyes and nostrils. A low, electrical keening sounded from the remaining bulbs. One after the other, they flickered off until none remained. Lucas watched his shadow shimmer on the cold concrete floor, backlit by the empty radiance of the Situation Room. It looked shrunken, weak.

His heart was beating erratically, out of rhythm.

Mother Rebekah emerged from the darkness. She looked... different.

It was his last coherent thought before her aura took him.

Different.

More powerful. All powerful.

How like a god, he wondered, wide-eyed.

Like someone he should kneel before.

He was nothing in her presence. Unworthy.

Ripples of electricity crackled over his quaking body, arcing blue between segments of armor plate.

His heart was racing, the beat of it manic in his ears.

Where before her irises had shone gold, like enraged fireflies, they now also sparkled silver. He was enraptured by them. The auditorium, the lobby, the other men—they all disappeared, folded into a swirling vortex of black. But it was not an empty void. It shone with the brilliance of the lost heavens, a trillion stars, a great circular moon haloed by the distant sun. He wanted to weep—

"We need to talk."

Lucas wheezed as his lungs filled with air.

The sound of her voice penetrated his thin shell of flesh and metal, each syllable squeezing his arteries in turn. A single bank of lights reignited but remained dim, as though fearful to extend their emanations to the creature below.

He was breathing, hard.

Mother Rebekah stood between him and his men: four massive soldiers, the elite of the elite, all of whom had the look of a babe just sent to Hell and back. Their rifles hung limp in their hands. Each face was a pale, sweat-soaked permutation of abject terror—and adoration.

George's hand was on his elbow, tugging rhythmically at his arm. It was a reminder to breathe: four in, hold, four out. He had been doing it the whole time, even as the rest of those present crumbled.

The sensation passed, leaving him feeling cold and somehow... empty. There was only the sound of his own ragged breath and this woman standing directly before him.

Four in, hold, four out.

Lucas tried to swallow, his dry throat clicking in protest. Whatever moisture his drained body had left was dripping down his forehead, collecting in burning pools below his eyes.

Control. He had to regain control. And composure. He removed his right arm from George's grasp and dropped his left to his revolver, but there was no respite this time, none of the usual comfort he drew from his sidearm. It felt like a cane in his hand.

"Stand down, men," he called, forcing steadiness into his voice. "Mother Rebekah is a servant of God." The words—

slightly slurred and drawn out—were like poisoned daggers dragged along his soul. One by one, the guardsmen blinked slowly back to life, grateful for the lie.

The march back to his office was silent. Rather than normalizing his predicament with familiarity, the bright white light of the Situation Room felt harsh, out of place, its distant chalk lines insignificant. At the least, walking reminded his body how to function again. His men, too, had regained some of their composure. Everyone except George was relegated to stand guard outside, blocking access to both the meeting room and the adjoined hallways that led to an emergency exit. No one protested, even though their lord commander would be left alone with her.

What had changed? It was as though the woman he'd encountered last time was merely a shadow of the true creature that presented itself before him now. Doubt savaged him. Had Alexis seen this Mother Rebekah—this threat from the west— the whole time, while he was blinded by his stubbornness? He had admitted to his colleague a penchant for moving too slow, but perhaps his judgment was as impaired as his speed of action. Aleph was powerful, but at least it was a thing of the world, created by men.

"The drill has been canceled," George said, replacing the handset on the call box. "Readiness level *normal* has been restored."

Readiness level normal. The highest state of internal threat alert for Central Command, aptly named by George to seem innocuous if communicated under duress. There was no such thing as normal for the defenders of Bastion. All spaces were currently being reinforced by armed guards. Thick steel doors that hadn't shifted in years crept out from the walls, sealing every junction. Man-portable weapons would be deployed at every Legion entrance in the Metro, doubly so at Central

Station. No one was getting in or out, in theory. The alarm would also be communicated to the other seats of government.

"Do you feel better now?" Mother Rebekah asked.

Lucas exchanged a glance with his confidant. Deception was not in their favor, but at least their people would be as prepared as possible if need be.

The designated meeting room of the day was a large one, but it felt entirely inadequate. Even if they had met across the length of the Situation Room from each other, it would not have been enough. She stood at the far end, closest to the door, while Lucas and George sat at his desk. The thing—the *sensation*—that emanated from her was not heat or cold or anything natural he could pinpoint. It was more like... pressure. Waves of it compacted his body, joined to a relentless undertow that wrenched at his mind. Somewhere in between the tidal forces lay his soul, adrift.

Lucas tugged down his cuirass, wincing at the throb in his left arm. A tumbler of water sat tantalizingly close, but he refrained, clearing his throat instead with a series of raspy grunts.

"Why are you here?" he asked.

"We've been betrayed."

He smarted at her immediate response, exchanging a confused look with George.

"We..."

He was having a hard time focusing on her face. Any time he tried to deduce something of value from her body language, he was entrapped by her alien eyes. They were like twin radiation storms, boiling atop a field of blasted obsidian.

"You must have heard the klaxons from the citadel district the other night," she said.

Lucas blinked, clawing himself from her depths.

She was right. There had been an alert two days ago, and

another three days before that. He had been debriefed by the Ascendancy on both. The latter had been a cultist attack—a frighteningly bold one, certainly of concern and scheduled for follow up by the Order Sacramental—while the more recent one was a false alarm.

"I did…"

"And, I suspect, you think you know what triggered them."

Think you know. What was she getting at?

"Go on."

"Ascendant Benoit tried to kill me."

The pressure wave surged with violence. Lucas's eyes flared wide.

"What?" The question sputtered out of him before his brain could catch up. Her words were mired behind a growing wall of purple fog, which was steadily deluging his thoughts.

"That was the first alarm," she said acidly. "Fortunately, I was able to escape."

Escape.

A cultist attack, he had been told. When Lucas first "met" Mother Rebekah, ambushed within the archon's chambers, he had considered the possibility that she wasn't a foreigner at all but instead an agent—or worse, a *product*—of one of Bastion's growing number of cults. For all the Order Sacramental's claimed diligence, they had failed to suppress the tide. Maybe he had been right about her. Or worse, maybe she wasn't the only revenant sister that had infiltrated Bastion.

"The second alarm was me hunting down Ascendant Gauthier on behalf of my rescuers."

George sat upright in his chair. Lucas gawped, but no words were forthcoming. Something had his voice.

"Don't worry," she continued. "He's fine."

Fine! He should have been untouchable, along with the rest of the Ascendancy. Along with Central Command.

"I don't understand," he managed.

Of all the ascendants, Lucas was least familiar with Felix Gauthier. The Order Occult was repugnant, a malignancy within the Church. Were it his choice, the holy heptagram would be reduced by a couple of points at least. Regardless, the notion of any member of the Ascendancy being so casually targeted was alarming.

"A necessary ruse. While I cleaned up your cultist problem."

Lucas sank in a sea of confusion. His left arm felt like an anchor, dragging him into its depths. He desperately wanted to prop it on the table, but it was too heavy.

"A ruse," he wheezed. Every breath now was a wheeze. "But he lives."

"He lives and had much to say. Your alliance has been scrapped. The Ascendancy is corrupted."

Corrupted?

What could Gauthier know of it? The holy man was an enigma, one that Lucas had never desired to unravel. Too close to the enemy. As the lord commander was now.

Too close.

He couldn't breathe.

"Sir?"

George was there. George was always there.

"Lucas?"

He was drowning, body and soul. His vision turned as gray as the revenant mother's skin.

"What's happening?"

Voices in the dark.

"—having a heart attack—"

Call box buttons tapped out a staccato dance.

Click clack, click clack.

Slamming against their worn contacts, desperate to connect.

Threads of gold and silver streamed around him, undoing the clasps of his armor. Removing him from his station.

Undoing him.

"Send for Ascendant Clermont!"

"—can't be trust—"

A vortex opened around him, sucking him deeper into the sea, spinning faster until the threads became a blur.

Trapped between blinding brightness and the pitch of oblivion.

Spinning, spinning, unmoored from the world.

Then nothing.

Pain. Throbbing on and off, like the flashing engine light on his AARV's dashboard. Each *on* flattened him, crushing him like paste into the ancient concrete. Each *off* left him floating adrift in a sea of dizzying nausea.

On, off, on, off.

Waves of deconstructed flesh crashed against him, pulling him further into the sea with each retraction. Sloshing and churning, filling his ears with their hissing drone. Beneath the surface, whispers called to him. Blackened unintelligible words turned pink as they reached the surface of consciousness. Muffled, indistinct.

"This—"

Something hit his face, or his face hit something.

"—alive—"

He could see the engine light now. It glared through his lidded eyes, crackling fissures of swirling red in the black mass. Or maybe a different light—rotating in alarm from a cavernous ceiling as high above as the empty heavens.

"—over here—"

Ceiling. Blurry concrete bulkheads. The dim beam of overhead lamps smothered behind billowing clouds of bluish smoke.

The hangar? Where were the flags?

He was on his back but also moving, dragged by the heels. Blood and oil lubricated the way. Glimpses of puckered limbs no longer attached to their bodies. Smoldering metal.

The revenant mother?

He was locked into her gaze, vertiginous, as her pupils slowly dilated, enveloping him.

No, not Hub. A different hangar.

Bunker 23.

The Matriarch had sent her butchers, and he ran—away from Julia, away from his daughter. While the God-engine killed everyone around him.

A loud ping shattered his already sundered right ear, forcing his eyes open. A gunshot. Followed by the boiling crescendo of his tinnitus.

Sophus craned his head over, carefully peeling the left side of his face from the ground so he could hear better. If he had a voice, it would have screamed from the exertion. Someone else did it for him: a man amidst the rubble, crying out in awakened pain. By the liquid sound of it, he was drowning in his own blood.

"Reverend Father!" Someone standing nearby. Young, his voice quivering with uncertainty. "One of the Black Watch. He's still alive."

A shadow moved past him, pitching him back into darkness. Wandering blobs of orange and red coalesced in his blurred vision, forming the shape of a robed man. The bitter stench of unfamiliar herbs invaded his dust-caked nostrils.

"You know our orders," the shadow intoned. Flames danced around its head.

"But... the foreigners are one thing. These are our pe—"

"His Eminence was clear. There can be no counter narrative." The wounded man groaned again, gargling indistinct pleas for help. "You would be doing him a mercy in any case," said the shadow.

Sophus held still, locking his breath in place.

"God forgive me—"

The air evaporated in a flash of gunfire. He retreated behind clenched eyes as the burst blazed past his head, scorching his scalp. Something slammed to the ground beside him, landing with a fleshy thud. A noxious cloud of ammo fume billowed over his face, scouring his lungs. He began to cough.

"Drop your weapon, Overseer!" a third voice called out, just behind him.

"How dare you!"

The shooter stood, stumbling noisily from a waterfall of debris. The two men circled each other—circled him.

"Put your gun down, Reverend Father."

The shadow unfurled around him, looking for an opening. He could feel its eyes on him.

"I am the right hand of Ascendant Benoit. You have no authority over me, Chaplain."

The third voice was trembling now. "This is your last warning."

Alternating cycles of high-pitched ringing and whispering static blew through his ears as the men faced off.

A sudden movement above, then a second burst of gunfire—from the other side of the hangar. The shadow grew as wide as the world, then crushed him, knocking what little breath he had from his chest.

"Father Valmor!" Another new voice, echoing along the cavernous bay. "Are you okay?" Followed by heavy-booted footsteps, running toward him. "Valmor?"

"Yes. Yes, I'm okay. I need to attend to Stratton." Sophus

could hear the man's teeth chattering. *Father*—one of their priests. "Help the heathen."

The shadow lifted off his body and was tossed to the side, leaving a soggy pile of residue on his abdomen. A pair of dark-skinned, heavily armored men were peering down at him.

"Can you stand?" one of them asked.

Broken words leaked out of his mouth, but he couldn't yet manage the string of curses he wanted to unleash. Metal-sheathed arms slid under his armpits, yanking him to his feet. His dislocated left shoulder shimmied in its sling, sending fireworks of agony flashing in his vision.

"Sorry," the soldier muttered.

Sophus held in his pain, straining to see what was happening. His eyes were burning, on top of all the other misery. Every blink felt like a layer of corneas being stripped off.

He was definitely inside the bunker. The entranceway was filled with oily smoke, wafting from the obliterated and still-burning ruin of a Bastionite APC half in and half out of the building. One of the enormous hangar doors had collapsed on top of it. There was rubble and molten scrap everywhere, strewn atop the dead. A second APC squatted behind them, seemingly intact.

"Stay with me, Stratton," Valmor said. Their red-robed priest —not also a redhead, which nixed his prior theory—was tending to a survivor. From the familiar sounds of the wounded man's agony, he was the one the *other* priests were about to execute.

What the fuck...

His addled brain kicked into gear.

"Sergeant, what's going on?" It was the man who had helped him up, directed at the other soldier. Sophus recognized them now: Deckard and Lafayette, the two subcommanders that had bracketed Baptiste at their fateful first meeting. Lafayette, the stoic one who seemed more a supervisor than a subordinate, was standing over the body of the man he had just shot to death.

"It's Rayos," Lafayette answered, wide brown eyes breaching his normally expressionless face.

"Rayos?" Deckard asked, aghast. "The confessor?"

"Two of them," Lafayette said, looking back and forth between the man that Father Valmor had shot and the one he had taken down. Where Valmor wore battle armor under his robes, these priests were clothed in some sort of black leatherette under theirs. The numeral *II* adorned their dramatically high collars. They almost looked like revenant sisters, only male, and not quite as corpse-like despite being very dead.

"Father Valmor," Lafayette said, turning to face his priest. "I just killed an OS overseer. I need to know why." There was an unmistakable flutter of panic in his otherwise stern voice.

Sophus expected a smug reply, communicated through obtuse scripture, but their holy man was clearly shaken by also having murdered one of his own people. He was distractedly pumping a handheld catheter to suction blood and bile from his patient's throat, ejecting the man's innards one load at a time onto the ground beside them. The soldier was gagging noisily, sending Sophus's stomach into his throat. A white-knuckled hand clutched the chaplain's robes, but by the end of it he was breathing again. Valmor rolled Stratton onto his side, driving his knee into the man's bare back so he could bandage a cluster of oozing shrapnel wounds. Each roll of gauze was sealed with a prayer.

Finally, the priest looked from his filthy fingers to the fresh corpses. Long moments passed before his shifting lips could produce words. "After you went in to get supplies, I heard a vehicle pull up outside. I told Private Stratton to stay put while I hid." The private's eyes were closed, his breath coming in rattles. "When I saw them, I was relieved. I thought we'd been reinforced. But then I saw they were Order Sacramental. Here... outside Bastion. It didn't feel right, so I stayed out of sight."

Deckard was nodding dumbly, but Lafayette was rapt, completely focused on his chaplain's retelling.

"They started rearranging the dead." Valmor crossed his arms over his chest, whispering a private prayer.

"Rearranging?" Deckard asked, confused.

Sophus took another look around, forcing his spine upright. Another graveyard. How many more would he walk before he was among the fallen, blown to bits, his headstone a slab of ill-gotten treasure? A spot of desert camo protruded from the ring of gray bodies surrounding the destroyed APC. His heart started thumping. He walked unsteadily toward the shape, beating down his own anxious thoughts.

It's not Julia. She escaped.

He was sure of it. He had seen Mace tackling her, bolting for one of the Greybull IFVs while someone dragged him back into the bunker.

He was sure of it... but also not.

Ingram's vacant eyes stared past him into the void. The gangly young man's body was broken in too many places, both feet turned all the way around, most of his torso gone. The smell—

Sophus threw up, barely turning his head fast enough to miss his subordinate's remains. He heaved it out, right arm on his leg while the other swayed uselessly in its sling. Bits of bluish road rations splashed onto the ground, near the shotgun Ingram was holding in his delicate long-fingered hand.

"What," he eked out, squinting at the firearm. Ingram was a junior mechanist, still a kid. He had probably never fired a gun in his life.

The soldiers watched him as he straightened back up, scanning the ruins for more familiar faces. He found Bridget's, closer to the splayed hangar door. Despite her proximity to the explosion, she barely looked injured other than a fresh bullet hole in her head. She, too, was holding a firearm.

She looked peaceful.

"They executed that one," Valmor called out.

"Executed..." Sophus repeated. "They?" He spat a lingering ball of vomit from his mouth and turned to face the Bastionites. A thread of rage wound its way from his rapidly beating heart to his throat. "Or you?"

Lafayette stared back at him, expressionless. Though the sergeant bore no swagger, he had an air of cold, efficient lethality. Sophus hadn't seen it before now. His indignance faltered immediately.

"Not us," Lafayette said.

Deckard was shaking his head. "I don't get it," he muttered.

"We've been set up," Lafayette responded, "somehow."

"Those were God-engines," Sophus broke in, gesturing past the broken hangar doors. Stale light crept through from the other side. "Only the Matriarch commands them."

"Matriarch?" Deckard asked.

"We need to get back," Lafayette said. "Quickly. Deckard, load up the supplies. Valmor, help him once Stratton is stabilized."

"Get back?" Sophus asked, his stomach readying for another round. He already knew the answer.

"To Bastion."

"Maybe we should wait," Deckard said. The man was clearly shaken.

"Move out, Sergeant," Lafayette replied, terse.

"But we're going to be reinforced right? We can get an escort back."

Lafayette pointed his rifle at the one they had called Rayos. "After this, we can't count on anything."

Deckard lowered his eyes, defeated. "Yes, sir."

Memories of the battle trickled back. Kai had started yelling like a fucking maniac. Sophus knew what was coming—certain death courtesy of Clan Greybull—so he gave the command to scatter. Flashes of violence, the impossibly loud cannons of the battle walkers. No, just the one—something was wrong with the other one. Carried on a tide of armored bodies back into the bunker, dodging past the rolling fireball of their ill-fated APC. Idiots... Poor idiots. It had no chance against a God-engine. Harper and Greybull vehicles fleeing, then an explosion, much worse than the last one, like the world was tearing open all over again.

"Where's your lieutenant?" Sophus asked, turning to look at the cracked-open hangar door.

Deckard walked up beside him. "With your people. They got away."

Your people.

Julia.

"I have to be sure," Sophus said, stumbling his way past the wreckage.

"We already checked for survivors," Deckard called after him.

Everything was scorched black right up to the point where the bunker met the exterior, then reverted to undisturbed gray. There were signs of battle beyond the door, but it was as though debris had been lightly sprinkled from the heavens. There were no craters, no blackened pockmarks to disturb the nothingness. A mostly empty expanse under an empty sky.

His legs wobbled as he stepped out.

Julia got away.

He probably didn't need to check...

Sophus hobbled forward, in the direction he remembered Mace running. The pulverized silhouettes of a Harper AARV and a Greybull Ironclad hung at the limits of his vision. They looked thin, two dimensional. Instead of smoking, they seemed to be disintegrating, their elementary particles reclaimed by the Deadlands.

There were no bodies, no ash, just bits of decomposing metal. Soon those would be gone as well. The bunker exterior was in rough shape, blasted down to the rebar all around the massive door. Now that it was exposed, he wondered if it, too, would be claimed by the Deadlands along with the secrets that lay within. Had Julia told the foreigners about the battle walker? He should never have left her. He should never have taken this mission in the first place. He should never have taken Roen on his Finder's Right...

"Endless fucking failure," he muttered.

Sophus shuffled back inside. As much as he hated the Deadlands, the abattoir within was little comfort. Stasis Bunker 23 was as much a rotting corpse now as the bodies it would forever entomb.

"*Set up,*" Lafayette had said.

First the revenant mother at Hub. That was bad enough, a repeat of something that was never supposed to be repeated. Now this. Had the Matriarch finally decided to wash her hands of the Union? It seemed impossible. Generations of coexistence wiped out just like that, because they couldn't keep their collective dicks in their pants. Whatever the intent, Clan Ramirez had fucked them again. Last time it was the Greybulls that fell for it. This time it was his own clan.

"We need to burn the dead," Valmor said. He was standing now, looking warily over the sea of human remains before him. His complexion was as pale as a Scavrat.

"No," Lafayette responded. "The Adv—"

"We must!"

"No, Father. There's no time. The Adversary will not touch them here. They'll return to dust on their own."

"This place is unclean. Their souls will linger."

"If *we* linger and more enemies come, we'll join them, and then they'll have died for nothing."

The priest looked broken. "Then let me pray, at least."

Lafayette nodded and turned to Sophus. "There's only the five of us. Father Valmor will need to watch over the private. Deckard and I need to man the guns." He peered at the other sergeant, a concerned grimace on his face. "Do you think you can drive this thing?" He gestured to the second APC.

It hunkered low on meaty tires, its sloped prow a battering ram that could annihilate anything standing in its path—anything except a battle walker, apparently.

Something sparked in Sophus's groin, a prior lust reawakened. When his crew had first encountered the Bastionites, he wanted nothing more than to investigate the shiny new vehicle. To feel something unfamiliar in his hands. He smirked, wondering how it had come to this. Chaos reigned, the passing of time counted with dead bodies. Everything he touched had turned to shit. And yet some dreams did come true, even if they cost him everything in the process.

REBEKAH-6

IMAGES IN THE DARK

Rebekah-6 limped across the gray wastes, broken and alone. The myriad systems that comprised her mechanical body had become necrotic: optical conduits clotted, electrical circuits enervated, polymer linkages straining with physical damage. They protruded from her blasted carapace, exposing her soft core to the nothingness beyond. Damage reports echoed in her mind, spoken in a voice that was once her own, relaying each point of failure in gruesome detail. It felt like pain—what she remembered of it.

Her once-spine curled upon itself, overgrown vertebrae choking her nerves, casting pins and needles down the length of her autocannons and hawklike legs. She could disconnect the synthetic viscera, numb away the discomfort, but what would be left then? Just her mind, wandering the graveyard of her own body. Until it, too, shut down, soaked through with caustic radiation from her strained power plant.

Mechanical heart failure. Mechanical arms; not even arms—instruments of death in place of fingers once long and articulate. Mechanical legs in the image of some ancient avian creature. An abomination, an affront. Everything she had once hoped for: to cut away her weakness and roam free, to see the world, to save the world.

To cut away herself.

A sheath of black gauze caressed her skin, rippling in the forced air currents of the operating theater, peeled back one limb at a time as she was made smaller. She had been heavily anesthetized, removed to a lightless abyss, but no Numbered was as powerful as she. Each touch of the scalpel, each cut of the saw was a flash of reawakened agony. She prayed—to Messiah, to God, to her mother—to end the suffering. None answered, so she endured—alone.

Alone, in the bowels of the machine, like so much human waste.

Alone, her sister destroyed, blind and stumbling.

Alone, motherless, in a cradle of steel and titanium. Swaddled in electrodes that pried at her every nerve and violated the terminus of each amputated limb.

"Wake up!"

Rebekah-6 gasped for air, gagging against her breathing tube —within the sepulcher. Within her flesh. Only this was the present.

Sensors malfunctioning. Acoustic, seismic only.

She had fallen back into her human body. A split second of Hell, bereft of the opportunity to scream.

Locked in. Buried alive.

Reset! Reset! Reset!

Her awareness lurched, scrambling through the sepulcher's cybernetic interface. The way opened, but all she could see were ghost images in the dark, trembling sine waves on a field of static. They shuddered with each machine-assisted draw of her lungs, crashing upon the shore of her consciousness.

Visual sensors offline.

She crammed her thoughts into the battle walker's ancient redundancies, prying open thick vault doors to subterranean circuitways never before traversed. Seeking, desperate, to patch herself into one of the uncounted access points where the dead AI's neural network once resided so that she might see. A node appeared, assuming the shape of a minuscule window upon an infinite plane of shimmering black. It would have to do.

Visual sensors online.

Barely, but still more than the void. A few meters of featureless dark gray appeared, forward-facing only, crackling in and out of pointless focus. The distant pounding of her heart eased. Was it dawn? Dusk? She had fallen asleep, exhausted by days on end of relentless concentration, past blended with present. Time had been lost along with direction after the explosion.

After her sister died.

The battle replayed in her memory at high speed, freezing at the frame just before the sky turned white. L-4 just standing there, waiting to die.

Unreconcilable loss strangled her. Within the machine, there were no tears. Anguish could only build, saturating her polymer tendons until extruded through speed or violence—or sleep. It ate at her like cancer. In the absence of proper rest, her brain would burn out long before her body did.

Rebekah-6 terminated the playback. Recentered within her machine body, she paused to look around, but there was nothing to see. Each turn of her torso brought the same myopic view: gray, horizonless. Her tutelage said little of the Deadlands, only that it was a barren emptiness left behind when the world fell, not to be lingered in, devoid of humanity and demons alike. A mirror of the void above.

She needed to rest. The escaped Union forces were long gone.

It should be okay to stop and sleep.

It should be safe.

So many *shoulds*. Out here in the open, on display for whatever malevolence made the Deadlands what it was. It should have been empty. And yet...

There was *something*.

She pushed herself to the boundary of the battle walker's carapace, extending her consciousness into its outermost antennae. Beyond her constrained vision was a shadow, a figment that did not register on any of her dulled machine senses. It lurked at the corners of awareness, unsettling the immutable pattern of cracked earth below her. It crept and wallowed. A corruptive presence, slipping between her metal feet, across the jutting plates of her splintered rib cage, into the fuming wound of her shoulder.

Her mind recoiled in horror, almost dragged back to the sepulcher.

I am blinded by the light of thy torches—

Light. She needed light. Rebekah-6 raced back to the chamber of redundancies, bypassing bundles of dead fiber, shunting power from weapons to auxiliary systems.

—and I praise the Lord—

Disconnecting neural pathways to her extremities, reducing herself a second time.

The rattle of wheelchair casters rang in her memory as her mother raced to save her from her fate.

—that I may see the beasts that cannot be seen.

Her central eye ignited, transposing the earth a deep red. A shape shimmered into existence amidst the gray—a tentacle, long and ethereal—then snapped back out of sight. Rebekah-6 spun around, hip joints grinding in protest, upper torso swaying ponderously back and forth to spread the light of her sacred lantern.

Nothing.

She turned again. Still nothing. A hallucination? Anguish and fatigue coursed like poison in her synthetic veins.

Reactor temperature elevated; life support systems interruption; reducing output.

Her own voice, condemning her to a slow death.

Rebekah-6 activated her vocal processors and screamed. It was her voice only by proxy, but at least it was audible, tangible. Over and over, she evacuated her terror and hatred into the nothingness, until it seemed enough.

Nothing echoed back at her.

Leah, what did you do?

Loneliness enveloped her. Symbiotes always traveled in pairs, protecting each other physically and mentally. It was a commandment, a sacrament not to be broken. Rumination led back to the sepulcher and could be defeated only with constant focus. Collaborative scriptural recitation served as a guidepost and mutual diagnostic, a constant stream of purifying data flowing between sisters, interrupted only by situational emergencies.

Leah-4 pushed those boundaries. Between psalms, she injected personal queries regarding Rebekah-6's human life: What did she look like? What did she eat? Did she have any toys? What were her tests like? Rebekah-6 had admonished her sister for her curiosities. Now she was gone.

"*I am called.*"

Her sister's final words before allowing herself to be destroyed. Before committing the cardinal sin of suicide. Though the sun shone upon Leah-4 as her body evaporated in flame, her soul would not ascend. It would remain forever trapped in this place.

Digital tears rolled across Rebekah-6's cropped viewport, zigzagging black and white.

Where are you, Mother? Was she also trapped out here, wandering aimlessly?

[R-6 > Open channel: Anyone, respond]

Nothing, not even the hiss of interference.

"Remember your prayers."

Rebekah-6 allowed herself a momentary controlled retreat into her sepulcher, enough to feel the movement of her own lips in silent prayer. Solitary staccato mantras cascaded through her mechanical legs, ushering them from their paralysis.

There was no respite here. She had to keep moving. She had no other choice save death, and this was the last place on Earth she wanted to die.

LUCAS
THE SAME SIDE

Buzzing, incessant buzzing. Something was swarming around his head. Flies. Bulbous, golden abdomens, antennae glistening black. Fireflies. Darting and nibbling, carrying the final bits of him out of the earth. Worms swam in his mouth, leaving burning trails of mucus in their wake. Bitter, tingling, up into his sinuses. Vermin climbing into his face—

Iridescent light exploded in his vision.

He was gasping, which meant he was breathing, even if he couldn't feel it.

Rays of blue, green, and purple spiraled down from a rolling floor lamp. The purple one hurt the most. He tried to turn his head so it would change to something else, but he was trapped.

"Stop. Moving."

Lucas shut his eyes again, trying to connect the movement of his chest with the air that must be in his lungs.

Four in. Three. Two.

One in.

No matter how small the number, he couldn't feel it.

"George, help me out here," someone called.

Strong hands grasped his own above his head, then lowered

them back down to his side. He didn't know how they had got there. Batting fireflies.

Lucas cracked his eyes open again, squinting against the offensive lamp.

"Bright," he croaked. It was the voice of an impossibly old man.

The spotlight disappeared, its afterglow fading into rows of diffuse bulbs stitched along a concrete ceiling.

"Welcome back, Lord Commander."

He blinked away the blobs cascading over his vision, trying to focus on the person standing over him. Dark hair streaked the same gray as his eyes, a permanently wrinkled brow, and a face deeply chiseled by years of caretaking.

"Francis..." Such a hard name to say. His uvula dragged along his tongue, threatening to gag him each time he spoke.

Four in. There it was.

Hold.

Four out.

George was at his side, hand on his forearm. Squeezing the breath count. Lucas's armor had been stripped from the waist up and warm compresses placed over his chest. He often had dreams—nightmares—of walking the streets unarmored, some-times even naked, his withered body on display for all to see. A mockery before Bastion, before God; a harbinger of its fall. Was that what this was?

"Thank you, George," he said, pulling away. "And you, Your Eminence." He nodded weakly to Ascendant Francis Clermont.

Francis nodded back, though he seemed restless, reluctant to make eye contact.

"Sir, I..." George began, but trailed off as Lucas felt his own gaze pulled to the side. To a dark corner of the hospital, where a figure was standing, nearly invisible in her black habit, her colorless face lit only by her own eyes. "I had no choice."

Francis muttered something to himself, a prayer maybe, turning his attention to her as well. "She can't be trusted," he whispered.

"And you can?" Mother Rebekah retorted, loudly.

The ascendant flinched as though struck.

"Easy, Francis," Lucas said. It was all he could muster. On top of the choking sensation, every word uttered made the next breath harder. His chest felt no less tight, even removed from its metal sheath.

More figures lurked in the shadows, though these were of a conventional variety. He crooked a finger in their direction, hoping George would understand the question.

"Ritchie called ahead, cleared as big a path as they could. Noncritical cases were transported to other care centers. The wi —the... Rebekah followed us." George grimaced, the woman's name like a bite of rotten fruit in his mouth. "She was cowled, but I'm sure word has spread by now."

Lucas sighed, closing his eyes. The fragile wall he had built around the truth had crumbled. Chaos was coming for them all.

"There's more," George continued, adjusting his position slightly so he could catch Lucas's full attention. "His Holiness is en route. As is Ascendant Blake." Special emphasis was given to the second man's name.

Alexis? It was reasonable that the archon would want to see him, whatever ugliness had transpired between them recently. He would do the same. But Xavier Blake... he hadn't liaised with the Order Militant in some time. Which could only mean one thing.

"We have prepared the way?" Lucas asked, gasping by the final word.

George nodded.

"Up."

George ratcheted up his bed, each clunk of inclination like a blow to his kidneys. The ascendant's face contorted in commiseration, but he knew better than to interfere. The lord commander could not be seen laid up on his back when the interlopers arrived.

———

Lucas was crushed by the weight of his armor, having insisted on donning it again for their guests. A buffet of "vasodilators," painkillers, and pungent herbals were plowing their way through his system, thanks to Francis. Just enough to get him on his feet, which turned out to be a lot. The herbals were the worst, harvested from the deepest, dankest bowels of the earth; they tasted of how the archon's incense smelled. The cocktail seemed to be working, in the same way the Legion's centuries-old tanks mostly worked, up until that fateful point where they had to actually shoot something out of their cannons.

He was seated on the side of his bed. Francis was taking his pulse, but Lucas didn't need to ask for the assessment—he could feel his heart chugging, raring stupidly for battle in its brief moment of reinvigoration. In either case, the head of the Order Somatic had withdrawn when he learned his colleagues were on their way. He seemed even more unsettled by their imminent arrival than he was by the hovering specter of Mother Rebekah.

"They're here," intoned George.

Lucas brushed the ascendant away and scooted slightly more upright, halfway to standing at least.

The remainder of patients had been removed, and all bay curtains were retracted, leaving the hospital wide open all the way from the small concourse at the front, past dozens of bed spaces to the back. A platoon of Central Guard had been dispatched around the floor, distributed between the main entrance, the exits, and his immediate vicinity. It was silent save for the electric buzz of the overhead lights.

Mother Rebekah had not moved from the corner. He watched her watching them. In this moment he realized he had not garnered any reassurances from her, but she had already been back to the Grand Citadel; if a bloodbath was her intent, she could have carried it out directly instead of relying on current events. Still, it felt like an ambush. All his available soldiers' eyes were on her, the darkness and distance blunting a small measure of her prior countenance.

Booted footsteps echoed down the hallway from the entrance—a considerable number of them. One of the guardsmen there turned and gave him a questioning glance. Lucas nodded, and the pair parted, making way for a regally armored paladin-captain of the Order Militant. Lucas didn't recognize him. The holy warrior was as imposing as any of his best guardsmen, resplendent in his burnished armor and deep-red cloak. He marched into the concourse and scanned the area, noting with a raised eyebrow each man of the Legion. A flash of surprise crossed his face as he found Lucas, followed by a minimal bow.

"Announcing His Holiness, Archon Alexis Levesque, and His Eminence, Ascendant Xavier Blake."

The pronouncement echoed around the emptied hospital. A train of paladins followed after their commander, eight in total, bracketing one of the most important men in the nation and another who imagined himself so. Other than their red cloaks and heraldry that emphasized the Church's heptagram over the Legion's crossed gauntlets, the Order Militant looked much like proper soldiers, which was by design. They were on the same side, after all, though the fact that they were wielding their rifles —patrol carry at least, pointed downward—cast that into doubt.

A ripple of discontent moved through the semicircle of

guards behind Lucas. For as long as he had commanded the Legion, he had never experienced such an imposition. There wasn't a censer-swinging, Bible-carrying preacher in sight; this was all business. Military business. Francis nervously rubbed his bare forearms, continually pushing the sweat-soaked sleeves of his cassock back up.

The train of holy warriors entered the hospital in perfect formation, but their ranks shifted as they noticed the force arrayed before them. Eyes darted, footsteps faltered, white-knuckled hands gripped their rifles tighter—*in shame perhaps*, Lucas thought. He hoped. They halted mostly in unison and snapped to attention.

Alexis and Xavier stepped forward together—in lockstep, as Lucas once had with his counterpart. Alexis looked as bad as Lucas felt. The archon's hair was disheveled, and his bloodshot eyes strained to free themselves from sunken pits of charcoal. Xavier was unreadable. He shared a curt nod with Francis, who was getting cagier the closer they got. As military leaders, he and Lucas shared a common heritage, but the ascendant's ecclesiastical allegiances were an impassable barrier to meaningful camaraderie. It was the way of the Legion and the Church: tight, but not touching.

"You look... better than expected," Alexis said. The archon's furrowed brow expressed the confusion his words did not. "We came as quickly as we could."

Lucas was on a fixed time limit. Francis had warned him not to push it, that the stimulants given to him would ultimately result in a crash with little advance warning. Also, the longer he delayed bed rest—Lucas cringed at the thought of it—the more likely he was to have another arrest, and the next one would be even worse. He had to prioritize, aggressively.

Mother Rebekah had given a scant outline of the Church's betrayal, as she saw it. He wasn't surprised by the actions of the

Order Sacramental against her. He wasn't even sure if he disagreed with them, as grotesque as Benoit's methods were. It was the secrecy that bothered him. Such a decision wasn't the Church's alone to make. Bonds had been broken after he ordered Aleph—and the archon, by proxy—to stand down. Broken worse than he may have imagined.

He was also unsettled by Gauthier's words, as reported by the revenant mother: their proposition rejected, an implied threat against their alliance with the Union. There was certainly betrayal here, deeper than the Ascendancy expunging a heretic from their midst without making a courtesy call first.

"Why is Ascendant Blake here?" Lucas asked, eyes fixed on Alexis. He gave private thanks to God as his voice emerged whole—strong, even—imbued with the power of purpose.

The head of the Order Militant chewed his lip, clearly irritated at not being addressed directly. His arms crossed imposingly over his barrel chest.

Lucas had also wanted to ask why they had brought armed paladins with them into a Legion facility, but he already knew the answer to both questions and was mindful of his abridged timetable.

Alexis cleared his throat. His right arm twitched several times as he restrained his usual nervous response; the bald patch on his chin had grown larger since Lucas last saw him.

"He is here to execute his mandate, as decreed."

Silence fell on the room. Even those soldiers shuffling around the edges of the hollowed-out facility seemed to be holding their breath.

His mandate. By law, in the event of the death or invalidity of the lord commander, where a successor had not been declared —Lucas cursed his procrastination—it was the mandate of the Order Militant to temporarily take command of the Legion.

"And yet," Lucas said, his voice cracking around the edges, "I live and breathe."

"You are lucky to be able to say the same," called out Mother Rebekah, stepping from the shadows.

The bank of lights directly above the woman exploded. An arc of splintered glass waterfalled around her, falling too slowly, as though trapped between time.

The revenant mother was in their midst.

Everyone's guns came up: first the paladins, followed by the guardsmen, pointed in all directions—many of which would have resulted in a court-martial under regular circumstances. Two of his guardsmen had taken up a shielding position in front of him, moving with lightning speed despite their size. George didn't move, but Lucas knew his confidant had his thumb readied over a very important button: a clarion call that, if pressed, had the potential to destroy everything the Triarchy had built.

Lucas raised his right arm and dumped most of his remaining energy into a bellowed command. "Stop!" He could feel Mother Rebekah's gravity pulling him sideways but held fast. "Stop immediately. The hammer and shield will not be striking at each other this day. Not while I draw breath."

The archon's contingent shifted posture, from aggression to trepidation, but Lucas knew better than to think it was his orders that stilled them. As far as he knew, none of them save the archon himself would have known about or interacted with a revenant mother. And then there was her... change. He could see it in their faces: the uncanny mix of terror and adulation the woman inspired. Holy terror. It was hard enough for him to reconcile the facts of her power, having had a few minutes to get acclimated. For those among the Church delegation still in their junior ranks, it must have been soul shattering. Even Ascendant

Blake was stricken dumb, his mouth agape. The archon had shrunken back two steps.

Lucas had to end this as quickly as possible.

"You harbor a fugitive," Alexis said, somewhere between a question and an accusation.

"A fugitive?" Lucas repeated. The more that was revealed by the archon himself, the better. Whatever his counterpart's accusations, he did not wish to appear swayed by the witch.

Alexis froze, trapped between lies.

"What have you done, Alexis?"

There was a ripple in the interlopers' ranks. It was forbidden to address the Holy Father by his first name in public. It was also intentional. The Metro, and everything in it, was the lord commander's domain. Lucas's domain.

The archon remained silent.

Francis finally broke from his shuffling and turned to Lucas. "Lord Commander, I'm sor—"

"Be silent!" Alexis commanded.

Ascendant Blake's expression had turned to uncertainty, eyes darting between his superior and his colleague. The Order Militant was just as intertwined with the Order Somatic as the Legion was. Francis was the glue that kept Bastion's defenders, both secular and holy, intact.

"Gather your things," Alexis said. "You will be returning with us to the Grand Citadel."

"Yes, Your Holiness," Francis replied, relief in his voice. He spared a final apologetic glance at Lucas, gathered up his bag, and crossed to the other side.

There would be no answers today, but status quo beat out the alternative. And just in time. A tremor was growing in Lucas's legs, threatening to topple him if he stood much longer.

Alexis locked eyes with Mother Rebekah, remarkably

resilient in her presence. "We will be leaving, Lord Commander," he said, unblinking.

She towered between them like an obsidian mountain, impassable from either side.

Their delegation exited in short order, those taking up the rear practically running.

Lucas slumped backward on the bed. George was there, as always.

He was no closer to his counterpart's schemes, but at least order had been reestablished—for now.

Order...

He snorted, looking with unabashed wonder upon the foreign influence in their midst. What was she, truly? Priestess? Demon? Something in between? She didn't belong there, definitely not in Bastion and maybe not anywhere in the world. If this was what the rest of her priesthood was like, battle walkers would be the least of his people's concerns.

"What now, sir?" George asked.

Everyone was watching him, waiting.

"What now..." he repeated, pausing to take another breath. His armor felt too tight again. "I need to call the chancellor. Then we go find my great-nephew."

Sophus got used to the foreign APC—the Crusader—quickly enough, after a brief tour and driving lesson from a skeptical Sergeant Deckard. It was powerful but geared for fuel efficiency, just like back home. Scarcity knew no borders. All in all, it wasn't that different from an AARV, other than having a horrible field of view. The Bastionites had opted for increased armor over driver visibility, leaving it to the vehicle commander and gunners to provide auxiliary nav. Not that Sophus was worried about meandering into any ditches in the Deadlands; he just didn't like being so... constrained.

When he had first complained about the tiny slit of a window, Father Valmor retorted with a cryptic warning about trusting one's eyes over their faith when facing the Adversary. Deckard added something about tentacles getting through the windows and not wanting his face sucked off. Sophus preferred the priest's reasoning.

The trip back—doable in under a day, he was promised—began quietly. The rest of the crew were out of sight behind the crawlway door, and no one had been eager to chat over the crew comms. The vehicle's drivetrain settled into a benign drone at cruising speed, leaving only the shifting hisses and tones of Sophus's tinnitus to keep him company. Even contained within the vehicle's metal shell, the nothingness of the Deadlands accentuated his personal soundtrack in the worst ways possible. The whispers were always there in the background, threatening to reemerge and ruin his day.

Sophus was also exhausted, on account of the restlessness of his over-crowded journey in Kai's IFV. Getting knocked unconscious during the attack hardly counted as sleep, though the fear of being murdered any time he shut his eyes generally kept him from nodding off.

He found his thoughts drifting to the Greybull warrior, wondering if he had made it out alive or if his corpse now constituted a few million of the dust particles ringing the bunker. Somehow, their common bond, born from Kai's brutal defeat of the revenant mother, had stuck. Magnus would have been happy—reconciliation at last! Though it wasn't enough for Sophus to stick around when Kai charged the God-engines.

Crazy bastard.

Crazy? Or brave? Without that diversion, things could have gone very differently. Sophus saw something of Roen in the man, and through that lens he saw something of what his daughter might have been attracted to: bravery, energy, a propensity to go willingly into the shit instead of succumbing to self-pity.

Like he had.

So many of them, dead. Bridget. Ingram. Who else? Nine Harpers had shipped out on the rescue mission, including him. They weren't soldiers. They didn't deserve this. And what about the rest of the Greybulls? Between the attacks on Hub and the bunker, they were dropping off at an alarming rate. It felt like a shitty race to see which clan was going to die out first.

Then there were the vehicles. Sophus winced as he counted

off everything they had lost since this endeavor began. Every AARV was the culmination of years of hard scavenging. Without recovery vehicles, there was no salvage. Without salvage, there was no Clan Harper. And the Ironclads were irreplaceable.

Sophus felt the loss of his people, but it was muted, stuffed under layers of pragmatism. He scanned his thoughts like a machine, looking for grief, maybe hidden behind a veil of shock, but he kept coming back with logistics. Anna had always given him a hard time for being robotic, for "stuffing down his feelings." He could never explain to his wife that, yes, he had emotions, he just wasn't controlled by them. Even when she lay dying, when Sophus held his squirming newborn daughter in his hands, when Julia was screaming with hunger, there was no time for grief—

A burst of static shouted from his headset, sending him momentarily swerving. Then another, and another.

"Motherfucker!"

"Everything okay?" came Lafayette over the radio.

Sophus blinked, squinting out his tiny window. Julia was still there, mewling, begging for comfort. He gripped the wheel hard, forcing himself back to the present.

Gray. Gray, as far as he could see—which was not very far, whatever the false horizon of the Deadlands suggested. Still, he stared until the nothingness wiped the painful memories from his mind.

"Do you see anything out there?" he croaked.

A faint shudder resonated around him as the sergeant pivoted his guns over and around his side of the APC. "Negative, we're still a few hours out according to the chronometer. Do you need a break?"

A few hours... May as well be a few weeks in this place.

"I have to piss."

In truth, he had to take a shit. But given the nature of the onboard facilities, that could wait.

"Deckard showed you the facilities?"

"Yeah…" Sophus eyed the plastic hose clipped to his seat, adjacent a rusted metal bedpan. It was an atrocity compared to what his clan offered. Onboard toilets were a critical component of long-distance travel, and he was proud to say he had a big hand in their development. His ill-fated AARV sported a convertible seat with actual plumbing and even a pressure-driven bidet. It was magical. "Keep in mind I've only got one good arm. We'll have to stop."

"Right. Controlled deceleration. Stratton's touch-and-go back here. And make sure you stay on course."

A few degrees off and they were liable to get lost. Lost meant dead, or worse. Stopping was always the worst part of travel through the Deadlands. At least while moving, you could distract yourself with other things—vehicular noises, chatter. But as soon as you stopped, the nothingness came for you. He hated it.

Sophus brought the APC to a halt, grimacing as it jerked backward at the last. A muffled curse came through the tiny doorway.

He wriggled his way out of his zipper, fumbling to maneuver his suddenly very anxious penis into the urination tube. An initial sigh of relief broke into a curse as the ochre liquid sprayed right back at him, dribbling all over the thin vinyl seat cover.

"Son of a bitch!"

"Don't forget the valve," Lafayette said.

He had forgotten the valve.

Sophus reached under the tube and twisted it, then drained himself while cursing the whole time. He thought he heard laughter from the crew cabin.

Lafayette continued the conversation after they got going

again. Sophus didn't know if it was because the soldier was worried about his new driver's capabilities or if he was trying to keep his mind from drifting too far outside—or back to the bunker, to the scene of his crime. Killing one of his own had clearly affected the man, corroding some of the usual impassivity he wore like a shield. There was also the matter of Sergeant Deckard, who seemed worse for wear before they even disembarked. The young man clearly didn't relish the idea of another journey through the gray. Talking was a welcome distraction—for everyone.

Importantly, Sophus got caught up on current events. This second mission was officially sanctioned by Bastion's government, which sounded like a complicated bureaucracy rife with mismatched priorities. He hadn't been surprised to see the foreigners when his so-called rescue party arrived at the bunker. If anything, he had expected the whole thing to be a trap and to see the battle walker chassis loaded up onto an enemy flatbed. He had not expected diplomacy. They even sent a civilian negotiator, who was presumably on her way back to Hub now with Julia and their lieutenant. Their vice chancellor was supposed to invite a delegation back to Bastion for formal negotiations, that's all Lafayette knew. Sophus was now that delegation.

The prior bunker mission—somehow arranged by Clan Ramirez, a mystery that continued to elude him—had been a test to make sure their people didn't murder each other on the spot. There were legitimately no conditions other than an eventual report of their findings, which Julia and Mace had apparently not disclosed. The engineering bays had been resealed, and Lafayette's crewmates said nothing about it, other than Deckard muttering at one point about how much of a waste of time the whole operation had been.

Sophus had been allowed to retrieve some of his own stashed

gear before they left. He didn't have any, of course, but it was an opportunity to scoop up as much of his daughter's work as possible. He grabbed a pair of ancient hard drives and an archival-quality notebook. The hide-bound tome catalogued necessary components missing from the prototype battle walker, along with reassembly analyses. Julia's penmanship was pristine, her lines as straight as a machine's. His fingers recalled the hand-drawn diagrams with awe, each fragmentary schematic a promise of the future. It was beautiful work, even better than her mother's.

He had also retrieved a few of Julia's personal items: an ornate silver comb passed down by Anna, a faded scarf he had clumsily knitted when she was a teenager, and, most importantly, her sniper rifle. The ridiculously long weapon garnered raised eyebrows from everyone aboard, but Lafayette ultimately allowed it. This was the balance of his daughter. But she was okay. She came into the world too early, to a useless father, and had thrived; she could survive anything. She was probably back home by now.

She had to be.

Sophus tried to focus on the nothing ahead of him. Each time he blinked too long, he saw the overseer's shadow hovering over him, ready to murder him in his sleep.

"What about the priests?" he asked over the comms.

Lafayette didn't respond immediately. The sergeant hadn't divulged any more details on that matter since they left the scene of the crime. Dead air turned to whispers in the absence of conversation. Sophus stretched his jaw from side to side in hopes of quieting the torrent in his ears.

"The one I... killed was Overseer Rayos, a high-ranking priest of one of our orders."

Sophus sighed with relief at the man's voice. He was resilient —maybe more than most, given recent experience—but he knew he was bumping up against his limits. The Deadlands claimed everyone in the end.

"Orders?" he asked.

"It's complicated."

The priests had come in an armored car—sleek, deadly, parked around the corner from the blasted bunker door. Sophus immediately recognized it as the same one that accompanied the APC on first contact. No one had exited the vehicle that time; it merely watched them as its turret cycled between targets. They had siphoned its fuel before leaving, but Deckard reported the vehicle otherwise empty. Valmor didn't go near it.

"It was unusual," Lafayette continued.

Sophus snorted. "Unusual? I'd say it's fucking unusual to have one of your own crew try to kill you."

"Not just that," Lafayette said. "I don't know how your people operate, but priests of... that sort don't normally work with us. With the military."

Sophus could tell the man was thinking hard, probably way outside the bounds of his codified parameters. It seemed Bastion had problems of its own. Problems neither he nor the Union needed.

"So, are you expecting trouble when we get there?" Sophus asked. The deep unease he felt when they'd first embarked on this journey returned in full. They could be barreling right into a trap.

"We'll see..."

Not the answer he was hoping for.

They continued the rest of the way in silence. The eventual transition between Deadlands and regular shitty wasteland was fuzzy, like always. The landscape simply changed at some point, transitioning from endless gray to a barren charcoal lowland. They were traveling along the faded remains of an ancient highway, bracketed by a lifeless spill of rubble and jutting stalagmites of volcanic rock. Occasionally, the calcified remains of ancient forest crept out from the wastes, but the blighted trees were long dead and showed no sign of resurrection. An ugly, abbreviated mountain range lumbered from the northern horizon. Huddling within its shadow was a speck of man-made linearity: Bastion.

Sophus's gut clenched. Humanity scattered far and wide after the War against Hell, but why come here? It felt like the ass end of the world, his own home impossibly far away.

A crack of static came over the radio, followed by a robotic-sounding female voice. "This is Bastion Control. Identify yourself."

Sophus swallowed nervously. Would he ever show up somewhere announced?

Lafayette took over. "This is Black Watch One-Two, Sergeant First Class Lafayette in command."

"Hold for instructions."

He hated not being able to see the rest of his crew. Was Lafayette nervous?

His crew. The reality of his situation still hadn't sunk in. At some point his mind was going to crumble worse than his body already had.

"Sergeant Lafayette," the voice continued. "Report location of Lieutenant Baptiste."

"MIA," Lafayette responded, clearly expecting this question.

Sophus wondered who was sitting on the other side of the radio. The sergeant's tone was all business.

"Report location of Third Platoon."

This seemed to trip up Lafayette. Sophus had no idea what they were talking about.

"Say again, Control?" Lafayette asked.

"Lieutenant Gerard's platoon was dispatched to your location this morning."

Dispatched to our location?

A click in his headset indicated Lafayette switching to internal comms.

"Sophus?"

"I didn't see shit. Trust me, I wish I had."

"You're sure?"

"Of course I'm sure. How many vehicles in a platoon?"

"Three, normally."

Three. Three bursts of static. Had they somehow passed each other without anyone noticing?

Fucking Deadlands.

Lafayette switched back to radio. "Negative, Control."

"Hold for instructions."

An eternity passed while they waited for a response, still barreling ahead. Bastion grew larger, betraying little behind its massive curtain wall. They could have been preparing artillery on the other side for all he knew.

The operator blipped back on. "Approach through South-west-3 and proceed directly to Central Command."

"Acknowledged, Control. Southwest-3."

The signal disconnected. Not exactly a warm welcome.

"Are we good, Sergeant?" Sophus asked.

Lafayette breathed deeply, sending a wave of static rolling through his headset. No one else spoke. They were all listening in, waiting for the answer.

"I guess we're about to find out."

Alexis Levesque, Archon of the Church, Shepherd of Bastion, was trembling. Rage, fear, insecurity—it all tumbled through his veins, leaving him senseless. The journey back from Central Command had not cleared his mind. If anything, the sight of Mother Rebekah disoriented him more over time, as though her simple presence was a slow-acting poison in his blood. Benoit had said she disappeared underground after his failed assassination attempt.

Underground.

What lay beneath his own city that could so invigorate someone such as her? Maybe Cathedral was already in their midst. Or something worse.

Her eyes...

Bowls of incense smoldered around the room, but instead of imparting calm, they asphyxiated. He waved annoyedly at the choking spirals.

"Where is Gauthier?" Benoit asked impatiently.

They were sitting at the circular table of ecclesiastical governance: Alexis at the head, Ascendant Blake two seats to his left, and Benoit at the opposite end. Ascendant Gauthier had been summoned but was thus far absent. The other seats remained empty, uninvited. Alexis tried not to linger on them. Secrecy between the Church and the Legion was bad enough, an emergent rot; if it became habit within the Ascendancy, it could destroy them all. Clermont's spot seemed particularly dark.

"Patience, Jean-Paul," he muttered.

The white-haired man bristled at the familiarity, tugging at his chasuble. He seemed less composed than usual, maybe even a little frantic.

Ascendant Blake was silent. He stared forward, occasionally mumbling something under his breath and frowning. The big man was the only one of those summoned who had not yet met the revenant mother prior to their confrontation with the lord commander. That altercation would have been bad enough without her bursting from the shadows like a conjured demon. Who knows what she had already whispered to the head of the Legion. The same poison that coursed through Alexis now was no doubt corrupting Lucas, eating away at his heart.

Benoit.

Blasted Benoit and his zealotry. They should have waited until the report came back from Black Watch before moving on her. All they had to do was wait for war to show up on their doorstep. Aleph's deployment had been imminent, but now it was all at risk.

One of the great doors opened, depositing a harried Ascendant Gauthier. Like Benoit, he seemed less composed than usual. How strange those two were, so similar and yet ever at odds. Even by appearance, Benoit as pale and white-haired as a ghost while Gauthier was as black as night. The tall man sat himself adjacent his counterpart, neither of them acknowledging the other. Blake said nothing.

"Apologies, Holiness. I came as fast as I could."

"Indeed," Alexis replied. "Let us begin then, this informal conclave of the Ascendancy to discuss the matter at hand."

Blake snorted derisively.

"The witch returns?" Gauthier asked, leaning in.

"You know full well she returns," Benoit snapped.

Gauthier was rubbing unconsciously at his finger. Alexis noticed the ascendant's ring of governance was missing but set aside his curiosities; there were enough questions already and little time.

"I need to know exactly what you all know," Alexis said. "What she told you, as pertains to the plan or otherwise." He gestured at Benoit. "Begin."

Ascendant Benoit's nails dug into the table. The man hated appearing anything less than his colleagues, and recent events had cast aspersions on his capabilities. "We moved to eliminate her. As *agreed*, following delivery of the message to Cathedral."

Blake shifted in his chair as Benoit reiterated their plan—Aleph's plan. The Orders Militant and Somatic had voted against it, but Xavier was a loyal servant of the Church. Maybe more so than the other ascendants present today. He would comply.

"She managed to escape the Grand Citadel," Benoit continued, "and was subsequently rescued by Gauthier's prodigy."

Gauthier's smooth skin folded into a scowl. "You mean the one who's cult you supposedly burned out."

Benoit scowled in return. Blake grumbled impatiently, ready to smash the men's heads together any second.

"Enough," Alexis interjected. "What words were exchanged before she escaped?"

"What His Holiness is trying to ask," Ascendant Blake cut in, "is if you gave away all of our secrets as part of your premature victory monologue."

"I'm not an idiot," retorted Benoit. "I merely sought to put her in her place."

"You should have let me send my adepts," Gauthier said.

Alexis shivered within his robes. The Order Occult was a uniquely opaque subdivision of the Church. It had been designed as such to protect the sanctity of the other orders while carrying out its "essential work." Felix Gauthier had led the order since before Alexis was archon and probably would long after. The enigmatic man's cherished servants—the adepts that guarded his library and chambers—were no less mysterious than he was.

"Are they immune to lead?" Benoit asked, gesturing at Blake.

"You left my paladins little choice," Blake grumbled.

"Enough!" Alexis yelled again, slapping his palm down on the table. They were like children, perpetually squabbling. For a moment he regretted not inviting the other ascendants. Though the men before him held the most agency in dealing with this mess, there was a delicate balance between the seven orders. Absent any one point of the heptagram, order teetered into chaos. "Gauthier, what of you?"

Benoit's hands clenched as he restrained his usual retort.

"She meant to murder me," Gauthier began, "as has already been reported to Your Holiness."

"And yet you somehow swayed her," Alexis said.

"With what in trade?" Benoit snapped.

Gauthier sat still, overly long fingers steepled upon the table. *Where is his ring? Did she take it?*

His expression hadn't changed through the entire conversation and betrayed no more now than before. "I offered to help her get out of the city," he said. A flicker of rage crossed Benoit's face. "A favor to us all, since we seem otherwise incapable of ridding ourselves of the heretic."

Blake snorted, a grim smile at the edges of his mouth. "He's not wrong."

"And yet she stayed," Alexis countered.

"Yes…" Gauthier's emerald-green eyes pierced him. Something shifted in his gut, dislodged by the man's stare. "She said she had unfinished business."

Benoit licked his lips, his anger regressing into fear. He looked suddenly haunted, even more pale than normal.

"Ascendant Benoit?" Alexis prompted.

"We received reports yesterday, from District Thirteen. Strange light, inhuman screams. We're still following up."

Inhuman…

Her eyes had been different this time. They were always inhuman, celestial, reflecting heavens that no longer existed. But at the hospital, they had been even… worse. She radiated power, more so than when she had first come to him. He could feel it. He was terrified by it.

Alexis turned to Blake. "What of the Legion?"

"Am I a spy?" Blake asked, incredulous.

"You are out of order, Ascendant Blake," Benoit said.

"Order," Blake repeated, huffing. "This is no conclave." The big man shuffled in his seat, his armor and the narrow cushion suddenly incongruous. Alexis waited, knowing the man knew more than he would ever let on about the movements of his military counterparts. "They sent a rescue mission. What remains of the Black Watch."

"Timeline?"

"Maybe two days, there and back. Assuming nothing is waiting for them."

Two days. How far would Mother Rebekah's poison travel in that time? The Church was her enemy now. Would it also become the Legion's?

"We should move now," Benoit said.

No one argued this time.

"How do we justify it?" Blake asked.

"We tell the citizenry," Benoit said.

Alexis recoiled.

"Not of our plan, of course, but a portion of truth: the enemy in the west, battle walkers marching on our territory. We will be vindicated when the rescue party returns empty handed."

The truth. Alexis plucked vigorously at his chin, anxious to clear-cut the few hairs that remained. Each graying bristle felt like the withered residue of a lie, preceding him wherever he went, for all to see.

"How do you know they'll be empty handed?" Blake asked, squinting across the table.

Alexis looked up from his malaise. Benoit's eyes darted between him and the head of the Order Militant. His mouth remained open for a moment before responding—too long a moment.

"My agents spotted two of Cathedral's so-called God-engines en route. Our men are brave, but those are not winning odds."

Our men. The words sounded insincere—revolting even—coming from the ascendant's mouth.

Blake did not seem satisfied. "What of the heathen forces? The Scavrats?"

"Inconsequential," said Benoit, but his usual tone of confidence was marred by fear. It was subtle, but Alexis knew the man well enough. He cleared his throat noisily. "In any case, we will know soon enough."

"Yes," Alexis muttered. "Aleph and I have discussed the details—as confusing as they are—of reviving the balance of his platoon. In truth, the process has already begun."

"You're sure you can trust it?" Gauthier asked. "Such a mind—"

"I am as certain of Aleph's loyalty as I am of all of yours. Everything he knows is by my hand."

Gauthier looked unconvinced but shrugged, leaning back into his chair.

"What of the Legion forces stationed outside our base?" asked Blake.

Alexis turned to his colleague. Even now, so close to the brink, the man was seeking an out. Compromise. It was admirable. Futile, but admirable.

"The Order Militant will mobilize, as it did at the genesis of our great nation. The citadel district will be cordoned off. The remainder of your men will march with us as we accompany Aleph from the gates."

"Into their cannons," Blake said, dubious, though clearly moved by the invocation of his order's essential legacy.

"God will be with us." As would the greatest war machines of ages past and present. "The Legion will stand down. Two battle walkers will stand guard at the Grand Citadel. Two more will be dispatched to hunt down and destroy our attackers as a sign of good faith."

"Good faith," Blake muttered, looking down at his hands. They rubbed absently at the point before him, gingerly tracing the inlaid numeral *IV* that represented his noble order.

"So that the lord commander does not think we are attempting a coup," Alexis returned.

Blake looked up. "Aren't we?"

A tremor ran up Alexis's back. The room was silent, all eyes on him. His dreams would be realized: Aleph and his brothers unleashed, the promise of more battle walkers, a foreign enemy beaten back, and most importantly, the Church attaining true parity with the Legion.

Parity? Or superiority?

The fallout would be severe. But it was necessary. He could

handle it from a position of power. Assuming Mother Rebekah did not intervene.

He looked at the handful of men seated around him. Their participation was crucial.

"We must prepare for chaos," he said, catching each ascendant's eye, "so that order can rise."

SOPHUS
INTO THE DEN

Lafayette had directed them to a massive portcullis cut into the city's patchwork curtain wall. The defenses looked nothing like Cathedral's, whose geometric, crenelated towers and pleated concrete were as meticulous as the sisterhood itself. This was the product of raw necessity. Uneven lines of repurposed ruin, scavenged stone, brick, and concrete were layered into the wall like geological strata, cataloguing the lifespan of a civilization painstakingly resurrected. Bastion and the Union seemed more alike than not on first impression.

The portcullis opened into a narrow barbican with a second set of iron bars on the interior side. They loitered there, under a threatening array of murder holes, for what seemed an eternity, stewing in their own anxiety. Sophus eyed the facilities again as his nervousness moved into his bladder.

"Processing," Deckard had called it, joining them on the comms now that the sight of home had stabilized his mood. But no one ever emerged to process them. Instead, the second gate eventually opened on its own, ushering them into a subterranean roadway. The sun set behind them as they descended belowground.

Sophus rasped out a chuckle as he navigated his unlikely crew through the sparsely lit tunnel. It was all too familiar. Lowly Scavrats were never permitted into Cathedral proper; they transacted within a series of cordoned-off trade and engineering stations segregated from the rest of the Matriarch's glorious civilization. Deprived of the option to return home, he had hoped at least to see something of this *other* civilization—one that supposedly wanted them around—but it appeared that their invitation into Bastion did not extend to the surface. The similarity of his surroundings to Hub imparted little comfort. This was an unfamiliar den, potentially rife with snakes.

Eventually, they emerged into a tight, low-ceilinged vehicle hangar. Sophus instinctively ducked his head down as they exited the tunnel, while Lafayette and Deckard rolled their cannons from the Crusader's roof onto its sides. Several other APCs were stationed there, but again no personnel.

"Park in the first open bay," said Lafayette.

"Where is everyone?" Deckard muttered, scanning the deck from his side.

"Don't know," replied their stoic commander. "Deckard and I will check it out. The rest of you stay here."

Sophus situated their vehicle between two painted yellow lines and squirmed in his seat while the sergeants exited out the back. He craned his head around the too-small window but saw nothing of note. It was getting hotter. The shit that had previously calcified in his bowels started to stir as he moved around, blood returning to his organs. He looked again at the vehicular bed pan and cursed his life.

"Everyone out," called Lafayette from the rear of the vehicle.

Finally.

Sophus pried himself from the cockpit, grimacing as his bum shoulder caught on the portal to the passenger compartment. Deckard was helping Valmor remove the stretchered private. He staggered after them, resorting to hand and knees by the end. The air beyond reeked of diesel and sweat.

Two men stood opposite their vehicle—red robed. Sophus froze, not knowing if these were the good kind of priests or the murder-you-while-unconscious kind.

"Father Andrite," called Valmor, recognizing one of them.

Andrite.

The name was familiar. But he seemed to be... blind? A broad strip of fabric the same color as his robes was tied over his eyes. Above it protruded a matt of orangey-red hair. Whatever had happened to the holy man, it explained his absence on the Bastionites' return mission.

Valmor stopped in his tracks, noting some minuscule adornment on Andrite's robe. "Or should I say Reverend Father. Apologies, Your Grace." He bowed his head slightly.

"No need, Father Valmor. It is good to see you."

See you. Odd turn of phrase for a blind man, yet no one seemed to notice. The priest turned his head toward Sophus. Sighted or not, he could feel the holy man's gaze burning into his soul. Goosebumps flickered to life along his bare arms.

"We meet again," Andrite said.

Stratton started coughing. Sophus took the opportunity to peel himself away from the priest's attention. Their wounded private looked like shit. His complexion had yellowed significantly since they left the bunker, and rivers of sweat were running down the shrapnel-chiseled grooves of his face.

"We need to get your man to the infirmary," said the second priest.

Lafayette turned to Deckard. "Deckard, you stay here with Stratton. We'll continue on to Central Command."

Deckard nodded and worked alongside the chaplain to move Stratton to a wheeled gurney stationed alongside the lot, then hurried him down a dimly lit hallway.

Andrite's peaceable composure dissolved as his colleague's footsteps faded, his forehead wrinkling with concern. Lafayette shuffled back and forth, seemingly as uncomfortable as Sophus under the man's scrutiny.

"Where is Lieutenant Baptiste?" he asked.

The interrogation was starting early. Sophus wasn't surprised—the bond that this priest shared with his lieutenant had been evident. Hopefully Lafayette had not delivered his ass here as a sacrifice.

"We were attacked," Lafayette said.

Andrite's posture stiffened, his head tilting toward Sophus. "Attacked…"

Lafayette shook his head. "Not them. Cathedral."

Sophus's asshole unclenched.

"The westerners. So it's true," Andrite muttered.

"Say again?" Lafayette asked.

Andrite steepled his hands over his mouth, then intertwined them over his chest. His knuckles were white as chalk.

"Battle walkers?" the priest asked. "As the lord commander warned us about?"

"Yes," Lafayette said. "Two of them."

"Your news precedes you," Andrite said quietly.

Something wasn't right.

"Precedes us?" asked Sophus.

"Earlier today, His Holiness made an announcement, a public broadcast to the whole city. An attack on our territory. We are at war."

"War," Lafayette repeated, eyes widening.

"We just got here," Sophus said. "How could anyone know we were attacked?"

The foreigners exchanged awkward glances. Sophus looked around again, wondering at the emptiness of the place. Something was up, something well out of the ordinary. Whatever unity may have once existed here was fractured.

"I..." Andrite began but trailed off.

"Where is the garrison?" Lafayette asked.

Andrite lowered his head as though praying, fingers still intertwined. "A situation has developed. The Order Militant has been deployed, and all ecclesiastical personnel have been recalled to the citadel district. The Legion has moved into the rest of the city."

"What?" Valmor asked.

Lafayette squinted, struggling to understand. "But you're still here."

Andrite nodded. "His Eminence, Ascendant Clermont, countermanded the Holy Father's decree."

"Countermanded?" Valmor asked, aghast.

"He directed all chaplains to"—Andrite paused, clearly pained by the recall—"follow our hearts. He dropped out of contact thereafter."

"God save us," Valmor whispered, crossing his arms over his chest.

"Most of us remained at our posts, with the Legion, but the choice is yours, Father Valmor."

Valmor swallowed loudly, turning to Lafayette with a knowing look. The sergeant's eyes quivered with indecision. The two men were so similar: rigid, by the book. The clusterfuck at hand was doing a number on them. Sophus shifted his weight from one leg to the other, unable to find his equilibrium. The pressure of the low-ceilinged vehicle hangar was exacting a toll on his eardrums.

Finally, Lafayette shook his head. "We've been directed to Central Command," he said, clearly anxious to remove himself to familiar territory. And reluctant to divulge whatever betrayal had occurred at the bunker.

The ceiling lights flickered, dipping them all into darkness for a second before returning with a loud buzz. Sophus squeaked out a panicked fart, clenching his buttocks immediately after. Whatever was happening here, he needed to find a toilet—fast.

"Yes. There's a powered car waiting for you at the substation."

Or not.

Fuck this place.

"Will you be okay, Reverend Father?" the sergeant asked, genuine concern in his voice.

Andrite straightened, regaining his prior composure. "Yes. And we'll take care of your man, Sergeant."

Lafayette hesitated, eyeing the Crusader as though considering abandoning this place and getting the fuck out instead. Sophus would not have argued. The sergeant turned from Andrite to his reduced crew. A strange trio indeed.

"Let's go."

"Wait," Sophus said. "I need to get my gear."

"It'll be safe here," Lafayette said, moving off.

Sophus backed up toward the APC.

The sergeant stopped and turned, jaw twitching in irritation. "You have my word. The lord commander was very clear on this."

Sophus glanced back at the vehicle and the treasures that lay within. There was enough information there to make progress on battle walker tech even if they never made it back to Bunker 23. Assuming the Deadlands hadn't already swallowed it whole. If it was lost—

"Now, Sophus," Lafayette ordered.

Sophus winced.

Not your fucking soldier.

His hands were tied, in any case. He was in a foreign den now. He just hoped the snakes weren't poisonous.

———

Sophus gripped the railing adjacent his metal seat as they clattered their way down the subway tunnel. An overworked diesel engine chugged behind him, driving them deeper into the den. The Metro was the beachhead that allowed Bastion's ancestors to take back the ruined city above. Deckard had bragged about it while they waited in processing—justifiably; it was impressive. Hub was replete with tunnels and subterranean transitways, but nothing compared to this. Importantly, the substations that connected the network to the Legion's facilities also included latrines, though the emptiness in his bowels was quickly refilling with anxiety.

His mind wandered, sedated by the rhythm of their movement along the tracks. Julia might be back at Hub by now, along with her own mismatched crew. What awaited them there? He had left his home in chaos after the appearance of the revenant mother, and her subsequent beheading.

Kai, you crazy bastard.

There would be a price to pay for Clan Harper's actions, which his daughter was now on the hook for in his absence. He cursed under his breath. The priest had said they were going to war with Cathedral, but who was the Matriarch after, Bastion or the Union? Hub could lock down if it needed to, just as these people had, but they wouldn't last long on their own, not anymore. They had become too dependent on the Matriarch. And if she was truly in it to punish them, her God-engines could just park outside their home indefinitely and pick off expeditions as they emerged.

His eyes grew heavy as the trauma just past dragged him into the abyss of exhaustion.

God-engines... They should have been called demon-engines. Infinitely black, like the void of the night, empty heavens opening into Hell. Carapaces gleaming, entrapping his mind in interleaving layers of perfect, impenetrable geometry.

The one that had spoken—*spoken*, of all things!—had glared at him. He could feel its malign presence, somewhere behind its glowing red eye. Human? Machine? Something in between. All-seeing as they tried to swarm it. The fury of its guns, power unseen since before the World War. Exterminating them like vermin—

"Sophus, we're here."

Sophus jolted awake, wincing as his neck whiplashed backward. Both his arms were numb, the left already inept from his shoulder down and the right now joining it thanks to nodding off against the car's railing. Stretching against pins and needles, he wiped the sleep from his eyes.

They were surrounded.

A veritable army of dark-skinned soldiers was stationed all around them, some on the tracks, some above in defensive emplacements on a much larger substation to their right. Concrete barricades had been set out on both sides of the tracks. Valmor squirmed beside him, one hand tightly gripping his Bible, whispering prayers under his breath. All eyes were on the two of them: traitor priest and alien.

Lafayette was standing at attention before another man, who stood at least a head taller than the sergeant and two taller than Sophus. They were exchanging tense words, interspersed with suspicious glances his way from the commanding officer—apparently none of them were to be trusted.

Finally, Lafayette returned to the car. "We have clearance. Let's go."

Valmor rose immediately, eager to extract himself from what must have been quite the role reversal. Sophus lumbered after him, doing his best to walk in a straight line despite the swaying of his uncooperative limbs. Curious looks turned to disdain—*look here at this troglodyte, emerged from his cave.* Someone spat behind him. Murmured epithets followed in their wake—heavily accented but universally recognizable by their tone.

He kept his head down, snarling at the floor. Whatever budding fellowship had developed on the drive back withered under the onslaught.

Fuck these people.

They may as well have been revenant sisters. Arrogance followed those who lived in the sun, as though they alone merited the right to civilization. Whatever came of this arrangement, the Union would always be alone. And they would outlast every single one of these self-righteous pricks.

Lafayette led them through the defensive cordon, down a series of broad tunnels, until they emerged at another nexus, also guarded. One of the guardsmen gestured for them to follow, leading them through the broad entranceway.

The noise hit him like a hammer. It looked like a hospital, with a series of makeshift workstations crammed between bays —a temporary command station, maybe. People everywhere, speaking into corded terminals, interfacing with messengers and soldiers alike. An intricate painted map six meters square hovered over the scene, assembled from dozens of tiles and swarmed over by a handful of cartographers. It must have been the city above, subdivided into numerous districts and pockmarked with magnetic figurines. Sophus toggled on his analytical brain, scanning as much detail as he could for later recall, while they wound their way around the maelstrom.

The monstrous guardsman halted before what looked like another temporary structure: a set of framed metal panels forming a room-sized box with a single door. He turned to Lafayette, arms crossing over his chest. There was a look in his eye that didn't belong to someone so formidable, a look of fear. "Prepare yourself, Sergeant." He nodded to Valmor. "Father."

Ignoring Sophus, the soldier knocked in a particular pattern, waited for a muffled acknowledgment, then opened the door and stood to the side. They walked in, single file: Lafayette, Valmor, then him. The room was lit from above, but its corners were shrouded in shadow. There was something off about the light. Though it shone yellow, it became iridescent—palpable— as it descended.

Lafayette snapped to attention. "Lord Commander."

An elderly man was seated on a hospital bed that had been converted into a workspace, bracketed by a second stout man on one side and—

Sophus's throat clenched. The world fell out from under him. He swayed, suddenly unsure if he was facing forward or up. The sounds beyond the room evaporated, consumed by a growling surge of tinnitus. There was only him, standing—or lying, he couldn't tell. And a pair of purple eyes, inset into the void, supplanting the heavens. Beams of gold and silver coiled around his soul like a colossal snake. Choking him. Ushering his spine from his body.

Greybull bodies were everywhere. The revenant mother murdered them all. He had never seen death before, and it came in spades. His mother tried to shield his eyes, but the horror burned past them, into his soul. He wanted to breathe, but his lungs wouldn't expand. He wanted to run, but his legs wouldn't move. They were trapped, in her presence.

The Chiefslayer was here.

Death was here.

"Oh fuck..."

Everyone had huddled around the radio, waiting as the channel hissed and crackled. The guardsmen present cradled their rifles, sweating with uncertainty. George was seated beside him, reviewing the latest batch of district statuses, printed on color-coded plastic cards and delivered by courier from the Situation Room.

The daily news was due any second, and with it a sense of what the future held. Chancellor Maddox had informed Lucas in advance that her office would not be broadcasting today. Instead, the address would be coming from the Grand Citadel, by request of the Ascendancy. Normally, daily broadcasts were delivered by Parliament, but *normal* was far from sight. As was Central Command. Lucas wished he could detach himself from this place and govern like a proper lord commander, but his sputtering heart demanded otherwise.

He caressed the handle of his revolver, awkwardly, as the holster pushed up around his waist. The IV tube in his bare arm flexed with each stroke, pinching his wrinkled flesh, its incessant drip fraying his already tattered nerves. He wriggled in the bed, craning over to look at the crank and confirming for the millionth time it was as upright as possible. If a second heart attack didn't kill him, his low back would.

A long tone buzzed from the radio, followed by two more, then a synthetic-sounding voice. "Good day, citizens. We interrupt our regular programming to bring you a special announcement from His Holiness, the Archon. Please stand by for an important message."

As promised. The radio clicked as it switched to another source, presumably Alexis's office.

"Brave citizens of Bastion. It is with regret but also great hope that I bring you the news of the day.

"We have ever been vigilant in our daily toil: workers and servants of the Triarchy alike, aspiring to the day of redemption when God will grant us his mercy. For generations we have rebuilt our holy city, fortifying ourselves against Hell as we await the return of the stars in the heavens.

"Our lot is not an easy one. Each district bears its purpose, as they have always done. And within each district, each man, woman, and child strives and struggles. For the People. For the future. A future that is now at risk.

"Our enemies have ever been known: the beasts of Hell that beat upon our walls and their faithless minions who lurk within them. Throughout our short history, the hammer and shield have kept us safe. But today I must inform you of another enemy, a new threat from the west.

"As we know from the chronicles of the past, humanity fractured on the close of the Great War. God spoke to our progenitors then, and those who heeded his word—his promise of redemption—traveled east, to Bastion. Those who rejected it fled west. We thought them lost, physically and spiritually. Sadly, we were wrong.

"Two days ago, we were attacked by these very heretics of legacy. A vital outpost, essential to our self-defense apparatus.

The attack was savage and unprovoked, and it is with a heavy heart that I reveal there were no survivors. We do not know our new enemy's motives, but we may judge them by their actions. In attacking us, the People, they do the work of the Adversary. They mean to drag our holy nation with them into Hell, to subjugate prophecy.

"I regret that my words today will bring fear to your hearts, maybe even despair. But the Church has ever been the guardian of Bastion, and I declare that we shall overcome this challenge as we have all others. And we shall not do it alone. God sees his people. God loves his people. And God has delivered to his people a weapon with which to repel this new enemy.

"There have been rumors of movement in the eastern storm wall. These rumors are true. As the clouds shifted, a great gift was revealed: an arsenal, left for us in state from the Old World, preserved from the sundering for our time of need. The Order Militant rises to the task, as it has always done, now wielding the most powerful weapons on Earth. Our vengeance wakes and is being deployed at this very moment, both to pursue the enemy and to bolster our defenses. You will learn more of this in the coming days. In the meantime, we must do what we have always done: work, pray, prepare, endure. For we are at war."

———

The archon's actions were unprecedented. After failing to place his man in "temporary" command of the Legion, Alexis had instead directed Blake to take control of their shared facility beneath the Northern Ridge. Paladins had moved in with overwhelming force, displacing both the platoon stationed on watch over Aleph and the armored troop on the other side of the exit. It was a bloodless confrontation, thank God, but Lucas seethed, nonetheless. The Legion had been expelled from the citadel district and everything north of it. He was blind, in addition to laid up, though Alexis's announcement confirmed his suspicions: the battle walkers to be released, not just Aleph but its slumbering platoonmates as well.

Every man of the Legion not assigned to wall defense had been deployed, swarming from the Metro to take whatever territory the Order Militant had not already claimed. As it stood, the Church controlled a third of the city. Parliament, as ever, was caught in the middle. The chancellor was doing her best to maintain order, but between the archon's speech and their counter-mobilizations, the citizenry was on edge.

Whatever justification Lucas's former friend and counterpart in the Triarchy might present, there was no going back from this.

A sharp knock on the door roused him, reverberating along the room's flimsy paneled walls. George crouched toward the rifle stowed at his side, tense until the designated pattern completed.

Mother Rebekah stood silently in her corner, like a ghoul. The enigmatic woman had not tarried far since the Church's stillborn coup, as eager as he for news from their second mission. When word came of Black Watch's return, she had installed herself into his temporary office. The space was far too small. Though she was tucked into the shadows, her presence was all-consuming.

"Come," Lucas called, thankful for an imminent airing out.

The door opened, depositing SFC Lafayette, a chaplain identified as Father Valmor, and...

So, this was a Scavrat.

The epithet fit. Everything about the man spoke of the cave dwellers' impoverishment. His complexion was almost as cadaverous as the revenant mother's, pale hair the hue of wilted straw framing a narrow face. He hobbled with an uncertain gait, swaying from one side to the other as though unused to walking on a straight floor. But there was intelligence in his black-rimmed, deep-set eyes—something beyond animal cunning.

The operator had told him there were only four Black Watch on board, plus the foreigner, and no Baptiste. That fore-knowledge did little to prepare him for the sad state of this ragtag crew, or for the unexpected tremor in his chest at the confirmation of his great-nephew's absence. The lot of them stank of smoke and sweat. Lafayette was keeping it together, but just barely. His skin was sallow, his stubbled cheeks hollowed out. The Deadlands spared no one, no matter how resilient.

Mother Rebekah floated from the corner just as the sergeant addressed him, freezing the survivors in place with her gaze. Lucas cursed at his preempted introduction. The Scavrat fell back as though shoved, his already thin body collapsing upon itself. The sinewy man's eyes began to water, filled with pain—and recognition. Lafayette merely gawped. The chaplain's arms were locked over his chest, eyes clamped shut against the sight of her.

George stood, interposing himself between the revenant mother and the fragmented platoon.

Damnable bed! It was a prison.

"Welcome back, men," George said hurriedly. "We appreciate your expediency." He gestured to Mother Rebekah, careful not to stray too far into her sphere. "And we apologize for not being able to warn you in advance. There is much to discuss."

"Too much," Lucas said, attempting to straighten his posture, "in too little time."

Too little time. And too little breath. He had reassumed his armor for the meeting, and it dragged him down with every syllable.

The trio remained speechless.

"I imagine we've all seen things now that our imaginations

have never before suffered. Things that require much explanation. But circumstances require the short version."

He nodded at George.

"This is Mother Rebekah," George said, "an exile from Cathedral. She is the one who warned us about them, and she was instrumental in arranging the meeting between our two peoples." He nodded at the Scavrat, who was dumbstruck.

"But. Sir—" Valmor began.

Lucas raised a hand. "I know, Father. We live in strange times, but she is an ally."

Ally. How many times had he used that word of late? It had become frivolous, nearly meaningless.

"Ally..." It was the Scavrat. He was staring at Mother Rebekah with a mix of terror and abject hatred.

She squinted back at him from the folds of her cowl, unearthly eyes seeking out his face in her memory.

His long fingers retracted into fists. "Murderer."

"You were there," she said. The revenant mother's voice slipped between them like a volcanic wind, scalding every exposed pore of his skin.

"There?" Lucas asked, exchanging a concerned glance with his secretary.

"A regrettable incident from my past," Mother Rebekah explained.

The Scavrat's mouth opened and closed, chewing on her words. Whatever this was, it would have to wait. Lucas gestured for George to continue.

"Did you hear the broadcast?" George asked.

Lafayette shook his head, nervous attention fixed on the man before him. "No, but Father Andrite mentioned a lockdown. And war..."

George nodded. "We need to know the truth of it. What happened at Bunker 23?"

Lucas writhed impatiently in his bed. "Where is my great-nephew?"

Lafayette licked his lips, eyes blinking with fatigue. The man desperately needed sleep; they all did.

"We were ambushed," he started, "just after the Union delegation arrived. Battle walkers, as you had warned. Two of them."

"God save us," Lucas whispered.

Mother Rebekah stiffened, her scrutiny turning to the sergeant.

"I've never seen anything like them," he continued. "Machines, but... something else as well. One of them spoke, demanding our surrender."

The revenant mother's agitation was growing, and with it the pressure in the room. "Did it say its name?" she asked.

Say its name?

Lucas recalled the woman's description of Cathedral's battle walkers. Unlike Aleph, they were supposedly human-piloted—or augmented. Children, unbelievably. An abomination in any case. What would these ones be to her?

"Its name," Lafayette repeated, sharing a confused glance with the Scavrat. The pale man was hunched into a ball, compulsively scratching at his slung arm. "No. Sophus commanded his people to retreat. It was chaos after that. One of the machines attacked. The other seemed to be malfunctioning. We counterattacked—us and the Union—but the losses were severe."

"Philippe," Lucas prompted.

"We got him into one of the Union vehicles, along with the rest of the delegation. They escaped."

Relief fought against fresh panic. A Union vehicle. So very far from home. But alive, presumably.

"Go on," George said.

"The Union forces managed to destroy one of the battle walkers."

One of the room's metal panels popped, dislodging from its frame. The walls were vibrating.

"Destroy," Mother Rebekah said. She was blinking rapidly.

A hint of a smile touched the Scavrat's face—the cold malevolence of victory. These people clearly hated each other.

Destroy, indeed. Meaning, for all of Mother Rebekah's fancy stories, Cathedral's so-called God-engines were as vulnerable as any conventional enemy when enough firepower was brought to bear. Bastion just needed more of that power—under human control.

"We made it back to the bunker before it blew," Lafayette said. "The few of us left."

Black Watch was facing extinction. His most trusted unit, second only to the Central Guard, had suffered greatly of late, between the fiasco at Drill Site 7 and now this.

"What about Third Platoon?" Lucas asked. After much debate, he had finally sent Lieutenant Gerard on a rescue mission. George advised against it, given current circumstances, but his patience had been expended. He should have listened.

Lafayette just shook his head. Somehow, they had missed each other, despite their paths intersecting.

Damn the Deadlands.

Lucas had so many questions. Bullet points—it was how he operated best. This was all going too slow, but every wheezed question from his lips was rewarded with pain.

"You said the battle walkers showed up after the Union," Lucas said.

Lafayette nodded. "Almost immediately."

Lucas peered at the Scavrat—Sophus.

Sophus scowled back. "Don't blame us. You're the ones who got us in this mess."

George stiffened at the man's disrespect, but Lucas waved it away.

He looked to Mother Rebekah, the great engineer of this disastrous plan. The interior of her cowl was aglow with swirling light—purple, gold, silver—appearing and disappearing between blinks. Her mouth remained flat.

"I was discreet," she said.

Sophus straightened out of his misery, inching closer to the revenant mother. The wiry man looked like he might actually assault her, fueled by his hatred. "Discreet. *Discreet*. Is that why the Matriarch sent another one of you to Hub?"

The woman blinked, brow furrowing with momentary surprise, but held her tongue. Everyone's eyes were on them, shocked in various degrees by the nerve of this bedraggled scavenger, laying accusations upon the most powerful person in the room—in Bastion, even.

"Is this some trick to kill us off once and for all?" Sophus asked, taking a small step forward.

George grasped the man by his slung elbow. He opened his mouth to speak, but Lucas raised a finger, silencing him again.

Lucas knew so little of Mother Rebekah and her ilk. All that he knew of Cathedral had been via her own deposition, lent credibility by the assurances of the archon. Was there some other scheme at play here? Trusting her had been a mistake, but it wasn't too late. He wasn't dead yet. If they could just catch her off guard—

The sleeves of Mother Rebekah's mantle rippled in absent winds. Her gaze locked onto his, pupils dilating. He felt his eyes peel open like the rind of a fruit, spilling forth his conspiratorial thoughts.

"Don't let her—" Sophus began.

George turned. The revenant mother blinked.

Lucas fell back in the bed, as though he had been physically lifted. His left hand tingled with the memory of her death grip.

"I have betrayed no one," she said.

"Sir." It was Father Valmor. "If I may."

Lucas shivered. His head felt leaden as he turned to the chaplain, who looked lost without a Bible in his hands. His heart had started pounding again. "Proceed," he said, barely above a whisper.

Father Valmor stepped forward to stand beside his sergeant. "I believe we *are* betrayed," he said, shrinking as the woman's attention turned his way, "but not by her."

Lucas nodded for him to continue.

The chaplain cleared his throat several times before regaining his voice. "Sometime after the attack, we were preparing to leave. I heard a vehicle approach and thought we were rescued. But it was not your men, Lord Commander. It was the Order Sacramental—Overseer Rayos and a subordinate."

"Rayos? Benoit's man?" Lucas asked.

Alexis had made a special request to include the Order Sacramental on their first contact mission, to ensure the integrity of the foreigners' souls. He didn't like it but ultimately conceded, deferring to the presumed wisdom of his counterpart. They had not been invited back. Not by him, at least.

The chaplain's fists were clenched. "They..." He faltered, glancing askance at his sergeant once more before continuing. "They started rearranging the bodies. To make it look like the Scavrats had attacked us, alongside Cathedral."

"What?" Lucas gasped.

"Then they started executing the survivors. All of them."

Lucas had no words, nor any breath to speak them. Though Mother Rebekah hadn't moved, he felt himself pulled toward her, spinning end over end. He clutched the bed rails for support.

"Benoit," she whispered, acid in her voice. "That snake."

"I overheard him saying something about a 'counter-narrative,'" Father Valmor said.

George was staring at the priest, a grim expression on his normally neutral face. "No survivors..."

"God save us," Lucas said.

Lafayette shifted uncomfortably. "This is how Cathedral knew."

"They set us up," Lucas said, aghast at his own words.

Lafayette nodded.

They. The Ascendancy. Alexis.

But how?

He locked eyes with Lafayette. "What did you do?"

Lafayette moved slowly to attention, eyes fixed forward. His lower lip had split and glistened with blood. "We killed them, sir."

Killed them. Hammer against shield. The unthinkable had come to pass after all.

Lucas tried to process it all, but his brain felt saturated, unable to absorb more horror. Bastion was truly at war, from within and without.

Lafayette was shaking. Under normal circumstances, there was only one punishment for murder within the ranks.

"At ease, Sergeant. You did what you had to."

The sergeant relaxed, but only fractionally.

The room had begun to stink of incense. It wafted from the priest, souring his nostrils. Lucas glowered at Valmor, suddenly uncomfortable in the man's presence. "You knew nothing of this prior?"

Valmor's mouth dropped open, his expression contorting between indignance and horror. "Of course not! Lord Commander, we would never..."

Ascendant Clermont—this man's superior—had wanted to

tell Lucas something earlier, something that had been eating at his soul. If Francis had been a part of this, it was possible he didn't know the full extent of the conspiracy.

Does Alexis?

Instigating a war—in whatever putrid manner they had managed—was one thing. But to murder your own people in cold blood... The thought of his old friend stooping to such degradation hurt his heart worse than his failing health.

And what about Blake? The man was many things—bitter, stubborn, power-hungry maybe—but he was no traitor. He would no sooner kill his own people than Clermont would.

Everyone was staring at him, awaiting his command. Grimacing, he forced his enervated legs from the bed, waving away George's assistance as he stood. His revolver slipped back into place at his hip, lending its reassuring weight to his stance.

The sidearm had been passed down to him by his father, and each father prior for five hundred years. It had survived two great wars and the ending of the world, serving those who would see civilization succeed.

Bastion needed him. He could die later.

A rhythmic rapping sounded from the door. George pried his way past the others and cracked it open, listening intently as a guardsman murmured to him from the other side.

"What is it?" Lucas asked.

George closed the door and turned slowly. His complexion had paled considerably. "The Order Militant has opened the northeast gate. Two battle walkers have been deployed within the citadel district."

"Two..."

So it was done. Aleph's platoon had been revived, each of them—what, a clone? Of its "downloaded consciousness"? Whatever madness had taken him, the archon gave his heart and soul to teaching Aleph their ways. Lucas prayed that instruction would carry forward to the machine's siblings.

"You have battle walkers?" Sophus asked, wide-eyed. His question was reflected in the faces of the Black Watch survivors.

Deception was everywhere, by his hand as much as the archon's. Though Lucas had informed his senior staff after the machine's test deployment, the truth of their resident artificial intelligence had been kept from the rank and file. A mistake. All of it, from the very beginning.

"The short version," he had called it. *Lies* by any other definition.

Hurried explanations filled his head, but none were sufficient. He simply nodded.

"We need to get word to Blake," he said, "before this all goes too far. Before he starts another war from which no one will recover."

"You've killed us all," Sophus muttered.

Allies. Dragged from the outset into chaos. He'd be lucky if Bastion didn't have two new enemies by the time this was resolved—assuming they didn't self-destruct first.

"Father Valmor," Lucas continued, ignoring the Scavrat, "I'll need you to return to the Grand Citadel."

Valmor nodded, understanding the unspoken directive. They had to get to Clermont first, assuming Benoit didn't have any more surprises planned. Hopefully, the snake would be lying low in light of the unexpected survivors' arrival. As for the archon—

Mother Rebekah glided past him, sending the hairs of his arms flailing as she moved to leave.

"Mother Rebekah!" he stammered, more excitedly than intended. The woman was a curse, but her vendetta against the Church could be useful. His blood curdled at the private admission, retreating from the numbed claw of his left hand. "The Legion could use you."

She half turned, scalding his flesh with a baleful stare. "You've all used me quite enough." Switching to the Scavrat, her expression unexpectedly softened. "Are you coming?"

Lucas stared in shock.

Sophus recoiled, his scant brows knitting together in confusion. "Coming?"

Dozens of small blue arcs shimmered around Mother Rebekah's legs, as though she could just snap her fingers and disappear into a magical vortex.

"It's time for the Chiefslayer to return to Hub."

REBEKAH-6
ALL OF OUR SINS

"Again."

Rebekah-6 flinched, the cavern walls blurring under her tears. Mother Leah had retrieved another cat from her attendants. That was the name given to the animal she'd just allowed to fall to its death, and the two before it. The new cat's frightened cooing thrummed painfully in her ears, the same sound the others had made before dropping into the abyss. Her heart beat hard in her temples, slamming in fits against the electrodes placed there.

It was her first experience of death—at her hands. She had tried her best, but the machine she inhabited was too hideous. She was too hideous—bulging human eyes staring out from the open guts of an obscenely humanoid machine, crippled as she was. Her metal hands were too cold, like the tools of a surgeon—

Distant stars exploded as the nerves of her arm were severed, muscles parted, blood vessels dissected to make way for the surgeon's saw.

This one was black and white with a mottled pink nose. It shivered atop the platform, tiny hairs swimming in the hot draft of the pit. Green eyes pleaded at her.

"Again," Mother Leah repeated.

It was the first time she had failed a test. She was never supposed to. Her personal attendants always spoke in low voices, but she knew their thoughts: *the most powerful of her kind, Great Mother's favorite*. However normal they tried to behave in her presence, tending to her in her cell, it was a façade. She was feared. Now that fear was her own: fear of failure, judgment, and subsequent reprisal. Terror ran the abbreviated length of her body, culminating in manic swirls of arcing electricity where she plugged into the machine. The sweet stench of burning hair drifted into her nostrils—

The wailing screech of the cranial perforator filled her ears. She tried to hide, folding herself back into the blanket of unconsciousness, but it was too loud. The vibration was like an earthquake in her skull.

What would her punishment be? Perhaps this was it: witnessing one tiny life after another snuffed out until she succeeded. Shriveled reflections of herself, absent their mothers, absent love. It was torture enough.

Mother Leah was beside her. Like Mother Rebekah, she was radiant, magenta eyes burning under a pulled-back curtain of obsidian, her skin flawless alabaster. She looked like an angel, hewn from the walls of this place. She was the only revenant mother Rebekah-6 had known other than her own.

"You can do it, R-6." The woman's voice was gentle, unexpectedly so, eyes fixed on hers. Within that constellation of golden stars, she saw empathy, grief, and cavernous yearning. The woman's hand was on her arm—on the machine's arm, too far removed to deliver any warmth to her shaking human body. She wanted to grasp it with her thoughts. Another blink, and the woman was gone as quickly as she had appeared, resuming her position of authority behind the exosuit's hulking shoulder.

Rebekah-6 nodded, minuscule movements within her cage. She turned once more to the creature—to the cat. It was waiting for her. She was its hope, its way. She breathed deeply, reasserting control over her biological body. Releasing the muscles of her brow, jaw, neck, and overloaded spine. Releasing doubt and crushing anguish. She observed the creature through glazed vision, allowing herself to fall away slice by slice as her consciousness floated upward, into the body of the machine—

The surgeon lowered his tools. She was complete. Her lips quivered around the breathing tube in an autonomic mantra, mouthing prayers of gratitude.

Hands reaching forward. Capable, powerful, her own but cast in metal. Extending through the void, navigating a primordial river of chaos—blinding with prismatic light and even brighter blackness—whose undertow sought to pull her into oblivion. Inhuman whispers called to her from beyond the boundary of space and time, countered by her own. Beads of bloody sweat trickled along her distant lips.

The platform materialized before her, a shimmering island of silver in the dark. Upon it, salvation. The creature existed only as light: pure, patient, expectant.

It was waiting for her.

She grasped it.

"Rebekah."

Whispers. In the dark.

The creature's energy filled her hands, iridescent. Imagined softness that she could never truly feel, brushing against the titanium joints of her fingers.

[Leah > Rebekah: ...]

The light dissolved, sizzling into a wave of static, pulling her from the memory. Someone had spoken—a voice, synthesized in her mind from distant radio waves.

L-4?

The testing chamber fell away, as had the Deadlands.

She was out.

The gray was gone, in its place an indistinct blur of silver on the horizon, scraping the sky. Every tiny movement sent it spinning. Her visual sensors, once myopic, had become fixed at maximum zoom. Rebekah-6 stumbled, falling back to emergency gyros as she felt her body tipping forward. The earth was crumbling, ready to pitch her into something she could not see, even as it sprawled directly ahead.

[Leah > Rebekah: Come home]

Rebekah-6 twisted herself about, swinging her arm cannons in a desperate maneuver to pull herself from the precipice. The groaning of degraded joints and flaring turbines echoed back at her.

From the chasm below.

It projected onto her subconscious—a vast crater mapped out in primitive lines by reawakened geographical sensors. She had left the nothingness of the Deadlands behind. This was somewhere new. Somewhere she had never been.

Far from home.

Her orientation stabilized. Rebekah-6 stepped back, carefully, as she attempted to unlock her optical zoom. The subsystem required a reboot, which meant she would be blinded again. Anxiety inflamed her joints. Imagined pins and needles, clawing at her distant throat. She had no choice. It would only take a minute...

Reboot optical subsystems.

Counting her way through it would make the wait longer. Instead, she focused on her acoustic sensors, listening for any indication of where she was. There was something there: susurrations, like flowing water, but not the kind that would have calmed weary travelers in ages past. Not an oasis in the desert. Voices: distended, polyphonic—millions of them. Their volume increased as she probed, rising to meet this new observer. She reduced her input gain, but the oceanic wail penetrated her armor shell, transmitting itself through vibration, shaking her to the core. There were too many. She wanted to scream again, to release her fear into this place. But to do so would call attention from whatever was gathering at her feet—

Reboot complete.

Praise the...

Prayers of gratitude dissolved as Rebekah-6's vision was restored. The world fell away before her, an enormous cliff cut into the earth from east to west, descending into a nightmarish inland sea. The dark, shambling horror of it glowed red under the trembling midday sun: seething masses of deconstructed flesh, flayed limbs, screaming mouths chanting litanies of suffering. Beyond the abyssal gulf was an unreachable city of silver, perched atop a narrow peninsula.

She wished for blindness again. Violence had been ingrained in her since birth, but not this. Circuits blazed and died as she retreated from herself, intentionally caving in the neural pathways to her sensory antennae.

"Come home," Leah sang, her dead sister's voice scything through her mind.

Something moved at her feet, following the outlines of her backsteps. She tilted downward, revealing the same monstrosity from the Deadlands, only this one was plain to see. A bloated tentacle, the color of rust, skittering across the earth like a millipede. Thousands of joints made up the whole, stuck through with delicate bones that chattered in the wind. The outline of a face screamed from its carapace.

Instead of flitting in and out of existence, it burned its way through reality, igniting everything around it. Purple smoke lifted from her lower torso as layers of paint bubbled and blistered into rivulets of smoldering lava.

More tentacles followed it, dozens of them, clambering over

the cliff face like a tsunami of the damned. They carried with them uncountable faces, each singing its own tale of agony.

She could not think.

She could not move.

She could only watch, paralyzed, as the wave encroached upon her, tentacled viscera conjoined into ever larger appendages and distended sacs of rancid flesh. Superheated air currents surged around the unholy mass, howling at her like a wolf on the wind.

She had come so far, for this. It was not the destiny she had been created for—not alone and broken. Grief squeezed her human heart as she imagined the Eternal One's disappointment. She had let her sister die, and now she would die as well, not even returned to the accelerant to swim in eternity with her other fallen sisters.

"You might hold all our fates in your hands one day."

The Hellmouth would never be closed. Humanity would never be saved.

Mother...

Shuddering reticles overlaid her nightmare, a multitude of red crosshairs struggling to find targets as the wave grew taller.

Help me, Mother.

"Remember your prayers."

She had no prayers left. The Deadlands took them, along with her destiny.

I'm sorry.

In the absence of hope, dismay turned to hatred. An artificial sun burned within her chest. The scorching heat of it channeled through her arms, prying the cooling fins from her mechanical biceps. Unrestricted power rippled along the synthetic tendons of her legs.

Right autocannon nominal; left autocannon damaged, fixed firing only; PDCs online.

She would not go quietly.

Rebekah-6 sidestepped, removing herself from the snapping maws at her feet as she brought her point defense systems online. Heavy machine gun fire erupted from her prow, the recoil of each round pulsing back into her sepulcher. The first tentacle burst apart, its innards crumbling to ash as it separated from the whole. It did not scream, so she screamed in its stead, projecting her synthesized voice like a battering ram. Words were not important, only that the Adversary knew it faced a servant of Cathedral—Great Mother's wrath.

Thunderous fire rang out from her arms, blowing massive holes into the demonic wall, revealing a twisted latticework of metal beneath. Sinew and steel crashed against her, raking at her skin before dissolving back to oblivion. No one had ever explained to her why some demons were biomechanical. It was taken for granted that the beasts of Hell were a composite of everything that came before: creator and creations alike. There was so much still that she did not know—

Left autocannon offline.

She had expended the last of its chambered ammunition, the remainder unable to feed through the vicious gouge in her shoulder. A gouge torn wider by the millisecond as she pirouetted away from the probing appendages of the thing, maneuvering the battle walker well beyond its tolerances. She continued to fire and to scream as the distance between her and the growing army of snapping claws diminished.

Tentacles whirled around her, exploding from the dry clay below, smashing into her back, barbed and vicious. Seeking, metal wrapped in putrescent flesh. Slithering past her pockmarked exterior to violate the delicate mind within. Rebekah-6 lurched, bringing her guns to bear, but there were too many. A final burst of holy fire erupted from her right arm as her ammunition ran dry. The small cannons protecting her vulnerable belly had also quieted.

Mother!

Her viewport turned dark as she was smothered.

Mother!

Her arms were bound, squealing in throes of metallic agony.

Mommy!

Her mind screamed along with her voice.

"You will always be my miracle."

Something was inside her, hijacking the neural pathways of her communication systems. Something alien. Rebekah-6 wished only for tears. She had to die, now, before the Adversary took her soul. There was no returning to the accelerant. Messiah would greet her beyond the veil.

It had to be true.

There had to be something else waiting for her. Not just the void.

Not that.

The instructions stammered out of her: *Initiate self-destruct.*

It was not fair. She had so much left to do. She was so little.

Reactor temperature increasing beyond safe thresholds.

She had to save her soul.

Reactor temperature critical.

She had to die.

Steel pitons gouged into her legs. The demon was climbing her, mounting her, seeking vengeance for its pulverized brethren—

Before being pulverized itself, sundered by the holy flame of L-4's short range missiles.

Her world was fire.

Leah?

No. Leah was dead. L-4 was dead.

The thing in her mind took form: a voice; twin voices, in perfect synchronicity.

[Unknown > R-6: There is no need for that, Sister]

The world shook as munitions exploded on every side of her, scorching the air within centimeters of her carapace. She froze, watching as her viewport sizzled white before dropping offline. She was blind again. Her remaining sensors shuddered under repeat shockwaves: deafening bursts of distortion, heat upon heat, earthquakes cascading through her sepulcher.

Then silence.

The alien signal returned, traversing threads of her cybernetic interface she thought as private as her own brain. It was cold, but without malice—without any emotion at all. She followed the signal down unfamiliar conduits, through imagined archways constructed of light and data, into vast unconceptualized areas of the battle walker—of her extended self. They landed together upon a tessellated field of black polygons, infinite below an equally black void. She waited, lost in the expanse.

The signal stirred. One by one the polygons opened, projecting blinding beams of light toward the void. The world—the real world—sprang up around her, rebuilt one virtual atom at a time. She could see everything, in all directions, despite the destruction of her visual sensors. There was no vertigo, only the perfection of the simulated image. For the first time since symbiosis, Rebekah-6 did not feel like a host in another body; she *was* the body.

The sea of screams was at her back, an impassable moat around the silver city. The earth had been scorched black, cremated viscera piled to the edge of the cliff.

Before her stood two battle walkers. They were all gray slab, unadorned with the filigree of her kin, absent the glory of the Eternal One. Their weapons were pointed in her direction.

Rebekah-6 queried her own armaments and found herself defenseless.

Squalls of hot ash billowed between them. She waited, but they were silent. Whatever—whoever—they were, they had saved her, given her sight, and deactivated her self-destruct. The shock of that near death numbed her to their foreignness.

[R-6 > Unknown: Are we enemies?]

[Unknown > R-6: That remains to be seen]

One of the battle walkers strode forward, stepping past her to observe the nightmare below.

[Unknown > R-6: What are they?]

Rebekah-6 turned, though she could see in all directions once more. With great effort, she limped over to the other war machine. No more demons ascended the escarpment. There was only the mournful wailing of those below, carried on the wind.

[R-6 > Unknown: All of our sins]

They swirled to and fro, pulled below the surface by vicious whirlpools, then vomited up again in new configurations of torment.

[Unknown > R-6: There are too many]

[R-6 > Unknown: Yes]

Rebekah-6 desperately wanted to reach out, as she would with her mother, to know the mind of this creature.

[R-6 > Unknown: What should I call you?]

The alien battle walker turned its upper torso in her direction, its singular amber eye piercing through her armor to her soul. An ancient intelligence lay therein.

[Unknown > R-6: My name is Aleph. But you may call me... Brother]

AFTERWORD

Holy cats!

I remember very clearly when my wife spoke the words, "You should write a book." This in response to many years of wanting to reboot my original gaming world of Dark Legacies™, plus all the vignette storytelling I had started doing on social media.

At the time, it seemed insane. How could I possibly write a book? Crazy job, crazy kids, and more than enough health issues to keep one very occupied (i.e., mired in misery). But then I did it, slowly but surely, with a great deal of support from said wife and a great deal of fretting along the way.

If you've just finished reading Book 2, then that means you read my impossible debut novel (hopefully, otherwise you're probably confused as hell right now!) and I thank you from the cockles of my heart. It also means, well, that you've read my second novel. (Or you're some kind of weird heathen that reads afterwords first.) So, again, I say, holy cats!

Writing a book was an accomplishment that I'm extremely proud of. But many authors will tell you their first one feels like a fluke, no matter how well received it is. It's easy (for us) to wave it away as years of pent-up ideas and procrastination finally given life. But two books... now it feels real.

I hope you enjoyed reading it as much as I enjoyed writing it. And I hope you join me again when it gets even more real, i.e., Book 3. Until then, please consider leaving a review and spreading the word, and feel free to reach out on my socials. I'm always happy to chat all things Rebekah-6.

May you walk in the light.

ABOUT THE AUTHOR

Yuval Kordov is a chronically creative nerd, tech professional, husband, and father to two revenant sisters. Over the course of his random life, he has been a radio show DJ, produced experimental electronic music, created the world of Dark Legacies™, and built custom mechs with LEGO® bricks.

facebook.com/yuvalkordov

x.com/yuvalkordov

instagram.com/yuvalkordov

ALSO BY YUVAL KORDOV

The Hand of God

The World to Come